Cross My Heart

Pamela Cook

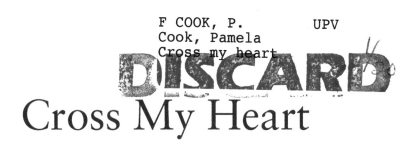

WILDWORDS
PUBLISHING

Cross My Heart

POD: 9780648523505
EPUB: 9780648523512

Publishing services provided by Critical Mass
www.critmassconsulting.com

In memory of Kathie.
So greatly missed, forever in my heart.

Do you remember the time we found that baby bird?

We were sitting on a rock by the creek. Cicadas were singing and the bush mint was making my nose itch. There was a shrieking noise from over near the scribbly gum. I jumped up and ran over, and there he was all puffed up in a ball. You reached down and picked him up. A magpie, you said, or maybe a butcher bird. It was hard to tell because he was so young. His body was grey, but his tail feathers were black and white. You held him so gently, and he stopped squawking and watched us, with eyes like rusty pebbles. There was a cut in his chest and he'd been bleeding. We looked around, but his parents were gone. He was an orphan, you said. I held out the bottom of my T-shirt like it was a hammock and you rested him in there, and he just sat like that all the way home.

Remember we dug up worms from the garden and tried to feed him? Except he wouldn't eat. We put him in a shoebox with some straw and I tried to stay awake to look after him, but I fell asleep. When I woke up he was still and cold.

Like you.

One

Even now, the click of a closing door could make her flinch. One long, deep breath, and the familiar citrusy scent of furniture polish was enough to pull her back.

Home.

Safe.

A faint glow softened the darkness beyond the hallway. The proverbial light at the end of the tunnel. She hurried towards it, the heels of her boots beating a staccato rhythm on the polished timber, the wheels of her suitcase drumming along behind. She stuffed her keys into the handbag dragging on her shoulder, dumped it on the living-room floor and heaved a sigh of relief. Her hands found the nape of her neck, rubbing out the kinks—the usual long-haul gremlins. Something cracked beneath her fingertips—sinews, bones, muscle, maybe all three—and she groaned. A massage would be perfect right about now.

Finally, a movement from the far corner of the room. Josh spun around in his chair, pulling the headphones from his ears, the screen of his laptop shining brighter as he turned.

'Shit, Tess, you scared the hell out of me. I didn't even hear you come in.'

The knot between her shoulder blades tightened. 'Yeah, I noticed.' She dropped her hands to rest by her sides. The last thing she wanted right now was an argument. 'What are you doing working so late?'

'Trying to make some headway on this project. Not getting very far.' He swivelled his chair back to the desk in front of him. 'How was the conference?'

Same old question, but at least he bothered to ask. 'Fine.' Same old answer, but it was too late to bother with details. She walked over and stood beside him. Once upon a time, she would have laid an arm across his shoulder, leaned down and brushed a kiss to his lips. Once upon a time, Josh would have greeted her at the airport—or at least the door—with a dozen red roses. She'd never had the heart to tell him the scent of them made her gag. It was crazy how some things never changed even when so much time had passed. She swallowed down the burn in the back of her throat.

'Did you dazzle them all with your brilliance?' A smile in his voice. His eyes glued to the screen.

She coughed. 'Naturally.'

'Have you eaten?'

'I picked at a few things on the plane.' To be honest, she could do with something decent in her stomach, something that didn't come from a foil container and smell like it belonged in a soup kitchen. Something they could share over a chilled glass of wine while they sat side by side on the couch, catching up on their respective weeks. Laughing. The fridge, no doubt, would be empty, and in all probability she'd be eating alone.

She gave her neck another twist, closed her eyes and waited for the pop. Blinked her way out of her daydream. It was late and they were both tired. 'Might just have a shower and collapse into bed.'

Josh half turned, one of his hands hovering on the touch pad, the other cradling his chin. Had he sensed the note of disappointment in her voice? Was he about to shut up shop and suggest a nightcap?

'What?' His head angled slightly in her direction.

'Nothing.'

'I won't be long.' He was already back to work, fingers tapping against the shiny surface of the desk.

How many times had she asked him not to do that? And it was a lie, of course, about not being too long. He'd be up all night. As always when a deadline was looming. Then again, when wasn't one?

She lifted her suitcase, a cramp stabbing at the arch of her foot, and grabbed the bundle of unopened mail from the island bench. A veritable mountain.

Was it that damned hard to open a few envelopes?

She glanced back to where he sat, completely absorbed with the numbers on his spreadsheet. She could strip off and dance naked around the room and he probably wouldn't even notice. The suitcase thumped against each step as she dragged it upstairs. She didn't bother lifting it to dampen the noise. Josh was totally in 'the zone', with any extraneous distractions, including his wife, completely blocked out. It wasn't like she could complain. They were as bad as each other when it came to work. Focused. Determined. Driven. It was what had drawn them together in the first place. Five years of marriage and they were both still the same in that sphere of their lives.

Even if other things had changed.

There was no point thinking about it all now. Not when the spray of hot water on her skin was beckoning, closely followed by the cool weight of high-thread-count sheets against her arms. She tossed the mail onto the bed, the dozen or more envelopes falling like a hand of cards across the crisp white doona. Probably bills or bank statements; nothing that couldn't wait. She undressed and headed for the ensuite, her bra and knickers hitting the tiled floor as she stepped into the shower. Hot water, almost scalding, streamed onto her scalp and she moaned. She sounded positively R-rated. Luckily there was no one around to hear.

Certainly not Josh.

Oh, the irony. Over a week, she'd been away. They'd shared plenty of phone messages, some of which could only be described as sexting, and now here they were under the same roof barely able to utter two words to each other. Not that she was up for anything anyway, it's just that the option would have been nice. Having *some* sort of conversation would have been even nicer. How long had it been since they'd talked about anything meaningful? She tipped her head back and let the heat pummel her face, to wash away her question. A few more minutes of mindless soaking and she turned off the taps and reached for a towel.

White, thick, fluffy and perfectly arranged on the rail. She gave her body a quick once-over before rubbing it across her head. As a kid she'd been scolded for going to bed with wet hair, told she would catch 'her death of cold', whatever the hell that meant. It had stayed with her, though. That grandmotherly warning still niggled behind her closed lids whenever she defiantly pressed her freshly washed head against the pillow. Now that it was cut short it hardly mattered. A quick shimmy and just like that, it was almost dry. The bathroom was surprisingly clean considering Josh had been home alone. Everything gleaming and in its place—no smears on the mirror, floor without a mark, the lid down on the toilet seat. Of course. It was Thursday, so the cleaner had been. Yes, it was an extravagance she'd justified to her mother on more than one occasion; the office hours they both kept didn't leave much time for household chores. Hard work might be its own reward, but a floor you could eat off and clothes pressed by an ironing service weren't too shabby, either.

She tossed the towel in the laundry basket and pulled on her pyjama top. The usual remnants of airsickness lingered from the flight; she knew they'd be gone by morning. Once she'd had a good night's sleep and sorted out her body clock.

Lamp on, light off.

There was something so comforting about your own bed. Even if you were in it alone. She sank into it, pulling the covers up to her chin as she curled into a ball on her side and closed her eyes. Serious bliss. A rustling noise had her eyelids flickering: the unopened envelopes scattering to the floor. No problem, they could be dealt with in the morning. Everything was easier to deal with in the bright light of day.

'Missed you.'

Josh's breath was damp on her cheek and the evidence supporting his words firm against the small of her back. Tess shifted forward, struggling against the heaviness of an arm draped across her middle. She cracked open one eyelid. Then another. Watery pre-dawn light leaked through the blinds. How could it be tomorrow already? Hadn't she just gone to sleep?

She reached over and switched off her bedside lamp. 'God, what time is it?' Her voice had the groggy, slurred sound of someone who'd stayed at the bar long after closing time. Jet lag was a bitch.

'Time we said a proper hello.' A hand rubbed at the underside of her breast and his mouth against the curve of her neck made her rouse. She could argue it was his fault their reunion last night had been more like colleagues passing in the coffee room than a married couple who were actually pleased to see each other. But at least they were connecting now.

She closed her eyes and drifted as his fingers floated across her skin, a warm, familiar thrum between her legs. Blood heated her cheeks, and the other parts of her body with which Josh was quickly becoming reacquainted. She dropped her hand to join with his. Her habit of wearing no underwear to bed and his of sleeping naked, often led to early-morning sessions. Not that she minded. Not at all. She pulled the singlet over her head, tossed it onto the floor and rolled over to where he lay, propped up on one elbow.

'Hello there.' She looked up at him, a smile forming.

He replied with a wicked curl of his mouth and a raised brow. His eyes, normally a sweet shade of caramel, had darkened into something more like treacle. Something in which she could happily drown. 'Is that the best you can do?'

She ran a hand greedily through the silky strands of hair at the back of his neck and followed up her earlier perfunctory greeting with a longer, deeper kiss.

'Hmm ... that's more like it.'

His body engulfed hers and she arched into him. Gripping his shoulders, she hooked one calf around his and gave him a quick shove, flipping them both over so she was the one looking down. She reached between his legs, positioning him in just the right spot, and with one single, sharp upward thrust he was inside her. Her chest billowed. She flattened her hands against the hollows below his shoulders and he rocked beneath her until they became a sweaty, ragged tangle of limbs, and she was completely overwhelmed by the glorious bone-shattering ache she'd been chasing. Josh followed quickly after, his palms searing her hips, his limbs rippling. She collapsed on top of him, her forehead nestled against the dark stubble of his jaw. Even after hours at the computer, minimal sleep and a sweaty round of wake-up sex, he had that just-washed, deliciously minty smell.

She rolled over and lay on top of the sheets, her hands tracking the rise and fall of her ribcage as she waited for her heart rate to return to somewhere this side of normal. The room heaved with their tandem panting. A horn bleated from the street outside, and another echoed back. The world was out there, ready and waiting, demanding attention, but she remained still, eyes closed, willing it away.

'Now *that's* a good morning.' Josh sat upright, reached for his phone from the bedside table and switched off the beeping alarm. He looked like a Cheshire cat. 'Best I've had all week.'

She stretched her arms above her head with a languid yawn. 'Certainly beats *Good morning, ma'am, this is your five am wake-up call.*'

'You've got the accent aced.' He laughed. 'I'd better get moving. I've got an eight o'clock meeting.' He threw her a wink before sauntering off for a shower, wiggling his bare backside more than was strictly necessary.

Tess snuggled back under the covers, any sign of the tension her body had stored up during the flight—and afterwards— now vanished. Sex had always brought them closer, stitched them back together even when their relationship had frayed. Her mind leap-frogged to those looser threads—the days, nights and weeks that sometimes rolled by when they barely saw each other. Hours spent working or doing their own thing: Josh with his cycling crew while she procrastinated about the gym by watching mindless reality-TV shows. More and more it felt like the seam holding them together was splitting, yet they were always able to patch it up with a workout between the sheets. It was how they found their way back to each other.

But was it enough?

She stared at the vacant space beside her, placed her hand on his empty pillow, the cotton cold beneath her palm. A weight heavier than the doona settled on her. She shook it away. There was nothing to worry about. Life had its ups and downs. They were all good.

Something crinkled under the sole of her foot as she swung her legs over the edge of the bed: the mail she'd been too tired to deal with last night. She gathered it up and shuffled through the envelopes. As predicted most were bank statements addressed to them both, one was an electricity bill—overdue—and a few were for TDS. A thrill tripped through her veins. It was the same whenever she saw the acronym, especially in logo-form, the letters entwined with a rough sketch of a heart: *Team-Driven Solutions*. A play on her own initials joined by the *heart* of her own human resources consultancy, which just happened to be going gangbusters. Not bad for a thirty-five-year-old. Even if it was Plan B. One last envelope fell from her lap as she stood. This one addressed to Ms T. De Santis, her full name, and while it looked official, it didn't seem to be a bill. She slid her finger under the seal and ripped, unfolding the single-page document.

FACS, Department of Family and Community Services.

Why would they be writing to her? Her stomach hollowed as she skimmed over the first few lines, and she dropped back onto the bed. She needed to read from the beginning, but each word sucked her a little further out of her own skin, so by the time she reached the end of the letter she was watching herself from somewhere outside her body.

She stared down at the signature and the department-speak at the bottom of the page, the muscles in her chest tightening as if a too-small elastic band had been wrapped too many times around her heart.

This could not be happening.

No.

It was *not* happening.

She folded the paper back into the torn envelope and placed it deliberately on the bedside table, pinching the points of her elbows tightly as she crossed her arms, holding herself together.

'Tess?' Josh's voice came to her through a cotton-wool fog. 'What's wrong?'

Somehow he was right there, standing by her side, already showered, the brown waves of his hair wet and towel-ruffled.

'It's …' She tried to pick up the letter, but it fell from her grasp like a hot coal. Her hand flew to her mouth. If she didn't say the words then they wouldn't be true, would they?

'Tess … what is it?'

As much as she didn't want it to be real it was right there at her feet, black print blurring into a haze of grey. She pressed her fingers against her palms, scoring the soft pads of flesh with her nails.

'It's Skye.' The name was foreign on her tongue after all these years, like a rare fruit she'd tasted long ago, in another lifetime, and then forgotten. But it wasn't as strange as the answer to Josh's question. It came out quickly in a strangled cough, a bitter seed she couldn't stand to swallow. 'She's dead.'

Two

A crescent moon of white arced at the base of her thumbnail, below the navy gloss. Regular manicures might draw attention away from her ravaged cuticles, but they didn't change her disgusting habit. One day she might stop chewing the skin until it was raw and red. One day. Not today.

Josh leaned over, picked up the letter and sat beside her, the paper taut between his hands. 'Jesus.'

Somewhere outside a garbage truck rumbled, the bang and clatter of bins reverberating like a set of cymbals. Tess coiled back in on herself as the noise ebbed away.

'What happened?' Josh's voice was muffled, as if he was speaking from a distance. 'Tess, when did you last talk to her?'

She shook her head and let out a long, slow breath. 'I'm not sure. Six months … longer maybe.' It was July now. Had it been this year or last when she and Skye had spoken? 'She wrote to me, a while ago.' But was that letter before or after the Christmas card? The one she'd replied to with a promise to visit soon. The same promise she'd been making for the last eight years. Her stomach plummeted.

Josh moved closer and tried to draw her into his embrace. She pulled herself upright, and he settled for resting his arm across her shoulders. 'I'm really sorry. I know how much you cared about her.'

Did he know? Really know? How could he when Josh had only met her friend once, when she had barely mentioned Skye in the entire time they'd been together. Not talking about her didn't mean she didn't think about Skye, though. Her memory hurdled over the intervening years back to earlier days, a series of disconnected images flickering like an old home-movie reel to a soundtrack of childhood laughter. Those dark spiral curls, the pale, freckled face, eyes that shifted like the sea on a hot summer afternoon—clear and blue one minute, grey and stormy the next.

'Guess you'll have to call them first thing. The letter's dated almost a week ago.'

The letter. She clenched her teeth until her jaw ached. If he'd bothered to tell her about it on the phone, she might have asked him to open it then and there. She jerked at her shoulder, forcing his arm to fall away.

'So what will you say?'

'I'm sure you have some suggestions.' The words came out in a hiss and Josh sprang from the bed, the towel around his waist slipping to his knees. He secured it back into place, hooking one thumb into the fold below his hip. 'Well, I mean you'll have to tell them we can't do it.' He was floundering now, flapping the letter around in the air, but a sharper, more defiant edge had crept into his voice. 'You either do that over the phone or go in and see this person. End of story.'

He'd already made up his mind. Presumed she agreed. That piece of paper in his hand was asking about *her* intentions in regard to Grace, asking if she would be honouring the agreement *she* had made to be the child's legal guardian. Skye was dead; her daughter was now Tess's responsibility. This was her decision.

She pushed herself up from the bed. They were almost exactly the same height when she wasn't in heels, making it easy to stare him down. 'So we're not even going to discuss it?'

'Tess, come on.' He dipped his head, raked a hand through his hair and snorted—actually snorted—as if this was some kind of joke. 'There's no way we can take on someone else's kid.'

'It's not just *someone*. It's Skye.'

'No, it's not Skye. It's her daughter. Shit, the kid is ten years old. When was the last time you even saw her?'

She couldn't look at him anymore. Couldn't stand that I-know-better-than-you jut of his chin and the tell-me-I'm-wrong tone in his voice. She covered her bare breasts with one arm and bit down hard on the inside of her mouth. The last time she'd seen Grace the little girl had been a pre-schooler, but so what? It didn't change the facts. 'That's not the point. I signed the papers when she was born.'

'Well, that was your first mistake.' And right on cue, there it was, the pointing finger. 'You should have thought it through more carefully in the first place. That was a legal document.'

'Skye didn't have anyone else.'

'A simple no would have worked.'

His same old attitude, everything black and white. She was the one who'd signed the papers, made the promise, not Josh. This was not his call to make. She wanted to grab a handful of that dripping hair and yank it out of his stupid fucking head. Not that it would change anything. Josh had total tunnel vision when it came to his life plan, and right now he was on track to corporate stardom. Nothing—and no one—would be getting in his way. She whipped her top off the bed and pulled it on, shoving past him as she stalked to the window.

The padding of feet on carpet signalled his retreat to the ensuite. Tess folded her arms and peered down at the street. People were out there as if nothing had changed. Women in coats and scarves braced against the winter wind. Men in smart suits striding along the pavement, mobiles to their ears, brows furrowed as if the future of the world depended on their every word. All of them going about their lives, oblivious to what had happened. Skye was dead and yet everything outside was completely normal.

Across the road Rocco, her favourite barista, popped up an umbrella out the front of his cafe. A young woman in a short denim skirt, black top, fishnet tights and Docs pulled up a chair. Rocco tossed his head and laughed at whatever joke passed between them, before he gave an exaggerated bow and ambled back inside, leaving the girl to her phone. A peacock tattoo covered the bare skin of her upper chest. Her short-cropped hair was dyed the darkest shade of black. Boots and tats. Almost a replica of Tess's own teenage self. Light years ago, well before Skye had asked her to be Grace's guardian. The request had seemed so lovely at the time, but she'd never considered it legally binding. Could she actually turn around now, a decade later and change her mind? Apparently, Josh thought that was perfectly fine. From the sounds of the opening and closing of drawers in the room behind her, he'd already moved on with his day. She turned to watch him do up his tie in the full-length mirror inside the wardrobe door.

Almost fully dressed now, he stuffed his wallet into the back pocket of his perfectly pressed pants and shrugged on his suit jacket. 'Tess. I get that you're upset, but you need to be practical. We both work crazy hours, live in an apartment, don't have any children of our own. There's no way we're equipped to look after a kid we don't know, who doesn't know us. I've never even laid eyes on her.'

She edged back towards the window, let his words percolate through the layers of emotion the letter had exposed. *Was* it stupid to even be entertaining the idea? She'd really only seen Grace a few times herself: when Skye came down to the city to buy her first lot of school supplies, briefly as a toddler at Skye's grandmother's funeral service, and before that in those early weeks of her life as a newborn. A tiny baby with fresh pink skin and that puzzled where-am-I expression. Totally helpless and completely dependent on her mother. Who could she depend on now if Tess didn't step up? 'She's going to be fostered out to total strangers.'

'Babe, to her, we are total strangers.' The cloying scent of his Armani aftershave was suddenly too strong, too close, but at least he was smart enough not to attempt to touch her. 'Don't you think she'd be better off with a real family? People who actually know what they're doing.'

Tess closed her eyes as the shrapnel from his 'real family' grenade cut deep. Kids had never been on his agenda. He'd made that perfectly clear the minute they'd become engaged. He didn't want to risk creating another broken home, he'd said, like the one he'd come from, and it had suited her at the time, when the concept of bringing innocent children into the world had made her insides quiver. They hadn't discussed it since, had rolled their eyes and changed the subject when others had brought up the b-word, but never seriously talked about it again. So when she'd married him, hadn't she implicitly agreed to the no-kids deal? Anyway, they were a pair of workaholics who had hardly any free time and lived in the inner city with designer furniture and white walls. None of it was conducive to raising a child, and if it didn't work out it wouldn't be fair to dump Grace back into foster care, would it?

Across the street the peacock girl's perfectly gelled hair gleamed in the winter sunlight. In ten years' time she might regret that tattoo, or other choices she'd made. People's lives can take such different directions to what they'd imagined. The Tess who'd signed the guardianship papers had been living out some kind of Disney godmother fantasy, but now that bubble had well and truly burst, leaving behind the cold, hard stain of reality.

'I'll call the woman …' She cleared her throat. 'Tell her to make other arrangements.'

'I am sorry about Skye.' He squeezed her shoulder, as if that was supposed to make her feel better. 'Maybe they can tell you more about what happened with her when you call. It would be good for you to have some closure.'

Closure. Psycho-babble for 'The End'. Everything all neatly packed up in a box, stored away and forgotten, exactly how Josh liked it. The bedside clock clicked over. Seven-thirty. Time was slipping away. Josh needed to get moving, and she needed space. 'You'd better go.'

He pressed a kiss to her cheek and was gone, no further urging required. In an instant the room, the whole apartment, was quiet, the kind of quiet she imagined that followed the felling of an ancient tree in a forest or the deafening seconds of silence that come after a raging, calamitous storm.

Or perhaps before.

She made her way to the bathroom. Only ten hours ago, she'd stepped into the same shower and scrubbed away the exhaustion of the flight. Now it was something much deeper she needed to remove, something no amount of body wash or exfoliant could cleanse. How was it possible that someone was here on the earth one moment and gone the next? *Skye.* The letter didn't even give the cause of death. A razor-sharp pain pierced her chest, swelling into a lump stuck deep in the base of her throat. She opened her mouth, tried to sluice it away, but it refused to budge. She'd always meant to get in touch, meant to check in on her friend and see if she was doing okay. Plan an actual visit. Now it was too late.

Hunched over, naked and dripping, she watched the water swirl around the drain and disappear. A sob broke from her mouth, echoing against the tiles. There was only one thing she could do: rip off the Band-Aid, the faster the better. The FACS office from where the letter was sent was in Redfern, which wasn't far away. She would call in before her scheduled meeting and see the caseworker. Explain the situation.

And find out what happened to Skye.

Jabbing away at the traffic button wouldn't make the lights change any quicker, but it was vaguely satisfying. Cleveland Street, as usual, was a virtual car park. A bus lurched past, spewing out a stream of black vapour, making Tess's stomach roll. Most days she could handle the noise and fumes—it was part of the fabric of the suburb. Chaotic. Loud. Colourful. One big noisy carnival. Surry Hills was so far removed from her childhood in southern Sydney, it was like another planet. As far away from suburbia as you could get. That word, 'suburbia', was as bland as the notion, and thankfully she and Josh had been on the same page about where they'd wanted to live. Granted, the craziness wasn't for everyone. Certainly not Skye. Her idea of heaven was the total opposite: sustainable living on an isolated country property, homeschooling her daughter, sculpting and painting, making just enough money from her artwork to survive.

Two completely different worlds. Was it any wonder she and Skye had drifted apart?

Tess pressed a hand against the ache in her chest. 'Drifted apart' was such a handy euphemism. Made it all sound so gentle, so inevitable. So okay.

The beep of the walk signal jolted her forward and across the intersection through the throng of pedestrians. On the corner, a wolfish-looking dog lay sprawled on the footpath beside his owner, who was scraping a squeegee across the windscreen of a car. People rushed past, heads down, absorbed in whatever was flashing on the screens of their phones. Worker bees, all part of the Sydney hive.

She stopped outside a nondescript building, number 219. It was already after nine am, so the FACS office should be open. She pulled the letter from her bag, ignoring the contents as she searched for the name of the person she needed to see. Regina Martin. A woman—a stranger—who had been appointed by a government department to supervise custody arrangements for Skye's only child, who was now an orphan. Like her mother. History repeating itself in some sick, cruel joke. Skye's grandmother had loved her like she was her own, but it couldn't possibly be the same. Tess's thumb throbbed. She pulled it away from her mouth, wincing at the blistered skin, and wriggled it to get the blood circulating. Where would Grace be right now? Probably stuck in some awful orphanage, or had she already been placed in foster care? All those stories you heard on the news about kids being shoved from one home to the next, at the mercy of people who only wanted to collect a payout ... or worse.

Under the cool silk of her long-sleeved shirt, the fine hairs on her forearms stood on end. Surely there were good, honest people out there who did want to do the right thing? People who genuinely wanted to provide a stable, loving family; care for a homeless child. People who were better equipped for parenting than she and Josh were. Of course those people existed. Procrastinating wouldn't help anyone, certainly not Grace.

Slipping through the automatic doors, Tess checked the directory and made her way up in the elevator, the folded document pulsing like a heartbeat against her palm.

The woman at the reception desk gave a tight-lipped smile. 'Can I help you?'

'I need to speak to Regina Martin.'

'Do you have an appointment?'

'No ... no, I don't.'

'I can make one for you if you like.' Her fingers skipped over the keys as she scanned the screen. 'I can get you in to see her next Tuesday at three forty-five pm.'

Tuesday was four days away. Far too much time to consider her options. Reconsider.

'I need to see her urgently. It's in regard to a guardianship case.' She handed the document across to the receptionist.

A few flyaway hairs sprang from the woman's centre part as she bowed her head to read, frowning behind her thick-lensed glasses. 'And you are the guardian named here? Tessa De Santis?'

'Yes.'

'Take a seat.' She rose from her chair and disappeared, the letter still in her hand.

Tess settled back against the hard plastic seat. The waiting room was too warm and reeked of disinfectant. Photos of children of various ages lined the walls, some holding hands with an adult, all of them looking happy and contented. Were they real kids who had been placed in homes, or idealised versions the department wanted the public to see? A door opened and closed along the hall and the receptionist returned, resuming her seat without a word.

'Ms De Santis?' A second woman appeared in the waiting room. 'I'm Regina Martin. Please come in.' She had a faint accent, maybe Spanish, a lusciously thick set of dark brows, and an air of absolute authority. A bright-orange scarf was wound around her neck and her ripped jeans, definitely not traditional work wear, were a sharp contrast to the tailored charcoal of Tess's business suit.

The caseworker led the way to her office and waved Tess into a chair. 'I thought we might have heard from you sooner.'

Snippy, but probably best not to fight fire with fire. Tess put her bag on the floor, took a breath and pasted on her best conciliatory smile. 'I'm so sorry, but I've been overseas for work.' Considering the gravity of the situation, it was hardly surprising the woman would be questioning her tardiness. 'I only got back late last night.'

'We did try to contact you on the phone number found at Ms Whittaker's house, multiple times.'

Those few missed calls while she'd been in LA, the voicemail she hadn't bothered listening to. Tess cringed inwardly. No wonder the woman was snaky. Regina Martin leaned forward and shuffled through a pile of manila folders, slid one out and flicked it open. A computer and a wooden carving of an elephant were the only decorations on the desk. Tess plucked away a piece of white fluff caught in the weave of her skirt while the woman read through paperwork, probably re-familiarising herself with the case. She looked drawn, slightly harried. It couldn't be easy dealing with such fraught situations day after day. Eventually she looked up, rested her elbows on the desk and balanced her chin on the arch of her clasped hands. 'So, you are Grace Whittaker's legal guardian.'

Was she asking a question or stating a fact? Either way the answer was yes. 'That's right.'

'There's no father involved?'

'No. Skye fell pregnant when she was travelling. It was an accident, but she wanted to have the baby.'

'And when is the last time you saw Grace?'

Tess shrank back into the chair, shifting again as it creaked. The heat in her cheeks was a dead giveaway. She'd read somewhere that if you acknowledged the blush it would subside. And yet her face remained on fire.

'Ms De Santis?'

'About five years ago, I think.'

'You think?'

The incredulity was well warranted. 'No, it was. I mean … I know it was. In Sydney.'

Regina Martin sat back in her chair. 'And you haven't seen her since? Haven't visited? They didn't visit you?'

'No.'

The caseworker tipped her head to the side and frowned. 'So, I'm curious as to why Grace's mother would leave her in your care.'

'We were friends, close friends.' Tess sucked in a breath. The explanation sounded totally lame, considering the length of time since they'd actually seen each other. 'Skye had an aversion to the city and I've … well … I have a very busy job.'

'I see.' Regina Martin pursed her lips as she considered the documents in front of her. 'It's my job to make sure that the child is placed with the right people.' She glanced at Tess's hand. 'You're married?'

'Yes.'

'Do you have any children?'

'No.'

She was noting down every word. 'And what is it you do for a living?'

'I'm a human resources manager. I have my own consultancy.'

'So you would be financially able to care for Grace?'

'Yes. Absolutely.'

Another scribble in the file. Surely financial stability had to count for something? 'Have you discussed this with your husband?'

'We've ... talked about it.' Finally, they'd come to the point of the meeting. She'd started off on the wrong foot, given the wrong impression about why she was here. 'To be perfectly honest ...'

'Let *me* be totally honest with *you*, Mrs De Santis.'

The sudden, incorrect change in title niggled, but there were more important issues at stake. If the woman wanted the floor, she could go for her life. In the end, the outcome would be the same. Tess crossed her legs and gave a slight nod.

'If there was any extended family in this case, we would prefer Grace be placed with them. Are you aware of any relatives who might be able to take her in?'

'No.' The short, single syllable came out far too loud and Regina Martin widened her brown eyes. Tess's stomach hollowed. She made a conscious effort to lower her volume, soften her tone. 'I was the closest thing to family after the death of Skye's grandmother.' It was the absolute truth. Family wasn't just about blood. She was right there in the room when Grace was born, watching on as the midwife laid the tiny bundle on her friend's chest, those smoky eyes looking up into her mother's. Days later, as they had sat together on the lounge of Skye's rented flat watching the baby sleep, Skye had taken her hand.

Promise me you'll take care of her if anything happens to me.

Those had been her exact words.

'And you are one hundred percent sure you can provide a safe, loving, long-term home for the child, as her mother wished?'

'Yes.' The word sprang from Tess's lips, the same answer she'd given her friend. Wherever it had come from, there was no taking it back. Not then. Not now.

'In that case, I'm going to need to set up an interview with you and your husband.'

'But he isn't listed as a legal guardian.'

'No, but since I assume Grace will be living with both of you … there are protocols we need to follow.' Regina Martin gave a soft smile. She seemed to be thawing. 'I'm sure you understand.'

'Of course.' This conversation was not what she'd intended when she'd walked inside the building. Or was it?

'I suggest you talk this through very carefully. Taking on someone else's child is no picnic.'

How the hell was she going to break the news to Josh?

So, babe, I'm sure you won't mind, but …

I know this wasn't what you were expecting …

Can we talk about this calmly …?

'And there's something you should know about Grace.' The serious tone in the woman's voice drowned out the practice questions. 'She's extremely withdrawn. Hasn't spoken a word since she's been taken into care.'

22

'Isn't that normal, though, considering she's just lost her mother?'

'Yes. And no.' She folded her arms and tapped the pen against her bottom lip. 'You just need to be aware, there could potentially be some deep-seated emotional or behavioural issues.'

With all the focus on guardianship, there'd been no discussion of how this whole situation had come about in the first place. A part of Tess didn't want to know, wanted to just sign on the dotted line and get as far away as possible. But if she was going to be Grace's foster-mother she needed to know the details, for better or worse. And wasn't there a tiny part of her that wanted to know the truth? She ran her tongue over her lips and forced herself to look straight at Regina Martin. 'Do you know what happened to Skye? How she died?'

'Didn't the police inform you? You were named in the legal documents they found in the house.'

'I haven't been contacted by anyone except this department.' Tess scrunched her toes inside her shoes. Josh always harangued her about not listening to her phone messages. Maybe he was right.

'Grace was the one who reported her mother's death.' Regina Martin sighed, the air leaving her body like a deflating balloon. 'She found her, in bed. The coroner requested a postmortem, but I'm not sure what the outcome was in the end … There was some evidence to suggest it might have been suicide.'

The room began to spin. Tess gripped the edge of the desk, tried to anchor herself by staring at the small wooden elephant, but it blurred into a trio. She closed her eyes to focus on her breathing, and when she opened them again a tumbler of water appeared in front of her. Regina Martin was looking down with motherly concern.

Tess held the glass with two hands and took a sip. 'Thank you.'

'I take it the news has come as a shock. I'm so sorry.'

She should ask for more information, find out the details, but an image of her friend's lifeless body was already forming. She stood and placed the half-empty glass on the desk. 'How quickly can the approval interview be arranged?'

Regina Martin took up her seat and peered at the screen of her computer as she typed. 'I can definitely organise something for Tuesday next week.'

'Nothing sooner?'

'Today is Friday. Tuesday at eleven am would be the earliest.'

Naturally, the wheels of officialdom did not spin on weekends. 'Alright. We'll see you then.' *We.* Tess and Josh. The new parents. 'What's the procedure after that?'

'Assuming you're given approval, you should be able to take Grace home by the end of the week.'

'Next Friday?'

'Correct. Paperwork takes time, I'm afraid.' She shook her head apologetically. 'Nothing moves quickly in community services.'

'So what happens to her in the meantime?'

'Grace is being looked after by a qualified carer in a transitional facility.'

'An orphanage?'

'We no longer have orphanages. The children are placed in temporary care in strictly supervised homes.'

So Grace was grieving and alone. Friday was another week away. 'Is there any chance I could visit her over the weekend?'

Regina Martin drummed her short, neat nails against the desktop, a soft light growing in her eyes. 'Look, it's not something I'd usually approve.' She spoke conspiratorially, as if she was afraid the room might be bugged. 'But since this case is quite unusual, I suppose I can allow a short visit in the morning.' She pulled a Post-It Note from a holder on her desk, jotted something down from the file and handed it across to Tess. 'Here's the address. I'll let the carer know you and your husband will be there at ten am.'

Tomorrow morning. Josh had a bike trip this weekend. 'Ah …'

Regina Martin was already moving out from behind her desk. 'Keep in mind that Grace is in a very fragile state. Don't make any promises and don't mention anything about what happened to her mother.'

Right. No promises. No mention of Skye.

'I'll see you and your husband back here on Tuesday.' The door opened and they stepped out into the overly heated hallway. 'And, Tess …'

The sudden use of her first name pulled Tess up short. 'I'm very sorry about your friend.'

There had been a few difficult moments during the interview, but this woman had a heart. Summoning a smile was simply too hard. 'Thank you.' She made her way downstairs and out onto the street, leaning against the rough brick of the building as she tried to process what had happened. Had she really just agreed to be a foster-parent? How would Grace react to meeting her? And what was she going to say to Josh?

And then there was the question she needed to ask above all the rest but didn't want to know the answer to at all.

Why did Skye kill herself?

Three

The bus scraped against the kerb and Tess shuffled forward on autopilot along with the crowd of late-afternoon travellers. Most of her day since arriving at the office had been the same: people talking at her and her mouth moving in response, her face forming the appropriate expressions, but behind the mask was the feeling of having just been dumped by an errant wave. And not quite surfacing. Processing the meeting about Grace was one thing, the news about Skye's death was something else completely. Work had provided the necessary distraction, but now that she was wedged against the window, staring out at the evening bottleneck of traffic through finger-smeared glass, the horrible finality of it all was unavoidable.

Suicide.

Skye had killed herself. Or at least that's what the police suspected. There would be a coroner's report, based on the post-mortem and whatever evidence was found at the time, but it wouldn't include the cause, the truth concealed deep inside such a desperate act.

A bell chimed on Tess's phone and a calendar notification appeared on the screen. *Dad's Birthday dinner seven pm.* Shit. Sitting through a cheery family gathering was the last thing she needed tonight, especially when she had far more urgent matters to discuss at home. All day she'd resisted the urge to throw up, had swallowed it down through meeting after meeting, but now she was being dragged back onto this morning's rollercoaster of emotion and there was a good chance she would actually heave. Closing her eyes and trying to breathe only made it worse: the sour tang of body odour from the man beside her sent her stomach into a spin. Jumping to her feet, she climbed over the top of her fellow passenger and hit the buzzer, weaving her way down the aisle until she reached the front of the bus. Thank God the driver had the good sense to pull up at the next stop. Right outside a pub, where she no doubt looked like she'd had one too many, but the rough brick façade was as good a wall as any to lean against. Keeping down the meagre morsels of food she'd consumed today was far more important than keeping up appearances.

The buzz of a phone.

A text from Josh. *Going to be late. I'll Uber and meet you at your parents'.*

He'd remembered the dinner. She texted back, *Okay. See you soon.* Surely he would know better than to mention anything about what had happened in front of her family. Best to make sure, so she added a second message: *Don't mention anything about Skye at dinner. Might spoil the party.*

Time was getting on. She needed to get back to the apartment, pick up the car and get to her parents' place on time, or her head could very well be served up on a platter along with the tiramisu. She cringed at the mental image: far too frivolous in light of today's news. A taxi appeared in the stream of cars and she hailed it down, climbing in and resting her head against the back of the seat, finding refuge in the chatter of drive-time radio. All she wanted to do was go home and crawl into bed, wake up in some new existence where the last twenty-four hours had never happened. Pray for a sliding-doors moment so she could hop in the car this weekend and do the four-hour drive to Weerilla to see her old friend again.

Alive.

The cabbie jammed his foot on the brake, jerking her forward, and she braced herself against the front headrest.

'Sorry, love.' He had the grace to look mildly apologetic as he shrugged in the rear-view mirror.

Tess slumped back against the seat, sighing aloud as they started moving again. There would be no road trip to the countryside, no warm and fuzzy reunion. No more chances to make amends. And there was no avoiding the truth about Skye. Or Grace. For the next few hours at least, she could hide behind her father's birthday celebrations, delay the inevitable, awkward conversation she would be having soon with Josh and continue doing what she'd become so skilled at over the last twenty years.

Pretend.

'Is that you, Tess?' Her mother's voice cut through the babble coming from the kitchen.

Tess paused by the hall stand, checking her face in the mirror. Dark shadows circled her eyes, standing out against the ghostly pallor of her skin. She gave her cheeks a good, hard pinch. Maybe the rush of blood would make her look a little less like an extra from *The Walking Dead*.

'Tessa?'

There it was, the frantic tone, the soundtrack to every family function. Her reflection frowned back at her. The pinching hadn't exactly worked—in fact, it had given her two angry patches rather than a healthy glow, but that would have to do.

'Yeah, it's me, Mum.' Judging by the voices making up the kitchen chorus, she was the last—almost—to arrive. The closer she got, the louder the volume and the more she wished she'd called to say she was feeling sick. It wouldn't have been a lie.

'Hello, darling. I was getting worried. Where's Josh?' Her mother's face was as flushed as her own was pale.

'Sorry, I meant to call.'

Her mother scowled, then recovered with a welcoming smile.

'Josh should be here soon. Don't wait to serve, though.'

'Hey.' Rob appeared from behind, poking Tess in the ribs before dragging her into a suffocating hug. 'How's my little sister?'

'Your *only* sister is fine.' She rubbed at her face as he let her go. 'You might want to think about shaving sometime soon.'

'Nah, Ally likes me rugged.' He gave her a goofy grin. It was hard to take him seriously when he looked like Bear Grylls. 'You look like crap by the way.'

'Yeah, long-distance flights followed by a day of meetings will do that to you. Where is your better half anyway?' Usually, the family banter bored her senseless, but tonight the dependable monotony of it was a soothing balm.

Rob nodded his head towards the living room. 'Just changing Ethan. Giving Dad a few pointers.'

'I could never get him to change his own children's nappies, so I wish her luck with that!' Her mother's indignation was the perfect accompaniment to the lavish arrangement of food on the bench.

'Now, now, Beth, don't go defaming a man when he's not around to defend himself.' The birthday boy appeared, carrying his grandson, who had a fist in his mouth and drool coating his chin.

'Happy birthday, Dad.' Tess hugged her father while the baby flashed a gummy smile.

'Thanks, princess.'

'Tess might want a cuddle with Ethan.'

'No, not at the moment.' Her mother never missed an opportunity to drag her into the baby thing, but she'd perfected the art of ducking and weaving. 'Might just grab a drink.'

'Fine. Dinner's ready.' Her mother rushed past, a huge dish of steaming lasagne in her oven-mitted hands.

There was a frenzy of movement and plate passing as they all took their seats. Ally popped through the doorway, blew Tess a kiss and slipped in beside Rob. She was a tiny woman, her long blonde hair pulled up into a ponytail so tight her head must be seriously aching. She leaned across to Ethan, now strapped into a high chair, and wiped his face with the Spiderman bib slung across his chest. Everyone was in their allotted place, Tess in the seat she'd sat in all her life, opposite her brother and to the left of her father, with her mother at the other end of the table. The seat beside her was conspicuously empty.

'So, where's Superboy?' Rob asked.

Tess really was too tired for Rob's teasing tonight. After a lifetime of being the youngest in the family, she'd learned how to let it go. She made sure her voice was light when she answered. 'He's been caught up at work, but he shouldn't be long.' Thankfully, Adrian was off somewhere in the wilds of South America climbing mountains, so there was only one of her brothers here to do the tormenting.

'How was your trip, Tessie?'

Good old Dad, breezing through life with his rose-coloured specs firmly in place.

'Busy but good.'

Her mother's eye roll was standard. She always carried on about how Tess needed to slow down, take things easier, even though she had no idea about life in the corporate world. One day she *might* get over the fact that Tess had refused to become a teacher, or carry on the family tradition and become a teacher-librarian. Probably not. You'd think she'd be satisfied with having a daughter-in-law who taught kindergarten, but it only seemed to make her more irritated with her own daughter's choice of career. Tonight was not, however, the night to tackle that particular issue. Tonight was all about survival.

The table was crammed with the usual menu: pasta, garlic bread, gnocchi, polenta. It was all too much, especially when the Italian blood was on her father's side and he was as Anglo as a shrimp on the barbie. Tess picked at her food, staying firmly under the radar as the conversation bounced from stories about her absent brother's mountaineering adventures to Ethan's latest growth spurt, Rob's new building project and her father's current exploits on the golf course.

When the doorbell chimed, her mother was out of her seat and practically running down the hall in a matter of seconds. She had a huge crush on Josh, despite having two sons of her own. Was it sweet or sickening? If Tess had turned up this late for a special dinner, her mum would have given her the silent treatment for hours.

'Not a problem at all, love, I'll just pop your dinner in the microwave. You sit yourself down. Would you like a beer?' So much fawning. Definitely sickening.

'Thanks. That'd be great.' Josh appeared, brushing a kiss against Tess's cheek. 'Hey, sorry I'm late.' He continued on to the end of the table, clapped her father's shoulder and shook his hand. 'Happy birthday, Tony. Had a good day?'

'Thanks, mate. Not bad. Got in a round of golf, beat the pants off the other blokes, and knocked back a few brews at the club.'

'Excellent. Better than a day at work.' Josh hovered, pushing his tortoise-shell-framed glasses up the bridge of his nose. He'd loosened his tie and rolled up the sleeves of his business shirt, trying to bridge the gap between work wear and family dinner. If Rob made the tired joke about him being Clarke Kent's doppelgänger again, there was a pretty good chance Tess would lose her shit.

'You're not wrong.' Her father was still rambling. 'Retirement's the best thing that's happened to me.'

'Is it, now?' Her mother plonked a plate on the table beside Tess and an opened beer on the coaster. She turned to Josh with a saccharine smile. 'Watch the plate, love, it's hot.'

Tess bit into a forkful of gnocchi, the metal grinding against her teeth. Her mother's eternal fussing was almost sycophantic. Why was she the only one it seemed to bother? The conversation rolled on, with a backing track from Andrea Bocelli until Ethan pitched his rattle across the table and it landed right in the middle of Tess's plate, sending a splash of tomato sauce down the front of her white shirt.

Great. The evening was getting better by the minute.

Muffled laughter erupted around the table. Tess grabbed a serviette and dabbed at the stain. Nothing better than being the butt of everybody else's joke.

'That's a first-grade bowler's arm, right there.' Rob beamed.

'Sorry, Tess.' Ally, at least, looked vaguely embarrassed.

Tess wiped the rattle and, resisting the temptation to aim it at her brother's head, passed it back to the baby. Ethan squealed and a bubble of warmth expanded inside her chest. He really was the cutest little thing and she never bothered paying him much attention.

'He must keep you on your toes.' Awe, and maybe a hint of fear, permeated Josh's contribution to the conversation.

'That's an understatement. But parenthood is the best thing that's happened to *me*.' Rob winked at his father. 'Apart from marrying my beautiful wife, of course.' He put an arm around Ally and gave her a hug.

Ally elbowed him in the side, but the corners of her mouth lifted in a coy smile. Despite their ten-year age difference, they were a very well-suited couple.

Rob chugged on his Corona and banged it on the table. He'd clearly been here well before dinner and downed a few birthday bevvies. 'Speaking of which, are you two all set for your starring roles?'

'Starring roles?' Josh looked at her, equally puzzled.

'Sunday fortnight.' Her mother piped up, positively bursting. 'I'm sure they're both looking forward to it. Make sure you're not late, though, Tessa. Father Rafferty likes everyone to be on time.'

Oh shit! The christening. Grace would have been home with them for just over a week by then. Would it be a good idea to take her to such a huge family gathering so soon? Probably not, but she could hardly announce that now, even if they had been railroaded into being godparents. *There was your first mistake*, Josh had said this morning in reference to her saying yes to the same request from Skye. In this case he was actually right. The whole thing was a farce. 'I don't really get why you're having him christened, to be honest. It's not like either of you is religious.'

'I really don't know why you'd say that, Tessa. You were all christened and it's never hurt any of you.' Her mother had her scolding voice well primed. No doubt she'd had a hand in organising the whole shebang.

'No, but, well … we are both Catholic, and it's just something we want to do.' Ally looked as if she was about to start crying.

Oh Lord, please let it end. 'I never said it hurt anyone.'

'Anyway … Since we are having him dunked, thanks again for agreeing.' Rob de-escalated things before they could get any worse. 'I know kids aren't really your thing, so it means a lot.'

'Our pleasure, mate.' Josh raised his hand and the two of them clinked bottles across the table. 'It's an honour to be asked.'

'And I'm sure kids *are* their thing.' Her mother lifted her fingers into air quotes. 'They just haven't gotten around to it yet. Being godparents will be good practice for when you have your own.'

Josh was a straight-out liar, and as for her mother, if only she knew it was *him* providing the roadblock to her additions to Nonna's Brag Book, she might not treat him like God's gift to the De Santis family. Josh dropped his gaze to his meal and began eating with gusto. No help there. Tess let her knife and fork clatter onto the centre of her plate.

'You can't put it off forever, darling.'

'And you can't help yourself, can you, Mum? Maybe you should just mind your own business for once.' Even as the words fell from her mouth, she wanted to suck them right back in, rewind the conversation to the usual inane topics, but it was already too late.

Her mother lifted a hand to her chest, her eyes wide as the room held its breath.

'Now, Tessie ...' Her father jumped in.

'You must be exhausted, Tess.' Ally rushed in, playing peacekeeper. Confrontation had never been her forte. 'I don't know how you stay on your feet half the time with the hours you do.'

'Probably a little jet-lagged, aren't you, love?' Her father smiled softly, the warning tone now gone from his voice.

'Yeah, I am actually.' Under the table, Josh put a hand on her knee and squeezed. A reminder to count to ten. Or twenty. More likely a thousand the way things were going. Her dad had provided the perfect excuse for her appalling behaviour. She raised what she could of a thankful smile in both their directions and shot a more apologetic one at her mother. 'Sorry, Mum.'

Knives and forks scraped again as life returned almost to normal. Josh sipped quietly at his drink. Ally wiped Ethan's cheek with her napkin and tickled him under the chin, releasing a burst of giggles. The small amount of food Tess had managed to keep down sat like a boulder in the pit of her stomach.

'You do look pale, though, darling. Are you sure it's just from the flight?'

'It's been a tough day.' Finally Josh was speaking up, saving her from wreaking any more havoc. 'Coming home to the bad news about Skye.'

A wave of heat rolled beneath Tess's skin. She locked her hands in her lap. Physical violence in front of her whole family would not go down well.

'Skye Sullivan who you went to school with?' Her mother, not surprisingly, was first to respond.

Josh turned, waiting for her answer, and realisation rippled across his face. 'Oh, sorry.'

'Yes, Mum.' Tess looked up. 'That Skye.' Her mother had never known about Skye's decision to change her name after her grandmother's death. 'She died.'

'Oh. What happened?'

'I'm not sure.'

'That's awful, love.' Her dad sounded genuinely concerned. Rob narrowed his eyes. 'Didn't she have a kid?'

'Grace. She's ten.' If she spoke in short syllables, kept it factual, she might just manage to keep it together.

'Yes, she was a single mother.' Never one to miss an opportunity for moral judgement, her mother shook her head. 'Poor little mite. What's going to happen to her now?'

Josh was busy finishing off his lasagne. It would serve him right if Tess dumped him in it, announced his new status as a father here and now, made him deal with it in front of her whole family. But then she'd be dealing with it, too.

'She's, um, been made a ward of the state. They'll find a foster home for her.' *Please let Ethan start projectile vomiting, let his head spin and his screams be ear-splitting, anything to make this conversation end.*

'Wasn't there another relative?' Her mother squinted. 'Surely they could take her.'

A shrill ringing started up in Tess's ears. She shook her head, simultaneously willing it away and answering the question.

'She was a bit weird, wasn't she?' Rob picked at the crack between his two front teeth, removing a piece of parsley and wiping it on his napkin. 'Into all that new-age crap.'

'For fuck's sake, Rob, just because someone doesn't fit your idea of normal does not mean they're weird.' Tess shoved back her chair, picked up her plate and made a beeline for the kitchen. Scraping her leftovers into the bin, she turned on the tap too hard and sent a shower of water spraying across the parquetry floor.

'Why don't we have the cake in the lounge room?' Her mother's voice was an octave higher than usual as she circled the table collecting the dishes. 'You all head in and we'll be there in a tick.'

Tess leaned against the sink, eyes closed, waiting for the knot in her chest to loosen. Even with the jet-lag excuse, her reaction had been uncalled for, bordering on hysterical. She was usually better at keeping things under control.

'I'm sorry to hear about Skye.' Her mother mopped at the floor with a tea towel, sounding mildly sympathetic.

'You never liked her, anyway.'

'That's not true, Tessa. I had no problem with her when she was younger, but she did go a little off the rails when she left school.'

'I think *wayward* was the adjective you most frequently used to describe her.' She took the soaking cloth from her mum, wringing it out in the sink until her fingers hurt.

'Well she was, Tessa. Even you have to admit that. Out at all hours of the night, worrying her poor grandmother out of her wits. Is it any wonder I didn't want you hanging around with her?'

They were both upright now, her mother shuffling dirty plates into the dishwasher, Tess stationary against the bench. She should muster the energy to help, but her legs refused to move. Skye had been the scapegoat for her 'going off the rails' as a teenager, for her 'wild' behaviour, the tattoo, and the Goth phase her mother had so detested. It was a mutually convenient rationale that Tess had never bothered to challenge. 'It was all a long time ago.'

'Yes, it was. And I am sorry to hear she's died. She didn't have an easy life. And that poor child of hers.'

Children were her mother's Achilles' heel; her concern for Grace was genuine. Maybe confessing her decision to her mum would be good practice for telling Josh. She peered back over her shoulder into the lounge room. Josh seemed to be occupied, deep in conversation with Rob. Now was as good a time as any. She took a deep breath. 'I never told you this, Mum, but I'm Grace's guardian.'

Her mother, retrieving dessert bowls from the cupboard, literally froze mid-movement. 'Do you mean guardian as in *legal* guardian?'

Tess nodded.

'No, you didn't ever tell me that.' She placed the bowls down without looking up.

'We were going through one of our no-speaking stages at the time. I never really thought it would matter that much, but now ...'

Her mother took the cake from the fridge and placed it on the island in the centre of the kitchen. You could almost hear the wheels clanking inside her skull. 'So, what does that mean exactly?'

'A letter came from Family and Community Services. It's up to me—well us,' she motioned towards the lounge room to include Josh, 'to decide whether or not we want to foster her.'

'And what does Josh think?'

'He pretty much dismissed it without a discussion.' This morning's conversation, the letter, all of it was still surprisingly raw. She folded her arms across her chest.

Her mother placed the birthday cake on an engraved silver tray and positioned gold candles around the circumference, her frown lines deepening by the second. This could go either way, but it was better to give her mum time to think it through before jumping back in.

'Taking on someone else's child is a huge decision, Tessa, especially a child of her age. And it's not like you and Skye were that close anymore.'

'This is a little girl we're talking about, a little girl I agreed to look after if anything happened to Skye.' She shook her head. Why had she expected her mother to understand? How could she? 'Anyway, you're always saying you want me to have kids.'

Her mother walked across the kitchen and picked up a box of tissues. She sat down on a stool, patted the one beside it and waited.

Snatches of conversation filtered through from the lounge room punctuated with an occasional baby squeal. This was her father's birthday celebration and she shouldn't be making it about her own problem. She was being selfish. Petulant. Acting like the spoilt child she'd been once. Her mother seemed to be waving a white flag. It would be foolish not to offer one of her own.

'I went to see Grace's caseworker today.' She sucked in a short breath as she sat on the proffered stool. 'There's a possibility that Skye killed herself.'

'Oh no.' Her mother's hand came to rest on top of her own.

The touch bolstered her courage. 'I told them I'm willing to go ahead and foster Grace.'

'But I thought you said Josh was against the idea?'

Tess met her mother's gaze. 'He is.'

A look towards the other room, an unexpected gleam in her mother's watery eyes. 'Well, sometimes things happen for a reason. It's not the ideal way to start a family, but I'm sure Josh will come around. And who knows? It might be the push you both need to start a family of your own.'

A raucous squeal rang out with almost perfect timing.

Grabbing the cake in one hand, her mother stood and handed across a stack of dessert plates. 'Come on, let's get the birthday boy to blow out his candles.'

And that was that. Her mother breezed out of the kitchen, leaving Tess alone and floundering. Had she really just suggested that fostering Grace could be a good idea? And then used it as ammunition for her baby campaign?

Tess made her way to the lounge room, moulding her expression into party mode and mouthing the words of 'Happy Birthday'. As her father blew out the candles, a starry-eyed Ethan nestled on his lap, she looked around for Josh. He was huddled in the corner at the far end of the room, a hand over one ear, an intense expression of concentration on his face as he spoke into his phone. Work, no doubt. It was always work. There was barely room in his life for her, let alone a child. Would he really agree to take on someone else's daughter? Someone else's possibly disturbed ten-year-old daughter?

Hip hip hooray.

Hip hip hooray.

Hip.

Hip.

Hooray.

There was only one way to find out.

Four

The drive home was painfully silent. Josh pulled into the underground carpark and they stepped into the steel tomb of the elevator, Tess watching the neon numbers increase as they stood on separate sides of the lift. She'd been the classic ice queen ever since they left her parents' house. It was their tried-and-tested method of dealing with an issue. Usually she was the first one to thaw; there was no way that was happening tonight.

'I'm sorry I let slip about Skye.'

He must really be feeling guilty to back down so soon, but if he thought that a simple apology was going to cut it he could think again. 'I did ask you not to say anything.'

'I just said I'm sorry, didn't I?'

The doors slid open. She pushed past him and strode along the landing to their apartment. This was not a conversation she wanted to have in a public space. Inside, she headed for the kitchen while Josh gravitated towards the lounge, their respective corners separated by the island bench. Bizarrely, it struck her how good he looked in a suit, the same thing she'd thought when she'd first met him—the sharp, straight lines of his shoulders, the long, muscular stretch of his legs. Even at eleven pm he was scrubbed and polished, his honey-brown hair perfectly coiffed, only the light shadow on his jawline giving away that it was over twelve hours since he'd dressed for work. This morning's conversation was long forgotten if tonight's dinner fiasco was anything to go by, yet for her it had been silently simmering all day. He'd been so sure she'd agree with him, and at the time she'd almost convinced herself she did. Then she'd stepped inside that office and everything had changed.

'I spoke to Grace's caseworker today.' It came out so casually, like she'd had a lovely chat with an old work mate in the middle of the street. She grabbed a glass and filled it from the chiller in the fridge door, let the rattle and clunk of the ice machine fill in the gap left by her opening statement.

'And?' He peeled off his jacket and laid it over the back of the lounge, then began undoing the buttons on his shirt.

Tess took a mouthful of water. There was so much riding on this conversation, she had to get it right. But which piece of information should she lead with? Starting at the beginning, the reason this was even happening, made the most sense. 'Skye ...' Another sip. 'She killed herself.'

'Shit.' Josh pushed his hands into his pockets. 'How?'

'I don't know.' She should have asked for more information, or called back later, but it had been so much easier to hide behind her workload. It still didn't seem real, except the visible tremor running through her limbs was proof this was more than a bad dream.

Josh took a tentative step forward and ran a hand roughly across his chin. 'What about the kid?'

'Grace.' Blood pounded in her ears. She placed her glass very carefully on the bench as she waited for the noise to recede. 'Her name is Grace. She's been temporarily declared a ward of the state.'

He nodded. As if that fact was actually okay. 'Must be tough for her.'

Tough. Like losing a teddy bear or scraping a knee. Was he actually fucking serious? 'Yes, I'm sure it is. That's why I told them we'd foster her.'

His eyes rounded, then narrowed again. 'You did what?'

'I made a promise. I'm going to honour it.'

'Except it's not just you, is it? There are two of us here, last time I looked. You know how I feel about this, Tessa, we discussed it this morning.' A tiny ball of spit rested on his bottom lip as he came closer, hands perched on the back of his hips.

'No. You made a decision.' If he wanted a shouting match she was happy to oblige. 'Without knowing the full story. Without even asking how *I* felt.'

'I didn't need to know the story. We decided years ago we wouldn't be having kids.'

'Again, you decided.'

'And you agreed.'

She glared right at him. Let him see the challenge in her eyes. Let him work it out for himself.

He turned away, his shoulders heaving as he paced across the room and then rounded on her. 'Are you telling me you lied? That all this time you really did want kids?' His voice was deathly quiet now, his cheeks a giveaway shade of crimson.

She rubbed at the bony arch of her eyebrow. Had she lied? Maybe. Or maybe she just hadn't thought it through because it had suited her still-raw disgust with the world. Before she'd learned to put it under lock and key. But this wasn't about them having their own kids, this was about Grace. About

Skye. It was about something she had to do. Her decision this morning in the FACS office might have been impulsive, but there was no question she'd made the right choice. 'She doesn't have anyone else, Josh.'

'Tess, this is huge.'

'I know.'

He sighed, his body slumping as if an enormous load had just been dumped on him. In a sense it had, and at least he was trying to be honest. They'd always been about the plan, especially Josh, and this was so far left of their plan it was hard to comprehend. She squeezed his arm. 'It scares me shitless, too, but I'll never be able to live with myself if I don't do this.'

He remained rigid, unreachable, as he gripped the back of the chair, head bowed. Putting any more pressure on him would be a mistake; it was better to let him process. Tess let her hand fall and finally he straightened up. 'I need some time to think about it.'

'Okay.'

'I have the bike trip tomorrow. I'm going to bed.' He walked away from her and up the stairs.

The bedroom door banged shut and she let out a breath. Sleeping would not be an option for her tonight, so she may as well have a coffee. Nothing had been resolved really and there was the visit to Grace in the morning. Yet another lie of omission, but one best kept under wraps for now. The kettle droned robotically as she scanned the pristine space of their apartment. Would it pass muster when Regina Martin came for the inspection? Would she and Josh, for that matter? All those happy snaps hanging like question marks on the wall of the FACS office. Were the two of them really up to parenting Grace, even if Josh did agree to come along for the ride? *Traumatised. Withdrawn. Possible emotional issues.* All details she'd neglected to share with her husband, the foster-father by default. Water bubbled, violently rattling the stainless-steel kettle until it switched itself off with a high-pitched *bing.*

Instant would do the job at this time of night. She heaped in a generous spoonful and filled it to the brim. It tasted like dirt but had the zing she needed and the liquid burn she craved. *I don't know if I can do this*, Josh had said. And yet, for her it seemed almost like a gift. A second chance at getting things right. Whatever it was, she couldn't let Skye down again.

An ordinary suburban house in an ordinary suburban street. Hardly the stuff of nightmares, and yet Tess's insides were quivering like jelly.

She needed to get over herself, stop being such a wimp. Her fingers tightened around the handle of the gift bag she was carrying as the gate opened with a whine and clanged shut behind her. It wasn't just the prospect of meeting Grace that was making her sick to the stomach, it was the whole situation. There'd been no opportunity to resolve things with Josh before he had headed off with his cycling crew. Any further discussion about fostering would have to wait until late tomorrow, but at least if things went well this morning she could give him a positive report. Two more short steps to the door and she pressed the bell before she could change her mind. The carer had gone through the rules when Tess had called to confirm the visit and let her know she'd be coming on her own: *keep the conversation light and neutral, don't ask any potentially upsetting questions, and above all, don't make any reference to adoption.*

Or Skye.

The front door swung open and a round-faced woman smiled from behind the wire screen. 'You must be Tess. I'm Kirsten. Come on in.'

'Thank you.' She seemed nice, normal, like the house.

'Grace is watching television.' Kirsten started down the hallway, tucking a strawberry-blonde strand of hair behind one ear. She was wearing jeans and a sweatshirt, possibly a better option than Tess's skirt and boots topped with a mohair jumper, the third outfit she had tried on before leaving the apartment. They stopped in the kitchen and Kirsten leaned close. 'Correction. Grace is sitting in front of the TV, but I'm not sure she's actually taking anything in. I gather you've been filled in on the situation?'

Tess nodded. 'Yes. Ms Martin told me she's quite withdrawn.'

Kirsten pursed her lips. 'Maybe a visitor will perk her up.' Her eyes were soft and her manner warm. She stepped through a timber-framed alcove into a wide rumpus room at the back of the house, its walls lined with shelves of books and an assortment of toys. Canned laughter pealed out from a television at the far end of the room. Slumped in a brown velvet beanbag was a waif of a girl, a curtain of long, dark curly hair tumbling over her shoulders. Her body was angled away, concealing her face. If she'd heard any voices she didn't react, didn't turn around, but remained inert. The soles of Tess's ankle boots squelched on the linoleum and she cringed, tiptoeing the rest of the distance to join the foster carer as she bent down, hands clasped in front of her. 'Grace, you have a visitor.'

No movement.

Kirsten shifted closer and laid a hand on Grace's shoulder. The foam beads in the bag rustled as the little girl shuffled sidewards. 'Grace, this is Tess. Remember I told you she was coming to see you?'

An ever-so-slow turn of the head. Tess's breath hitched and for a few unbelievable seconds her heart stopped beating. The pale complexion, the smattering of freckles across the nose, the blue-grey eyes. Grace was an absolute replica of her mother; the perfect image of Skye when she'd arrived at the school in third grade. Except for the patch of pink skin on Grace's left cheek. Although the birthmark she'd been born with had faded, it was still there. An angel's kiss, Skye had called it, laughing as she'd stroked a finger over the bow-shaped blotch.

A sharp pain in the centre of her chest reminded Tess to exhale. 'Hi, Grace, you wouldn't remember me, but my name is Tess.' Kirsten nodded. *So far, so good.* 'I got you a little something. I hope you like it.' She held the gift bag closer, but Grace just looked down at her hands.

What now? The present was no big deal, just an icebreaker. Still, it didn't seem to be opening any avenues of communication. She glanced at Kirsten, who gave a not-so-subtle roll of her fingers. *Keep trying.*

Tess sank down onto her calves, ignoring the crack of her knee bones, and placed the gift on the floor. Grace's lips twitched. A worn brown bear slipped from under her arm as she tentatively reached out and hauled the bag into her lap. The bear lay there staring up with his one good eye. Just as Tess moved to rescue him, Grace lunged, gathering him into her arms and holding him to her chest.

'How about you bring your present up to the table when you're ready and we'll have some morning tea?' Kirsten winked and stood. She was clearly using a diversion tactic, giving Grace some time alone. Tess pushed herself upright, angling her head in the child's direction and smiling, still getting no response.

In the kitchen, the kettle was already boiling.

'Tea or coffee?'

'Tea, please. White, no sugar.'

Either Grace was hungry or super obedient. Gift bag in one hand, bear dangling from the other, she was up and moving, light-blue skinny jeans clinging to her thin legs, her dark mane of hair hanging loose, almost to her waist. She pulled out a chair and deposited both bear and bag on the table. Tess hovered in the doorway. Joining Grace on her own could be too unsettling. Kirsten came to the rescue, carrying a loaded tray, and leading the way with a cheery grin.

'So you and Grace's mum were old school friends?'

Wasn't that subject a no-go zone?

Grace slurped at the milk Kirsten had placed in front of her, looking up in Tess's direction and then back to her glass. Maybe that was a good sign? Maybe she did want to hear about Skye.

'Yes, we were. We met in primary school and went all through high school together. To Year Ten, anyway. Actually ...' She dug around in her handbag and pulled out an envelope, then began fishing through the contents. Watching Grace, she laid out the snapshots and eased them across the table. 'I found these last night.' Skimming through boxes of old photos after Josh had gone to bed had been a good way to pass the witching hours when sleep refused to come. Until the faded polaroids of Skye and her had become too much. She'd shoved them in an envelope and this morning, despite the rules she'd been given, had slipped them into her bag. Just in case.

Grace reached out to pick up the closest photo. She stared at the image, her expression neutral.

'That's your mum when she was about your age. You look just like her.'

Kirsten looked wistful. She had such a kind, gentle manner, it was easy to see she'd make a good foster-mother.

Grace blinked. Resting the photo in one hand, she traced the outline of Skye's face with her index finger.

How could Skye have deserted her only child when she was so young, so vulnerable? Tess reached out a hand to stroke those silky locks of hair; Grace tipped her head and edged away.

Touch was a no-no, but the photos still held Grace's interest. 'And this one is of you when you were a baby. I was there when you were born. You were so beautiful, and Skye … your mum … was so happy. I'd never held a newborn before and you were so small, it was like holding a bundle of feathers.' A cough from the other side of the table. Oh God, she'd got carried away with herself and gone too far.

'Are you going to open your present?' Kirsten nodded towards the still-unopened gift.

Without making eye contact with either of the adults, Grace picked up the bag and sat it on her lap. She pulled out the white cardboard box, letting the bag itself drop to the floor, unfolded the edges of the lid and removed the contents: a wooden jewellery box, its lid inlaid with flowers and butterflies of mother-of-pearl. It was the first thing that had caught Tess's eye in the giftshop, something she would have loved herself when she was young. A shadow flitted across Grace's face.

'There's something inside.'

'Would you like to take a look?' Kirsten was really trying to help, even though Grace remained mute.

This was not going well. In the backyard, a swing set and slippery dip sat beneath a huge old maple tree. It was like astral travelling back in time to Tess's own childhood. Swings, trampoline, pool—her parents had provided their three children with the works. Bikes, scooters, rollerblades. Hours of entertainment and a garage overflowing with 'things'. They hadn't been rich, but they'd certainly been comfortable. An idyllic, stress-free life. She had no idea what Grace's childhood had been like up to this point. Some godmother she'd turned out to be.

'How about a cookie?' Kirsten, on the other hand, was total magic. She moved the jewellery box aside and replaced it with a plate of choc-chip biscuits.

A small hand crept towards the plate. Grace sat back and nibbled at a cookie like any normal kid. *Yes!* Such a small thing, and yet the very ordinariness of it seemed to dissolve the mounting tension.

'So, what do you usually do on weekends, Tess?' Kirsten was keeping the conversation flowing.

'Well, I work pretty long hours during the week. So I try to catch up on house stuff on weekends, or my husband and I sometimes have coffee, or go for walks if he's not out on his bike.'

'He cycles?'

'Yes, he's in a club. They're away riding this weekend, in Kangaroo Valley. His name's Josh. He's a software designer.' It was more information than Kirsten had asked for, but there was no harm in sneaking in some extra details. Not that it seemed to have any impact on Grace—she'd finished the cookie and was licking the crumbs from her lips.

'And what's your line of work?'

'Oh, I'm in human resources.' That would mean nothing to a ten-year-old. 'I have my own company, run training programs, consult, that sort of thing. I've just come back from Los Angeles.' Should a potential mother figure be jetting off to foreign countries? Oh God, she was totally screwing this up. Cartoon voices squealed from the far end of the room, the perfect opportunity for a change of topic. 'I used to love watching cartoons when I was your age, Grace. I loved *Scooby Doo*. Do you have a favourite?'

Nothing. It was as if Tess had not even spoken.

'Grace didn't have a television at home, so she might not be all that familiar with what's on,' Kirsten explained.

Well done, Tess. You're really on a roll here. 'Ah, I see. I don't watch much myself these days. I prefer reading books to watching a screen.' Was that a tiny flicker of light behind the girl's eyes at the mention of books? 'Do you like to read, Grace?'

A nod. Small. But a nod just the same.

Finally, some common ground. 'Maybe we can go shopping together sometime soon. I can show you my favourite bookshops.'

Grace swiped a finger across the milk moustache left behind by her drink, her hand almost hiding the slight curve of her lips. At last, a connection.

'Let's wait and see.' Kirsten glanced down at her watch. 'We'll let you get on with your morning, Tess.' She rose from her chair, signalling the end of the meet-and-greet.

Fair enough, she'd possibly over-stepped, but her business wasn't quite finished. Tess crouched down again beside Grace's chair. 'It was so lovely to see you after all this time, Grace. Can I come back again?'

A slight shrug.

Not a yes, but not a no. 'Okay, well, goodbye.' Tess pressed her lips together and squeezed her hands around her kneecaps.

It didn't seem right to leave without some kind of touch or a kiss to the cheek. Grace gave no indication that either would be acceptable and her wishes had to be respected.

'I'll see you out.' Kirsten gestured towards the front door.

It was time to leave. As she followed Kirsten into the kitchen she touched a hand to the other woman's arm. 'I'm so sorry if I said anything wrong. This is all new to me.'

'I understand. It's new to her, too. We just have to take baby steps and ease her into the situation.'

Tess sighed. 'I don't want to make things worse for her.'

'The book idea seemed to click. You could possibly bring her a book next time? Not that I think the way to a child's heart is through gifts, but in this case it might be a way in.'

Next time. That sounded positive. 'Is it okay if I come back tomorrow?'

'I'm afraid not. You'll need to organise that with the office. But it would be good if you could come and see her again before everything is finalised. She needs to get to know you— and vice versa—if she's going to live with you. Can your husband come along?'

'Of course.' Tess's smile was so tight her cheeks ached.

Kirsten laid a hand on her shoulder. 'Don't look so worried. I'm sure it'll all be fine. She just needs time to adjust.'

'I hope so.' Together they looked back to where Grace was seated at the table. The lid of the jewellery box was open and the gold necklace Tess had placed inside was dangling from Grace's fingertips, the small heart-shaped locket resting in her other palm. She considered it for a moment before tossing it back in the box and banging down the lid, then turned away to stare out the window.

The tiny bud of hope starting to unfurl in Tess's heart snapped shut. It was only a necklace, and she hadn't been trying to buy the girl's affection, but secretly she'd wished for a better reaction. She said goodbye to Kirsten and headed back to the car, as wrung out as if she'd just run a marathon. Regina Martin had warned her not to expect anything, and she'd been right. The dull light in Grace's eyes, the complete lack of interest in anything Tess had said—apart from the one brief spark at the mention of books. It wasn't much, but it was something. Something to grab onto when there was very little else to celebrate.

Five

The laptop was taking forever to boot up. Meanwhile, the smooth merlot Tess had found in the wine rack was going down a treat. It was a 2013 bottle. The year she and Josh had married. It was handy that his father owned a vineyard and could supply both the wine and the venue. The day had been everything she'd dreamed of and more. Josh, so very Mr Darcy in his tux; her dad's eyes shining as she had taken his arm at the end of the bespoke aisle; the rustic pergola dripping in purple wisteria they'd stood beneath while they had swapped their vows. A light breeze had jostled the flowers and a few wayward petals had settled on her shoulders like mauve jewels against the champagne silk of her dress. They'd decided on only one attendant each since Skye was the only person Tess could think of who fitted the brief, but she'd been unable to come at the last minute. Grace had taken ill with a bout of measles, so Ally had stepped in and saved the day. Her mother had managed the necessary alterations in between mutterings about ridiculous people who refused to get their children vaccinated. So, apart from the missing bridesmaid, it had all gone according to plan.

Much like their lives afterwards. Until now.

The update finally finished and it was time to google, but she had no idea where to start. A name was as good a place as any. She typed out the letters and within a few seconds a list of possibilities appeared—Skye Whittaker on YouTube, Facebook, Twitter, Instagram, Vimeo, Soundcloud. There was no point in checking any of them. Skye's refusal to indulge in anything remotely resembling even twentieth-century technology meant there would be no social media profile of any kind. There was page after page of listings, a bucketload of images of women and girls who were not her Skye, but nothing worth clicking on until page eleven. A report in the *Central Western Times*, the newspaper from the area in which Skye had lived. And died. Tess moved her finger across the touchpad and let it hover. Her gut clenched. Opening the link was a risk, but something inside her needed to know. One quick press of her finger and there it was.

Local Woman Found Dead

Police were called to a location outside the township of Weer-illa yesterday where a woman was found dead in her home. The deceased has been identified as Skye Whittaker, a thirty-five-year-old mother of one. The woman's daughter has been taken into the care of Family and Community Services. Police say there are no suspicious circumstances surrounding the death.

No suspicious circumstances. Found dead. Police jargon for presumed suicide. Tess sat back and let the mellow tannins of the merlot rinse away the sting of bile. What possibly could have driven Skye to do such a thing after all this time?

Or who, was probably the better question.

Footsteps sounded from the far end of the apartment. She closed the laptop and sprang from the lounge, knocking over her wineglass as she stood. 'Shit.'

'Tess?' Josh's voice grew louder as he made his way down the hall.

Grabbing a tea towel from the kitchen, she raced back out, managing to stem the flow of crimson liquid oozing along the coffee table before it hit the edge of the shagpile rug.

'Good save.' A kiss to the top of her head; a broad hand, warm across her back.

'How was your weekend?' She shifted her computer out of the way and mopped at the wine.

'Great. Exhausting, but we had an awesome time.' He was in the kitchen now—rummaging around in the fridge.

'That's good.' She dumped the cloth into the sink and held the half-full bottle towards him. 'I managed to save some.'

'Might have one with dinner. I feel a bit grotty. Think I'll shower first.'

This was the first real communication they'd had since Friday night, apart from a few quick texts when he'd managed to get some reception. She stepped closer and kissed him, lingering. 'You're right, you do need a shower.'

'That's a nice way to greet your husband.' He had that wounded little-boy face he was so good at, but the smile in his voice was a good sign. He seemed calm, happy after his time away. Maybe even in the mood for a civil discussion.

'Go shower while I get dinner. Then you can tell me about your weekend.'

'Deal. And you can tell me what you've been up to.'

She spun back towards the sink, flicking on the hot water. Up to? He made it sound so underhanded. Sneaky. Not that he was far off track. She rinsed the cloth, wringing it until her palms burned and Josh was out of earshot. 'I can't wait to tell you all about my visit to meet the kid you don't want.'

About how she'd already booked them in to sign the official papers without bothering to consult him first.

She closed her eyes and downed the rest of her wine. She was making a complete balls-up of things. Broaching the subject again wasn't going to be easy, but it had to be done, and it had to be done tonight. The half-full bottle was on the bench. She was already light-headed, only a few hours of sleep last night and not much to eat all day. But a little more liquid courage wouldn't hurt.

By the time they'd finished dinner their conversation had covered the highlights of the bike trip, the pros and cons of riding in winter and the finer points of Tess's boring weekend of housework. They were both being extremely polite and hugely interested in what the other was saying, but the one thing they needed to talk about chafed at the pauses between their sentences.

The Chill playlist on her computer shuffled onto one of her favourite Ed Sheeran songs, 'Perfect'. Destined to be played at a zillion weddings, smitten couples gazing lovingly into each other's eyes as Ed warbled away about them being made for each other. She looked across at Josh, his cheeks pink from hours in the sun, hair slicked back from his forehead. When they'd first met he'd been her idea of perfect. Solid. Secure. Safe. He was still the same man she'd married. Exactly the same. And therein lay the problem she needed to address.

'Josh, we need to talk.'

'Yeah, I guess we do.'

Don't think about it. Just start. 'So I—'

'I'm sorry about the way I reacted the other night.' His habit of talking over the top of her hadn't changed either. 'I was just taken by surprise, I think. In shock.' He rested his hands on the edge of the table. 'I know you say it's what you want, but I'm still not convinced it's a great idea, Tess.'

So much for the apology. Had he even bothered to think about it while he was away? She needed to stay calm if she had any hope at all of convincing him. She needed to make him see they could do this. She raised her chin, made sure her voice was low and steady. 'I met her yesterday.'

He frowned. 'Met who?'

'Grace. I went to the Emergency Care Home where she's staying.'

Josh turned one knuckled hand over and studied his fingers, as if he was contemplating the length of his nails. He inhaled slowly as he looked up. 'And?'

'She's sweet. Looks exactly like Skye. It was a little freaky, to be honest.'

His eyes were dark, unfathomable. Only the set of his jaw gave away what was going on inside his head. Appealing to his sense of compassion, his basic human decency was the way to go. 'She's very quiet. Withdrawn. But I guess that's understandable.' Saliva pooled beneath her tongue at the memory of the newspaper article.

Josh rested a fisted hand against his mouth.

'I know this isn't what we planned, but sometimes life throws things at you and you don't have any choice.'

'Except we do have a choice.'

'Do we? Really? Could you live with yourself if we say no to this, knowing that we can offer Grace a perfectly good, stable home?' Her composure was rapidly evaporating, but the

58

time for calm and common sense had passed. She had to make him understand. 'What if she ends up with some dodgy foster-family?'

'There are plenty of good people out there who want to foster kids, Tessa.' He was using his settle-down-you're-getting-hysterical tone. The one that made her want to punch him.

'And there are plenty of people who are just after the money. How many stories do you hear about kids being shunted from one home to the next and ending up on the streets or emotionally damaged—or worse.'

'From what you say, Grace is already damaged.'

'She probably is, so why make it even harder for her?'

'And you think we're fully equipped to deal with a child with potentially serious issues? Us, with all of our extensive parenting skills?'

Why did he have to be such a smartarse? She scrubbed a hand across her forehead. He was right, of course, they didn't have a clue about child rearing. Three years of an unfinished psych degree at uni hardly qualified her as an expert, but that wasn't the point. 'Nobody knows how to be a parent before they are one. We're not stupid, Josh, we use common sense and FACS provide support. We wouldn't be doing this on our own.'

The soft sounds of an acoustic guitar hummed in the background. Their wineglasses sat empty on the table. She leaned across and reached for his hand, and for a moment neither of them moved. Josh inched his hand towards hers, finally resting his palm across her fingers. He looked like a frightened little boy, perhaps the little boy he'd been when his own parents had pushed and pulled him in the tug-of-war custody battle they'd staged in his early teens. Her heart swelled. Was it fair doing this to him? Forcing him into a life he didn't want?

But *not* doing it wrenched at something even deeper inside her, something she couldn't even begin to unravel. Or explain.

She flipped her hand over and twined her fingers between his. 'We can do this, I know we can.'

Josh let out a long sigh. 'I guess we can give it a try.' His voice was so low she could barely hear him.

They sat at the bench, neither of them daring to speak. The decision had been made and now everything would change. It felt like the end of something, but also a beginning, the future unfolding before them like an invisible map they would some-how have to learn how to read.

Six

'Here we are. Let's head up and show you your room.' The chirpiness of Tess's voice was all bravado. Bringing Grace home was one of the scariest things she'd ever done, but there was no way she was going to let it show.

The engine stopped and Josh climbed out, the banging of the car door jarring in the near-empty parking garage. Grace's eyes remained fixed on a point somewhere beyond the backseat passenger window. Tess coaxed her out with a wave. There was no point in trying to take her hand: she'd made it clear she didn't like being touched.

Josh popped the boot. 'You girls go on ahead. I'll grab the bags.'

'Okay.' He'd been so helpful over the last week, an absolute model of politeness through all the meetings, police checks, personality assessments and home inspections. Even meeting Grace, he'd been more than pleasant, yet there was something about his manner that didn't seem quite right, as if he was trying too hard.

Weren't they both?

Tess held her smile all the way to the basement foyer, Grace walking by her side and hugging her bedraggled bear.

The lift doors slid open and Grace froze.

'In you go.' Josh balanced a pathetically small suitcase in one hand and a plastic shopping bag with a few toys Kirsten had bequeathed in the other.

Grace's knuckles blanched around the teddy's arm. The doors began to close and she stumbled backwards into Josh's legs.

'Shit.' The expletive fell so easily from his lips. So much for the conversation about watching their language.

As Tess pressed the button again realisation dawned: Grace may never have been in a lift before—it was probably like stepping into a spaceship for the poor kid, like being abducted by aliens.

She crouched down, tucking her hands in, resisting the urge to reach out. 'It's okay, Grace. Nothing will hurt you. Hop in and we'll be up to our apartment in a few seconds.' This time she held the door, and her breath, as Josh stepped inside and then Grace shuffled in to join them, her face ashen. No one spoke as the elevator rose, but when the doors opened again Grace was the first out. Tess moved past her and led the way along the landing. A few more seconds and the three of them would be inside the apartment, heading into the un-charted territory of being a family. A spark of adrenaline burst through Tess's veins as she pushed the key into the lock, and her smile was completely genuine. All the checks and inter-views had taken longer than anticipated, so Grace had been with Kirsten two days longer than planned, making the whole process even more nerve-racking. But they were here now and it was a new start for all of them. It needed to be positive.

'I left the sandwich on the table next to the bed.' Josh slouched against the back of the kitchen stool. There was a definite note of irritation in his voice; he was letting his mask slip. 'She didn't even look at it.'

'Must be strange for her.' Tess poured a second cup of coffee, slid it across the bench to him and inhaled the dreamy scent from her own mug.

'She's not the only one it's strange for.'

'We have to be patient with her, Josh. Give her some time to adjust.'

He shrugged. 'I've got some work to do.' Picking up his mug, he walked over to his desk in the far corner of the living area. He had the lean, lithe gait of a panther, almost a lope. Another one of the things she'd found attractive when they'd met. Sexy, even, along with his smouldering eyes. Funny how, now that she was starting to assess him more from a parenting perspective, none of those things mattered anymore.

Parents. They were actually parents. Not quite officially, but the paperwork was being processed and in the interim they'd been approved as legal guardians. Not of a squirming baby, one they'd conceived and watched grow, but a fully formed ten-year-old girl. Although Tess had no idea what morning sickness felt like, nausea seemed to be her default state of existence these days. Some days were worse than others and the current bout was an eight out of ten. She shot a glance up the stairs, her teeth dragging at the inside of her mouth. One of them had to try to connect with Grace and it wasn't going to be Josh.

'Hey, there.' She poked her head inside Grace's bedroom door, keeping her voice just above a whisper.

Grace was perched by the pillow on the edge of the bed, the bear in her lap, the untouched sandwich and full glass of milk still on the bedside table. 'Not hungry?'

Only a blink.

Before she could second-guess herself, Tess took the three steps to the bed and sat down near the end. She was a big fan of personal space herself and she could sense the need for it in Grace. 'I hope you like your room. We haven't finished decorating it yet, thought we'd wait until you got here so we can go shopping together. I couldn't resist the quilt cover, though. It reminded me of the one I had when I was a little girl.' She ran her hand over the patchwork bed cover. Bouquets of dark-blue roses against a field of powdery-pink daisies.

No response.

'It's a new bed, too. I hope it's comfortable.' Converting the spare room from a storage space into a child's bedroom had been a rush job and the smell of fresh paint lingered.

Some fresh air wouldn't hurt. Tess walked to the window and slid it open, the usual traffic noises filtering into the room. A gruff voice yelled some sort of abuse. She and Josh had become immune to the sounds, but what would a girl who had lived in the country all her life make of them? If the noises bothered Grace she showed no sign, but then she showed no sign about anything. Beneath the window sat a set of shelves, bare except for the few books Tess had bought as welcoming gifts. It was worth a try. Selecting one, she moved back to the bed, sitting a little closer this time, but still maintaining a safe distance.

'This was one of my favourites when I was your age.' She angled the book so Grace could see the cover. *The Lion, the*

Witch and the Wardrobe. Her own copy was still on a shelf in her old room at her parents' house. Re-gifting it had been a possibility, but the pages were tattered and the cover half off. You couldn't go wrong with a new book and a classic seemed the best choice. What wasn't there to love about Narnia?

'Do you know this story? Would you like me to read you some of it?'

Reading aloud had been one of her favourite things to do as a kid—her mother had later used it as ammunition as to why she should go into teaching. Josh had laughed out loud when she'd once suggested she read to him in bed, saying there were plenty of things he wanted her to do in bed, but reading wasn't one of them. Apparently, Grace didn't have any objections, so Tess cleared her throat and began.

'Once there were four children, whose names were Peter, Susan, Edmund and Lucy.' In an instant, she too was climbing through the wardrobe, back in that fantasy world of childhood where everything was magical.

At the end of Chapter One she came up for air to find something miraculous had happened. Grace had shifted closer until their arms were almost touching. She gazed down at the book, a dreamy light in her eyes as she reached out and gathered it into her lap. Carefully, she turned one page and then the next, her reverence for the object in her hands more than obvious. She might not be speaking, but she was responding to the story. This was good. Better than good.

She had to tell Josh. Running from the room and cheering like a crazed football fan would not do much to reassure Grace. Better to stand slowly and talk very quietly.

'I'll leave you to yourself for a little while. If you need anything give me a shout. Or just come downstairs.' Another page turned as Tess left, leaving the door slightly ajar.

Yes! This was an absolute win. A total buzz stayed with her all the way down the stairs, to where Josh was on a conference call. He frowned when she tried to speak and her dizzy excitement evaporated. Her news would have to wait. Now was probably as good a time as any to check her emails, to keep herself busy. She'd taken the next few weeks off work so she could settle Grace in and try to get her head around the whole mothering gig. Being your own boss had its perks, but there was still admin to be done.

She scrolled through her inbox, concentration only half on what she was doing, until she decided to empty her spam, and there it was: *State Coroner's Office: Skye Whittaker.* Her stomach twisted itself into a knot. Even though she'd known this was coming, had been told to expect it and provided her email address, seeing it right there in black and white was too much. Skye's body had been taken to Newcastle for an autopsy and a coroner's report had been completed. There was a backlog, it would take time, they'd told her, and she'd pushed it to the back of her mind, concentrated on getting things sorted with Grace. The room narrowed to the page in front of her, then to specific words and phrases as she skimmed the email, taking in only snippets.

Coroner's finding.

No inquest.

Overdose of prescription medication.

Death certificate.

Funeral arrangements.

Contact mortician.

Tess sat back, absorbing the ramifications of each phrase. As practised as she was at avoidance, this was one thing she was going to have to face. She was the executor of Skye's will, but more than that she was her friend. Giving her a proper funeral, making sure her last wishes were carried out was the least Tess could do. Right now, Skye was lying on a slab in a morgue waiting to be transferred back to the local funeral home and it was up to her to organise it.

But when?

They'd just brought Grace home. Uprooting her and dragging her back to where her mother had died could make things a whole lot worse. Ruin the chance of them building any sort of relationship. Skye had to be buried and shouldn't Grace have the opportunity to say a proper goodbye? Bringing Skye's body to Sydney could be an option. Tess was way out of her depth here. She looked across to Josh. He was rambling away on the phone, happily lost in discussions of budgets and financial reports. No help there. Professional advice was what she needed and there was only one person she could trust. Eleanor. Another friend she hadn't spoken to in years. Not in person. Only the occasional 'like' or comment on Facebook. Now was the time to look her up.

A few clicks and there she was: a clinical paediatric practice in Glebe and the contact number was right there on the screen. It was a Monday, early afternoon, so a perfect time to call, but the familiar feel of her phone in her back pocket was gone. Damn, she must have left it upstairs.

All was quiet as she approached Grace's room, not that she'd expect anything else. She peeked around the corner to see what was happening. The plate was empty and the milk gone, and Grace lay on the bed, fast asleep with her bear, the book facedown beside her. She looked so peaceful, with her hand tucked under her chin. An ache throbbed inside Tess's chest and she had to work hard to keep it there, stop it creeping its way up and out. Half an hour ago the picture in front of her would have brought a smile to her face, but now all she could see was a lost little girl whose mother had probably killed herself, sprawled out on someone else's bed. Tiptoeing into the room, Tess picked up her phone from the bedside table, pressed two fingers to her lips and transferred the kiss to the corkscrew locks of hair falling across Grace's forehead. So soft; so beautiful.

She dialled Eleanor's number on her way back downstairs, before she could think too hard, ignoring the all-too-familiar tingling in her limbs. Psychologists weren't her favourite people, but her own issues would have to be sidelined, her old doubts forgotten. Right now, Grace had to come first.

Seven

It was a relief to finally be alone in the waiting room now that Eleanor's receptionist had clocked off. The woman had made her feelings more than clear about Grace being squeezed onto the patient list at the last minute: her boss was highly respected, had a waiting list 'as long as your arm' and was doing an enormous favour by fitting Tess in to her already overloaded schedule. Why did medical receptionists always treat their employers like some kind of divine being who needed protecting from the mere mortals who dared to enter their sanctum? Now there was an irony. In her younger years, Eleanor Carter had been far from celestial. At uni she'd spent most of her time drunk, hopping in and out of bed with their male classmates and barely passing her undergrad courses. Which only went to show how much people changed. Eleanor was now one of the most sought-after paediatric psychologists in Sydney. Tess, on the other hand, had achieved only HDs in the same subjects then opted out.

But that was another story.

The waiting room was exactly what you'd expect. Subtle hues of blues and greens, black-and-white images of beach scenes dotting the walls. Did Eleanor still surf now that she was a hotshot psychologist, *the* woman to see if your kid had a problem? If the décor was any indication, the answer was yes. Grey velvet chairs were arranged around a small round table decorated with shells and one of those transparent glass paperweights with a wave curling inside. An aromatherapy jar with a bunch of skewers protruding from the top smelled suspiciously like reef oil. A few kids' books and magazines were strategically placed on a side table, with a lamp setting off a gentle glow. Calm and relaxed. The sort of feeling you always got around Eleanor herself. Hopefully, Grace would react to her in the same way.

Tess tossed the magazine she was blindly flicking through onto the table. What was going on in there? She'd begged to be allowed into the office for the session, but Eleanor was adamant she wait outside, citing the importance of patient confidentiality and trust building. She got it, of course, but the whole point of this exercise was to find out how Grace was feeling about her mother's death, and if there was a chance she might actually say something, Tess wanted to be there.

The hour was almost up. Not much time to sort out the problem, but that was the limit on the session, and according to Eleanor, about as long as children Grace's age could handle. She picked up her phone and thumbed through her messages, all work related, stuff she could deal with later. There was radio silence from Josh. No checking in about the appointment, or Grace. Or anything.

The office door swung open before she could process that thought any further. Grace emerged, eyes down, a book tucked under her arm with Eleanor standing behind. 'Can we have a chat?'

Grace sat in a chair and peeled open the book. Was it okay to leave her out here on her own?

'She'll be fine.' Eleanor tipped her head in the direction of the office and Tess followed her in, taking a seat on the patient side of the desk.

'So, how did it go?'

Eleanor moved her head from side to side as if she had a crick in her neck. 'So-so.'

'What does that mean?' Tess hadn't made it as far as the clinical studies in her psychology degree, but she'd done enough to have her warning antennas twitching at Eleanor's ambiguous response.

Eleanor gestured towards the desk, where an assortment of picture books cluttered the surface.

'Books?' Tess raised her eyebrows. 'You spent the session reading books?'

'Not entirely. You said books seemed to be the only thing she was interested in, so I thought I'd try something different.'

Tess picked up the one closest to where she was sitting. *Possum Magic*. An old favourite when she'd been a kid. A very young kid. 'El, she's ten. Isn't she a little old for this stuff?'

Eleanor's eyes lit up and she sprang from her chair, gathered up two piles of books and placed them side by side. 'Yes, but if Grace *is* into books it means she's been exposed to them as she's grown up.'

Okay. Maybe she had a point. Tess nodded for her friend to continue.

'So, I was hoping that presenting her with some of the books she might be familiar with could spark some kind of reaction, facilitate conversation, since she wasn't very forth-coming.'

'Not very forthcoming' was a polite way of saying 'mute'. Eleanor was the real deal now with all her talk of 'exposure' and 'facilitating'. She obviously knew what she was doing. Tess sat up straighter, a tiny hummingbird of hope fluttering inside her ribcage. 'And did it?'

'Yes and no.'

Urgh. 'El, did it work or didn't it? Did you get her talking?'

Eleanor let out a loud sigh and moved around to the back of her desk, going into 'doctor' mode as she slid into the chair. 'It's not that simple, Tess. I told you there might not be a quick fix.'

'I get that. But did you manage to find out anything?'

Eleanor nodded. 'The books she chose were quite reveal-ing.' She pushed one of the piles across the desk, arching one eyebrow without moving the rest of her face, a skill of which Tess had always been inordinately jealous. 'Take a look at these. Note the illustrations in particular.'

The first pile contained five picture books and the theme emerged very quickly. A talking tree. A grasshopper. Paddocks dotted with black-faced sheep. Clouds floating across a cray-oned sky. A quaint old cottage perched high on a hill sur-rounded by wide green fields. Tess closed the last book and returned it to the pile. 'They're all set in the country.' You didn't have to be Einstein to work it out. Or Freud.

'Touché. And these …' Eleanor picked up the second pile. 'Are all set in the city.'

'Did you give her these books deliberately? Did you know what she'd choose?' Tess held up a cautionary finger. 'And do not say yes *and* no.'

Eleanor laughed. 'To begin with I just gave her random books, but then I noticed there were quite a few with rural scenes and I started thinking about where Grace came from, what she might be into … so I let her choose them herself.'

'And it worked? I mean, she reacted in some way?'

'Her expression changed as she was reading them, became less distant. Softer. She even giggled at one point.'

'Giggled? Really?' In the three days Grace had been with them, Tess hadn't seen her smile, let alone emit any sound even vaguely resembling a giggle.

'Yep.' Eleanor made a popping sound, emphasising the 'p'. 'And the one she has out there with her she pretty much refused to part with, so I told her she could keep it.'

Where was Eleanor going with this? Of course Grace was a reader. The collection of books Tess had bought were about the only things she seemed interested in, but it didn't exactly provide any clues as to how she was feeling. 'Did she actually say anything about her mother? About what's happened?'

Eleanor clasped her hands together.

'El, what?'

'I think she wants to go home.'

'Home, as in Weerilla?'

A slow nod. 'Grace is pining. She's in a totally foreign environment. Everything she's ever known is back where she grew up.'

'But that's where her mother died. Where she found her in the bed.' How could going back there help? Wouldn't it just make the trauma worse?

'Yes, she did die there. But she also *lived* there. It's where all Grace's memories are, where she feels comfortable, and based on her reading preferences and reactions, she's missing it.'

Tess's heart stuttered along with her breath. 'Are you saying I should take her back there to live?'

'Not forever, just until the two of you get to know each other. She'll feel more comfortable there and you might have more chance of connecting. I know you said you have to organise the funeral, and I do think she needs that closure. Staying on there for a while afterwards might help.'

So much to process. There was work to consider. And Josh.

Eleanor shifted her glasses up on the bridge of her nose. 'It's up to you, Tess. I'm just giving you my professional opinion as to what might work.'

Tess dropped her chin and looked down to where her hands nestled in her lap. Her rings were twisted and she spun them back around, rubbing her finger across the diamond-crusted surface of her wedding band. Weerilla was way over the other side of the Blue Mountains, a four-hour drive. A tiny country town in the middle of New South Wales, and from what the caseworker had told her, Skye had a property somewhere in the surrounding district, out of the town precinct. She'd bought there when Grace was small, when she'd decided to escape the city. Now it had all been left to her daughter, and as her guardian Tess was the one responsible for the property. 'There's a lot to think about.'

Eleanor nodded. 'There is. I'm heading overseas for a holiday, so I won't be around for the next week, but if you need me you can email.'

'Where are you off to?'

'Lying on a beach in Fiji.'

Tess followed Eleanor's gaze to the photo on the desk—a family shot at the beach, with her partner, Kayla, and their two young kids. Who would have thought?

'I'm guessing that involves surfing?'

Eleanor's face split into a toothy grin. Underneath the professional façade, the beach bum still lurked. 'Can't keep an old surfer off her board.'

'Enough with the old. That would make two of us.' It was good to connect with her friend again, even if the circumstances weren't exactly social. 'Have fun. And thanks for fitting us in. I really appreciate your help.'

'No problem, Tess. It's good to see you again.' Eleanor opened the door, then paused, her eyes narrowed. 'I always wondered if you'd change your mind and finish your psych degree, go into private practice yourself.'

A too-loud laugh broke out, but she reined it in with a shrug. 'Turns out HR was my calling.'

They stepped out together into the waiting room, where Grace was hunched over the book Eleanor had given her, the shadow of a smile fading as she closed its covers.

'Let me know what you decide.' Eleanor placed a hand on Tess's back and kissed her cheek. She still wore her signature scent of patchouli, mixed now with something a little more refined.

'I will, thanks again.'

Grace headed straight for the door, book in one hand and her treasured bear in the other. The cover of the book was facing out: two small children sitting on a patch of grass looking out over a canvas of hills and sky, the title floating above it in flowing white script. *All the Places to Love.*

The traffic was annoyingly snail-paced, but it gave Tess a chance to observe Grace, post-counselling session. Securely seat-belted on the passenger side, she was looking down at the pages opened out on her lap, her fingers tracing over the illustrations, almost caressing them.

'It looks like a beautiful book. Maybe we could read it together later on?'

Grace blinked a number of times before turning the next page. Was Eleanor right? Would Grace be different in her own environment? Would she feel secure enough to start to open up? This was a little girl without a mother, or father, or grandparents. Not a soul in the world who cared about her.

Although that wasn't exactly true.

Skye had known that Tess was the one person she could trust. Completely ironic considering how that trust had ended up eroding their friendship, and yet Skye had never changed her wishes. Tess's own future had become inextricably bound to Grace's. To all intents and purposes she was now someone's mother. Her pulse raced and she sucked in a quick draught of air. Whatever it took, she had to help Grace. Even if it meant uprooting herself and, for the time being, moving west. They both needed to say a proper goodbye to Skye and a chance to get to know each other in a place where Grace felt safe.

Finally, they reached their street and Tess slowed to a stop inside the carpark. She let the engine idle as she focused her attention completely on her passenger and spoke as softly, as gently, as she could. 'Grace, would you like to go home?'

Grace's hands fell to the centre of the open book and she hooked her fingers around the top edge like she was clinging to a life raft. For a few breathless moments, it seemed as if she was going to speak. Then, without looking up she gave a silent but definite nod.

Tess clasped her hands together to stop them trembling and a shaky laugh fell from her lips. 'Okay.'

Inviting her mother shopping might not have been the best idea, although in reality, she had pretty much invited herself. She was in an absolute tizz over the christening, happening in two days' time, so Tess had avoided announcing that she was taking Grace back to Weerilla, just as she'd avoided telling Josh. The last thing she needed was an interrogation about the ins and outs of the funeral, which she'd managed to set a date for after speaking to the mortician. Today was all about playing nice—and as long as her mother did the same everything would be fine.

Grace walked along beside her like a well-trained puppy, minus the enthusiasm. Reading her body language was getting easier the more time they spent together. That old saying about eyes being the window to the soul was definitely true. Grace's had widened more than should have been humanly possible as the train rattled into Redfern station and screeched to a halt. Once they were on board, the panic seemed to fade. There was a brighter light as she scanned the signs on the wall of the carriage, and studied the faces of their fellow commuters. And there was no doubting the mild amusement shining out as she watched the toddler sitting opposite in his pram stick his fingers into his mouth, pull it watermelon wide and waggle his tongue. Now, heading down King Street, Grace's eyes shifted from stranger to stranger, and every now and then her hip bumped against Tess's leg. Not exactly a huge deal, but one Tess couldn't help smiling about, at least on the inside.

'So, my mum's really excited to meet you.' Tess leaned down as she spoke, reeling Grace's attention away from the crowds.

Nothing.

'We can have lunch first then do some shopping. There's a great kids' clothing shop up the road.'

Nada. Not a thing.

The visit to Eleanor had made up Tess's mind about taking Grace back to Weerilla, even though it hadn't made a dent in the cone of silence. None of the recommended books or websites she'd consulted had been much help on this whole non-communication thing, either. Even the guidelines for adopting parents didn't explain how to deal with a child who had recently found her mother dead. The best advice she could glean about 'damaged children' was to persevere, be patient, give them space. So that was the new plan. Carry on as normal, make conversation even if there was no response and take some time off. Claudia could manage everything at work for the next month: throwing your trusty assistant in at the deep end was certainly a way to find out if she was good under pressure.

The ornate gold lettering of the Wicked Sips sign quieted the chatter of Tess's monkey mind. Her mother, ever punctual, was already seated at a table. Her light-brown hair was cut into one of those blunt mum cuts, longer at the front and cropped shorter at the back. In her turquoise shirt, smart black pants and leopard-skin loafers, she was the epitome of retiree chic. A love of shoes was the one thing Tess and her mother had in common. Lifting her head from the menu she was studying, her mother waved so furiously it was clear she was in one of her potentially overwhelming moods. Grabbing Grace's hand and bolting was tempting. Tess plastered on a smile and went with the next best option: pushing through.

'There you are.' As if they were half an hour late instead of right on time. She stood and held her arms out towards them, signalling her intention to engulf them in a group hug.

That was not happening. Tess stopped short, pulling the strap of her bag across her chest, elbow out.

A cloud fell across her mother's face, but she caught it before it darkened too much, arranging her mouth into its brightest smile.

'Grace, this is my mum, Beth.' Tess hovered a hand vaguely behind Grace's shoulder. She wasn't a touchy-feely person, but this whole distance thing was so weird. And if she found it hard, her mother was going to be positively horrified by the no-contact rule. If she could keep her hands to herself it would be a miracle. 'And, Mum, this is Grace.'

Beth bent down, both hands resting on her knees as if she was midway through a yoga pose. 'Hello, Grace, it's so lovely to meet you. Welcome to our family. You can call me Nonna.' She straightened up, continuing to talk. 'It's such a beautiful day out there, isn't it? And look at that lovely jumper you're wearing.'

Her mother was trying to be welcoming. Maybe once she saw how withdrawn Grace was she'd keep a lid on the game-show-host enthusiasm.

The three of them settled into their seats and her mother flapped a napkin, proceeding to lay it across Grace's lap. Grace stiffened, pinning herself to the back of her chair. Tess resisted the urge to sigh. It was going to be a long morning. Only the smell of brewing coffee held some glimmer of hope. She waved to the waitress, who frowned but sauntered over, iPad poised as she looked out the window. 'Anything to drink?'

A double vodka on the rocks would definitely go down a treat.

'Flat white, please.' Her mother was taking the more conventional option.

'Skim cap for me, with an extra shot. Would you like a juice or a milkshake, Grace?'

Grace was looking up, completely stunned.

What was the problem? Tess followed her gaze to the waitress. Thick black pencilled eyebrows drawn over heavily lined eyes. Electric-blue hair pulled up into a top-knot above the fringe. A battalion of piercings in her ears, lips and nose. Nothing unusual for the inner suburbs, but probably not a common sight in a tiny country town. Still, the overt staring was more than a little awkward. 'A chocolate milkshake, please. We'll order some food in a minute. Thanks.'

The girl scowled as she took their order and left.

'So …' Her mother beamed at Grace as if nothing had happened. 'Have you been shopping yet?'

'Not yet.' Jumping in to answer would hopefully give her mother the hint not to ask Grace direct questions. 'We thought we'd have something to eat first and then attack the shops. We're going to buy Grace some new clothes.' The idea of the withdrawn child sitting beside her 'attacking' anything was completely absurd, but retail therapy had been known to work wonders, so who knew? 'How's Dad?'

'Oh you know, out on the golf course trying to improve his handicap, as usual.'

'Mutual retirement not all it's cracked up to be?' For years it was all either of her parents had talked about, but like most things, the vision didn't quite match the reality.

'It's just as well I still get my casual days, otherwise I'd be sitting at home twiddling my thumbs half the time.'

'Good for you, Mum.' Why she had retired in the first place was a mystery. She was healthy, good at her job—apparently the kids adored her—and not one to sit around idle.

'Once Ally goes back to work I'll be busy with Ethan, of course.'

'Are you minding him all week?'

'Five days a fortnight. She's going back part-time.'

'That's a big commitment, Mum. Doesn't leave you much time for yourself.' Sometimes it seemed her parents had that baby more often than his own parents.

'Well, I don't mind. The way things are going he could be the only grandchild I get.' Her mother punctuated her point with an exaggerated roll of her eyes. 'Of course we do have a new granddaughter now.' She reached across the table and patted Grace on the shoulder.

'Mum!'

'What? She's part of our family now, aren't you, darling?'

Grace coiled into a ball, shoulders hunched, head hanging. The arrival of drinks was perfectly timed. Food needed to be ordered before Tess said something she might regret. 'We'll have a bowl of chips to share and a couple of the toasted ham sandwiches, please.' Her mother ordered her usual caesar salad, and by the time the menus had been gathered up the air was a little clearer.

Brunch ticked away with small talk about the family, the weather and the upcoming christening. Her mother did most of the talking, choosing her topics more carefully. Grace picked at the bowl of chips, ate only half the sandwich, but did manage to down the whole milkshake. Working out her food preferences was a process of elimination, based primarily on what was left over. Tess's mother pursed her lips as she eyed the remnants on the plate. If she mentioned anything about starving children in India, there was going to be one hell of an explosion.

Time. Patience. Perseverance. Tess's new mantra was going to be played on repeat all afternoon. And not just because of Grace.

King Street was an ice box when they stepped outside the cafe. Winter was the pits. Frozen fingers, short days, long nights. The only upside was the fashion: boots, jackets, scarves. Tess pulled her new Burberry plaid scarf a little higher to sit below her chin. Her skin tingled despite the layers. Shopping was her favourite guilty pleasure, and shopping for Grace was more exciting than she would ever have anticipated.

A passing bunch of schoolkids crowded the pavement and one dropped the f-bomb loudly as they passed, setting her teeth on edge. Normally, it wouldn't bother her—she had a potty mouth herself at times—but Grace didn't need to hear it.

Her mother tutted, sending the boys into a chorus of riotous laughter. 'I really don't know what happens once they get to high school. No discipline.'

Not far down the street Tess found the shop she was looking for. Girlzone. Headless mannequins ranging in size from babies to teens, wearing dresses, jeans and T-shirts crowded the window. Bright, funky patterns. Flamingoes. Hawaiian prints. Paisley. The sort of thing she would have loved to wear when she was ten—had her mother not insisted on dressing her almost permanently in pale-pink frills. 'This is it.'

'I'm not sure there'll be anything suitable in here.' Her mum looked like she'd just swallowed a fly.

'Let's go in and find out, shall we?'

Taylor Swift was warbling through the speakers. All that whining about yet another heartbreak, but at least she had the guts to send them packing when they didn't measure up. Did that make her a good role model for tweens?

'Take your time, Grace. Look around. Tell me if you see anything you like.'

Grace squinted, taking in the racks, jam-packed with stock.

For Tess, one outfit stood out from all the rest: a houndstooth checked pinafore over a black turtleneck, something T. Swizzle herself might wear. Perfect with a pair of ribbed tights and boots. Maybe Grace would go for it without any prompting.

'Oh, look at this.' Her mother pulled a dress from its hanger: a rosebud-print bodice over a white satin skirt. Cute if you were going for the princess look. But was that Grace's thing? All there'd been in her suitcase was jeans, jumpers and a few old tees and skivvies. 'Grace, this would be gorgeous for the christening. And it's a size ten. Why don't you try it on?'

Grace stood in the centre of the shop, as inert as one of the dummies in the window.

'I don't think it's her style, Mum.'

'But it's beautiful. What little girl wouldn't love it? Come on, let's try it on and see, shall we?' She grabbed at Grace's hand.

'Mum. Don't.' The warning came too late.

Grace ripped her arm away, lashing out like a feral cat. She backed up against the nearest rack, turning a starker shade of white than the skirt of the chosen dress.

Beth recoiled, clutching at the offending garment.

Tess stepped into the space between the two of them. 'Let's just take a minute here.'

'Is everything alright?' The shop assistant joined them, looking completely flummoxed. Grace crept out from her hiding place and Beth gave them all a defiant smile. 'Yes.' She pulled at a strand of hair caught in the hinge of her glasses. 'Everything is fine.'

The girl shifted her attention from the dress to Grace. 'Would you like to try that on?'

Grace stared at the floor.

'You don't have to if you don't want to.' There was no way Tess was going to let her mother bully Grace into following orders.

'Tessa, let the child make up her own mind for heaven's sake. It will only take a minute to try it on.' The look Beth was fixing on her new 'granddaughter' would have made even the toughest opponent wither.

Without looking up, Grace nodded.

'The fitting rooms are right over here.' The shop assistant took the dress and smiled sweetly at Grace. Taylor had moved on to a song about having the best day ever with her mother. The situation would have been hysterically funny if it wasn't so fucking horrible.

Tess's mum perched herself on a lounge chair outside the change room like a queen on her throne. For Tess, it was a toss-up between staying as far away as possible and keeping close to maintain damage control. Close was the safest option.

'I see what you mean about her being withdrawn.'

Only a couple of metres of carpet separated them from the flimsy curtain of the change room. Hardly an effective sound barrier. 'She's not deaf, Mum.' Tess made sure she kept her own voice to a whisper.

'Can she even speak?' Her mother continued, not bothering to lower the volume. 'I mean, maybe she has a proper disability, something she's had since birth.'

'We've been through this.' Did she ever listen? 'The FACS people had a doctor take a look at her and as far as they can tell there's nothing physically wrong.'

'Has she said anything at all since you picked her up?'

Tess shook her head. 'Yes and no a few times, but that's about it.'

'Well, she has lost her mother, the poor little mite.' She heaved out an overly loud sigh. 'Who knows what's going through that head of hers?' She turned her own head and exhaled noisily, a sure sign that whatever she was about to say was terribly important. 'Tessa, I know I told you to go ahead with this adoption thing, but now I'm not so sure. I mean, she's obviously troubled and you and Josh aren't experienced parents.'

This was so typical of her mother. Changing her mind whenever something—or someone—didn't exactly fit inside the perfect little box she'd packaged it in.

'Mum …'

Her mother rose to her feet. 'I don't think you understand what you're doing here. This isn't a game, Tessa. This is a child's life. Not to mention your life—and your husband's. You have no idea what you're taking on.'

'And you have no idea what you're talking about.' Tess pushed herself upright from where she was leaning on the wall. With her heeled boots on, her mother was a good eight centimetres shorter and she was going to take full advantage of that difference. 'So you'd rather she went into some random foster home where she could be neglected or abused?'

'Oh, Tessa. That's such a cliché. I just don't understand why you're breaking your neck to do this? Wouldn't you rather have a child of your own? A baby of your own?'

'Is that what this is about? Me not having a baby?' Her volume was rising now, her decorum vanishing.

'Not entirely, but since you mention it …'

'I didn't mention it, Mum, you did.'

'So what if I did?' The woman was on a roll. All five feet and three inches of her puffed up like a bullfrog. And croaking just as loudly. 'It's perfectly normal for a mother to want her only daughter to have a child. I do want you to have a baby before it's too late, not a ten-year-old girl who clearly has problems that are only going to get worse.'

'Ah, ladies.' They both turned at once to see the sales assistant glowering in their direction. She'd obviously overheard their conversation. Which meant Grace, out of the fitting room and standing beside her, had too.

'Shit.'

'Sweetheart. You look so pretty.' Ever the expert chameleon, her mother changed her tone in an instant. 'Doesn't she, Tessa?'

It took one very long, deep breath for Tess to pull herself back from the brink. 'You look lovely, Grace. But it's your choice. Do you like it?'

Grace's chin quivered, probably nothing to do with the dress.

'It'll be perfect. My treat.' Beth showered them all with a victory smile. 'Pop it off and I'll buy it for you.'

A rush of heat spread up Tess's neck into her cheeks. If matricide wasn't illegal she could gladly strangle her own mother right now. What started as a potentially enjoyable day had turned into a total disaster. The sooner they could cut and run the better.

Grace scuttled back into the change room while Tess's mum rummaged around in her bag for her wallet.

Tess took a few steps away, waving at her mother to follow. Even though the damage was already done, Grace didn't need to hear any more.

Her mother held up a hand. 'I know. I shouldn't have said what I did.' Her voice was low, her tone hardly apologetic. 'Tessa, this young girl isn't a project you can fix with a management plan. She's a troubled little thing. You need to be prepared for a bumpy ride.'

Like the bumpy ride she'd had as a teenager while her own mother was completely clueless? She wanted to scream at Beth, regale her with a list of good old home truths, tell her how if she'd been a different kind of mother maybe Tess could have talked to her about more important things than the nightly dinner menu or what time she needed to be home. Maybe things between them might have been different.

The curtain shifted and Grace emerged, eyes brimming. If only she would be comforted with a hug, if only she would let Tess in.

Patience. Perseverance. Time.

Her mother was right, she didn't have any experience with kids. All she had were her instincts, and right now she was letting them lead her in what she hoped was the right direction. She kneeled down and inched as close as possible without scaring Grace away, creating a space just for the two of them.

'I'm sorry you overheard that. This is a big change for all of us …' She glanced over to the counter where her mother was paying for the dress. 'Remember, I am on your side no matter what. Okay?'

A solitary tear slid down Grace's cheek and it was all Tess could do not to sit on the floor and weep. She held herself together and waited.

The nod was small but clear.

Tess gave Grace a hopeful smile as she ever so slowly reached out her hand and curled it around the girl's shoulder. There was no smile in return, but for the very first time Grace didn't pull away.

Eight

'Remind me why we said yes to this.' Josh's hushed voice cut through the drone of the sermon.

'If I remember rightly, you were the one who jumped at the offer.' He'd answered as soon as the question had been asked: *We'd be so honoured, thank you so much for asking.* 'That's what you get for being a yes-man.'

'What else could I say? We were cornered. And you didn't exactly veto the idea.'

It was true. Rob and Ally had ambushed them and they'd taken the path of least resistance. Now they were paying for their cowardice. The church reeked of burning wax and someone had been far too zealous with the pew polishing, making sitting still quite the challenge. Her mother was seated further down the row, on the other side of Josh and Grace. Tess hadn't spoken to her since the shopping fiasco and, of course, Beth was acting as if nothing had happened.

Admittedly 'the dress' was very pretty, the faint greens and lavender tint of the leaves setting off the blue tones in Grace's eyes and the pink rosebuds brightening her pale complexion.

What must she be making of the man in the floor-length gown, the candles, the strange hymns? Skye had been an atheist for years, so there was no way she would have exposed her daughter to any form of religion, especially Catholicism. And who could blame her? Despite her quasi-religious upbringing, Tess wasn't exactly a fan. They just needed to get through this christening ceremony, make a brief appearance at the after-party and then get the hell out. The whole godparent thing was purely a formality. Ally's entire family would knock both Josh and her senseless to get their hands on Ethan if anything ever happened to his parents.

God forbid.

A shiver ran across her scalp. It wasn't a joke. People did die and their children did become orphans. She above all people needed to take this whole thing a lot more seriously.

'We're on.' Josh grabbed her hand and started moving up to the dais, but Tess pulled back and leaned down to speak quietly to Grace. 'We won't be long.'

'Tess. Come on.' Josh squeezed harder, motioning towards the front of the church with his free hand.

Ally, dressed to impress in crimson silk, held a squirming Ethan in her arms. Rob and the second set of godparents stood on the opposite side of the font, glowing like a trio of angels. They all repeated the pledges they were promising to make as the baby's guardians. While Josh went particularly quiet at the 'I believe in God the Father almighty' part, Tess glanced across to the front pew. Grace hadn't bothered to fill the gap between herself and her new *nonna*—if anything she'd shuffled further away, but her head was angled, her eyes glued to the baby. Ethan let out a high-pitched cry as the priest poured a full cup of water over the poor kid's head, the crowd clapping and cheering as if they were at a rock concert—things certainly had changed since Tess had spent a Sunday morning at mass. They all smiled dutifully through what seemed like a thousand photos as her mother watched, eyes glistening, from the front row.

'You looked lovely up there,' she murmured as they swapped places on the altar. It most definitely wasn't a reference to Tess's pant suit or the darker shade of her newly cut hair, but best to let it go.

The organ started grinding out 'Oh, Happy Day', and the ceremony, thank the Lord, was over. As they joined the throng of people heading outdoors, it was impossible not to notice the looks and whispers directed their way. Word was out about Tess's own new addition and it looked like she was going to have to smile and wave her way through the entire event.

Small clusters of people gathered to chat. Josh joined a group of Rob's mates, removing any chance of a quick exit. If she hovered around the gate long enough, maybe he'd get the message. At least at the after-party there'd be places to hide.

'Tess.' Ally's sister, Renee, zoomed in, kissing her on both cheeks. 'How are you? Al told me about your news and I think it's so great what you're doing.' Words bubbled out of her like champagne fizzing from a shaken bottle. 'And this must be Grace?' Renee bent down, hands on her spray-tanned knees. 'Welcome to the family. I mean, we're not exactly family, but almost, right?' She stood again, redirecting her questions to Tess. 'How is she settling in?'

'Good thanks, Renee. We're still getting to know each other. Taking things one step at a time.'

'It's so sad what happened to her mother. Lucky you and Josh can afford to take her in. Must be freaky when you don't have your own kids, though. Maybe this will get you going.

Ethan would love a little cousin to play with.' She drew a breath and shot a glance over her shoulder to where her partner was swapping man-stories. 'Although, he will have one soon. We haven't really announced it properly yet, thought we'd wait until the christening was over, you know, let Ethie have his fifteen minutes, but Jase and I are pregnant.'

Tess swallowed back a sigh. 'Congrats, Renee. That's great news.'

'What's great news?' Her mother joined them, gossip radar on high alert.

'I'm having a baby.' Renee, glowing prematurely, dropped a hand to her perfectly flat stomach.

'Oh, that's lovely.' Her mother tipped her head to the side as if she was looking at something in the distance. 'When are you due?'

'I'm only eight weeks along. Shouldn't really be telling anyone yet, but it's too exciting to keep a secret. I was just saying to Tess how great it'll be for Ethan to have a new cousin to play with—and maybe another one on your side of the family soon.'

Her mother's eyes brightened. You could practically hear the squeal echoing around in her skull, as if Renee's proclamation was a statement of fact.

A diversion was drastically needed. 'You were right, Mum.' Saying those four words was like choking on a furball, but desperate times called for desperate measures. Tess waved a hand in Grace's direction. The poor girl had been ignored long enough. 'The dress is beautiful.'

Taking a step back and holding a hand to the base of her throat, her mother drew in an exaggerated breath. Way too much, but infinitely preferable to more baby talk. 'Darling, you look absolutely gorgeous. I knew it would be perfect on you.' Her gaze dropped to the worn pair of leather sandals strapped to Grace's feet and her enthusiasm waned. 'We'll have to get you some nice black Mary Janes for next time.'

What Beth De Santis giveth with one hand, she taketh away with the other. Admittedly, the shoes didn't exactly match the outfit, but another shopping trip had been out of the question.

People were starting to leave. Tess extended her arm to the space above Grace's shoulders, an action so well practised Grace had learned it was the signal to make a move. 'We'll see you at the party.' They walked towards the carpark, leaving Josh behind to cadge a ride. All they had to do was get through the next few hours and then they could go home and pack for Weerilla. Where there'd be another ceremony to attend. And organise. Tess had managed not to think about that for most of the week after ringing the mortician and setting a date, but once today was over that luxury would be gone.

Volunteering the family home for the baptism lunch had been her mother's idea, even though Rob and Ally had a perfectly good one of their own. But that was Beth, always right in the centre of things. Running the show. Thankfully, there were enough guests for Tess to be able to stay out of the spotlight. Her dad, manning the barbeque, beer in hand, was surrounded by a posse of mates, including Josh. The queen of the kitchen had more than enough help, leaving Tess free to escape the well-wishers and busy bodies.

Word had spread and just about everybody had expressed an opinion on the new family member. All of them positive, of course, although judging by the strained facial expressions accompanying some of the words of welcome, not all of them heartfelt. Ally seemed a little miffed about Ethan's limelight being stolen. Another good reason for Tess to keep a low profile, but not as crucial as protecting Grace from the mostly well-meaning guests. The more attention she got the more she shut down, like a flower closing its petals at nightfall. It was too much, all the fussing, all the noise. The nook tucked away at the end of the deck was the ideal spot for both of them to hide: Grace reclining in a round garden chair, reading *The Hobbit* to her bear, and Tess people-watching without being seen.

Down in the man-huddle, Rob handed the star of the day across to Josh, who propped Ethan against his hip as if he was holding a bag of groceries, a sight almost as rare as one of him holding a baby. Tess had agreed to his no-children edict, but seeing him here now, relaxing his posture, the stiffness fading from his jaw, was like watching another version of him. One who might have existed if his fractured family hadn't left him so emotionally bruised. If he only had the courage to deal with his issues rather than let them determine the whole course of his life.

If only they both did.

'Tess. Tessa!' Her mother's voice was shrill and perilously close. Red-faced and flustered, she marched around the corner of the house. 'There you are. Didn't you hear me calling you? Lunch is being served.'

Such drama. 'Oh, no I didn't hear you. Sorry, Mum.'

'Where's Grace?'

'Just over …' The chair was empty, the closed book sitting on the decking beside the abandoned bear. 'She was there a minute ago.' Tess's stomach twisted itself into a knot. Where could she be? Clusters of people were moving towards the pergola, where multiple platters of food had been laid out. But there was no sign of Grace.

'She can't have gone too far.' Declared as if she knew every move the girl made. 'Check the bathroom. Bring her out for some lunch.'

Tess gave a mental salute as her mother rushed back down the stairs to join the party and she set off in search of the missing child. Of course Grace would be in the bathroom. It wasn't as if she would have suddenly got the urge to play with the small group of kids who were here. Not unless there'd been a radical transformation. All the rooms she passed were empty, but the bathroom door was closed. She crooked a finger and rapped on the timber.

'Just a minute.' A distinctly adult, male voice. Definitely not Grace.

'Sorry.' This was not good. She retraced her steps, checking every room, looking behind doors and under beds, opening wardrobes in case Grace was playing some odd game of hide-and-seek.

No sign of her. Anywhere.

In the backyard, the chatter of voices grew louder, the volume turned up too many decibels. Tess scanned the tables. There were people here she didn't know. Men she didn't know. She gripped the railing to steady herself, willed the flapping creatures inside her belly to settle. That was a stupid way to think. They were all friends and family. Grace must be here somewhere. She had to be.

And there was Josh: plate loaded, taking a seat at a table, flashing his poster-boy smile. Totally oblivious. Some 'father' he was turning out to be. Taking on Grace might have been her idea, but he had agreed, so would it hurt to help out just a little in the parenting department?

She strode to the end of the deck and down the far steps, searching the courtyard to the side of the house. Bird of paradise plants along the fence line tilted their strange, angular heads of orange and purple. Violets bloomed beneath them, their tiny flowers scattered like stars through the garden. A slight movement caught her eye and she bent lower, peering under the house to where Grace was sitting cross-legged in the dirt, the family tabby planted between her legs. The blank, often haunted expression that seemed to permanently mar her face was gone. Instead she looked peaceful, almost happy as she gently stroked the cat behind his ears.

Tess let out a long-held breath. 'Hey there, I see you've found Wilson.'

Grace looked up, slightly startled, then returned her attention to the cat.

'Lunch is ready. Want to come get some?'

For a few long seconds Grace sat still, patting the cat. Pensive.

'You can play with him again afterwards if you want.'

Hands around the cat's middle, Grace lifted him from her lap. Wilson tipped his head and she gave him one more scratch under the chin before crawling out from under the house on her hands and knees, wriggling through the gap between the posts. As she pushed herself up from the ground, a ripping sound made them both freeze. A huge hole had appeared in the dress, the skirt stained with dirty patches matching the ones on Grace's hands and knees. Smoothing it down only wiped more marks across the plain white skirt, and her face fell.

It didn't take a genius to work out what was on her mind. Tess was thinking exactly the same thing.

Beth.

They had two options. Front up to lunch with the dress ruined, or retreat out the side gate without a word. Either one was a risk, but disappearing was possibly slightly more dangerous. Anyway, what did it matter? Sweet as it was, Grace would probably never wear the dress again.

'Don't worry.' Tess forced a cheery tone. 'We can wash it later and get it mended. Let's go eat.' She took a chance and held out her hand. Poised midair, it was a silent, hopeful invitation. The clamour of voices dimmed, replaced by the frantic hammering of her heart. Millimetre by wonderful millimetre, Grace stretched out her arm, and for a few joyous moments after their palms kissed neither of them moved. Together they walked towards the tables, although for Tess it was more like floating. A tiny but significant miracle had occurred. Grace was holding her hand.

Plates piled high, they wound their way through the maze of tables looking for a place to sit. The guests were too busy eating and talking to pay them any attention. Tess bounced along the path like a moonwalker, her hand still warm from Grace's touch. Who would have thought such a small thing could make a person so happy? She started towards a couple of empty seats when her mother's shrill voice stopped her in her tracks.

'Oh, Grace, what have you done to your dress?'

If she'd known her mother was in the vicinity, she would have taken a different route. Twisted around with one hand on the back of the garden chair, the other resting against her sternum as if she was having trouble breathing, the woman looked ready to blow a gasket.

Chatter died, heads turned.

'Mum.' Her warning was almost a bark.

'Well, really, Tessa, look at the stains.' She reached out and picked at the flap of material torn by the nail. 'And this. What on earth was she doing?'

Chasing the cat. Having fun. Stuff normal kids do. The words stuck in Tess's throat, but her glare would be answer enough.

Anyone who had still been talking now stopped. Her father, seated to her left, rose to his feet. She needed to defuse the situation as quickly and as quietly as possible.

'Mum, it's fine. I'll get it cleaned and repaired. It's just a dress.'

'A dress I paid good money for.' The volume of her mother's voice was rising in inverse proportion to her own. This wasn't just about the dress.

'Leave it, Mum. Come on, Grace.' She reached out to take the girl's hand again but left her move too late. A growl burst from deep down in Grace's throat. She threw her plate on the ground, sending meat, pastry and hundreds and thousands swirling through the air like confetti, before she turned and ran down the aisle between the two rows of tables, up the steps and into the house.

Silence devoured any remaining scraps of conversation.

Her mother's chair dropped to the concrete paving as she stood. 'You need to do something about that child. Get some professional help.'

And you need to mind your own fucking business and learn some compassion. She wanted to scream it out loud, but the stunned faces in her peripheral vision rendered her speechless. What she needed was a mother who supported what she was doing rather than trying to shoot her down at every turn. What she needed was help instead of criticism. But why should she expect that now when it had been absent her entire life?

'For your information, I have had professional help, which is why I'm leaving tomorrow to take Grace home.' She took a step forward, zeroing in like a hawk about to dive on its prey. 'And I can't wait to get her as far away from you as possible.' With a jerk of her wrist, she tipped her plate over and slammed it down, mimicking Grace's action, scattering the contents all over her mother's black suede pumps.

Nine

A flash of lightning ignited the darkness of the living room. Tess stopped on the bottom stair, unclenching her teeth as she waited for the inevitable clap of thunder. Pale light shone from the computer in the corner of the room. Sunday afternoon and there he was poring over an Excel spreadsheet. How could he concentrate on work after all the crap that had gone on today?

A low rumble shook the glass on the sliding doors. The sky was a solemn shade of slate, and rain had turned the balcony into a wading pool. Drawing the blinds, she made a mental note to call the body corporate about the drainage.

'Is she okay?' Josh, finally, lifted his head from the screen.

Grace hadn't said a word since their hurried departure from the christening. Not unusual for her, of course, but everything about her body language said misery. A state Tess could totally relate to right now. So much for the hand-holding euphoria. 'She's reading.'

'You should eat something.'

Memories of the afternoon—her lunch strewn across the pavers, her mother's new shoes smothered in tabouli, the embarrassed buzzing of the guests swelling behind her as she stormed off—were doing little to induce her appetite. As much as she liked to think she and Beth were so very different, they shared the same quick temper, and were both too fond of using it when it came to each other.

She backed up against the island, the edge of the marble bench cold against her waist. Josh turned back to the desk and resumed his typing, clacking away at the keys as if the conversation was finished. When it hadn't even started.

'So, are we going to talk about what happened?' They hadn't spoken since leaving the party, had sat in silence all the way home in the car, Tess in the back beside a shell-shocked Grace, not touching her but close enough to hopefully be a comfort. Josh had turned on the radio, some mind-numbing music on Triple J, the sort he knew she couldn't stand. And then, following their well-worn pattern, they'd gone their separate ways.

She folded her arms tightly as he stood, agitation etched into every line on his face. Probably more to do with his work session being disrupted than anything else.

'Tessa ...'

Her full name. The one he used when she'd done or said something he didn't like. 'I'm in trouble am I?'

'Jesus, don't start.'

'Don't start what? I'm not the one who's done anything wrong, Josh. In case you hadn't noticed, it was my mother who picked this fight.'

'You didn't have to react the way you did.'

Her rough laugh echoed as she met him in the centre of the room. 'So you think I'm the bad guy?'

'You did make quite a scene.'

A scene. An embarrassing scene that might give people the 'wrong' impression. She stabbed her fingertip against the solid bone of her diaphragm. 'I wasn't the one who carried on about a bit of dirt on a fucking dress. She humiliated Grace in front of all those people.'

'Tess …' He lifted his hand to her elbow, let it fall away. 'I know she was over the top. Grace is a kid, of course she's going to get dirty.'

There was a 'but' coming.

'But …'

And there it was. Heat flooded her body, rendering her speechless. She shook her head, waiting for it to subside.

Josh ploughed on. 'I just think it would have been better for Grace if you'd let it go.'

'Let it go so my mother would think she has permission to belittle her anytime she feels like it? To talk about her like she isn't even there? You didn't see Grace's face in that store, Josh. She heard every single word and she looked totally devastated. And then Mum gives an encore performance today, just in case Grace didn't get the message the first time that she doesn't measure up.'

'That's not entirely true.'

'Don't be so bloody patronising.'

His cheeks reddened and he clenched his jaw. If there was one thing he hated it was being accused of chauvinism, but right now his attitude was doused in a heavy helping of male superiority. A message notification sounded from the desk behind him.

'Leave it.'

Only the slight turn of his head gave away how much not checking his phone was costing him. Whether or not he liked it, this needed to be discussed. Tess needed to know he was on her side. That she could count on him. Not just today, but next week, next year and for all the years after. For her, and for Grace. Outside, thunder rumbled. In the dull cave of the living room his face was in shadow, but she could still see the rapid darting of his eyes as he weighed up his decision. This was a test: he knew it as well as she did. Another beep from his phone. And then, like a time-lapsed photo, muscle by rigid muscle, his body relaxed as he nodded and let it go.

'Thank you.'

Annoying though it was, the interruption gave them both time to calm down.

Tess ran the heels of her palms over her hips. 'You agree with her, don't you?'

'Agree with who?'

'Mum. You agree with her that Grace isn't normal.'

Josh gave a weak shrug. 'I wouldn't say that, exactly.' His gaze shifted warily. 'I know she's been through a lot, but it's not normal for a kid to not communicate at all.'

He raised a hand as soon as she opened her mouth to speak.

'Hear me out. Your mother was definitely in the wrong about the dress. That was a whole lot of bullshit.' He trained his eyes on hers. 'But I do think she's right about Grace. There's something wrong.'

'It's called grief, Josh. People shut down when bad things happen. To protect themselves.' It wasn't a revelation, wasn't anything you didn't learn in Psych 101, but the undeniable reality of the words made her catch her breath. 'She just needs time. And love.'

Was that true? She'd been so sure she could handle this, had wanted desperately for there to be some sort of invisible connection between Grace and her, but she'd been fooling herself. Although there'd been a few baby steps forward, there'd also been a whole lot of gigantic strides in the opposite direction.

'Maybe we should reconsider.'

'What?'

'We said we'd give it a try and if it wasn't working we'd talk to the social worker about finding a better home for her.'

'Are you serious?' Less than one week and he already wanted to bail? She stared at him until her eyes began to water. He didn't need to speak. The hard line of his mouth made the answer perfectly clear.

'I don't think I can do this, Tess.'

'You mean you don't want to do it.'

He ran a hand through his hair, a single, stray lock falling back onto his forehead, not saying a word.

Something soft inside Tess started to shrink, leaving behind the tough, brittle shell of her armour. 'I'm taking Grace to Weerilla first thing in the morning, for the funeral, and then we'll be staying on for a while. The psychologist I took her to said it would be for the best.'

The colour drained from his face. 'How long is a while?'

'I don't know.' *However long it takes.*

'But I'm leaving for the conference first thing tomorrow.'

'I know.'

'Will you be okay out there on your own?'

No *I'll cancel my work trip.* No *we can work this out together.* Just *I* and *you*. Separate and divided. His phone began ringing again, neither of them moving as it continued to buzz. How it must have been killing him not to take the call. Part of her wanted to drag this out, make him suffer, but in the end, the result would be the same.

She shook her head. 'Just get it.'

He spun around and practically lunged for the phone. 'Hey, Aaron, how's the job going?' His work voice. Keen.

Interested. Completely opposite to the dry, strained tone of their domestic conversation.

A half-drunk bottle of red sat on the bench by the stove. She reached into the cupboard for a glass, and poured a generous slug.

Josh had made it blatantly obvious from the get-go that Grace was her problem to fix. She'd known that all along, so his reticence now came as no real surprise. Just as her mother's behaviour was no real revelation. In fact, after today's showdown, it had all become infinitely clearer. She couldn't rely on her mother. She couldn't rely on Josh.

When it came to helping Grace, she was on her own.

Ten

A few leftover drops of rain wobbled on the wipers before being swallowed by the wind. Showers had chased them all the way from Sydney, but now they were well past the Great Dividing Range and the clouds were starting to part, leaving a haphazard patchwork of grey and blue in their wake. According to the numbers on the dashboard, it was three pm with two kilometres to go until they reached the turn-off to Skye's house. Despite the coffee Tess had had in Blackheath, keeping her eyes focused on the road was becoming a challenge. Chatting to her passenger might have helped—if that passenger was so inclined. Grace was asleep against the door, her head resting on the scrunched-up orange cardigan she'd turned into a makeshift pillow, the apples of her cheeks rosy against her freckled skin.

The car jerked, skating over the edge of the bitumen and bumping along the rocky verge. Tess caught her breath, turning the steering wheel hard to get them back on the road. Grace let out a quiet groan, but then settled back into sleep. Had she just nodded off herself? Maybe one of those microsleeps they talked about on the driver-fatigue ads. She straightened up and forced her eyes to open wide. Stopping was probably the safer option, but they were so close now, it was better to push on.

When the side road appeared she leaned forward, straining to read the faded letters of the sign: Longman's Track. This was it. The Audi bounced along the dirt road, winding through deserted paddocks of stubbly grass. There were no farm animals, just dry land stretching into the distance dotted with occasional clusters of bush. Bare. Barren. Monotone. And a fifteen-minute drive into the nearest town. Skye had moved here for a reason, but surely such isolation wasn't really warranted. Or safe. What about at night, when it was as black as soot outside, and not a soul within screaming distance? Tess's skull shrank at the thought. Admittedly, an intruder would have to be pretty desperate to bother coming all the way out here, but still, there had better be strong locks on the doors and windows.

It took another two kilometres before the road curved around a bend and there, smack bang ahead was a house. More of a shack, really, perched behind a post-and-rail fence, a yard and an assortment of trees forming a buffer from the surrounding landscape. Blotches of rust darkened the corrugated-iron roof over the porch. A few determined leaves clung to the gnarly vine twisted along the supporting posts and eaves. Smoky-blue weatherboards wrapped around the frame of the building, and in the centre between two colonial-style windows was a purple door. Aubergine, it would be called in a paint catalogue. A set of wind chimes made from old spoons and forks swayed this way and that in the breeze. It was very arty. Very quaint. Very Skye.

'How did you live here, girl?' Tess whispered the question as she pulled to a stop in the patch of dirt in front of the house.

You're about to find out. The answer came from wherever Skye was, out there somewhere, or maybe inside her own head.

Grace sat up and yawned, unravelling her long limbs like a cat stretching awake. She blinked. Jerked up straight. Rubbed the sleep from her eyes and in a split second she unclipped her seatbelt, threw open the car door and raced to the gate. Her curls spiralled in the wind as she bounded up the two cement steps and threw herself against the door, rattling the knob, racing to one curtained window and then the next, cupping her hands to the glass as she banged her fists against the walls.

Did Grace think her mother was inside?

Nausea billowed in Tess's stomach. This was all wrong. They shouldn't have come back. Her own mother had told her she had no idea about being a parent and she was right. The engine was still running. She could race out and grab Grace and drive away, write off this whole idea as a mistake.

But then what?

Eleanor had said it would take time. And Skye's funeral still had to be organised. She owed her friend that much … and more. They would have to stay, at least in the short term. Regardless of the pain it caused them both.

An icy wind stole her breath as she climbed out of the car. In the warm cocoon of the Audi, they hadn't needed jumpers and the thin sleeves of her cotton shirt provided no protection.

'Grace?'

The front yard was empty. Cutlery chimes danced in the wind, clanging like a kindergarten orchestra. Tess's footsteps vibrated against the old timber boards as she marched to the end of the porch and peered around the corner. Not a sign of Grace anywhere. Her heartbeat quickened, pumping adrenaline through her veins as she jumped down onto the grass, the heels of her boots sinking into the damp soil. Grey suede perhaps hadn't been the best idea, but she hadn't been thinking of the practicalities when she'd dressed, only how Grace would react when they arrived. Vanishing into thin air hadn't even occurred to Tess as being one of the possibilities.

A jumble of terracotta pots painted in rainbow colours edged the back lawn. Two timber sheds bookended the far end of the yard, one purple, like the front door with a floral mural painted across the fibro. The other was a chook shed, minus the chickens, a flurry of white-and-brown feathers stubbornly clinging to the wire.

One bare stone step sat outside the back door of the house, painted the same shade as the one out front. Skye always had an eye for colour.

Leaves rustled on the far side of the cottage.

Tess turned to find Grace rifling through a camellia hedge, a hailstorm of pink petals littering the grass. She scrambled for a few more seconds before sitting back on her haunches, whimpering like a frightened animal.

'Sweetheart.' Tess kept her voice low, soothing. 'What's wrong?'

'She's gone.'

Gone? Did she really still think her mother was alive? This was exactly what Eleanor had warned her about. No closure. Tess kneeled down and placed a hand on Grace's shoulder. 'Your mum isn't here anymore. She's not coming back.' She said it as gently as she could, but it came out sounding way too harsh.

Grace lifted her head, confusion clouding her eyes. 'Tiger. My cat. She's gone.'

Tess dropped back on her heels, allowing herself a minute to regain some sense of equilibrium. Grace must think her a total dimwit, but the drama at the christening made sense now: the obsession with the cat, her commando crawl beneath the house to find him. Wilson had reminded her of home. The FACS people had said nothing about a cat. Nothing about anything much at all. Only that Grace had found Skye in bed and called … a friend. And that friend might know the where-abouts of the missing Tiger.

'What was your friend's name? The one who looked after you when … before you came to Sydney?'

'Jules?' Grace answered with a question as if she wasn't sure what Tess was talking about.

'That's the one.' A burst of hope made her skin tingle. Not only was Grace speaking, a coup in itself, but if they could find Jules they might find the cat, and Grace would have something familiar to cling to, something she loved. In the absence of *someone*. There was no point getting too excited just yet. The cat might not even be there—might not be anywhere. Tess needed to keep the whole thing low key, but at the same time try to be reassuring. 'So how about we get our stuff out of the car and head over and see Jules. She might be able to help.'

Grace's face instantly lit up. She gave an enthusiastic nod, pushed herself upright and walked away without another word.

But that was okay. She'd spoken. Little by little the ice was cracking.

Sparse. Basic. Rustic. If Tess was being polite, they were the words she would use to describe the interior of the cottage.

But since the place was not exactly inducing civility right now, the three words were completely different. A fucking dump. How the hell had Skye lived here? And more to the point, how was *she* going to live here?

The house was straight out of *The Man from Snowy River*, the entire thing lined with bare timber—floors, walls and ceiling—making it dark and dingy. At the end of the main room was a wrought-iron double bed covered with a crocheted throw, opposite which stood a battered old piano, partially covered by an equally ancient-looking quilt. On the wall above it, dozens of photos covered a cork board, the corners of some of them bending inwards, pinned at different angles. The wonky arrangement set Tess's teeth on edge. Neatening that up was going straight on the to-do list. And by the look of the place, the list was going to be long.

A combustion fireplace sat along the wall between shelves made from planks of wood stacked one above the other on bare bricks. More photos of Skye and Grace, this time in frames, decorated the shelves along with rows of books, some stacked vertically, others in horizontal piles. Candles and knickknacks completed the chaos. Tidying shelves: job number two.

Footsteps sounded from behind as Grace entered the house. Tess followed her gaze to the far end of the room. Was that the bed where Skye had died? This would be the first time Grace had seen it since then, and yet she'd wanted to come back. Eleanor had said there would be layers of complicated emotions, but she hadn't explained exactly how Tess should deal with them. Parenting was like being thrown out of a plane into the middle of the jungle and trying to navigate your way home without a compass. There was no guidebook for this, but Tess was the one who would have to lead them both out of the wilderness. Squaring her shoulders, she turned and took a few steps forward, to where Grace stood, motionless.

'Grace?' Her voice trembled. Not exactly oozing confidence. Or inspiring it. She cleared her throat before trying again. 'Sweetheart?'

No reply. Instead Grace made a slow walk, as if in a trance, towards the bed where she stopped, reached out a hand and ran it over the mound of the pillow. Tess held her breath as the little girl's head drooped and a shudder racked her tiny frame.

A baby bird coming back to an empty nest.

Seconds ticked over. Something solid in Tess's gut told her not to approach, to let Grace have this moment of grief. All she could do was look on silently. She had no idea how long would be long enough, but outside daylight was fading, so pretty soon she would need to put operation Find the Cat into action.

'Shall we go and find Tiger?' As soon as it was out she cringed at her own question. What if they couldn't find the cat? What if it was dead? She'd have to learn to phrase her questions more carefully.

Grace's shoulders rose, then fell again. She turned around and looked up with dry, vacant eyes. Some pain was much too deep for tears.

The diversion had worked. Now they just needed to find Tiger.

'So, do you know how to get to Jules's place?'

Glassy eyes staring straight ahead, leg jittering against the leather upholstery, Grace nodded.

If Tess had learned anything over the last week it was that trying too hard with Grace got her nowhere. Sitting back, shutting up and waiting was a far better way to get even vaguely close to whatever was going on inside the girl's head, so she cranked up the heating and trusted the directions would come when they were needed.

Late afternoon had brought a bank of angry clouds, a dramatic backdrop to the swathe of yellow grasses flanking the road. Thin rays of sunlight gave the landscape an eerie, almost ghostly glow. The countryside was so different out here. As soon as they'd crossed the Blue Mountains the scenery had opened up. Everything was vast. The farms, the open space, the sky. Even the quiet was more intense. Driving on the one-lane track without a soul around, with no sound except the humming of the engine, was slightly unnerving. By the time they returned it would be dark, and judging by the colour of the clouds, possibly raining. She should have left a light on inside the house. If she'd had any sense she would have left the search for Tiger until tomorrow, but if tracking down the cat was going to bring even a glimmer of a smile to Grace's face it would be worth the effort. And she did have a light on her phone to get them back inside.

At the turn-off to the main road Grace pointed left and in ten minutes they were in the town of Weerilla. Not a car in sight. A real-life ghost town. Right on cue, Grace lifted her arm, spectre-like, and pointed again.

'Is that the way to Jules's place?'

A nod.

Tess drove cautiously in case another direction came out of the blue. It gave her a chance to take in the sights: wide streets, an iconic pub with wrought-iron verandahs, stone cottages with picket fences and cottage gardens. There were even restaurants and cafes, actual civilisation. Skye would have been better to buy here, in town, where there was access to real food, real coffee and real people. But access worked both ways, didn't it?

'Here.' Grace pointed to a federation brick house set back from the road behind a hedged fence. Tess pulled to a stop. A sign hung from a post by the gate: *Jules Starkey. Art Studio. Classes and Commissions.*

So, Jules was an artist.

For the second time that day, Grace was out of the car before Tess could unbuckle her seatbelt. She ran straight up the cobbled path and yanked on the old ship bell dangling by the front door. Tess followed, wriggling her fingers to keep the cold at bay. Gloves would have been wise, but personal comfort hadn't been her top priority. Movement sounded from inside. The door opened and Grace launched herself into the arms of a woman who returned the embrace, closing her eyes as she rested her cheek against Grace's head. The affection between the two of them was obvious. Something prickled beneath Tess's skin. She folded her arms and waited for the love fest to end.

The woman swayed backwards, stretched out her arms and took Grace's face between her hands. 'Look at you! I swear you've gotten taller.' Instead of pulling away, Grace actually edged forward, snuggling into the woman's knitted poncho.

Just yesterday Grace holding her hand had felt earth-shattering, but seeing her here so comfortable with Jules stripped away any illusion of progress. Strange how something you never thought you wanted could so quickly become something you craved.

Wind rattled through the garden, sending a pile of fallen leaves scurrying across the lawn. The woman looked up and smiled. She had an old-fashioned, cherubic face, like a model from a Rubens painting, and a mop of grey curls pulled up into a rough bun, tied with a leopard-print scarf.

'Hello, you must be Tess.' She kept one arm around Grace as she spoke.

'Ah, yes, I am. But we haven't met before.' Strange that the woman knew her name.

'I ...' The woman looked down at Grace, the worry lines between her brows deepening. 'The FACS office told me you were caring for this little one was when I called to see how she was doing.' She hugged Grace to her side. 'It made me so happy to know she was being so well looked after.'

Everything about the woman said comfort. It was a good thing for Grace to have someone so lovely looking out for her. 'I take it you're Jules?' Tess reached out her hand and Jules gave it a firm shake.

'You're freezing, you poor thing. Come in, come in.' She waved them both through the door. 'I have someone here you'll be wanting to see, Gracie.'

For one brief, beautiful moment, an image of Skye popped into Tess's head, but she shook the vision away as they walked inside. The house was as welcoming as its owner, a zillion degrees toastier than outside, totally divine and delightfully heritage. Walking down the hallway was like visiting an art gallery. If this was all Jules's work, she was more than talented. The tour came to an end in a huge country-style kitchen complete with a butcher's block in the centre and an enormous pot bubbling away on an Aga. The combined, mouth-watering scent of chilli and garlic wafted through the room and Tess's stomach gurgled. She clamped her hands across it to mask the noise. Nobody else seemed to notice, or if they did they were too polite to say.

A cat fast asleep on a purple chair cushion lifted its stripey head and meowed. Grace actually squealed. The cat arched its back before jumping off its throne and winding itself around the girl's legs. She reached down and picked it up, burying her face in the fur. Tiger purred like a lawn mower.

'I'm guessing someone was missed.' Jules kept her voice to a whisper as she watched Grace cuddle the cat.

'I had no idea until …' Tess didn't want to get into that whole scene at her mother's. The wound was still too raw. 'Until we got to the house and she went searching for the cat. I'm so glad you have her.' The alternative did not warrant thinking about. 'It's good to see Grace smiling.'

Jules pulled out a chair and gestured for Tess to do the same. 'I'm guessing things haven't been easy?'

The look on Tess's face must have said everything she couldn't. Jules closed her eyes and gave a brief nod. She rubbed her hands together. 'Well, I've got an enormous pot of goulash soup on the boil. And some freshly baked sourdough. How about you two join me for dinner before taking Tiger home?'

'Oh, we shouldn't, I mean we haven't unpacked or anything and …' Coming up with an answer that didn't sound like an excuse was tricky, but Tess was eager to get settled. Grace, cat in arms, stepped closer and gave her a pleading look. 'Would you like to stay?'

A nod and a faint smile.

Her stomach rumbled again, much louder this time, right on cue. Even her own body was on the other team. So much for taking charge. She gave Jules a grateful smile. 'That would be lovely, thank you.'

'Gracie, why don't you and Tiger catch up while you watch some tellie in the lounge room.' She glanced up at the enormous railway clock on the wall above the Aga. 'I'll call you when dinner's ready.'

Grace slid from her chair and disappeared into the next room, perfectly at home. Jules was obviously more than an acquaintance. She'd been the one Grace had called when she couldn't wake her mother. She knew the layout of the house. And then there was that effusive greeting. None of it fitted with the image of Skye as a recluse. Tess studied their host as she stirred the goulash. A few well-worn lines on her face, a little thick around the middle—not quite her own mother's vintage, but she'd have to be in her late fifties. No kids around Grace's age, so that wasn't the link. It must be the art connection. She waited until the volume rose on the television before asking, 'So, were you and Skye close friends?'

Jules gave a weary sigh and motioned for Tess to take a seat. She pulled a bottle of wine from a rack on the bench and held it up for inspection, barely waiting for approval before she filled two huge Mexican-style wineglasses and handed one across. The merlot was peppery and smooth, an instant panacea to the stress of the long drive and arrival.

Jules took a mouthful, licking her lips before starting to speak. 'We met a few years ago, not long after I first moved here. I had a small exhibition of some of my artwork and Skye came along.' She shook her head. 'Gracie would have been about seven, I guess. Wandered into the gallery dragging this shaggy-looking toy dog behind her on a lead. The damned thing was filthy. Patted it and talked to it as if it was a real animal. Skye was wearing this amazing multi-coloured jacket and she had that wild mane of locks. They both did. Quite the pair. I couldn't take my eyes off them.'

It was exactly how Tess had felt that first day, when Skye had appeared in the classroom. All the other kids—herself included—had been neat and ordinary, but Skye's out-of-control hair and dreamy expression had made her so different. Mysterious almost. Jules was right, Grace had inherited her mother's aura.

'I hadn't seen her around town before, so I assumed she must have been passing through.' Jules looked into her wine-glass as if she was conjuring her story from its contents. 'Surprised me to hear she was a local. She was very interested in the gallery and, I could tell by the questions she asked, she knew what she was talking about.'

'She was always good at art at school.' Better than good. Ms Flowers, her art teacher, had been so disappointed when she'd left school early, had moaned endlessly about it being such a waste of talent and had harangued Tess about why Skye wasn't coming back to do her HSC.

Jules nodded, as if she was joining the dots. 'She started calling in to the studio every now and then. She'd come and watch me paint and we'd talk about different techniques, styles, that sort of thing. Always had Gracie with her. She was guarded, didn't give much away about her personal life. I got the feeling she was testing me, sort of trying me out. Then one day she asked me to her place for morning tea, to give her some help with a piece she was working on.'

Skye had mentioned years ago that she was doing some painting, but it had only been in passing. There'd been no evidence of any artist's tools at the house. 'She painted at home?'

'Painted, sculpted, potted. In the shed.'

Ah, the one with the mural. 'Was it good?'

'Really good. She started making some pieces for me to sell in the gallery. Built up quite a clientele. Tourists passing through would pick up a piece and then order something else online. Skye always insisted they order through me, never direct. I kept telling her she needed to set up a website and treat her art as a business, but she wouldn't hear of it.' Jules returned the glass to the table and folded her arms. 'We almost fell out over it at one stage, but I let it go. Settled for having her sell through the gallery, although I refused to take any commission.'

'Did she earn enough to make a living?'

'Enough to supplement her inheritance. She said it wasn't much, but it bought her the house and kept the two of them going. Grew her own veggies, had chickens, tank water, a wood fire. The extra bits she got from her art sales usually went into buying clothes or school supplies for Gracie. Their lifestyle was pretty simple.'

One look at the place made that obvious. Skye could do basic. She'd done it when she'd travelled: she had simply thrown on a backpack and ventured off for years at a time. Material objects, possessions, meant nothing, not unless they had some sort of sentimental value. Like the gift Tess had given her for her sixteenth birthday: a fine silver chain, two hearts intertwining on the clasp. A friendship bracelet Skye had treasured. Tess's stomach twisted. She'd meant it then, friends for life. But friends were people you could count on, weren't they? People who were there for you when you needed them. People like Jules. She was warm and fuzzy, and arty and crafty, and all round wonderful. Everything a mother should be. Everything Tess wasn't. Why hadn't Skye left Grace with her?

Jules's voice began to recede as the room started to spin. A hand rested on her knee.

'Are you okay?' Jules was looking down at her.

She put down her wine, pressed her index fingers against the bridge of her nose and waited for the dizziness to pass. 'Sorry.'

'No, I'm sorry. I should have been more sensitive. Rambling on like that. This must be such a terrible shock for you.'

Jules was so right. There'd been no time to find out why Skye might have done what she did, why she'd chosen to end her own life and abandon her only child. No time to process that decision, or what it meant. The sound of a neighing horse drifted through from the television in the next room as Grace, cat stuck under her arm, appeared in the kitchen. Her eyes shifted from Jules to the pot on the stove and back again.

'You hungry, Missy?' Jules stood, taking the hint. 'Let's eat.'

Tess cleared her throat and jumped to her feet. Action was always the best cure for introspection. 'Can I help with anything?'

'Plates and cutlery are in there.' Jules pointed to the top drawer. 'Gracie, you grab yourself a glass of milk. Tiger might like a saucer while you're at it.'

The cat managed to escape the stranglehold and snooped around the base of the fridge. In a few minutes, they were all sitting around the table with steaming bowls of goulash and oven-fresh slices of crusty bread. The smell alone was completely mind-blowing.

'Dig in, ladies.'

If action was the best distraction, food came a close second. It tasted as good as it smelled and Tess savoured each mouthful as they fell into a comfortable silence. The bowls were all mismatched ceramics, nothing like the fine china her mother always used or the plain white sets in her own cupboard. Grace devoured her dinner, flicking her eyes constantly from her bowl to the cat lapping up its milk in the corner. Tiger was not going to be let out of her sight for quite some time. Jules urged them both to help themselves to seconds and they did, Tess mopping the last of the soup with yet another slice of bread and dropping her hands to her stomach in surrender when her bowl was wiped clean. There was something to be said for homegrown country cooking.

'That was amazing.'

Jules looked genuinely pleased. 'I'm glad you enjoyed it.'

Grace too had left an empty bowl. She yawned, hand over her mouth, before rubbing a scrunched fist over her eye.

'You tired, sweetie?' Tess had no idea where that particular endearment had come from, perhaps some dormant maternal spring she'd never needed to tap into, but it seemed to be popping out of her mouth surprisingly often.

Grace nodded.

'You've both had a long day.' Jules began clearing the table, waving Tess away when she attempted to help. 'I'll do this. You get going before it gets too late. Take little Tiger home to bed.'

Home to bed in the cabin in the middle of nowhere. Jules's place was getting more appealing by the minute, but Grace was already pulling on her coat, gathering Tiger into her arms, and Jules, who had left the room briefly, was already opening the door to a cat carrier.

'No complaints, Missus, you're going home.' Jules shoved the cat in and clipped the locks shut. 'I'll bring her out to the car for you.'

Outside the temperature had dropped along with the wind. Tess wound her scarf a little tighter around her neck. Was it the cold or the vision of the empty house she was returning to making her shiver? She stared down the street into the night. So quiet. So black.

Jules deposited the cat carrier on the back seat and Grace slid in beside it. 'Thanks for looking after Tiger.'

'My pleasure.' Jules's voice cracked. 'I'll come out to see her soon.' She closed the door and blew Grace a kiss before handing Tess a business card. 'If you need anything just call.'

'Thanks.' They stood side by side on the footpath, two women who didn't even know each other, connected now by an orphaned girl, until Tess broke the spell and headed around to climb into the driver's seat. The load of her new reality pressed down on her like a solid slab of cement. The sensation wasn't a new one—the trick was to keep moving before it became too hard to shake it off. She sucked in a quick draft of air and started the engine.

In the rear-vision mirror she could see Grace smiling down at her four-legged friend, now out of its cage and sitting on her lap. Thank God for Tiger. Thank God Jules had kept her safe. Tess turned her eyes back to the road, the hum of a contented cat murmuring behind her, and drove off into the darkness.

Eleven

Every noise seemed to echo in the quiet of the night as they pulled up outside the house. The banging of the car doors, the crunching of gravel underfoot, even the whistle of Tess's own breath through her nostrils. Whoever came up with the torch app was an absolute genius. She opened the door and fumbled around for the light switch. A yellow glow lit the room and her shoulders softened a fraction. They were out in the sticks, but at least there was a lock and four solid walls between them and the rest of the world. Of course there was the chance they could both freeze to death—the fireplace was conspicuously empty and there was no way she was going on a kindling expedition at this time of night. Layers and blankets would have to suffice.

A beaded curtain separated the living area from the one single bedroom. Grace grabbed her suitcase and headed straight into what must be her room, cat in tow. If Tiger objected to being dragged around like a ragdoll, she kept it to herself.

Small mercies.

Only one other bed existed in the place: the double at the far end of the room, the one that must have been Skye's. Tess wrapped her jacket tighter around her body. The only other option was the couch. Or the floor: the rough, cold wooden floor. Couch it was, if she could find some blankets. A timber box at the base of the bed was the most likely storage place. She flipped up the lid and the faint scent of lavender wafted out. A pile of woollen blankets was stacked beside sets of sheets and a couple of spare pillows. She might have to sleep on a lumpy lounge, but at least she'd be warm.

There was a movement in her peripheral vision. Her stomach flipped as she spun around. She dropped the bundle she was holding, letting out a mouse-like squeak. Grace had crept out so quietly she hadn't made a sound and was standing right behind her. Well, in front of her now. Tess lowered her hand from her chest and heaved out a sigh. 'You scared me. I didn't hear you come out.'

Sorry. No words, but that's what her expression meant.

'Silly me.' She could hardly blame the child for her own paranoia. 'Is everything okay?'

Grace was holding the cat as if it was a baby, paws over her shoulder, head tucked beneath her chin. 'Can I sleep out here?'

A question. An actual out-loud question. 'On the couch?'

Bottom lip drawn between her teeth, Grace shook her head. She walked the length of the room and stopped beside the bed.

'You want to sleep there?'

A small but distinctive nod.

Tess flicked her eyes from the bed to Grace and back again. Was that healthy? Letting a little girl sleep in the bed where her mother had died? Where she'd found her? She swallowed hard. Her phone was right there in her back pocket. She could call Jules and ask her advice.

Grace put the cat on the bed and turned back around, eyes narrowed, lips pressed together in a pout. She'd sensed Tess's hesitation. Was this her version of a tantrum? Tess had been the queen of them as a kid, although hers had been a lot louder, involved a lot more wailing and thrashing, and generally took place on the shopping-centre floor. In her own quiet way, Grace was just as good. She was standing her ground. What was the point of saying no? Maybe it would be a comfort to her. Maybe it was her way of staying close to her mother.

'Okay.' Keeping it light, she reached back into the blanket box. 'Let's make it up fresh.'

Grace picked up the cat and gently deposited her on the floor.

Agreeing with Grace's request was easier than following through. Heart hammering, she pinched the edge of the crocheted cover and peeled it back. There were no sheets, just the pastel pattern of the bare mattress. She continued on, completely uncovering the pillow. Skye's face was crystal clear before her, dull eyes open. Unseeing. Lifeless.

Not a sound in the room, but the thunderous pounding of blood reverberated through Tess's temples. A hand fell gently on top of her fingers and she jerked her head up to meet Grace's gaze. Skye's eyes, and yet her own. Blinking. Gleaming. Alive. Tess mustered a small smile. Grace was made of tough stuff. She was most definitely her mother's daughter.

She took a breath to calm the clattering of her pulse, then step by step, they gathered up the clean sheets and made the bed together. Grace climbed in and Tiger jumped up to snuggle beside her.

Grace's eyes were already falling shut. It had been a huge day. In every imaginable way. Tucking Grace into bed here was so different. At the apartment she'd usually rolled on her side after reading her book, so clearly closing down that Tess had never been game to do anything other than whisper goodnight and switch off the light. But here, in her mother's bed, she lay flat on her back, her head tipped to one side, a purring, real-life Tiger tucked in beside her along with the wounded bear. There was something gentler, more relaxed in the angles of her face. Something Tess couldn't resist. Reaching out, she stroked a few wayward locks of hair back off Grace's cheek. So smooth. So innocent. She leaned down and kissed the sleeping child on the forehead.

'Sweet dreams.'

Grace wouldn't hear her, she was already asleep. But the feel of her new foster-daughter's skin beneath her lips was sure to make her own dreams a little easier.

The house grunted and moaned like a galleon being tossed about on a wild sea. Tess lay in bed, eyes bulging, arms locked across her middle. Lamplight drew long shadows on the wood panels lining the walls, creating a strange other-worldly effect. She focused on the brightest point, tried to block out everything else. Meditation had never been one of her strongest talents, but one technique she remembered was to focus on everything in the room first. Grace's bedside lamp was made from stained glass, covered in butterflies, like the ones on the jewellery box Tess had given her that first day they met. Presumably, Grace had packed it with her things to bring home. If it did make an appearance it would go perfectly with the room. A total fluke.

Another loud creak sounded as the timbers shifted. She jumped up, pulling the doona closer to her chest. Cold air nipped at her cheeks, the only exposed part of her body, the rest of it layered in tracksuit pants, shirt, hoodie and finally, blankets. The weight of it all was comforting, yet still not enough. She dragged her gaze back to the original spot on the ceiling. Pictured the butterflies coming to life and flitting around the room, herself as a butterfly, wings beating, drawn to the light. People talked about white light appearing when you died. Had it been like that for Skye? Was she afraid even though it had supposedly been her choice? The questions floated in the half-light as she drifted on the currents of sleep, pausing on one memory and then the next ...

Skye in the school playground, sitting alone with her lunchbox on her lap, her unruly hair bunched into two ponytails. A shy smile lighting her eyes at their first hello.

At the park, her head tipped back, arms taut against the metal chains of the swing as she arced up and down, the two of them side by side seeing who could go higher.

Walking along the street, her face drawn, shadows rimming her eyes, and the quiet desperation on her face as she clutched Tess's arm.

Each memory put her right back there with Skye, her eyes growing heavier, dragging her down into a deep, dark dungeon of sleep: doors opening and closing, the sound of her own breath echoing inside her skull, a voice hissing venom into her ear.

She surfaced into the bleary light of morning, her T-shirt damp with sweat. Rubbing a hand across her face, she picked up her phone and blinked at the numbers on the screen—it was almost eight. Much too late for a responsible parent to be rising. Plates and cutlery clinked in the kitchen. She sloughed off the covers and sat up, taking a minute for her blood pressure to settle. Her phone buzzed with a message from Josh. *I assume you got there safely*. Curt. Like most of their conversations since she'd said she was coming to Weerilla. She should have messaged him to let him know they'd arrived, but then they'd got here and Grace had freaked out and they'd gone in search of Tiger and …

She typed back a quick apology and a promise to call him later. Her temples ached and her head was as heavy as a bowling ball. How much sleep had she actually had? Only a few hours at most. She blinked away the residue of her nightmares and switched off the lamp. Time to get moving. Today was going to be all about taking things easy and making some headway with Grace. Now that the cat had been found and the first night was out of the way, things were sure to get easier.

By the time she stumbled out to the kitchen in bed socks, Grace was already eating breakfast—a standard bowl of Weetbix and banana, drowned in a swimming pool of the milk she must have retrieved from the esky—and a book was laid open on the table.

'Good morning. Sorry I slept in, that drive must have taken more out of me than I thought.'

Grace kept reading, slurping cereal off her spoon.

Back to square one. Tess rummaged around in the box of stuff she'd brought from home and dragged out the plunger and filter coffee. On a scale of one to ten, today's need for caffeine was around nine-point-five. She flicked on the kettle and folded her arms as she surveyed the space. The kitchen was tiny, set at the back of the house, divided from the lounge area by a rectangular table with bench seats. A set of cast-iron frying pans hung from hooks below open shelves storing cups, glasses and plates. A white trough sink set into a timber bench sat beneath the single window facing out onto the backyard. She straightened as she peered through the glass. What was all over the grass? She could have sworn it was a dull shade of green yesterday when she'd followed Grace out there on the hunt for Tiger. Now it was a powdery white. She leaned into the window for a closer look. Wait, was that …?

'Frost?' She turned to Grace, hooking a thumb over her shoulder. 'Is that frost out there?'

The usual nod, then back to the book.

Freaking hell. The whole yard was covered in a sheet of tiny crystals, under a woolly blanket of grey sky. The house was cold enough, but it looked positively arctic out there. Tess crossed her arms, rubbing at her elbows, her palms eventually warming from the friction. A cloud of fog appeared when she blew on her knuckles, then quickly evaporated. So that was why Grace was wearing a scarf, beanie and gloves. They needed to get that fire going before they did anything else. Before they froze. The kettle whistled and she filled the plunger, closing her eyes and inhaling. The last time she'd been anywhere remotely rural was at her father-in-law's winery, where the accommodation was more designer luxury than rustic cabin. A gas fire had ignited with the touch of a button and the heated travertine tiles beneath her feet had been positively a gift from the gods. Here all she had was an empty pot-belly and bare boards turning her socked feet into slabs of ice. It was like visiting an alternate universe—one that had a climate reminiscent of the North Pole.

Grace scraped the final remnants of cereal from her bowl. With Tiger perched on the chair beside her, book at her fingertips, she seemed perfectly content. Maybe, just maybe, coming back would be the therapy she needed. Maybe she would feel closer to her mother here and that would help her deal with Skye's death. Once the funeral was over, they could focus on getting to know each other.

Tess needed to phone the mortician and finalise arrangements, but settling Grace back in at home was her first priority.

She closed her eyes and chugged back a large mouthful of coffee, scalding her throat. This was all such new territory. The only other deaths she'd experienced had been her paternal grandfather and her maternal grandmother. She'd been young for both, a kid and then a teenager. Although losing them had been hard, there was something inevitable about an older person dying. It was something you could accept, part of that whole cycle-of-life thing. But this was different. This was her friend. Someone she'd grown up with, someone who had survived the worst and deserved to live. Funny then how this death hadn't moved her to tears, yet every time those two words—*Skye* and *dead*—came together in her brain, a solid lump of gristle settled at the base of her throat. It was there now, a mass not even the strength of the coffee could dissolve.

So what must it be like for Grace?

Her mother had left her. Not by leaving the house, by removing herself from life. Why had Skye gone to such lengths to protect her child—holed them both up in the wilderness with barely any connection to the outside world—if she was going to throw Grace to the wolves? It didn't make sense. Or did it? Did the past eventually catch up with you no matter how hard and fast you ran? How diligently you hid. Perhaps some things were just too horrible to live with no matter how much—or who—you had to live for?

129

The downy hairs on the back of Tess's neck bristled. She tightened her grip on the cup. Morbid thoughts were not helpful. She needed to take control of the situation and get shit done.

'So, how about we get a fire happening?'

Grace lifted her head from the book, but made no attempt to move. Tiger took the opportunity to jump from the chair and scoot across to the back door, letting out a high-pitched meow. That was enough to get her owner mobile. She walked to the door and opened it, the cat slinking out with a quiet trill, as if saying thank you.

A shot of cold air blasted into the room. Tess sprang forward and pushed the door shut. 'Brrrrr. I hope poor Tiger doesn't freeze her little butt off out there.' What looked suspiciously like a grin tugged at the corners of Grace's mouth. 'She doesn't run off, does she?' Another frenzied cat chase in what amounted to polar conditions was not on today's agenda.

Grace gave a shake of her head.

'Good to know. So, we should probably get some wood.'

Grace marched to the fireplace and returned with the empty basket. Tess reached for the door, pausing before stepping outside. She was only wearing socks. Not the best form of footwear for wood collecting, or traversing a frost-covered yard. Outside, Grace pointed to a shoe rack beside the step, where two pairs of rubber gumboots sat. Tess gave the larger set a good upside-down shake before pulling them on. She was literally stepping into Skye's life. Her daughter, her house and now her boots. Coffee swirled inside her otherwise empty stomach.

Grace left her no time to ponder as she headed off across the yard. Tess followed, blades of grass crunching like shattered glass beneath her feet. Even the fruit trees along the fence line were coated in frost, miniature icicles glittering on their naked branches. The morning air burned her lungs and she held it there for a few seconds before huffing out a mouthful of fog. Her eyes stung and she swiped away the beads of water settling against her lower lashes. Birds chirped high up in the gums and higher still, a crow cawed.

Everything was fresh and clear and crisp. Breathtaking, in the best possible way.

By the time she reached the woodpile at the back of the shed, the basket was already half-filled with neatly cut logs. Grace shook her head when Tess went to help, and continued on with the job, pulling a bundle of sticks from a pile stacked up beside the abandoned chook pen. The pile was waist high and a metre or so wide, probably enough timber to last a good few days. How long did wood take to burn? If she'd been a Brownie instead of a ballerina, or if her dad and brothers had taken her away for camping weekends instead of leaving her at home with her mother, she might know the answer to that question. She might not be such a useless twit when it came to anything vaguely practical. Give her a staffing issue and she'd have it sorted before the office door closed for the day, but hand her a load of sticks and a box of matches and she'd probably freeze to death before she could strike a flame.

Taking one handle of the basket each, they carried the load inside. Once again, all Tess could do was watch as Grace scrunched up bits of paper and stuffed them into the grate, tossing in a few fire starters from a box on the floor before she reached for the matches.

Tess sprang forward. 'I'll do that.' Grace was a kid. Far too young to be mucking around with fire.

'I am not a baby.' Grace snatched her hand away, the match box firmly in her grasp.

131

'No, but you're not an adult, either.'

'Mumma always let me. It's my job.' She pulled out a match and struck it against the side of the box before Tess could react. Sulphur sizzled and a puff of smoke rose as Grace lit the contents of the pot-belly. She slammed the door shut and placed the closed matchbox back on the shelf, the look on her face blacker than the soot on the hearth. She stomped past, grabbed her book from the table and vanished into her bedroom, the curtain of beads clattering against the wall as she swiped them aside.

In the quiet of the lounge room, the fire crackled to life. Tess turned towards it, knees tingling as her muscles began to thaw. Had she and Grace just had their first fight? And if they had, how long would the cold war last?

Twelve

Right now, the big freeze was much more physical. Her fingers were frozen solid. She scrunched them into fists and then released them again, repeating the action as the blood began to flow. Once the blaze inside the pot-belly billowed into a full-blown fire, she had to take a step away. There was no point in scorching her trackies since they were the only comfortable—and warm—piece of clothing she'd brought.

Breakfast refuse littered the table. She could get on with tidying up, if she had any idea where things belonged. The heating system was remarkably effective, already warming the air out in the kitchen. As she collected her cup, Grace, changed now into a sweatshirt and leggings, breezed past, picked up her bowl and proceeded to rinse it at the sink. A shaft of sunlight streamed through the window onto her hair, creating a halo effect. Based on the way she was savaging the plate with the dish brush, however, her expression would be more demonic than angelic. Good to know she wasn't all sunshine and light. At least she had some spunk.

And she'd come out of her cave. That was surely something to celebrate.

Eleanor had suggested normality, and a return to everyday routine for Grace was homeschooling. One more thing about which Tess was completely clueless. Wasn't there already enough tough stuff to deal with as a parent without adding that onerous task? Skye had her reasons, though, and for the time being Tess would need to follow suit. Surely it couldn't be that hard. A bit of reading, a bit of maths, maybe some social science or whatever they called it these days.

'Would you like to do some school work?' That sounded too tentative. She tried again. 'I mean, if you have any school work I can give you a hand.'

Grace swished her ponytail and opened a cupboard beneath the bench, pulling out a plastic crate and unloading its contents onto the table. Books, pencil case, ruler. She arranged it all neatly, sat down and looked vaguely in Tess's direction.

This was a turn-up. One minute the kid was storming off to the bedroom and the next she was setting up a home office, but who was Tess to argue? She pulled out a chair, taking in the textbook Grace had chosen first. 'Great. I aced maths at school. Show me what you're doing.'

Grace opened the book and pointed. Fractions. She bowed her head over the page and got to work. Letting the student tackle each question on their own first, urging them to work it out for themselves rather than giving them the answers, was the technique Tess had used in her university days when she'd earned her part-time wage as a tutor. A few of her older kids had blitzed their HSC, more fodder for her mother's argument that she really should be a teacher and give the psychology degree away. Funny that in the end she had switched paths, despite it not relating to any great desire to follow in her mother's footsteps. Giving that dream a miss had nothing to do with her future and everything to do with her past.

Grace stared up at her, one eyebrow arched. *Is that right?* She didn't have to say it out loud for Tess to catch her drift.

She'd been miles away. She bent forward and checked over the tidily drawn figures. 'You've got it. That's so good for your age.'

Grace's eyes shone. Seeing her face light up was such a gift.

Giving her space to try things for herself was probably a good idea. Better than being one of those helicopter parents, hovering around and watching every move her kid made. Not that Grace was her kid … anyway. 'How about I do a bit of cleaning up and unpack the rest of my stuff, and you give me a yell if you need some help?'

A quick nod and Grace returned to her books. Perhaps this whole homeschooling caper wasn't so bad after all.

A smoky, not unpleasant, scent filled the cottage. Unpacking her clothes was a logical next step, but there wasn't a whole lot of storage room in the place. Apart from the wardrobe and an old chest of drawers in Grace's room, there was the blanket box at the end of the queen-sized bed and another wardrobe in the far corner. Ornate flowers were carved into its timber doors, their stems and leaves highlighted with mother-of-pearl. Such a beautiful piece of furniture. Like the butterflies on the bedroom lamp, the pattern was reminiscent of the jewellery box she'd bought Grace for their first meeting. This time almost identical. Was that why Grace had been so immediately enamoured with the piece? The living area must have doubled as Skye's bedroom, so her clothes would be in there, and possibly some of her more personal items, too. Goosebumps pimpled Tess's arms, creeping across the ball of her shoulder and up the base of her neck.

She flicked a look back at Grace, head down, still absorbed in calculations. It wouldn't hurt to take a quick peek and glean some idea of Skye's life. They'd shed their gumboots at the back door, so her socked feet made barely a sound as she glided towards the wardrobe. Her heart, on the other hand, was thumping away like a boom box. She paused mid-step and looked back into the kitchen. No movement. All good.

Two more strides and she was there. A small key rested inside the lock in the middle of the double doors. She pinched the clover-shaped end and gave a twist. One small click and both doors fell ajar. Key between her fingertips, she held her breath. What was she doing? Snooping, that's what she was doing, but for a good cause. Besides, no one would know. She inched the doors open. Two racks of clothes. T-shirts, cotton long sleeves, a sheepskin jacket and a Driza-Bone, all hung along on the top rail. Jeans and a few long skirts on the bottom. Arranged in a neat row underneath, was an assortment of shoes—sandals, ankle boots and uggs. Nothing fancy, nothing out of the ordinary. All well worn.

A single panel door was on the right. Again, Tess turned the key. Drawers filled the lower half of the space. She pulled each one out, inspecting its contents. Underwear, socks, jumpers, shorts, scarves. A few pieces of jewellery sat on a shelf around eye level—earrings, rings, a necklace of tiny elephants joined trunk to tail. Skye had always loved that style. Bo-ho, it would be called now, but when they'd been kids it had been plain old Indian. They'd stop in at Asian Affair on their way home from school, swoon over the sandalwood incense, trail their fingers over the dangling pieces of silver hanging from the rack on the counter, and chatter away to Mrs Novak, who owned the tiny store. Back in the days when they still had walked home together.

Tess shook her head. She needed to stay focused. Poking around towards the back of the shelf, her fingers landed on something she instantly identified. Her stomach whirled. Skye had kept it, after all those years of travelling, the almost twenty years between then and now. She slid out the bracelet and let it rest in the palm of her hand. Two tarnished silver hearts. The small ruby birthstone connecting them was flat and dull. She slipped it over her wrist, but the clasp was broken. If only it was a Tardis that could send her tumbling back in time, to the day or the week or the year before everything had changed. Things might have worked out differently. Skye might still be alive. She let the bracelet fall into her hand and tucked it back in the hidden depths of the wardrobe. Pie-in-the-sky daydreaming would get her nowhere.

Three more shelves to go. A couple of leather bags and an old wallet on the first, an array of knitted beanies on the next, and on the top shelf two brown wicker storage boxes sitting side by side. She reached up and pulled one down, tucking it against her diaphragm as she peeled off the lid and rifled through the contents. Photos, dozens of them. Grace's pixie face, smiling. Actually smiling. Grace cartwheeling across the frosty lawn. Grace climbing a tree. Joyful, playful, happy. So different to the Grace she knew now. She closed the lid with a sigh and returned the box to its place, grabbing its shelf-mate.

Documents this time. Fixing the lid beneath the box, she filed through the stack of papers. A receipt for the sale of Skye's grandmother's house back in Sydney, one for the house she'd bought here in Weerilla, Grace's birth certificate, and tucked away at the bottom was an A4-sized envelope, unlabelled and unsealed. She balanced the base of the envelope against the box and prised it open with her free hand, pulling out a collection of photocopied pages. The header on the first page showed it had been copied from the *Melbourne Herald* back in April. '*He has a daughter*' was scribbled across the top in bright-red pen. Underneath the headline, 'LOCAL BUSINESSMAN RUNS FOR STATE SEAT', was a grainy photo of a man in a suit, somewhere in his late forties, smiling tightly from behind dark sunglasses. A shorter woman stood beside him, the pair flanked by two boys who looked to be in their late teens, and a younger girl stood in front of the couple. She brought it closer, squinting at the grainy caption: '*Businessman and Property Developer Neil Harrison announces his …*'

Her head swam. Her vision blurred.

Oh God. It was him.

Her legs threatened to give way.

She rested her head against the wardrobe as she zoomed in on the image. Yes, it was definitely him. Older, of course, his blond hair cut short now, balding in patches above his temples. Paisley tie, dark suit. The image of respectability. If she'd walked past him in the street, she never would have recognised him. She closed her eyes. A voice buzzed in her ears. She rattled her head, trying to block it out.

'What are you doing?' A smaller, quieter voice sawed through the white noise.

Tess's eyes flew open, the envelope and paper falling back into the box.

Grace eyed her curiously.

'I … um.' She ripped the lid away from the base and jammed it back in place. 'I was just seeing if your mum left any important papers. Documents. Things that would need sorting out.'

'Did she?' No inflection to her question, just a dull monotone.

'Nothing much.' She cleared her throat. 'Just papers to do with the house, some old bills.' She shoved the box back into the cupboard and closed the door, turned the key and pulled it from the lock, then shoved it deep into the pocket of her pants. Locking it all away again was safer. For both of them. She faked a smile as she turned around.

'Okay. I'm going to do some reading.'

'Do you need any help?'

Grace shook her head and disappeared back into the kitchen. She'd accepted the explanation without question. So trusting. Skye had done everything in her power to protect her daughter from the horrible realities of the world and now it was up to Tess to do the same.

Fire roared inside the pot-belly as a whoosh of air blew through the flue. The room was suddenly, overwhelmingly hot. Slipping off her socks, she crept outside to the quiet of the front yard. A cool breeze washed across her cheeks and she drew in a few deep breaths. The frost was dissolving, leaving the overgrown lawn wet against the soles of her feet. A thin veil of mist hovered over the garden. She stood for a long time, watching it gradually disappear, vanish into the day, until there was nothing but a wide expanse of blue sky.

A movement in the long grass. Something brushed against her foot. She bent forward to look more closely: a rat, blood oozing from a puncture wound on its snout, writhed at her feet. A low, guttural scream burst from her lips. She kicked at the maimed creature and the cat sprang into action, pouncing, clamping her jaws down hard, and scurrying off into the bush. A crimson blotch stained the trodden-down patch of grass. Tess scrubbed at it with her toe, rubbing it away so that only a trace of it remained. So faint the violation might never have happened at all.

Thirteen

Silence suited Tess just fine as they drove along the main road into town. Lunch had been a late, sullen affair of sandwiches barely touched. Still reeling from the morning's discovery and shaken by the bloodied rat, she couldn't eat a bite; Grace had only nibbled, leaving a demolition ground of crusts on her plate. Topping up the pantry seemed as good an excuse as any to get out of the house, so she'd cajoled Grace into the car and set off for an afternoon excursion. Weerilla was only a tiny place, but there had to be a supermarket somewhere. A local version of The Gourmet Kitchen was probably too much to ask. It was her go-to on weekdays, with its delicious, healthy home-cooked meals for two. Since Grace's arrival, Tess had had to step up in the cooking department, and tonight they needed some comfort food, something like that delicious stewy soup Jules had served. Or maybe mac and cheese, and one of those packet puddings. And chocolate. Lots of chocolate.

The main street was almost deserted, but then it was mid-afternoon on a weekday in the middle of winter in a small country town. Bare-branched trees lined both sides of the road and a gnarly vine formed an arty sort of canopy outside a coffee shop called Café Diem, which had a handy parking space right out front. Tess pulled on her jacket and buttoned up. Grace was wearing the beanie she'd donned before breakfast and she'd added a duffle coat to complete her ensemble. She was quite the eclectic dresser, and had no problem mixing and matching colours and patterns. If she rocked up to a social gathering wearing that sort of gear in Sydney, she'd get more than a few guarded whispers, and not just from the mothers. That was one benefit of being homeschooled—no peer pressure, no judgement, no bitchy girl dramas.

Tastebuds on high alert, Tess walked up to the cafe door. She yanked on the handle, but it didn't budge. Grace pointed to a sign in the window: *Open 8 am–3 pm Monday to Friday, 8 am–1 pm Saturdays. Closed Sundays.* What kind of cafe closes mid-afternoon? Tess cupped her hands and peered through the glass. A guy cleaning the counter shrugged and shook his head, mouthing, 'Sorry.' If he was so sorry maybe he should try opening the door since it was only ten past bloody three. Tess kicked at the concrete wall of the building and growled, wincing when her big toe began to throb.

The corners of Grace's mouth curved ever so slightly. Nice that someone found the stupid opening hours amusing. Might not be so funny if the next store was closed and there was nothing for dinner.

'So where's the supermarket?'

Grace spun on her heel and walked off down the street, stopping outside a narrow shopfront: a grocery store doubling as a newsagent. Did the place even have stock on the shelves? There was only one way to find out. Tess pushed her sunnies onto the top of her head and ventured through the doors.

The store was a surprise, the aisles long and stocked with a good selection of foods, even a few things you might find hard to source in the city—organic pasta, farm-produced honey and fresh, locally grown grass-fed beef. Grace held up a few things for approval before dumping them in the trolley. The kid might have attitude at times, but her manners were impeccable. By the time they got to the checkout, they'd exchanged a total of about ten words. Not a bad tally.

Shopping done. Now what?

'Can we go and visit Jules?'

A full-blown question instead of a barely there grunt? Grace was doing that intense-staring thing she seemed to have mastered, but the fact that she even asked was a positive. Jules, though? Was it good to encourage a connection with someone else when Tess was trying to establish herself as the key adult in the girl's life?

On the other hand, there was no reason to rush home. The fire had been turned to low to keep the place habitable, Tiger was safely secured indoors so she wouldn't be murdering any more rodents, and there were still a few hours to go before dark. All that was waiting for them was the ghost of a woman yet to be buried and a locked wardrobe Tess wouldn't be re-opening anytime soon.

And when Grace was looking up at her with those pretty-please eyes, how could she say no?

Grace bounded out of the car as soon as it stopped outside Jules's place and Tess's heart sank. Walking in together would have been nice. Being the person Grace wanted to hang around with would be even nicer.

Be the adult, Tess, her mother's voice hummed. Even if they'd been on speaking terms, she probably wouldn't want to ask for advice, but years of maternal wisdom was firmly wedged away inside her brain and this admonishment was well deserved. Grace was the child and she was the adult. She needed to act like one. So she mustered a smile as she joined Grace on the front porch. The bell had been rung already, but it looked like no one was home.

'We can always come back tomorrow.' *Turn a negative into a positive.* Another one of her mother's pearls.

Grace sighed.

'Hello there!' Jules appeared from around the corner of the house, an emerald-green scarf draped around her neck, gold hoops dangling from her ears, hair pinned haphazardly in a pile on top of her head. The woman was a walking work of art. 'We're out back in the studio. Crafty Kids is on today. Why don't you come and join in, Gracie?'

Socialising with other kids? This was an unexpected opportunity. Tess pressed her lips together to stop herself talking. It had to be Grace's call.

Jules took a small step forward. 'We're making octopuses and hedgehogs.' Her voice was softer, more enticing than when she'd greeted them. Smart move. 'And even better, we're drinking hot chocolate with marshmallows.' Bribery—smarter still.

Grace shifted from one foot to the other. With her hair pulled back and the teal beanie low on her forehead, she looked much younger than her ten years. Pale and totally vulnerable.

Jules reached out her hand and wiggled her fingers. 'Come on. You loved it last time.' There was so much kindness in her expression, Tess was tempted to take her hand herself.

Grace must have felt it, too. She didn't reply in words, only nodded obviously enough for it to be yes. This woman was a miracle worker. Grace didn't exactly bounce out of her skin as she trailed along behind Jules to the back of the house, but she had agreed, so that in itself was a win.

Easy laughter drifted from inside the studio. Jules pushed open the door and clapped her hands three times, waiting to speak until the group of six children quietened. 'Everyone, you remember Gracie?'

She whipped out a stool from under a table bulging with fabrics, glue, paint pots, wire and tennis balls. An older teenage girl approached, two long blonde braids grazing the waistband of her patterned leggings, and sat beside Grace. The noise level in the room dimmed as the kids stopped to check out the newcomer, but gradually their attention returned to their creations and the chatter resumed.

Jules angled her head towards the door. 'Let's go make that hot chocolate.'

Tess hesitated. Was it okay to leave Grace out here on her own?

'Come on, she'll be fine. Erin will look after her.' Jules took Tess's arm and guided her into the main part of the house.

Walking into the kitchen was like stepping into a toasty warm hug. Tess peeled off her coat, twisting her neck from side to side as she rested against the island bench to watch Jules make the hot chocolate. Three gigantic mugfuls: a couple of marshmallows dropped into the first, one pink and one white, then reaching into the cupboard above her head, Jules dragged out a glass decanter and tipped a slug of amber liquid into the remaining two cups.

'Medicinal.' She winked and handed one mug across to Tess, placed the second on the table and headed out the door with the other. 'I'll be back.'

The rich chocolate concoction tasted like liquid silk with a strong, distinctly orange tang. Like drinking a melted jaffa. Sheer bliss.

'Good?' Jules returned and collected her own mug, smacking her lips together at the aftertaste. She waved Tess over to the table.

'Heavenly. What's the secret ingredient?'

'Homemade liqueur. My own version of Grand Marnier. I like to add a dash when I need a bit of oomph.' She peeked over the top of her glasses. 'And you look like someone who could use a bit of oomph.'

Was it that obvious? Probably. Being in the place where Skye had died, dealing with Grace's issues, setting up house with a kid she barely knew in a ramshackle, isolated cabin ... turning the key in the wardrobe door and finding that box. Not to mention all the crap she'd left behind in Sydney. And the impending funeral. Yeah, it was fair to say she could use some oomph. It would take a good few slurps for the elixir to do its work.

Jules smiled, as if she'd read her mind. 'Well, you don't need to worry about Gracie. She's out there making tentacles like there's no tomorrow. It's good for her, being around the other kids.'

It really was. How could anyone get through childhood without friends? Tess's own had been filled with all varieties— family, school, neighbourhood. Afternoons riding bikes, rollerblading, hanging out at the park. Simple, happy days. How things had changed. She'd be lucky to make five digits if she tallied her current friend list. Skye had always been on it, in theory. It was reality that was the problem. For both of them. She'd made herself too busy to have time for friends, while Skye had closeted Grace away and become a recluse.

As well intentioned as it might have been, somehow it didn't seem right. 'Does she ever play with other kids … as far as you know?'

Jules shook her head. 'Apart from me, the pair of them barely said boo to anyone in town. I did manage to get Skye to bring her along to a couple of classes a while back. I think Gracie herself might have been the instigator. They were here one day delivering some of Skye's pieces when one of the kids' sessions started and the little one's eyes lit up like beacons. She sat herself down and joined in. Didn't say much to the others, but I think she liked being in a roomful of other children, doing something fun and communal. Skye brought her back a couple more times. Reluctantly, I think, but she could see how much good it was doing. I even suggested Gracie might enjoy being at school.'

'Really? What did Skye say?'

'It was quite strange.' Jules shook her head and frowned. 'She didn't say anything at first, just watched Gracie sitting there painting, and then this odd look came over her face and she turned to me and said, "Once this is over." I asked her what she meant, but she just gave me this sad sort of smile. It bothered me later, when she died. I wondered if it had been some kind of clue, you know, as to what she was planning.'

The space between Tess's ribs shrank. Every time Skye's death came up, it was the same. Like she'd been put in a straightjacket and the belt was being pulled tighter and tighter. She had to get over this. Had to face up to what had happened. 'Taking her own life, you mean?'

Jules nodded. 'I don't know what was bothering her, but it must have been terrible to lead her to do something so drastic.' She stared into her mug, but then narrowed her gaze on Tess. 'I'm guessing you would know better than I do.'

Heat rippled up Tess's throat and burned her cheeks. There was nowhere to hide, no Grace to use as a diversion, but no solid answer to give, either. Everything about Skye was wrapped inside layers of carefully curated childhood memories. The older Skye was something more ephemeral, a shape-shifter Tess wasn't sure she even knew. But how did you explain that to an outsider, to someone who assumed you were who you were supposed to be: a best friend?

Honesty was the only way through, even if it was selective. 'Skye took off when we were still teenagers. Travelled the world like a gypsy for years.' All those postcards from exotic locations. Far, far away. 'When she fell pregnant to some guy she hooked up with in an ashram in Goa she came home. She was head over heels in love with that baby from the second Grace was born.' There was a distinct tremor in her voice, so she kept her gaze firmly on the handle of the mug she was holding.

Jules leaned forward and rested her elbows on the table. 'She told me she didn't have any family, said she'd come here after her grandmother died to bring Gracie up where the air was fresh and she could hear the birds singing. That was the exact phrase she used.'

Fresh air and birdsong. It had seemed almost sensible at the time. A new start. Or was it just running away? Convenient for them both. 'Her mother died when she was seven. That's how we met. She went to live with her grandma and we just clicked when she arrived at my primary school. Then we went to high school together.' She closed her eyes and waited for her lungs to fill before she continued. 'We were always friends. But I hadn't seen her for a while. Losing her grandmother really rocked her.'

She ran her thumb over the shiny French polish on her ring finger. The single solitaire diamond in her engagement ring glittered brightly. Here, in the quiet simplicity of a country kitchen, it was too flashy. Too much.

'Life got busy. Weerilla was a long way from Sydney. Skye didn't use the internet, so the only contact we had was the occasional phone call, or letter. But I ...' She stopped. All she was giving was a string of lame excuses. The truth was entirely different: *I was too busy living my own life. I didn't even send her a fucking Christmas card last year and I can barely remember when we last spoke. That's the kind of friend I was. The kind of friend who knew she was up here alone, bringing up a child by herself without a soul in the world to help, and I made zero effort to check in and see if she was okay.*

She bit down hard on her lip. She could say it all now, get it off her chest, but would it change anything? Skye would still be dead. Grace would still be without a mother. Her sins would not be absolved.

'Skye trusted you enough to leave her daughter in your care.' Jules's voice was gentle and soothing.

A laugh tripped up Tess's throat. There was the joke. Skye had trusted her, but for all the wrong reasons. 'I'm doing a crash course in Parenting One-o-one.'

'No kids of your own, then?'

'Nope.'

'And your husband?'

Another tricky question. The rings had given her away. 'Let's just say he's trying to get used to the idea of fatherhood.'

'I see.' Jules spread her palms against the benchtop and pushed herself up to stand. 'Well, as they say, friends are the family we choose. Might sound corny, but it's true. For whatever reason, Skye chose you.'

There was no arguing with that. She'd chosen her that very first day in the playground. Or rather, they'd chosen each other. No matter what had happened since, there was still that bond to honour. 'I have to call the funeral parlour tomorrow and finalise everything for Friday.' Sharing that particular piece of news made the load a little lighter.

'I'm happy to help.' Jules checked the clock and collected the mugs. 'Not the best way of saying it, but you know what I mean. I'd better go check Erin hasn't been eaten alive by the little monsters.'

Heading back outside to the studio, where everything was buzzing and lively, was the perfect cure for the melancholy the conversation had induced. Grace was working quietly on some sort of sea creature, looking at ease. Almost like a normal little girl. Despite there being nothing normal about her situation, she did seem to be enjoying herself. Skye must have seen it, too, which is why she had caved in to Grace's request to join the class.

The question was, why had she stopped coming?

Tess laid a hand on Jules's arm, drawing her attention away from the group. 'If Grace liked the class so much, why didn't Skye bring her back?'

Jules shrugged. 'I don't know. I never got the chance to ask.'

'How long ago was that?'

'Probably a couple of months ago. Or more. I hardly saw her after that.'

It was almost the end of July now, so a couple of months ago would have been the middle of May, not long after Skye had found the newspaper article and written those words across the copy she'd made. Were the two things connected?

There had been more papers inside that envelope, inside the box, inside the wardrobe, but opening that door again would be like opening an old wound, one that had festered for too long before it had scarred. She needed to bury Skye and deal with Grace. Right now, digging up the past was not something she could even contemplate.

One by one, the children were collected by their mothers. Fresh-faced women in a standard uniform of worn jeans and jacket, who took their kids by the hand and smiled as they said goodbye. Before long only Grace and a boy around the same age were left, both of them happily helping to clean up. Grace was right at home, packing away the various art-and-craft supplies. Jules shared a joke with the boy, who threw his head back and laughed, flicking long strands of fair hair from his face. Rushed footsteps sounded outside and a man appeared at the door.

'Sorry, Jules, I was doing some shoeing for Bill McKenzie. Took longer than I expected.'

'No problem at all. These two are doing a fantastic job, so you can't have him yet anyway.' A paint pot in each hand, Jules waved her arms like one of the octopi her students had been creating. 'Tess, meet Mitch Farmer.' She nodded towards her helper. 'And this larrikin is Toby.'

The boy held up his paint-covered hands and flashed a cheeky grin, before returning to wipe down the table.

The man, Mitch, reached out his hand then quickly pulled it back to wipe his palm down the leg of his jeans. 'Sorry.' He gave her an awkward smile. 'I'm a bit grubby.'

'That's okay.' She wasn't much of a hand-shaker and he wasn't exactly clean.

'Are you a blow-in?'

'Pardon?'

'New to the town.'

'Oh … yes, I am. Grace isn't … it's complicated.'

He nodded slowly, even though the expression on his face was one of total confusion. He had a windswept look about him, salt-and-pepper stubble covering his chin and a light sprinkling of grey through his dark-brown hair. Definitely an outdoorsy type.

'Did you say you were shoeing?'

'Yep.'

'Shoeing what?'

He frowned, pinned his eyes on her as if trying to work out whether she was serious or making a joke. 'A horse.'

'Right.' She nodded. *What an idiot!*

'I take it you're not a country girl.'

'Is it that obvious?'

The lines around his eyes crinkled like cellophane. Toby barrelled into him and grabbed him around the waist, burying his face into his father's belly. Mitch rested his hands on the boy's shoulders. 'Easy on, mate.'

'Sorry.' Toby's grin faded as he looked up into the man's face, desperate for approval.

'That's okay.' He roughed the boy's mop of hair. 'We'd better head home. Your mum will be wondering where we are. Might see you around town sometime, Tess.'

'Nice to meet you.'

'See ya, Jules, bye, Grace.'

Grace stood beside the table, hands hanging by her sides, watching Toby closely. He gave her a half-smile and lifted his hand to wave and she mirrored both his expression and action.

Jules turned towards her, hands on hips. 'So, Missy, will I see you here again next week?'

Grace's mouth drooped a little as she watched Toby leave, but she nodded a mildly enthusiastic reply. It was a good sign. She was interested in something, seemed happy about the idea of coming back. Perhaps she'd even made a new friend today?

Perhaps they both had. Thinking of Jules as competition for Grace's affection had been a ridiculous notion. They were on the same team, Team Grace, and with what lay ahead, Tess could certainly use an ally.

Fourteen

One tug on the curtain and Tess could watch the sunrise without getting out of bed. Beneath the silvery morning sky a soft blush dusted the hills, marking the outline of the distant ridge in a faint tinge of lavender. Yesterday's mist had returned, draping itself over the paddocks like a cloak, and another gossamer frost coated the tufts of grass closer to the house. The velvet throw rug she'd brought along for extra warmth was gentle and comforting, like the blanket she'd had as a child. Whenever she was sad or afraid she would snuggle into it and almost instantly she would feel safe and secure. The way Skye had wanted Grace to feel. It should have been so perfect, living a peaceful life out here, surrounded by paddocks and trees. All this space; all this beauty. Perhaps for a while it was, until the past had chased her down, chewing at her heels like a rabid dog.

A shrill cry sounded, high up. Tess shifted closer to the window. One solitary bird wheeled across the brightening sky. The night had been long, relentless. Lying there in the dark with everything red and black: the bleeding rat; those words flashing like a siren behind her eyelids. *He has a daughter.* Even when she tried silently singing to herself, she couldn't drown out Skye's voice saying it over and over with that same sense of shock she must have felt when she'd found the report in the newspaper. A Melbourne paper. How had she found it? And why had she kept it?

The second question was one Tess wasn't sure she wanted answered. A headache was already niggling. Not the best way to start the day, especially when she would no doubt be called on for classroom duty. To be fair, Grace was pretty self-sufficient, probably following the routine her mother had set up. How either of them stood the monotony of doing the same thing day in, day out was the question. As good as Skye's intentions had been, Jules was right, the child needed company, not to mention a decent teacher.

A new noise, like the tinkling of a bell, floated in from the living room. Time to get up and investigate. The welcome smell of burning wood greeted her as she stepped through the doorway and belted up her dressing gown. They had this fire thing nailed. Grace was sitting at the piano, her left hand resting on the keys, her right hand playing some high notes at the treble end. It was a beautiful instrument, an antique upright, in pristine condition, a lighter shade of walnut than the wardrobe. It looked familiar, but where would she have seen it before? Of course! It had belonged to Skye's grandmother. How was it only just occurring to her that the house was full of Jean's furniture: the wardrobe; the dresser in the kitchen with the leadlight doors; the double bed with its intricate wrought-iron bedhead; all of it had been in the house she'd spent so much time in while she was growing up.

Grace played on, both hands now on the keys, as she began to sing. The very first word stopped Tess mid-step. Her heart pounded out an erratic beat, like an overwound metronome, as she pictured the rainbow. Jean had sung the same song to Skye, and to her, when they were kids, the two of them crammed onto the armchair, watching the older woman's fingers caress the keys, the veins and brown spots patterning the back of her hands like the rivers and valleys of a foreign landscape. The rendition Grace was playing now was simpler, picked out mainly with her right hand with only the occasional chord added in the bass, but her voice, the sweet fragility of it, was achingly beautiful. Tess hugged herself tight at the mention of dreams and lullabies, bracing herself for the final line and the bluebirds flying away.

Finished now, Grace rested her hands on her lap, head bowed, like one of the porcelain ornaments her great-grandmother might have had on her mantelpiece.

'That was lovely.' Her own voice sounded like a croak in the silence of the room.

Grace turned around, her face the colour of the clouds in the winter sky. She stared into the distance, as if at someone else, someone standing at the far end of the room, but then turned to look at Tess. 'Do you think that's where she is? Over the rainbow.'

'Your mum?'

Grace nodded.

Tess stuck her hands in her pockets. Death was a subject she'd always tried to avoid. She had to come up with something and Eleanor had assured her she would be fine if she followed her instincts. She walked over and crouched down beside Grace. 'My *nonna* died when I was about your age. I was very sad. My dad took me outside and told me to look up and search for the brightest star.' Her father's hands were firm and strong on her shoulders, the endless sky sprinkled with light. 'It was a clear night, and there were thousands of stars out, and there was one shining so brightly I knew it had to be her. All these years later, whenever I look up and see a really brilliant star I know she's there.' She was fudging a bit, had in fact totally forgotten that story until she'd started speaking, but even if she didn't believe it now that she was a rationally thinking adult, it had given her solace as a child. 'So, I think when we lose someone we love they stay with us, always.' Somehow, she sounded like she was making sense.

'But where is her actual body?'

And just like that the small shred of self-satisfaction vanished. Tess dropped to her knees, steadying herself with one hand on the piano stool. How could she tell an orphaned child that her mother was still in storage at an undertaker's?

'We found a bird one time and it was sick, so we put it in a box, but it died in the night-time. We dug a hole and buried it. Is that what they did with Mumma?'

Grace had barely uttered more than a sentence at a time in the last ten days and now she'd decided to start talking with a whole lot of way-too-hard questions. Her voice was clear, her eyes alert. She needed answers, like any kid, so the best thing Tess could do was to just lay out the facts. Carefully. 'Well ... when she died they took her to a hospital.'

'So they could make her better?'

'No, sweetie. There was nothing they could do for her by then. When someone dies ... they like to find out why that happened. And because I was away overseas, and then meeting you, your mum hasn't been buried yet.'

'Is she still in the hospital?'

Tess swallowed. 'Yes.' It wasn't the strict truth, but there was no way she was about to explain the concept of a mortuary. 'And now that we're back here and things have settled down, we need to have a funeral for your mum.'

'Will she be put in the ground like the bird?'

An image of a broken, featherless wren flashed through Tess's brain and she blinked it away. Skye had specified her wishes in a handwritten will and they would have to be followed. How to explain cremation to a child?

Tess took her hand and Grace didn't resist. 'Do you know what a soul is, Grace?'

'Mmm-hmm. It's the invisible part inside that makes you who you are.' Her face lit up for just a few seconds. 'Mumma told me that when I was born I was an old soul. Like I knew things other babies didn't.'

'That's true.' Tess's eyes burned. She managed a faint smile and a pat of Grace's hand. 'Well, when a person dies their soul goes somewhere else ... over the rainbow, or up into the stars, wherever they dreamed of being. Their body gets left behind, only they're not in it anymore. It's like that bird you were talking about, the bones and feathers were still there, but the part that sang and chirped was gone. People choose to either be buried or cremated, which is ...' She took another deep breath, a fish out of water gulping for air. 'It's when the body is put in a fire and turned into ash and then the ashes are either buried in the ground or scattered somewhere special, somewhere the person loved.'

'Mummy loved being here the most.' Grace spoke in a low whisper.

'I know.' The title of the book Grace had spirited away from Eleanor's office suddenly made sense. *All the Places to Love.* She waited until she was sure the traitorous quiver lurking in her throat was under control. 'That's why Skye—your mum—left a letter asking to be cremated and have her ashes scattered into the creek right here at home.'

'When?'

'This Friday.'

The curiosity that had animated Grace's eyes for a brief time disappeared. It was as if a shutter had been pulled down across her face and locked firmly at her lips. She jerked her hand away and turned back to the piano.

Tess pushed herself upright. Sunlight spilled through the windows, glinting off the silver cutlery of the mobile hanging outside, a kaleidoscope of light dancing on the grey timbers of the verandah. Grace started back on the same melody, but this time without the singing. She couldn't know it was the song her mother had requested be played at her farewell, couldn't know that each clear chiming note was cleaving Tess's heart in two.

Organising a funeral, it turned out, was as easy as making a few phone calls. One to the morgue asking them to release the body and have it transported back to Weerilla. A second to the undertaker, who offered to sort out the cremation. A third to a local celebrant suggested by Jules. Then there was the matter of the guest list, but that too was regretfully simple. Apart from Grace, Jules and Tess, there was no one to invite. It seemed wrong to have such a small group to say goodbye. Josh was still in Europe at his software conference, but there was one other person who had known Skye and who might agree to come.

Merely looking at the name and number in her contacts list made Tess jittery. She and her mother hadn't spoken since the christening, but one of them had to be the bigger person. And tradition dictated it to be Tess.

The phone rang once, twice, three times. 'Hello, Tessa.' Her mother's voice, cool as a southerly buster, came on the other end of the line.

'Hi, Mum. How are you?' She was upbeat and cheery, keeping it light.

'Apart from the fact I've been worried sick about you, I'm just fine.'

The guilt trip was nothing less than she'd expected. Riding it out rather than fighting back usually worked, especially when she was the one who wanted the favour.

She moved the phone slightly away from her ear as the rant continued. 'When I couldn't get onto you I called Josh and he told me you'd taken Grace back home. I know you didn't like me saying what I did, but the least you could have done was let me know what was going on.'

Time had not dulled her mother's wrath. 'I'm sorry.' It wasn't entirely true, but it was the best way of soothing the wild beast.

As Tess listened, a magpie landed on the grass, striding towards the verandah, where Grace was sitting in the sun reading yet another book in the C.S. Lewis series. As soon as she spotted the bird she jumped up and ran inside.

'Grace?' This wasn't about the bird conversation they'd had, was it?

'Tessa, are you there?'

'Yes, Mum, I'm here. Things have been pretty crazy.'

The silence on the other end of the line held every syllable of 'I told you so'. Her shoulders tensed, as they always did when she and her mother were having a 'moment'. Or moments. Grace reappeared and sat on the top step. The magpie tipped its head to one side, fixing a beady eye on the bowl in the girl's hand. She plucked out a clump of meat, from the look of it the mince Tess had bought to make bolognaise sauce, and held it out towards the bird, who hopped forward and plucked it from between Grace's fingertips, throwing back its head and gobbling down the treat.

'Oh my God.' A laugh bubbled out as Tess watched the show. She'd had a phobia about birds ever since she'd seen the old Hitchcock film, but this was too cute for words.

'Tessa?'

'Oh, sorry.' That word again. 'I'm just watching Grace feed a magpie.' Her mother gave a gruff snort. 'Anyway, I was ringing to ask you a favour.'

'Go on.'

She stood and walked to the other end of the verandah, out of Grace's earshot. The poor girl had been utterly miserable since their earlier discussion, hadn't said a word. 'I've organised the funeral. There's only Grace, myself, and another friend from the town. It doesn't seem right.' She ran her tongue over her bottom lip and looked out across the garden, squinting into the glare. 'I was wondering if you and Dad might come up.' Not that she had a clue where she would put them, but she would worry about the practicalities later.

'When is it?' Her mother's tone was suddenly more conciliatory. She was always good in a crisis. The ones she didn't help create.

'Friday.' Two days' time. 'You could come up and stay for the weekend.'

'Your father has a golf jaunt booked down the coast.'

'Oh, right.' Tess kicked at a nail poking out of the decking.

'But I could come if you like.'

'Really?'

'You don't have to sound so surprised, Tessa. I do have a heart.'

'I know you do, Mum.'

'Is there anything you want me to bring up for you?'

She turned back just as the bird swallowed the last of its meal and flew away, leaving Grace to escape back into the pages of her book.

'A magic wand to make everything right for Grace again?'

'I'm sure you're doing perfectly well without one.'

Was that her mother's roundabout way of saying she thought Tess *was* up for the task of being a parent? That she was actually capable? The same feeling she'd had when she rode her bike without training wheels for the first time rushed through her veins. And the same goofy smile plastered itself across her face. 'Thanks, Mum. I'll text you the address.'

'Bye, darling, see you soon.'

'Bye.' And just like that her mother was coming to visit. It would be good to have a familiar face here for a few days, as long as they didn't get into another fight. Her dad was right, they were both as stubborn 'as the day was long'. Not that either of them would ever admit it out loud. She sent through the address along with a request to bring bedding and pillows, and dropped a cursory text to Josh. It was the middle of the night in Switzerland. Or was he in Luxembourg? Either way, he'd be in bed, probably sleeping off a business dinner. Either way, he wasn't here.

She stuck her phone into her pocket and leaned into the verandah post. The magpie had returned and was pecking at the grass in search of more food. This time Grace didn't bother looking up. Maybe the whole conversation about burials and cremations had been too much. It had seemed right at the time, the longest talk they'd ever had. But would she be dwelling on it all now? Would the knowledge of what would happen to her mother's body give her night terrors?

A shudder, like a page being wrenched from a book, ripped through Tess's body.

If only there was such a thing as a magic wand. If only she didn't need one.

Fifteen

No funeral was good, but there was something shockingly confronting about a funeral for someone your own age: the realisation it could be you lying there inside that cold wooden box; the certainty that one of these days it would be. Worse than both was knowing you would never, ever see the person again. Keeping her attention on the celebrant at the front right-hand side of the chapel meant Tess hadn't had to look at the coffin even though it was right there, front and centre. The woman in white had almost finished her welcome to family and friends. Not that there were many guests. Tess and Grace, her mother as promised, and then Jules and two other women who took classes at the art studio, who must have met Skye at some point. Such a small handful of people to acknowledge a death. A life. It would be laughable if it wasn't so damned sad.

'... introduce Skye's close friend, Tessa De Santis.'

She'd been so distracted she hadn't even heard most of the introduction. Now it was her turn. Every muscle in her body quivered. Ordinarily, she never would have agreed to do a eulogy, but this was one she didn't have to think twice about. Skye deserved a proper farewell from someone who knew and loved her. Tess could sense that those gathered were quietly waiting. She closed her eyes and inhaled. Boronia: the scent of the wild blossom was unmistakeable amongst the spray of native flowers—wattle, grevillea and gum leaves—resting on the centre of the coffin. When she was seated not looking at it had been easy, but as she stood and walked towards the lectern it was stuck there like a burr, pricking at the corner of her eye.

Five short minutes, a few well-chosen words and it would all be over. Unfolding the two A4 sheets she'd scrawled some notes on, she gripped them tight in a vain effort to stop her hands from trembling. She cleared her throat and looked up. Rows of empty pews filled most of the space apart from the cluster of four women and one child seated nearby. Grace had chosen her own outfit—a pair of Mary Janes bought in Sydney by her new 'grandmother', black tights, a knee-length denim skirt and a striped woollen jumper. The one concession to Beth's concern that she was dressed too casually was a red satin ribbon pinning back the ripples of her hair. Brilliant-yellow branches of wattle blossom sprouted from her lap. But more than any of that, it was the cupid's bow of her lips that stood out for Tess, the same perfect pout she'd had the day she was born. And the same look of total confusion in her eyes.

The celebrant, standing to one side, gave a not-so-subtle cough and tapped her watch. Time to start.

Okay.

'Thank you for coming here today to mourn the passing of my friend Skye Whittaker.' Her mum had suggested the phrase 'celebrate the life of', but nothing about today felt like a celebration. 'Skye and I first met back in primary school. She'd come to live in my street after the death of her mother. Her father died when she was a baby and so there was only Jean, her maternal grandmother, who passed away eight years ago.' So much death in one family. How was that possible when she herself had known so little? 'Skye and I became great friends. We walked to school together every day, and spent hours playing on weekends. I was the youngest of three children, and as both my siblings were boys she was like the sister I never had.'

The words blended into each other on the page. All she needed to do was say them out loud, but the more she read the more they caught on her tongue. Bits of truth cobbled together like papier-mache with gaps only she knew existed. So much of the story was missing. She reached for the glass of water sitting on the tabletop beside her, took a sip and started again. Sticking to the script just as she'd always done.

'Skye was one of the kindest people you could ever meet. Gentle yet strong, she faced every challenge in her life with courage and determination. When she left high school she worked three jobs and saved enough money to take off and see the world—Morocco, Tanzania, Portugal and Turkey—finding work where she could, and she loved every minute of her time travelling. But the real love of her life was her daughter.'

Tess looked up. Grace sat motionless, staring at the coffin holding her mother's body. Did she really understand what this was all about? How could she even fathom her future without the one person who had always been in her life? Tess's stomach clenched itself into a tight, hard fist. Focusing on her notes was the only way through. 'I was lucky enough to be present for Grace's birth and I will never forget the look of pure joy on Skye's face when they first met. She loved being a mother and did everything she could to protect and care for Grace. She moved to Weerilla to provide a safe, quiet place for her child to grow up.' A cold chill settled between Tess's shoulder blades, like a knife pressed against her spine, at the memory of those newspaper clippings.

Not now. Not. Now.

'The two of them were inseparable, spending their days reading, painting, walking and enjoying the beautiful environment they quickly called home. I know that Skye's greatest sorrow would be leaving Grace.'

In the front pew, Grace's head was bowed. Beth's eyes were red-rimmed, a handkerchief scrunched between her fingers. Behind them, tears washed across Jules's cheeks, and her two friends were equally affected. Somehow, Tess had managed to hold herself together. She was almost at the end. She didn't need to read the rest from the notes. She folded them in half and turned towards the coffin. And there was Skye. Hanging upside down on the monkey bars at school, holding the skirt of her uniform tight around her thighs so the boys wouldn't see her undies, her long hair cascading to the ground like a chocolate waterfall. Skye, sweat-stained and flushed from labour, a bright light in her eyes as she held her squirming newborn. Skye, the day of her grandmother's funeral, thin and harried, so frantic she was almost unintelligible.

This was not the time for that memory. Or perhaps it was. Leaning in, she spoke directly to her friend, as if it were just the two of them. Together again for one last time. 'I am so sorry. I miss you. I miss our friendship. I promised you back then I would take care of her.' She glanced across to Grace, but she was looking down at the floor. No matter. This was between Skye and her. She moved towards the coffin, resting her hands on the polished wood. 'And I promise you now that I will look after her as if she were my own.' Saying the words out loud made it all crystal clear. She would do whatever it took to keep Grace happy and safe. The ache in her chest deepened. She flattened a hand against the jut of her collarbone, lifted two fingers to her lips and blew a gentle kiss. 'Goodbye, my beautiful friend.'

Music drifted through the speakers as she moved back to her seat. Grace raised her head slightly and Tess nodded. Her breath hitched as the small figure walked up to the coffin. For most of the ceremony Tess had barely been able to look at Grace, but now she couldn't tear her gaze away. As the first bars of the song floated through the chapel Grace placed the bouquet of wattle, handpicked that morning, onto the lid as planned. She took a step back but didn't return to her seat.

Tess shifted forward. What was she doing? Grace's lips were moving, quietly singing along to the song her mother had sung to her since she'd been a baby. Muffled sobs from the row behind them accompanied the Eva Cassidy rendition. Tess's pulse quickened. Her mother was trying to maintain her composure, the handkerchief now pressed to her mouth in a vain attempt to contain her sorrow. Even the celebrant—Marla, the name came to Tess out of the blue—was crying. If only someone could contain themself long enough to stop the music, stop that small, wavering voice singing about bluebirds and rainbows and dreams. But the song rambled on. There was no way out. All Tess could do was slump against the hard wooden seat and close her eyes. Wait for it all to end. Skye was there waiting for her, that day at Jean's funeral, her nails digging into Tess's arm, her voice whisper-soft, razor-sharp …

'I have to go.'

Tess didn't bother pulling her arm away, telling Skye she was hurting her.

It had been over six months since they'd seen each other. Tess busy setting up her consultancy, Skye caring for Grace and her dying, now dead grandmother. When Skye had phoned her about Jean's death she knew she had to come. Her friend was thinner than the last time they'd met, and sadder. More on edge.

'I'm moving away. Out west.' Skye rocked the pram holding a sleeping toddler.

Tess dragged her gaze away from the manicured lawn crowded with headstones. Skye had been crying, mourning the loss of the one person who had always been there for her, but right now her eyes were dry. And fierce. Tess swallowed hard. 'What do you mean?'

Skye flicked a hurried look to the door of the church. 'Gran left me the house. I'm selling it and moving away. I've changed my last name and I've got a solicitor sorting things out. He has my papers, my will, my wishes.' Her words were tumbling out so fast Tess could hardly comprehend what she was saying. 'I'll write to you when we get settled, but Tess, you have to promise me you'll do what you said.'

Do what she said? Hadn't she already? 'I promise you, Skye, I've never told anyone.' Admitting it now, as an adult who knew how wrong it was, sent a surge of blood rushing to her face.

'No.' Skye shook her arm as if to jostle her into understanding. 'About Grace. You promised me when she was born you'd look after her if anything ever happened to me.'

'Of course.' She sighed. The second promise she'd made was so much easier. There was little likelihood of it ever needing to be kept. 'You know I will.'

Skye's shoulders dropped. She loosened her grip, both of them staring down at the three curved lines marring the smooth flesh above Tess's wrist. 'Sorry.' She gave a watery smile before pulling Tess into a long hug. 'I have to go.'

She hurried away then, packed a sleeping Grace into the car and drove off. As Tess turned back towards the church a solid man in a charcoal suit made his way down the stairs. She hadn't seen him when she arrived, just as the funeral was starting. Her stomach swirled as she made a beeline for the carpark, her hand covering her mouth. It wasn't until she'd pulled open the door of her car, turned on the ignition and done up her seatbelt that she dared to look in the rear-vision mirror. She lifted her hands to the steering wheel, glad for the grounding feeling the movement allowed, completely ignoring the ten-kilometres-per-hour signs as she drove out of the cemetery. When she pulled over, a few blocks away, the three red crescent-shaped marks on her arm were already forming into tiny bruises.

As the final notes of the song played now, in another chapel, another funeral, Tess glanced down to where her arm was draped across her waist. The skin on her wrist was no longer red, the marks no longer visible, part of a series of memories she'd long since locked away, but she could see them now almost as surely as she'd seen them that day. She could hear Skye's voice joining with her daughter's, quietly singing the final bars of the song.

The same old paralysis gripped her on the drive home. Judging by the deafening quiet inside the car, she wasn't alone. No wake had been organised, despite her mother's claims that you couldn't have a funeral without one. There would hardly be a crowd to invite and Tess was in no mood to make small talk with strangers who never really knew Skye in the first place.

As soon as they pulled up at the house Grace marched inside, grabbed her book and bear, and bolted straight out of the back door, letting it bang shut behind her.

'Do you think you should go and have a talk to her?' Beth placed her handbag down on the kitchen table. 'Or I could?'

'No.' The last thing the kid needed today was the woman who had shrieked at her about the dirty mark on her dress trying to cheer her up. The two of them had been polite to each other since yesterday afternoon, but there was still a lot of fine-tuning needed before their relationship could really get off the ground. 'She'll be fine, Mum. Give her some time. Books are her escape. It's probably the best thing for her right now.'

The barely-there nod suggested her mother wasn't so sure. Nor did the folded arms. 'How are you feeling?'

'Wrung out.' 'Wrung' was exactly the right word for the twisted sensation Tess had going on, as if someone had grabbed her insides from each end, pulled hard and turned them in opposite directions. She dropped into a chair with a thud. Her mother was standing in the middle of the kitchen, a single strand of pearls slung around the neckline of her plain navy dress like a Tupperware hostess waiting for the party to start. Hands pressed together in prayer position, she tapped her fingertips together in a gesture Tess recognised well. It was probably best to circumvent what was coming next. 'I could use a cup of tea, actually.'

Tea was her mother's favourite cure-all, and being useful in the kitchen was her specialty. She sprang into action. It was good to have her here for moral support. A backstop if things went awry at the funeral, not that it had been needed in the end. The adults had been the ones shedding the tears. Grace had been a bastion of composure. Only the pallor of her cheeks and the distant, vacant look in her eyes gave any indication of her mental state. And her current, obvious need to be alone.

'How has she been since you arrived back?' Teacups clattered onto their saucers and the kettle started to boil.

'Okay, I guess. She wanted to sleep in her mother's bed. I wasn't sure if it was appropriate, given the circumstances, but at this stage I'm letting her do what she wants.'

'Children don't always know what's best for them.' This, through pursed lips.

'I know that, Mum. But I'm still working out how she ticks. Coming back here must be fucking hard ...'

Her mother's face darkened.

'Sorry.' She wasn't, but it was easier to keep the peace. 'It must be very hard for her to be here without Skye.'

'It's all she's ever known, I suppose.' Beth turned and poured the water, leaving the teabags to sit and brew.

'True. She's led such a sheltered life, it must have been so hard for her being wrenched away to the city, dumped with complete strangers. Twice.' She sighed. 'I really want to know what's going on in her head, but she's just so ...'

'Closed off?' A wry smile. 'Like someone else I know.'

'We can't help who we are.' It sounded more defensive than she meant it to be. 'How Mother Nature made us, I mean.'

'But you weren't like that as a child, Tess. You were happy-go-lucky, open, chattering away all the time.' Her mother handed across her tea. 'It was only later that you changed. Got all sullen and moody. I know teenagers can be difficult, but you really laid it on. Oh, and that terrible Goth business.' She shook her head. 'Thankfully, that didn't last long.'

Tiny bubbles edged the liquid in Tess's cup. She watched them spin as she stirred in a half-spoonful of sugar and then one by one, they vanished. How the conversation had become about her own deficiencies wasn't such a mystery. Her mother was well skilled in the art of table-turning. And judgement. For a supposedly Christian woman, she certainly didn't hold back when it came to laying blame. 'Anyway …' Tess arched her eyebrows and stared daggers at her mother. 'This isn't about me. It's about Grace.'

'See? That's exactly what I mean.'

'What?'

Beth waved a hand in the air. 'You. Closing off. I make one small reference to your attitude and you shut down.'

The bang of the cup on the table jarred in the quiet of the kitchen and they both winced. 'I'm not shutting down, Mum. We started off talking about Grace and how hard this all is for her and then you go off on some friggin' tangent about me being a painful teenager.' Cropped hair dyed a few shades darker than normal, a couple of tats and a wardrobe of basic black hardly made you a threat to society. Still, it had been good to get under her mother's skin. Find a focus for her anger. Beth had responded with alternating bouts of hysterics and melancholy. It was the latter she reverted to now, sipping her tea and sulking.

'The point I was making …' she waited for the slight turn of her mother's head, 'is that Grace is introverted, probably by nature. Living in such an isolated place and then losing pretty much the only person she could count on, it must be overwhelming. So I'm giving her some space and time.'

Her mother nodded. It was so unlike her not to say anything, not to try to run the show. Perhaps she'd been given the keep-it-to-yourself lecture before the mad golfer had headed off for the weekend. If so, it seemed to have worked. They finished their tea in silence. Embers crackled in the pot-belly. The clock ticked above the kitchen window. Slowly, quietly, a mother–daughter truce, of sorts, was reached.

The light in the room had dimmed. Tess took her final mouthful of tea and tilted her head to listen. A light pattering on the tin roof gradually grew louder. Time to get Grace back inside.

A steady stream was already falling as she opened the back door. The bench seat beneath the white gum, where Grace usually liked to sit and read, was empty. 'Grace.' Tess stretched her voice over the drumming of the rain. 'Grace, are you there?' There was no sign of her in any direction.

'Where is she?' Her mother joined her in the doorway.

'If I knew that I wouldn't be calling her.' So much for their détente. Tess rushed back inside and opened the front door, stepped out onto the porch and called again.

No reply.

'Grace!' She called louder now, over and over, her heart-beat picking up pace along with her footsteps as she stalked up and down.

'Where could she be?'

The pounding on the tin roof was so loud it was hard to think straight. A grey circle of trees flanked the left-hand side of house. Out back, the shed was padlocked, so she wouldn't be in there. There had to be somewhere else, somewhere she might go if she was feeling like she wanted to be close to Skye …

The creek! From the way Grace had spoken, it sounded like it was within walking distance. But where exactly?

Rushing inside, Tess grabbed a coat and weathered old hat hanging on a hook by the door, raced out the back and pulled on a pair of gumboots. Almost as an afterthought she turned to her mother. 'I have an idea where she might be. You wait here in case she comes home.' Without waiting for a response, she dashed down the steps and darted around the yard, peering between the trees for a clue. Rain beat into her eyes, making it hard to see. Using her hands as a shield, she searched around for any possible sign of a track until she spotted a rough path leading through the bushes.

A voice rang out from the house, but the rain and the thumping of her own feet on the hard ground drowned out the words. The trail was narrow, arching trees on either side providing a brief shelter. Rivulets of water trickled along its edges, snaking into crevices and washing across the carpet of leaf litter, making the track hard to navigate. At the bend she almost slipped, saving herself by grabbing onto a branch of wattle, the sulphurous yellow baubles so intense against the drab, grey sky. Was that where Grace had come to pick the bouquet for the funeral?

The path veered to the right and then downhill through a wide expanse of paddock, forcing her back to a brisk walk. A sprained ankle would render her completely useless. At the bottom of the hill a creek cut across the slope, pulling her up short. Water swirled at her feet, over and around mounds of rocks and channelling into a tunnel of trees. Raindrops needled the surface and the creek burbled and sang. The sound was mesmerising. Even in the pouring rain it was a beautiful place, but there was no sign of Grace. Tess squinted into the distance. The trail followed the creek, further down the hill until it disappeared around a corner. She swiped away the water pooling in the brim of her hat and ran between the sparse line of trees fringing the banks, winding around in what felt like a full circle. This was getting her nowhere.

A sharp pain jabbed below her ribs.

'Shit.' She bent forward, hands on knees, waiting for it to pass. And then, as she straightened up she saw her, like a mirage through the teeming rain: a small, crumpled figure perched on a fallen tree trunk, staring into the murky pond.

Taking deliberate steps, Tess moved forward. She lowered herself down against the trunk a short distance away. Everything inside her was racing, her chest heaving from the exertion, her mind whirling with all the things she could say. All the ways she could get it wrong. Rain was dribbling into the little girl's eyes, her hair hung soaked, that damned red ribbon drooping by her temple. She was hunched up like a crab hiding inside its shell, but there was an unmistakeable quiver in her jaw. Moving guardedly so as not to startle her, Tess dragged her arms from the heavy coat and draped it around Grace. She was already wet through, but the protection it provided might keep her a little warmer.

'I thought she would be here.' Finally. Grace's voice shuddered along with her body. She turned, tried to blink the rain from her eyes. 'Remember? You said she would be in her favourite place. We always came here to the creek.'

All those special moments the two of them must have shared.

'But she's not here.'

There was nothing to say. No way to explain to a little girl that her mother was once solid flesh and bone, and now she was not. The earlier explanation had been a desperate attempt to make sense of something that could never be fathomed. But it had backfired, ended up with them both here freezing in the pouring rain and Grace's question still unanswered. What was the point in lying anymore?

'No, she's not.' A chill jolted through Tess's limbs. She flipped up the collar of her shirt to cover her neck, not that it would make much difference. 'What I meant was she'd be there in your memories, and in your heart.'

'She's never coming back.'

'No.'

Sometime soon they would both be here again, fulfilling Skye's request about her final resting place, but for now there was nothing more to say. Grace sensed it and scrambled to her feet. The coat reached down past her knees. She slid her arms into it and folded them across her middle. Her new shoes were covered in mud and her tights had a long ladder running all the way down to her ankle. Tess pulled the sodden hat from her own head and planted it on Grace's, more as a gesture than a practicality. She placed a tentative arm around the girl's shoulder and they trudged along together, heads bowed, all the way back to the cabin.

'I really think you should come home.' Her mother punctuated her advice, repeated now for at least the tenth time, with the slamming of her car boot.

Yesterday's rain was gone and the sky was blue and cloudless. A snarky reply rested on the tip of Tess's tongue, but she bit it back and dug her hands deeper into the pockets of her hoodie. Her mother had been harping on the same topic ever since Grace had gone to bed last night. 'I'll see how it goes. Like I said,' she paused as Beth climbed into the car and wound down the window, 'she needs some time.'

'You do have a job in Sydney.' The sage was clearly getting in everything she needed to say before she left. She'd been like Mother Teresa yesterday when the pair of them had come back dripping wet. She'd bundled them both into hot showers and towels, then made a batch of chicken soup to ward off any lurking chills. Today, she was more like her old self. 'And a husband, in case you've forgotten.'

'Josh is fine with me being here.' Tess stared down at the pattern she was making in the dirt with the toe of her boot. Circle upon circle. Round and round.

Her mother gave an exaggerated sigh. 'That might be what he told you, but it's not what he told me.' She took off her sunglasses and waved them around in the air to make her point. 'You need to talk to him, Tessa. You railroaded him into this situation. If you're not careful he might get jack of it all and walk away.'

'When did he tell you that?'

'I spoke to him after the christening, before he left for overseas.' She muttered the words without looking up. She'd gone over a line and she knew it, but in her usual fashion she kept charging ahead.

'Did you now? And what else did he say?'

'As a matter of fact, he said he didn't like the situation at all.' Her mother sat up, her posture drill-sergeant straight, gaining courage as she spoke, as if Josh was sitting there in the back seat cheering her on instead of living the high life courtesy of some big shot's expense account. 'That he was letting it go until after the funeral, but when he gets back he's going to have a serious conversation with you about it all.'

'And you agreed with him?'

Her mother dropped her chin, but it didn't hide the flushing of her cheeks. At least she had the decency to look guilty. 'Yes. And based on what I've seen since I've been here, I'm even more convinced he's right. Staying on out here is a big mistake.'

'It's none of your business.' Tess folded her arms and glared. The last thing she needed was her mother and husband gossiping behind her back, conspiring together like a couple of narky schoolkids.

'Is that all the thanks I get for coming all this way to support you?' Beth was livid, her face a dangerous shade of purple, probably a mirror image of Tess's own. This conversation needed to end.

'Yes. And now it's time for you to leave.' She pushed the words out through gritted teeth.

Her mother mumbled something under her breath, started the engine and drove off, spinning the tyres of her perfectly polished Mazda and sending mud flying. *Good riddance.* As much as it had been nice to have her around for the funeral, the sort of negativity she was currently spouting was not helpful, not for Tess and certainly not for Grace.

Now it was just the two of them again, and strangely, that was okay. She turned to go back into the house. The purple door was closed to keep the warmth inside. Grace was still in bed, resting after all the turmoil of the funeral and her flight to the creek. She did need space, but was so much time alone a good thing? Despite the occasional glimmers of connection between the two of them, little had changed since that first day they'd met in the foster home. If anything, after yesterday, Grace had shut down even more, curled up in bed with her bear and book and refused to speak. This was all such a freaking mess.

Tess reached for the doorhandle. It wasn't just Grace she had to deal with now. There was still the issue of the newspaper clippings lurking in the wardrobe. A hot wave of nausea swept through her body, sending her head spinning. Her legs went limp, as if someone had stripped the bone from the muscle. She took a step back, gripping the verandah post and lowering herself to sit.

The faint smell of smoke wafted from the chimney. Weeds cluttered the small garden fronting the house, where bees hummed around a couple of lavender bushes still managing to survive. It hadn't been that long since Skye had lived here and yet the home she had so carefully created, this tiny oasis she had carved out of the bush for her daughter and her was already being reclaimed by nature. She'd done such an amazing job of raising Grace on her own, and now she'd entrusted Tess with the task. Grace deserved the best life possible, even if that meant throwing her own life into complete disarray. She'd told her mother Josh was fine with adopting Grace, with the two of them being out at Weerilla, but that was a straight-out lie. She'd told *him* taking Grace on was a trial, agreed they would reassess once the funeral was over, but she'd already made up her mind. And her instincts were telling her she needed to be here at Skye's house, at least for now.

So what did that mean for her marriage?

Any heat the hoodie and trackies she was wearing provided ebbed away. A shiver ran from the surface of her skin deep down into her very core. Being a mother to Grace would have to come before everything else. Even Josh.

A sudden rush of air made her pause in her tracks.

A flurry of black-and-white wings.

A magpie landed on the birdbath to the left of the path. Beneath the clear pool of water, the base of the bath glittered in the morning sunlight. A riot of glass, pebbles and gemstones Skye probably had created into a mosaic herself. And the bird was no doubt Buddy, the magpie Grace had been handfeeding for the last few days. He dipped his beak into the water then flew down onto the path only a short distance away, fixing her with his questioning eyes.

What will you do?

He tilted his head, hopped to the base of the bottom step and looked up.

What. Will. You. Do?

Tess stared back at him, the answer rising up from somewhere deep inside. This was no longer a choice. The choice had been made the day she'd walked through the doors of the FACS office without telling Josh, confirmed in that first visit she'd made to Grace at the foster home, cemented the minute she'd bundled the child into the car and headed west. And after yesterday there was no going back. This little girl needed *her*. In some mysterious way, they needed each other. Yes, for Tess there was a debt to pay, and her promise to Skye, but there was something more. Some indefinable feeling she couldn't quite pin down. She heaved out a sigh and pulled herself up to her feet. The magpie inched back a few steps, dipped his head and took off into the crisp blue winter sky.

Sixteen

'Hey, Tess, how's it going?' Eleanor's voice on the other end of the line gave her an instant lift. 'Good timing, I just arrived.'

Tess flicked her eyes to her watch: ten past eight. 'Sorry, it's probably a bit early to be calling.'

'No problem. Normally, I don't get into the office until later on a Monday, but I wanted to catch up on my emails. There'll be a pile of them after being AWOL for ten days.'

'How was the trip?' Tess ran a finger along the top of the fence railing, wiping away the drops of last night's dew.

'Awesome. Whoever invented the concept of kids' club has my eternal gratitude.' There was a distinct smile in Eleanor's voice. 'But I'm sure you're not calling to hear about my luxurious holiday. How is everything going with Grace?'

Tess turned back towards the house. The door was shut, smoke curling from the chimney. No sound. No movement. Even so, she lowered her voice, just in case. 'Not so good. We're back in Weerilla. Things seemed to be slightly better until Skye's funeral on Friday, which has set us back light years.' The weekend had been very long and very quiet, with Grace returning to her silent self and Tess finding comfort between the pages of an old copy of *Wuthering Heights* she'd discovered on Skye's bookshelf.

'In what way?' Eleanor would be frowning right about now, tapping a finger against her chin or doodling an intricate pattern on a piece of paper.

'Every way.' She tucked her free hand under her jumper and paced across the yard. So much for getting used to the cold. 'Before the funeral I thought we were getting closer. She was talking more, seemed to be trusting me a little, but now she's completely shut down again, and I know you said it takes time, but I'm really floundering here, El.'

Although she wouldn't admit it to her mother and Josh wasn't around to tell, she felt like she was caught in a rip and being dragged far, far out to sea. If anyone could throw her a flotation device, it would be Eleanor.

'You've certainly taken on a challenge, my friend.'

Now there was an understatement.

'I'm just thinking, does she like animals? She seemed to, based on the books she chose when she was here in the office.'

'Yeah, she loves her cat, appears to have a pet magpie. Why?'

'Well ... there's something slightly left field you could try. Stay with me while I do a bit of googling.'

Left field didn't sound too encouraging, but at this stage she was willing to try pretty much anything.

'Here we are. Actually, there's a facility not far from you. It treats people who have suffered trauma of some kind, including adults and children who are dealing with grief.'

Tess peered up into the gum tree above her head where a white cockatoo was stripping bark from a branch. 'Sounds good. Is it like counselling sessions or group therapy?'

'A bit of both. It's called equine-assisted learning.'

'Equine.' The word appeared in a bubble before her eyes, floating up to rest on the branch beside the pesky cocky. 'As in horses?'

'Yes, as in horses. As in the four-legged beast that threw you off when we went on that trail ride back in the day.' Eleanor gave a hearty laugh. 'I wish I could see your face right now.'

Tess didn't have to see Eleanor's face to know what expression she was wearing. The serious mask had been ripped off and the person she was talking to now was the joker from their uni days. She shuffled from one foot to the other, her backside smarting with phantom pain at the mention of that one disastrous horse ride she'd somehow survived. Surely Eleanor wasn't serious. This wasn't exactly the life raft she'd been hoping for. 'You are pulling my leg, I presume.'

'No, I'm not. Honestly. I have the place right here on the screen in front of me—Affinity Horse Training and Equine-Assisted Learning Centre.'

'And this is something you, Eleanor Carter, science major and professional sceptic, are actually recommending?'

'Yes, I am. There's a lot of data being compiled to suggest that using animals as a form of therapy assists *in some cases.*' The psychologist was back. 'Horses are really intuitive animals, apparently. They sense anxiety and fear, a wide range of emotions. This place was on the news recently for some of the work they're doing with traumatised kids. Look, it's not something I'd usually recommend, Tess, especially not as this particular type isn't formally recognised as therapy. If you tell any of my colleagues I'm suggesting this I'll flat out deny it but it's worth a try, particularly since Grace already seems to have an affinity with anything four-legged and hairy. Pardon the pun.'

If Eleanor was recommending this place it couldn't be all bad, could it? It wasn't like there were a lot of other options presenting themselves right now.

'Do you have your computer up there with you?'

'Yeah, but the internet connection is a bit dodgy here.'

'Okay. I've just sent you through the details and some reference articles, so find some reliable wi-fi somewhere and have a read through, see what you think.'

'Can't hurt to have a look, I guess.'

'Exactly. You never know, you might discover your inner horse whisperer.' Another chuckle.

'Very funny.' Tess huffed. 'Thanks, El.'

'See ya. Let me know how it goes.'

Equine-assisted learning. And Eleanor Carter, a clinical paediatric psychologist recommending it? Curiouser and curiouser. There was no way the girl she had studied with would have gone for it, but then she was older now and more experienced, so if she said it was worth a try, who was Tessa De Santis, someone who hadn't even finished her own psych degree, to argue?

Even in her near-comatose state, the word 'library' livened Grace up. She climbed out of bed, pulled on some clothes and took herself out to the car where she sat facing the passenger window, fingers resting on the doorhandle as if she might pull on it if she needed a quick escape. Her face was a whiter shade of pale than usual and her angel's kiss more like an angry welt. There was no point in trying to jolly her out of her mood, so Tess pressed the button on the CD player and let the soothing sounds of yoga music fill the cavernous space of the car. The ambient notes meandered, and she mentally worked through each part of her body bit by bit, releasing the tension, just as she would in an actual class. By the time she reached the Weerilla Library, she was as relaxed as she could be while still remaining vertical and alert enough to drive.

Grace headed inside and disappeared into the children's section, leaving Tess at the front desk to enquire about using the internet.

'No problem.' The librarian smiled and led the way to the computer. 'Great to see young Grace again. So sad. You're her guardian, are you?'

The soft hairs on Tess's forearms stood to attention, like anemone tentacles on predator alert. *Warning, warning. Sticky beak about.* She smiled brightly down at the woman, who was a good bit shorter than her, and waited for her antennae to settle. 'Yes. I am.'

'How lovely.' The librarian peered at the screen, scrunching up her face as if she was in pain. 'I really need to go for an eye test. My husband says I'll go blind if I keep squinting, but between you and me he's the one in danger of going blind and it's got nothing to do with needing glasses.' Behind her hand, she gave a conspiratorial giggle.

Tess forced her mouth into a brief smile but let it die just as quickly. She had no desire to hear about this woman's husband's masturbatory habits.

'There, that should get you going.' The librarian stood upright again and gave a single clap of her hands, like a kindergarten teacher trying to get the attention of her class. 'Is it the papers you're wanting?' She batted her thickly lined lashes in Tess's direction. 'Like poor Skye?'

'Papers?'

'Newspapers. The Sydney and Melbourne ones. She'd sometimes spend hours in here scanning through them. Catching up on the news, I expect, since she didn't have a TV or computer of her own. I kind of get not having a computer, expensive as they are, but no tellie?' The librarian's expression morphed into one of utter horror. 'How could you survive without one? Especially living all the way out of town like she did. And on her own, well, with Grace.' Finally, she came up for air. 'Anyway, she must have been right into the news. She even photocopied bits of the papers sometimes.'

Tess nodded, more to herself than to the woman. So this was where Skye came to get access to information, where she found out what he was doing. 'Did she ever look up other sites that you know of?'

'Other sites?'

'You know, like family archives for instance.' What else would she access to keep track of him? 'Facebook. Or Linked In?'

The librarian's face reddened. She glanced over her shoulder and then back again, lowering her voice to a hush. 'Well, I'm not in the habit of spying on people while they use the computers, just to make sure, you know, but Skye sometimes forgot to close down the screen when she was finished and, well, I did notice that there was often one man's name she was always googling.' She pinched her elbows against her sides as she leaned forward. 'It happened a few times so I remember his name, Neil …'

Tess's hand flew upwards into a stop sign. She'd heard enough. 'I'm sure that was Ms Whittaker's business and nobody else's.'

The woman's cheeks shone like a pair of tomatoes left out to spoil in the summer sun. It was mean, flipping the blame when Tess had encouraged the conversation, but the librarian was revealing way too much.

'I'll leave you to it, then.' Mouth pinched, the librarian spun around on her ballet flats and scurried back to her desk.

Tess pushed the unwanted information to the back of her mind and focused on why she had come. The link Eleanor had emailed was ready and waiting. One click and a page packed with images of horses filled the screen. Riding them may not be her thing, but they certainly were magnificent creatures— glossy black manes, thick necks, a sense of power in their very being. The 'Home' page was all about their innate sensitivity, their historic relationship with humans and their ability to tune in to emotions. Much easier to read through all the information here than trying to run her computer from her phone back at the house. She shifted over to the 'Learning' tab. *Learning from horses? Really?* Group and individual sessions were available. And yes, they did deal with trauma and grief. The contact page gave the address—only half an hour's drive away—and a number to call.

She stared across to the reading section where Grace was seated, a pile of books stacked up by her feet. Every rational cell in her brain was screaming for her to close the page and go find *Parenting for Dummies* on the shelf. But Eleanor herself had recommended it and the proximity of the place was a bonus. And something else was going on inside her, like a mouse nibbling at a piece of cheese, telling her to give it a try. There was no harm in giving them a call. She typed the number into her phone, did a quick check of the rest of her inbox and closed the computer as soon as the urge to respond to all the work messages had her fingers itching. She'd notified all her clients before leaving Sydney that she would be unavailable for the next month and Claudia had reported just this morning that all was under control. Today was about helping Grace.

The librarian gave a jittery smile from behind the desk as Tess approached. Poor thing. She wasn't really that obnoxious and she was most likely starved of company locked away in this place all day with nothing to look forward to going home to but a wanking husband. No wonder she devoured her customers' computer leftovers to make her day more savoury. Grace appeared with most of her book selection clamped under one arm and a single tome clutched to her chest. One by one she placed them on the counter and waited for them to be processed.

'And that one?'

Grace put the last book down and slid it across to the librarian. Tess did a double take at the title. Another classic story she remembered well, although the cover had been updated since she was a kid. A white horse galloping across a moonlit field, the title etched in foil lettering across the cover: *The Silver Brumby*. Maybe it was a sign. Maybe that rodent gnawing away at her insides was her instinct, the one Eleanor had told her to follow, like the Pied Piper but in reverse.

Maybe this whole equine-assisted-learning thing wasn't so irrational after all.

Head in her book, Grace took zero notice of where they were going, so there was no need to explain the alternative route once they left the library. The woman at the horse place had been surprisingly friendly when Tess snuck in a phone call on the way out to the car, keeping far enough behind Grace not to be overheard. Within minutes Tess had plugged the address into her phone and they were on their way for a quick reconnaissance-style visit. It wasn't like the two of them had anything better to do. Sitting around the house wasn't very stimulating, and certainly wasn't doing anything for Grace's social skills.

The countryside rolled by as they headed further west, the ribbon of road rolling out between a patchwork of paddocks, sections of bush and the odd farmhouse. The recent rain seemed to have had an almost instant effect on the winter grass, which was springing to life before her eyes, although still with a distinctly straw-like tinge. There was absolutely something peaceful about being away from the city. As much as she loved the colour and movement and noise that went with living in Sydney, the rural lifestyle had its perks. Skye had taken it to an extreme, but there was a lot to be said for the quiet life and the therapeutic effect of so much space and sky. The half-hour trip disappeared as she drove and soon they stopped outside a set of gates.

Grace's head popped up as the engine idled and Tess opened the car door. 'What are you doing?'

'Getting the gate.' She followed Grace's gaze to the foal poking its nose through the rails of the fence. 'Unless you'd like to?'

A smile flickered across the girl's lips. Within seconds she unbuckled her seatbelt and jumped out. A chocolate-coloured horse, an almost identical but larger version of the foal, sauntered over to the fence to where Grace was giving the baby a scratch behind the ears.

Tess rolled down the passenger window. 'So are you getting that gate?'

Grace nodded, did the job and waited for Tess to drive through before she closed it again. When she hopped back into the car her whole demeanour was different: her posture upright, eyes alert as she peered through the windscreen. On either side of the driveway, behind neat white fences, horses of a variety of sizes and colours grazed on carpets of green grass. Straight ahead sat a white weatherboard farmhouse with a broad wraparound verandah, four chimneys topping its corrugated roof and beautiful leadlight glass decorating its windows. This was some property. Tess followed the curve of the road to the left and parked outside a fancy-looking stable block. An enormous dog was stretched out on the gravel, basking in the midday sun. At the sound of the car it hauled itself to its feet, gave a couple of lazy barks and then ambled over, wagging its tail. More sheep than dog, its eyes were hidden by a mop of shaggy hair. Grace couldn't get to it quick enough. The mutt wriggled his entire body as if he was belly dancing, making a low grumbling noise. Tess couldn't stifle her laugh. 'I think he likes that.'

'He'll take as much of it as you can give.' A stocky woman in a blue button-down shirt, an Affinity logo on the pocket, appeared from inside the stables. She stretched out her hand in greeting. 'Hi, I'm Max. You must be Tess.'

'Nice to meet you.' She returned the vigorous shake with what she hoped was a strong grip. 'Was it you I spoke to on the phone?'

'Sure was. My full name's Maxine, but I prefer the short version.' She rested her hands on her hips and nodded in the direction of the dog, currently being held in a death grip. 'And who do we have here?'

'This is Grace.'

'Hi, Grace.' Max whipped off her cap, gathered the scattered pieces of her auburn hair into her hand and pulled it back into a neat ponytail. 'That beast there is Jed.'

'He's big.' Jed reached almost to Grace's armpit.

'He certainly is. We think he's got a bit of wolfhound in him and probably some retriever. Other than that he's a mystery, but a gentle one. Would you like to meet some of the horses?'

Completely unfazed by not being filled in on why they were here, Grace nodded eagerly. So far, so good.

'We've just moved a few of them into the top paddock, so you're in luck. Not far to walk.' Max strode off like a Scout leader guiding her charges on a new adventure, Grace close on her heels along with new friend Jed, and Tess bringing up the rear. Tiny pebbles crunched beneath their feet as they passed the outbuildings at the back of the house, cut through a large undercover arena, then slipped through a gate into a grassed yard where three horses were grazing.

Max bent down so she was at eye level with Grace. 'Would you like to pat one?'

Eyes wide, Grace gave her signature nod. Jed stayed close as they approached a black-and-white horse with feathery legs. It lifted its head to reveal a pair of ice-blue eyes.

Tess gave an audible inhale. It was like an exotic supermodel version of a horse.

'Pretty, isn't she?' The voice, coming from her left, belonged to a bear of a man leaning against the fence, watching them all. His face hadn't seen a razor for a few days and salty flecks were scattered through the stubble on his chin.

'Oh, it's you.'

He dipped his chin and plucked at the front panels of his shirt with both hands as if to check, before fixing Tess with a smug grin. 'Last time I looked.'

Classic smartarse. He'd seemed pretty meek when they'd met at Jules's place. 'I find it a little unsettling, to be honest.'

She pointed at the horse Grace was now patting. 'The eyes, I mean.'

He shrugged. 'Everyone has their own idea of beauty, I guess.' He stood and walked towards her, taking up the same position on the fence. Max handed Grace a brush and showed her how to groom the horse. It was weird just standing and watching, but Tess had no desire to join in. She crossed her arms. Sitting next to someone and not saying a word seemed weird, too, so small talk was the only alternative. 'This is a gorgeous place you have.'

'Now that we do agree on.' He spoke quietly as he watched Grace move from horse to horse alongside Max.

What was his name? Clearly, it started with M—Michael? Mark?

'So is Grace your daughter? I was a bit confused about that the last time we met.'

'Well, she's my, um ... foster-daughter.' One day she'd get used to the description. She pulled her coat tighter against the chill of the afternoon wind. 'Her mother died recently. Grace has taken it hard, as you'd expect. I took her to see a psychologist when we were in Sydney, but it didn't help much, then we came back here. It's been difficult ... I don't have kids and I'm not really sure how to handle things.'

The man kept his focus on the horses and didn't respond.

'I explained the situation to your wife and she said she might be able to help.'

He swivelled towards her. 'You explained it to my wife?'

'Yes.' She tipped her head in the woman's direction. 'To Max.'

He shook his head and made a chuckling noise.

'I'm sorry?' He had a way of making her feel like a total idiot, a way that completely got her back up. 'I wasn't aware I'd made a joke.'

'Max isn't my wife.' He leaned a little closer as if he was letting her in on a secret. 'She's my sister.'

Turned out she actually was the idiot here. 'Oh my God, I didn't realise, I just presumed ...' Now it was her turn to laugh. Awkwardly. 'On the website it just said M & M Farmer and ...' She waved her hands around, gesticulating wildly. The Italian blood always came to the fore when she was under pressure. 'Sorry.'

'That's okay. Easy mistake.' He pointed to where Max and Grace were now grooming a caramel-coloured horse with a blonde mane and tail. 'She seems pretty comfortable with them. Has she had any experience with horses before?'

'I wish I knew.'

Her vague reply was met with an equally vague expression.

'I agreed years ago to be her guardian, but I hadn't seen her for a long time before this happened, so I don't really know much about her, what she likes or doesn't like. She does have a cat, though, and she loves it to bits.'

He nodded, watching Grace all the while.

'So, how does this therapy thing actually work?'

'It's not therapy and it's not an instant cure, if that's what you're looking for.'

Did she say she wanted an instant cure? What was with this guy? One minute he was laughing and making jokes, the next he was being all prickly. Well, she had plenty of thorns herself. 'No. It's not.'

He pushed himself up off the fence and moved a couple of steps closer. 'Look, I'm sorry. We get people coming here who want us to solve all their problems without putting in the work, but that's not what we're all about.'

'Well, that's not me.'

'Max filled me in after you spoke to her on the phone. If you—and Grace—decide you want to come back, we'll work out a program where the two of you interact with the horses in different ways. We don't have anything much scheduled right now, so we could start as soon as you want.'

Hang on. Was she hearing things? 'Did you say the both of us?'

'Since you're part of the massive changes Grace is going through, it would be good for the two of you to connect. The horses will help you do that.'

'Ah, I don't think so.' She shifted slightly so she could meet his eyes and calm the butterflies battering against the walls of her stomach. 'Look, I'm not really an animal person. It's Grace who needs the help with her grieving. That's why we're here.'

He held her gaze before staring down at his boots and shaking his head. 'So you're not really that serious about helping her.' He raised his eyebrows, turned and walked away, disappearing back into the shadows of the stable.

What the fuck? Her head was about to explode. Who the hell did he think he was talking to her like that? Not that it mattered. Max was clearly the one who would be doing the counselling, or whatever they called it here. He was probably the roustabout, here to keep the fences upright and the stables clean. Oh wait, no, he was a shoeing person. Spent his days cleaning the muck out of horses' feet and banging bits of metal onto their hooves. So his opinion counted for zilch. Shaking off his criticism, she headed over to where Grace was now grooming the third horse, a smaller chestnut.

Max turned to her. 'She's not scared of them at all. That's a great start.'

'So do you think you'll be able to help?'

'Definitely. Although Mitch is the primary practitioner here. I'm still an apprentice.'

Mitch. That was his name. Tess looked over to the stable block, but there was no sign of the man who had just given her what for.

The look on her face must have said it all. Max put a hand on her arm. 'It's okay. He knows what he's doing. He's worked with horses since he was a kid. He got into the assisted-learning work a few years back by accident when a friend of ours brought her autistic son over. Mitch worked wonders with him and loved it, so he put himself through his first course. Word got around. Now he does almost as much of that as he does breaking and training.'

'So is he a qualified psychologist?'

Max laughed. 'Definitely not. He's done heaps of studying, and the diploma, but most of what he does is hands-on stuff. Experiential learning. He says he doesn't need to spend hours at a desk and get a piece of paper to tell him what he already knows. But he went through the motions of doing the training so people would take him more seriously.'

It didn't exactly sound like they were in the right place. Eleanor had only suggested it as a last resort and there was no way she was throwing Grace into the path of a self-taught cowboy. She'd do some more research, find a better alternative. 'Grace, it's time to go, sweetie.'

Grace turned, the brush still in her hand. 'Do we have to?'

'You can come back again.' Max gave a reassuring smile.

'Can we?' Grace's face was animated, as bright as when she'd spotted Tiger laid out on the cushion that night at Jules's place.

The answer was a no, but Tess was not going to rock the boat in public. They'd sort out the details later. 'We'll see.

Come on. Let's go.' If Grace wanted to groom a horse there were probably plenty of places she could do that back in Weerilla.

She held out her hand, but Grace simply stared at it, returned the brush to Max and walked past without another word. *Oh dear.* Punishing silence would now be the order of the day. Not that Tess had anyone to blame except herself. Eleanor maybe, but she'd only been trying to help.

It was an effort for Tess to force a smile as she turned to Max. 'Thanks. It was nice to meet you.'

'You too.' Max put her hand on Jed's collar, stopping the dog before he had time to chase after Grace. 'Just call if you'd like to come back.'

'Sure.' Tess moved towards the car, flicking a look over to the stables where she could swear a figure was standing in the shadows, watching. If the guy wanted people to take him more seriously, as his sister had said, he might want to work on his own social skills. She heaved out a sigh. Equine-assisted learning, at least at this place, was not the answer to her problem. Her instincts, it seemed, needed an overhaul. And judging by the sour look on Grace's face, the battle lines were once again being drawn.

Seventeen

The rest of the week was long and torturous, with Grace making daily requests to go back to Affinity and Tess coming up with ever more creative excuses for why they couldn't go 'today'. Or, in fact, not so creative. *Too windy, too cold, too wet,* all of which were applicable at times, but today she'd had to resort to feigning a migraine and retiring to the bedroom with a damp cloth pressed to her forehead, news which was met with a scowl rather than sympathy. Grace threw herself into her school work at the kitchen table, not bothering to look up even when Tess emerged from the bedroom desperately in need of fresh air.

Silence lurked like swamp fog in the cottage, the air so thick with it Tess could barely breathe. Being outdoors was completely liberating, how prisoners must feel when they're allowed out for a yard break. She let the blissful winter sunshine roll over her while she leaned against the weatherboards, checking her Facebook feed on her phone while there was a vaguely good connection. Mostly, the usual inane memes and pictures of cats, a few of them making her giggle, until Josh's latest post appeared. Windblown and T-shirted on a yacht in the South of France, he really was living the life, making the most of his extended work junket. But you could hardly blame him. It wasn't as if there was anyone waiting at home with a pipe and slippers. Not that she would ever be that kind of wife, or that he'd expect her to be, but ... the thing was she didn't know when he'd be back now he'd taken up an offer to visit colleagues from the conference, and she didn't know if that even bothered her. A nagging ache throbbed behind her temples, the headache she'd faked becoming a reality. Punishment for telling lies, or so her mother would say.

She closed her eyes and let the day soak into her skin. Tiger was resting against her leg, doing what cats do best. Tess stroked her sun-warmed fur, humming along to the sound of a contented purr. So soporific. Orange light filtered through her closed lids, and she started to drift.

Car tyres sounded on the track beyond the fence. She cracked one eye slowly open and then the other. A VW beetle circa 1965, very similar to the one her dad once owned but in an iridescent burgundy, pulled up outside the gate and the door opened to reveal Jules. 'Hope I'm not interrupting anything.'

'Obviously you are. Some very important dozing going on here.' Tess crossed her arms in a mock display of annoyance. 'Nice car.' She stood to greet her guest, shoving her phone in her back pocket.

Jules made her way up the path and onto the porch. 'Thank you.' She beamed. 'Elsie. My pride and joy.' She quirked her head towards the house. 'Gracie inside?'

'Yep. Swotting as usual.'

'Still not talking?'

She let out a long sigh in answer. She'd already vented to Jules over the phone, filling her in on the progress of the drama. Jules hadn't questioned her reluctance to take Grace back to the horse place, just listened without comment.

'Well, art class is on this afternoon. I was on my way back from Orange, thought I'd call in and see if I could persuade Missy to come along.'

'Good luck with that.'

Jules blew a breath over her knuckles and polished them on her purple velvet scarf. 'Challenge accepted.' She pushed open the door and disappeared into the house. Probably better to let Jules approach Grace on her own rather than risk her being tainted by association with the enemy. Two full weeks had passed since Grace had been to the class. Last Tuesday she'd flat-out refused to come out of her room and had spent most of her time in there since, no matter how hard Tess had tried to prise her out. Tiger stood, arched her back, and twisted around Tess's leg. It was funny how she'd taken to Tess, and vice versa. She'd never been much of a cat person, but there was something about this one's take-me-as-you-find-me attitude that she quite liked. Apart from the rat incident, the two of them were getting along nicely. If only the same could be said for her relationship with the other human inhabitant of the house. The two of *them* seemed to be lurching from one stand-off to the next, the current one being about the horse issue.

Just the thought of joining in on the not-therapy session sparked a cold sweat across the back of Tess's neck. Back at uni, getting to the bottom of other people's problems as a career had seemed like such a great career choice—until she'd become a guinea pig for an older student's practice session and fled the room without a backward glance. She'd seen her course supervisor the very next day and switched over to a Bachelor of Human Resources, where there was no need to worry about anybody's emotional baggage—especially her own. She shivered away the memory. Robert Frost had definitely been onto something about that fork in the road. Where would she be now if she'd followed that first path? Where would she be now if she'd never met Skye? Or if she'd never made such a dangerous promise?

The door flew open and Grace appeared, her favourite crocheted poncho thrown over her shoulders, a wide smile stretched across her face. She skipped down the steps, leaving Jules behind to do the explaining.

'Righto, Gracie and I are off to the studio. She'll be ready for pickup at five-thirty,' Jules announced, and with a bounce of her grey curls she followed Grace out to the car. Throwing a smug grin over her shoulder, she licked the pad of one finger and chalked up a point on an imaginary scoreboard.

Tess poked out her tongue, not completely in jest. As the VW clunked into gear and disappeared into the distance, her smile faded to a frown. She was the one putting up with all the bullshit here day in and day out—the glacial stares, the cat's-bum mouth, the cold shoulder anytime she tried to start a conversation with Grace. And then Jules waltzes in and gets her complete cooperation, coaxes her out of her shell and spirits her away. Utterly and completely unfair.

She heaved out a sigh and waited for the feeling to pass. It was childish to let such a little thing bother her. Of course, she was grateful to Jules—it was good for Grace to be out of the house, so there was no use sooking about being runner-up in the parenting stakes.

Unfolding her arms, she stared out into the waning afternoon, fully aware of the ping-pong nature of her emotions.

A cricket chirped in a bush. A garden lizard skittered noise-
lessly across the verandah. It was strangely quiet now that she
was here alone for the first time in weeks. She'd always treasured her solitude, loved it when Josh texted to say he would
be home late. Her usual response was to open a bottle of red,
switch the TV to Netflix and scroll through her phone, checking out mindless social media posts. Anything not to have to
think. Here, in the middle of nowhere, with not a sound other
than the occasional birdcall, the lack of noise was slightly unnerving. She walked back inside, but her heart immediately
skipped a beat. The wicker box was still sitting there in the
wardrobe, its full contents yet to be revealed. She would get
to it, one day soon. When things settled down with Grace.
When she had time to consider what it all meant. There was
something much pleasanter she could do while the house was
empty and she didn't have to worry about how it would impact Grace. Something she'd been itching to check out since
she arrived.

Skye's art studio.

She grabbed the keys hanging by the back door and made
her way across the yard. An enormous padlock secured a bolt
slide on the shed door. She tried each key on the bunch until one slipped neatly into the barrel and the lock popped.
The door yawned open, the shed exhaling the pungent smell
of paint and turpentine. She wrinkled her nose and leaned
in, peering into the gloom while she fumbled around for a
light switch. When she found it a single naked bulb sprang
to life, cobweb threads dangling from the socket. A battered-
looking trestle table extended across the far wall, the surface
covered in tubes of paint, brushes, some half-finished canvases
and an assortment of clay sculptures and pots. She stepped
inside, pulling open the heavy hessian curtains covering the

one window for natural light. There was a busyness about the studio. Chaotic yet organised. Skye would have been in her element here, pottering around, losing herself in her art.

Tess ventured closer to the table, studying the paintings one by one. The largest canvas, a metre or so square, was an abstract bush scene, the trees suffused in a yellow aura, birds dotted through the branches against a background of violet sky. Another showed a small figure walking down a trail, the blue-grey leaves of the gum trees arching over her head, and a garden of brilliantly coloured flowers in stark contrast to the duller tones of the bush. It had a dream-like, mystical quality about it, as if the girl—Grace?—was walking through a sacred space. Other, smaller paintings were similar in style and theme—crowded with trees and flowers and birds. Bright and lively and lovely. No wonder Skye's pieces were in such demand.

On the wall opposite the window was another door; another padlock. She rotated her way through the set of keys until she found one to fit. This was a smaller, darker room, much stuffier. Stale air filled her lungs and she coughed it out. An eerie fluorescent glow filled the space as she turned on the light. Shelves holding paint supplies, blocks of clay and mosaic tiles cluttered the walls. An old blanket was thrown over something propped against the lower shelf. Tess crept closer, picking at a corner of the blanket and letting it slip to the floor. A shower of dust motes flew into the air and she fought the urge to sneeze before focusing on what she'd uncovered.

She doubled over, as if she'd taken a punch to the gut. Breathing out, she emptied her lungs so completely her next intake of air echoed in the hollow cave of the room. Her eyes burned as they took in the image splashed across the canvas in front of her: a close-up of a woman's face done with haphazard brushstrokes in varying shades of charcoal, the eyes closed, the mouth down-turned, the features grossly distorted. Waves of long hair fell to the bottom of the painting. And dabbed across the cheeks were what could only be tears. Dark-red glossy tears shining against the matte grey skin. Tess forced herself upright. There were more paintings stacked behind. Barely touching her fingers to the edge of the first canvas, she tipped it forward at enough of an angle to take in the next image. Her hand, resting on the corner of the board, shook, the tremors reverberating all the way to her elbow as she took in the darkened room, a shadowy figure silhouetted against a sliver of white light, and in the corner, another figure curled into a foetal position.

'Oh God.'

She choked back the overwhelming urge to vomit. She needed to get out. Run. As fast and as far as she could, but her feet were rooted to the floor, her entire being paralysed. She was back there, in that room at Jean's house …

Swimming up through an ocean of sleep, eyelids flickering. A shuffling sound. Bedsheets moving. The rustle of cotton and a low growl, like a wolf baring its teeth. She made her eyes open. Skye's bedroom was always so dark, the heavy curtains blocking any light from the street, making it hard to see even the outline of your hand. Another sound, this time more of a grunt. Tess turned slightly in the single bed, waiting for her eyes to adjust. Another movement on the other side of the room. She pushed herself up onto her elbows, peering harder.

Everything inside her turned to ice. Someone, a man, was lying on top of Skye, his hand covering her mouth. He was moving. Pushing against her. His face so close as he made those horrible noises.

She tried to lift her hands, cover her ears to block out the sounds, but she couldn't move. She had to do something. Say something. She swallowed once, twice, and then again until finally a single strangled syllable scraped across the rawness of her throat.

'Stop.'

Complete and utter stillness. Blinding, aching silence.

The man turned his head. Looked right at her through the darkness. She fell back onto her pillow, gripping the hem of her nightie. *Don't breathe.* The knobbly bones of her knees clamped together. The insides of her thighs knotted tight. She jammed her eyes shut as the shadow moved closer.

No, please no, please no, please …

A stream of air forced its way out through her nostrils. She took a quick breath back in, pretending to be asleep even though it was far, far too late. The bed creaked under the foam mattress as the acrid mix of tobacco and aftershave smothered her senses. If she just lay here, if she was still enough …

The rough pad of a finger followed the line of her cheekbone. A hand crushed the bones at the back of her neck.

A sharp pull yanked her head sideways. 'Such pretty hair.' His breath on her skin, hot and clammy and vile. 'You want some, too, do you?'

She shook her head. A ripple of pain.

No.

Her eyes were already closed. She shut them tighter and shook her head, but the memory refused to budge. It was there in the painting when she opened them again, in the wild strokes, the frenzied brushwork. A sudden, suffocating heat filled the small space. She flicked off the light, slammed the door shut, bolting and padlocking it again despite her trembling hands, and staggered through the studio into the world outside. Everything she'd locked away for all these years.

Skye had captured it all.

An hour, maybe two, later, she gritted her teeth and pinned her eyes to the road. She'd sat outside the shed unable to move until afternoon had waned into dusk and then into darkness. It was the same reaction she'd had that night after he'd left, pinned to the bed, not by any physical force, but by something much stronger.

Much more debilitating.

Something that had nothing to do with selflessness or friendship.

Now, as then, a violent shiver racked her body. She pulled over, keeping her foot on the brake as she let the engine run. She had to get a hold of herself. What good would she be to Grace if she ran herself off the road? There was no one else, or at least no one else Skye trusted enough to take care of her daughter, even if that trust was completely misplaced.

And her job right now was to collect Grace.

She hit the button on the CD player and the interior of the car vibrated with the booming voice of Adele. The songs washed over her as she continued on into town, calming her jangling nerves. Until the lyrics of 'When We Were Young' and the idea of facing your fears brought back all that she was trying to forget.

By the time she arrived, the blinds on the studio windows were drawn and the door locked. Jules would think her an imbecile, incapable of getting here on time when she had nothing better to do than laze around and keep up with her social media updates. If only she'd stuck with that rather than venturing out to the shed.

She straightened her shoulders, pulling herself up to her full height, as she approached the house, followed the instructions she gave her clients about creating the right impression. In this instance, the impression of a capable parent, not a paranoid nutter. A murmur of voices hummed inside the house: Jules had company. Excellent. She could just whip in, grab Grace and be on her way.

'Hi, anyone there?' She rapped her knuckles lightly against the wall.

'That'll be Tess.' Jules not-so-muffled voice sounded as she swung open the door, one arm flung out wide. 'Come on in and join the party.'

'I'm so sorry, Jules, I lost track of time and then …'

'You and me both.' A deep voice greeted her from the other end of the kitchen.

Jules nodded in the direction of her guest. 'Mitch was late, too. His penance was to shell the peas.' She grabbed Tess by the arm and dragged out a chair. 'Yours is to peel the spuds.'

'I, uh …'

'The kids are in there watching some TV.' Jules pointed towards the lounge room. 'And you're all staying for dinner.'

Oh no, that was so not happening. Playing happy families was not part of her plan today. She was way too on edge to be decent company. High-pitched giggles trickled into the kitchen.

'Is that Grace laughing?' The sound was so unusual she needed to make sure she wasn't hearing things.

Jules simply shrugged and turned around to attend to something on the stove. Something that smelled of onions and family and comfort. A second barrage of squealing. This had to be seen to be believed.

Tess walked to the doorway. Grace and Toby were sitting side by side, their legs flung across a plush blue ottoman nestled between the couch and the television. Whatever they were watching had the pair of them in stitches. Was that really the withdrawn little girl she lived with sitting there looking so happy?

She ran a hand through her hair to push it back off her face. As much as she didn't relish the idea of staying for dinner, dragging Grace away now would only make things worse at home.

Suck it up, Tess. Play along.

She dumped herself into the chair Jules had pulled out. 'So, what did you want me to do?'

A basket filled with potatoes appeared on the table beside a well-loved saucepan. 'You cut.' Jules didn't even try to disguise the glee in her voice. She was actually gloating. 'And I'll cook.'

'Right.' Tess snatched up a potato and scraped the blade across the hard flesh, letting the dirty peelings fall into a pile on the table while Mitch sat to her left, quietly shelling the peas. A Tupperware container appeared and Jules gathered up the fallen skins. 'Chooks'll love that. Speaking of which, you should get some.'

'Who? Me?'

'Yes. You. Skye had a brood, but they had to be moved on after … well, you know.'

That explained the empty pen in the backyard where the weeds were already turning into a jungle. 'What happened to them?'

'I've got a couple here. A few others around the place took one or two. I could probably steal them back.'

Tess picked up another potato. 'Not sure how long we'll be staying.'

'Are you heading back to Sydney?' Mitch had finished his designated job and was reclining in the chair.

'Maybe.' She sighed. She had no idea how long they'd stay. Long enough to 'heal' Grace had been the plan, but thinking that would happen in a hurry had clearly been naive. 'We'll see what happens.'

Mitch nodded slowly. 'With Grace?'

'Grace, my job, my ... a few things.' There was that not-so-small issue of her marriage, and the discoveries she'd made at the house, but there was no way she was giving voice to either. It was awkward enough after their last meeting.

'How are things going with you two?'

She chopped the last potato in half and half again, depositing the pieces into the waiting pot. If Mitch was trying to sneak in a little counselling session before dinner, he could think again. She downed the knife and looked across at him. Contrary to her expectations, there was a softness in his expression and nothing but concern on his face. Maybe he really was just trying to help. Maybe he was genuinely nice. It wouldn't hurt to give him the benefit of the doubt.

'Things are pretty much the same.'

'So she's still not talking?'

'Not talking, withdrawn, obsessed with her books.' She waved a hand in the direction of the living room, her internal thermometer rising with her voice. 'Do you know this is the first time I've heard her laugh properly since I met her?'

Jules turned, wooden spoon in hand. Sauce dripped from the end of it onto the hotplate and sizzled. Tess dropped her hands into her lap. She couldn't look at either of them right now.

'Her mother recently died,' Mitch said, very, very quietly. 'There's not much for her to laugh about.'

The truth of his statement punctured the blustering hot-air balloon of her anger, bringing her straight down to earth. Of course he was right. Grace had lost everything. But how to reconcile that with the fact that she was sitting in there with Toby chuckling away at a cartoon like a normal kid, when at home, with her, she was completely aloof. She jerked out a short laugh. 'Maybe I should get a TV.'

'Or you could bring her back out to our place for some sessions.' Mitch was looking at her intently, the deep-green forest of his eyes way too unnerving. 'If you didn't want to take part, that would be your choice. It would be good for the two of you if you could work through some things together, but at the end of the day if it's Grace on her own that's better than nothing. You'd be doing her a favour if you brought her back, helping her understand her feelings so she can deal with them and move forward.'

Horse whisperer or not, he was starting to sound like Eleanor. *This isn't about you,* is what he was really saying, *it's about doing what's best for Grace.* Wasn't that the whole point of being out here in the first place? And if that meant taking her to a few horse-crazy 'learning' sessions, then that was what she would have to do. He'd given Tess an out, said it was okay for her not to join in, so she may as well take him at his word. Besides, getting away from the house and everything lurking in its locked-up spaces was more and more enticing.

She met his gaze. 'Okay. If you really think it will help I'll bring her out for a trial session.'

'Good. We're free all day tomorrow, so come whenever it suits.'

Tomorrow could be a little too soon, but she would deal with that later. Maybe now was a good time to change the subject. 'So, you seem like you're pretty close to Toby.'

'He's a top kid.' His smile said everything he felt about his nephew, but it fell as he continued. 'Unlike his father, who is a total prick.'

'Really?' She sat up and raised both eyebrows. He came across all gentlemanly, with his George Clooney hair and mild manner, but there was obviously a more feisty side to Mitch Farmer.

'The bastard left Max high and dry when Toby was only a couple of weeks old. Couldn't handle being,' he hooked his fingers into air quotes, '"tied down". Bloody coward.'

'Were they married?'

'Nope. They'd been together for a while, though. Max thought he was the one.' From the short distance across the table, she could see his jaw tighten. 'I had to bite my tongue and stop myself saying I told you so when he cleared out and went back to the rodeo circuit.'

'Rodeo?'

'Riding bulls and horses around a ring. Kicking the shit out of them with sharpened spurs until they're covered in blood. Poking the cattle with electric prods to make them buck. Total redneck bullshit.'

Wow. He really was not holding back. His face was all sharp lines, his eyes like brooding clouds. Rodeos were something she'd only ever seen in Wild West movies. 'And he does that for a job?'

'In the States now. Hopefully, some poor steer he jabs too hard will make mincemeat of him.'

'Does he ever see Toby? Or help Max out financially?'

Mitch gave a wry laugh. 'That would require manning up and taking responsibility. Hard to do if you have no balls. She hasn't heard from him since the day he walked out. Best thing that ever happened to Max and Toby as far as I'm concerned.'

So Max was a single mother. 'It must be hard for her, though, being on her own with him.'

'Max was never on her own.' Jules moved around the table, laying out cutlery and place settings. 'This one here stepped up right away. More of a father than an uncle. And plenty of people around town to help. That's one lucky boy in there.'

'No, I'm the lucky one. He's a great kid.' Mitch slapped his hands on his knees and stood, scooping the remnants of pea shells into his cupped palm and dropping them in a container on the bench. Something in his suddenly coy manner suggested Jules may have touched a nerve.

When the food was ready, Jules called the kids for dinner and they came barrelling into the room, Grace freezing as if she was playing a game of statues as soon as she laid eyes on Tess.

'Hi, sweetie, sounded like you were having fun in there.'

Grace nodded shyly as she took a seat beside Toby, thankfully without the angry pout she'd perfected during the last week. Jules sat at the head of the table, leaving two chairs side by side for Tess and Mitch. He was taller than her by a few centimetres, and while he wasn't overweight there was a solidness about him that matched his sturdy character. If she had to pick a word to describe being around him, it would be *comfortable*. A surprise considering the way he'd stalked off at their last meeting. He was quite the enigma.

Dinner was a hearty casserole with lashings of mash, minted fresh peas and honeyed carrots. Good old family fare served up with a side of light-hearted talk about television favourites and art-class antics. By the time their knives and forks were scraping across empty plates, everyone seemed pleasantly stuffed.

'That was amazing, Jules, thank you so much.' Tess placed her cutlery in the centre of her plate and leaned back in her seat, hands resting on her stomach.

'My pleasure. Cooking up a storm is my favourite thing— after creating world-class works of art, of course.' She stood and began gathering the plates, Mitch rising instantly to give her a hand.

Works of art.

A cold wave spiralled around Tess, engulfing her so thoroughly her skin turned to gooseflesh inside her clothes. Since she'd arrived, the chatter and company had completely blotted out the discovery of those paintings in Skye's shed, but Jules's joke brought each image rolling back one by one, like a twisted horror-movie preview. She lifted a hand to her mouth, unable to catch the low moan before it escaped.

'Are you okay?' Mitch stared at her, the same concern he'd shown for Grace now directed at her.

His voice was enough to jolt her back to her senses. 'Oh, yeah, I … um … I think I've just eaten too much.' She collected the salt-and-pepper shakers, scanning the cupboards to work out where they belonged.

Jules considered her carefully. 'Middle shelf of the pantry, next to the sugar.'

She gave a shaky nod, stalling for a few seconds longer than necessary as she found the empty spot in the walk-in pantry. She needed to get a grip. These people must think her completely certifiable. Seasonings shelved, she edged back out into the kitchen.

'Can we watch one more episode?' Grace bailed Jules up with that how-can-you-resist-me face, and Toby stood behind looking equally hopeful. The two of them fixed doleful eyes on Mitch and her in turn. As much as she wanted to leave, Grace was a hard one to deny, especially when she looked happier than Tess had ever seen her. And it was rude to eat and run. 'Another half-hour and then it's home to bed.' She turned to Mitch. 'Is that okay with you?'

'Sure.' He moulded his expression into one of serious concern. 'But there's one condition.'

Faces blank, Grace and Toby waited for the deal-breaker.

'I get to watch too.'

'Yay!' Toby cheered. He grabbed his uncle's hand and pulled him towards the lounge room.

Mitch turned, laughing. 'Not that I'm trying to get out of doing the dishes or anything.'

'Yeah, right.' Jules threw a cloth at him as he disappeared after the kids. She picked up a tea towel and handed it to Tess. 'And then there were two.'

Suds filled the sink. A cloud of steam billowed into the kitchen as knives and forks clattered against the enamel basin. Television voices rang out from the living room, interspersed with comments and questions from Mitch, and Toby's patient explanations about who was who, and what was what. Every so often Grace would chime in, always on Toby's side. Since Mitch had joined them, the volume was noticeably louder, the trio of voices providing an easy soundtrack to the washing up.

'You took your time putting those salt-and-pepper shakers away.' Jules circled the brush clockwise and then back around the dish. She held the plate aloft in her pink-gloved hand, letting the suds drain away, before sliding it into the rack.

Tess sucked in her cheeks, trying to moisten her bone-dry mouth. She picked up the plate and rubbed at it with the tea towel, making the china squeak. Jules repeated the action, not once looking sideways. She was feigning disinterest, waiting for her victim to crack.

'Not really.' It was a lame response, but hopefully vague enough to stave off further questioning.

'You know, sometimes it's better to talk about things rather than bottle them up.' Jules shoved a handful of cutlery into the drainer. 'It can't be easy for you, stuck out there with a child you barely know and no family around to help out. I'm happy to listen if there's something bothering you.'

'There's nothing bothering me.'

Jules frowned. She wasn't fooled for a minute.

The plate clanged as Tess placed it onto the stack. She didn't have to explain herself to Jules. Looking after Grace when she'd been late and cooking them dinner did not give the woman the right to pry. She wiped the last of the dinner-ware, pushing the tea towel into the glasses and twisting it so hard her wrist throbbed. Job done, she hung the towel over the back of a chair. 'I'm pretty tired. We might get going.'

'No problem.' Jules wiped down the rivulets of water that had formed on the sink.

There was something infuriating about her calmness-and-light attitude, her refusal to push too hard. Tess had had enough for one night. She picked up her bag from where she'd slung it over the back of one of the dining chairs and strode through to the lounge room. 'Come on, Grace, time to go.'

'But you said we could watch one more episode,' Toby whined. 'It's not over yet.'

'Well, it's getting late. Let's go, Grace.' She could hear the abruptness in her tone, but she was beyond caring.

Grace stood and did as she was told, the slump of her shoulders saying everything she was feeling. Toby simply stared at the screen in front of him.

'We'll see you both tomorrow, then.' Mitch jumped to his feet and moved towards the doorway.

'Tomorrow?' What the hell was he talking about?

'At the farm.'

The light returned to Grace's eyes as she looked up. Tess was cornered.

'Yeah, see you then.' She'd agree to anything right now if she could just get out of here and have some time alone. 'Thanks for dinner, Jules.'

'Any time.'

All the way home in the car, Grace carried on about their imminent return visit to Affinity, rattling off the horses' names and rabbiting on about Jed the sheep-dog so eagerly, Tess found herself wishing the girl would once again stop talking.

Eighteen

By the time they got to Affinity, Grace was practically jumping out of her skin with an infectious energy that even Tess could not ignore. She hadn't told her why they were coming, just that Mitch had invited them back to see the horses. The simple joy radiating from the child was almost enough to make Tess forget her own trepidation. Almost. She hadn't bothered with breakfast, afraid to add anything to the squalling sea inside her stomach. Since then the nausea had subsided, but the closer they got to the training centre the stronger the caustic taste at the back of her throat became.

She had to keep reminding herself: this was about Grace.

Max greeted them with a wide smile. 'Good to see you again. The horses are all ready and waiting.' She held out a hand and Grace took it, without a single second of hesitation.

The few brief times Grace had taken Tess's hand had been nothing short of momentous. Since then there'd been nothing. Despite the time they'd spent together, the distance between them seemed to be growing, or at least stagnating.

Hopefully, things would turn around if this horse scenario actually worked. She stifled her sigh and followed along to the arena.

The black-and-white horse with the spooky eyes was busily munching hay. A much taller black horse was picking at a pile in the middle, and a smaller chestnut stood at the far end, reaching its neck through the fence to snag some grass. Mitch emerged from the stable block and gave them a wave.

'Hey there, Grace, good to see you.' He briefly flicked his gaze to Tess. 'Glad you decided to come back. Come on over.' He led them to a space in the middle of the shed where four chairs were set out. What was going on here?

'Would you like a drink, Grace? Juice, cordial, water?' Max asked.

Grace shook her head.

'Tea or coffee, Tess?'

'No, thanks.' Trying to keep anything down was probably not a good idea right now. The circular set-up of the chairs looked suspiciously like a group-counselling session. Shit. She should have stayed in the car. She folded her arms across her chest. Whatever happened next better not involve talking about their feelings.

'Take a seat, ladies.' Mitch sat himself down. 'Make yourselves comfortable.'

Grace sat, tucked her hands under her jean-clad thighs and crossed her ankles. She had a cheerful, expectant look on her face, the exact opposite of her usual demeanour and an extreme opposite of the expression Tess imagined herself to be wearing. Max sat beside her brother, leaving one chair vacant. Tess shifted from one foot to the other. She could make some excuse about a headache, tell them she'd wait in the car. Grace frowned, reached out a hand and shook the seat, the instruction clear. Damn. She was stuck. She fell into the chair, zeroing in on a horseshoe on the ground in the centre of the circle.

Until Max picked it up and began to speak. 'So, Grace, has Tess explained to you why you're back?'

Grace gave a slight shake of her head. Her hands were laced together in her lap now, but she still exuded the same excited air she'd had in the car, the electricity zipping through her veins almost audible.

'Okay, I'll explain.' Max continued with the preamble. 'What we do here is called equine-assisted learning. We help people who have something in their life they want to make better or who have feelings they don't quite understand.' She paused, presumably waiting for her words to register. They were registering with Tess: the f-word was already being tossed around in her head and they were only thirty seconds in. 'Horses are very intuitive—that means they can pick up on how a person is feeling and their reaction, and the way they behave around that person can sometimes help the person understand things better. Does that make sense?'

Grace's expression was completely blank. Mitch rested his elbows on his knees and locked his hands together. Mirroring Grace. 'We know you've had a really hard time lately, Grace, losing your mum, being taken to the city.' He smiled apologetically. 'Getting used to all those changes mustn't have been easy for you. We,' he gestured to the other two adults sitting in the circle, 'Tess and Max and I, we thought doing some work with the horses here might help you. It won't fix everything, but it might make you feel better. Would you like to give it a try?'

A whinny from the paddock outside sounded right on cue. Grace glanced in its direction, before her attention returned to the shredded denim in the knee of her jeans. She picked at a loose white thread. Was she debating? Working through the pros and cons in her head? Or was she just unsure how to say no.

'You don't have to do it if you don't want to, Grace.' The words jumped out of Tess's mouth almost of their own volition.

Mitch failed to hide his frown.

'No, of course you don't.' Max shifted a little closer, the legs of her plastic chair scraping on the rough cement. 'It's completely up to you. But just so you know, the session doesn't involve a lot of talking, it's all about you hanging out with the horses, spending time with them, and whatever happens, happens. We'll only talk a bit to start off and then it's you and whichever horse you choose.'

Grace lifted her chin. The spotty horse was standing, head drooping over the fence, peering in their direction as if it was eavesdropping. Tess kept her eyes glued on Grace, completely torn. If she said no they could be out of here in a flash and the knot inside her own chest could unravel, but if doing this could actually help, then her own anxiety was a small price to pay.

'Okay.' It was a quietly spoken assent, but an assent nonetheless.

'Great. Let's get started, then. To begin with, we're just going to let you get used to the horses.' Mitch tilted his head towards the paddock. 'You ready?'

Grace hopped up and walked along beside him.

Max indicated a couple of seats in the fenced area. 'We can watch from over here.'

'You don't go in with them?' Sending Grace off with a man she barely knew didn't feel right, but then again, Tess would be watching. Eyes open. In broad daylight.

'It can be a bit intimidating for the client if there are two of us in there. Besides, I'm still learning. Mitch is the expert.'

The sunlight was blinding after the shadows of the stable. Tess rolled her sunnies from the top of her head to cover her eyes and sat beside Max, watching through the railing. The three horses they'd seen on their way in were standing separately, seemingly indifferent to each other. When Grace and Mitch entered the paddock the animals raised their heads, eyeing the two humans. Mitch crouched down and spoke to Grace, but it was too far away to hear what he was saying.

'So, how does this work again?' The brief bits of theory she'd read on the website combined with Mitch's intro still didn't really explain how a horse was going to help Grace process her emotions.

'Watch and you'll see.'

She resisted the urge to roll her eyes, crossed her arms and settled into her seat.

Brush in hand, Grace walked over to the first horse, stopping a short distance away and pausing, not looking directly at them. The chestnut flicked an ear and gave a brief swish of its tail before dropping its head to the ground and sniffing at a leaf tumbling across the arena. It made no move towards Grace, and after a few minutes she moved on to the second horse, the spotted one. This one turned its head and fixed one blue eye on Grace, who reciprocated before looking away. Odd, but probably what Mitch had instructed her to do. Tess glanced across to gauge his reaction to no avail; it was hard to read, other than focused. The spotted horse shuffled slightly and let out a sigh, its tongue lolling out of its mouth. Grace lifted her hand and touched the horse's flank, resting it there before giving one gentle stroke. A smile flared before she dropped her hand and walked on, approaching the third horse, the black Friesian.

Tess shuddered. Her whole body tensed. The animal was positively enormous. If it bolted or kicked it could do some serious damage. She gripped Max's arm. 'Is this really safe?'

'Watch.'

Her cuticles were already ragged and gnawing on your fingers wasn't exactly an attractive habit, but the temptation to bite them was overwhelming. She stiffened her knuckles and pushed them down by her sides. This process was supposed to be about trust—trusting the horses, trusting the 'practitioners'—so she was just going to have to wait it out and see what happened.

Grace, apparently unfazed, maintained her stance. The horse's eyes were as dark as his coat, making it hard to see exactly where he was looking. He shuffled slightly from foot to foot before settling back into the same spot, one back leg slightly bent. Then something else started to happen. The spotted horse, the mare, made its way over, stopped and poked its head across the Grace's shoulder, nuzzling her cheek. Grace giggled. She lifted a hand to the horse's face and gave it a gentle scratch.

'She likes you,' Mitch called. 'Try going for a walk and see what happens.'

Grace dropped her hand and walked purposefully down the arena away from the two horses. The larger one stayed put, nudging the air with his nose, but the mare began to follow, always a few steps behind. Tess sat up straighter as the horse mimicked Grace's movements, tracing the weaving pattern she made as she walked along. Without warning, Grace broke into a jog and the horse started to trot, still keeping its distance.

221

'Wow.' This was amazing! Grace was laughing, loving every minute.

'Told you.' Max grinned. 'That's just for starters.'

The horse pulled up behind Grace at the far end of the arena. Mitch, hands in pockets, wandered down and stood a metre away to give the next set of directions. His voice was soft, reassuring.

'Looks like Whisky has chosen you. Are you okay with that?'

Grace gave an enthusiastic nod.

'Great. So now you can spend a bit of time getting to know each other. Groom her a little, talk to her, see if she wants to go for another walk. Whatever feels right. If you need anything I'll be right over there.' He pointed to the spot on the fence he'd just vacated.

Mitch gave a cheeky wriggle of his eyebrows as he looked across to Tess. The look on his face was pure satisfaction. And maybe a little bit smug.

'So does Mitch actually do anything else to facilitate?' So far so good, but there had to be more to this than brushing a horse and walking it around.

'Some discussion at the end of the session. His main job is observation, watching the way the horses respond, and then interpreting what's happening.' Max considered what she'd said. 'Or rather, guiding the client to interpret what's happened.'

'But Grace is only ten. I don't think she's going to have much idea about what's occurring.'

'Don't you? She looks pretty cosy out there to me. She might have more to say about it than you think.'

Grace was running the brush down the length of the horse's back, tracing the path with her other hand and, hang on … was she singing?

'She might not understand the technicalities, but she'll know what she felt at each step of the way. That's what Mitch will talk to her about afterwards. We also like to get people to journal about their experience. If they choose.'

This whole thing was mind-boggling. Her own experience with animals was minimal. Her family had never even had a dog. Beth had been bitten by one as a child and never re-covered, and only acquired the cat after Tess had moved out. And after that one disastrous trail ride Tess had sworn never to sit in a saddle again. Using them as four-legged counsel-lors was a fascinating concept, yet also totally bewildering. 'I know you said to watch and learn, but there are some things I'd like explained.'

'Shoot.'

'Why did Mitch get her to walk around like that at the start? Why not just pick a horse and get on with it?'

'Horses are prey animals, so they're wired to sense danger, notice what's in their environment, respond and react. If they see, or sense, something—or someone—as a threat, they'll re-spond by running. They also live in herds for protection, so they're highly attuned to what's happening with their herd mates. They can read behaviour, and intentions.' She pointed towards the horse being happily groomed. 'Whisky recog-nises something in Grace—a need, an emotion, it's hard to explain exactly what—but she feels some connection to her for whatever reason. And judging by Grace's response, it's mutual.'

Tess shook her head and let out a deep breath. 'So what happens next?'

'It's up to Grace. If she decides she wants to come back, we'll continue to build on the start she's made today. It usually takes a few sessions to make real progress.'

That made sense. It was early days, but if the smile on Grace's face was anything to go by, they were off and running. Probably better to reserve judgement, though, until she saw the actual results.

Once the grooming session was over, Grace wandered back to where Mitch was waiting, Whisky walking easily by her side. At the gate Grace leaned over and kissed the horse's face, whispered something into her ear and then followed Mitch back to the stable block. In a couple of minutes the pair of them came outside, Grace holding a small black book to her chest.

'Grace did brilliantly today. I've given her one of our journals to take home. She can jot down anything she likes about her time with Whisky along with any questions or things she wants to raise next time.' Mitch bent down and spoke directly to Grace. 'If you want to come back.'

Her eyes round and hopeful, Grace gave an emphatic nod.

'Great.' He turned to Tess and gave her a wink. 'Well, we're here whenever you want to book in next.'

Tess tucked a piece of hair behind her ear and waited for the inevitable flutter inside her stomach to settle. They were in this now. She would have to commit. 'Right. Um, how long should we leave between sessions?'

Max had vanished and Mitch was now doing all the talking. He shrugged. 'That's up to you. And Grace. Some people come once a week, others twice, whatever works best for the both of you.'

Grace bounced up and down on her toes, like a ballerina breaking in her pointe shoes. 'Can we come again soon?' She had that pleading look aced.

'How about Friday? That's in two days' time.'

Grace nodded.

'If that's okay for you, Mitch?'

He pulled his phone out of his pocket and tapped at the screen. 'Yeah, sure. It's Toby's birthday. We're planning a barbeque, so if you two wanted to come for the session in the afternoon and stay for dinner, I'm sure the birthday boy would love it.'

'Oh no, we wouldn't want to intrude.' Mixing business with pleasure was always a bad idea.

'No intrusion. Toby would love the company.'

'Please?'

Grace was looking at her so intently. How could she possibly say no? 'Okay, see you on Friday.'

Grace skipped all the way back to the car. She'd been excited to come back but was even more upbeat now. Tess climbed in beside her and started the engine. All in all the day could only be called a success, and yet there was still something not quite right, some abrasive feeling, like a massive splinter wedged somewhere down deep inside. Even as Grace yabbered on about Whisky on the drive home, even as Tess nodded and smiled back in all the right places, it pricked at her gut, stuck and festering. Refusing to worm its way out.

Nineteen

Dusk. For years, the fading of day into night had always made Tess's heart beat slightly faster, her breathing a little shallower, filling her with an urgency to get home, lock the door and turn on all the lights. But that was in the city, a whole other lifetime ago. Out here, the end of a day was something entirely different: a melting away of light, a gradual transformation from one state of being to another, calming the rush of blood through her veins. At Affinity it was even more beautiful. Marshmallow-pink clouds streaked wide across a lilac sky. Black birds silhouetted against the luminous horizon. A gentle quiet, tranquil as a lullaby. The cool evening breeze caressed her cheek as the horses, back out in the paddock, worked their way through their feed bins. She shook her head. Where had all this poetic daydreaming come from? And could the real Tessa De Santis please stand up?

Grace was nowhere to be seen. No doubt she was off with Toby somewhere, probably checking out his birthday stash. Today's session with Whisky had been much the same as last time, but with a few additional tasks. An obstacle course, through which Grace manoeuvred the mare with only a little help from Mitch and a good fifteen minutes where the horse once again stood completely still while being groomed from top to tail. Who would have thought that brushing a horse could be so meditative? Grace's mood had definitely picked up over the last two days, so who was Tess to argue?

'Today went well.' Max appeared at her side and held out a tumbler of white wine.

'Oh, thanks.' The glass was cold against Tess's palm. 'Yes, it did. She seemed to enjoy it.'

'Has she said much over the last couple of days?'

'No.' Despite Grace's euphoria after her first session on Wednesday, she'd remained mostly mute at home even though she seemed happier. Tess looked out across the lush carpet of grass to the grey mist settling in the distance. 'She didn't say much at all. Raved about Whisky in the car on the way home and then nothing.'

'But she wanted to come back, so that's a good sign.'

Max was a classic example of someone who always looked for the positive. 'I guess so.' Although there was a strong chance that seeing Toby was the reason. The two of them were as thick as thieves. Which was surprising, given the minimal contact Grace must have had with other kids. But then who knew what was going on in the girl's head? Tess downed another mouthful of wine. If anyone could help in the parenting stakes, it was Max. 'So, Mitch told me you've been a single mum for a while now.'

'Yeah, like from the time Tobes was born.'

'Is it hard? Doing it on your own?'

Max faced her, staring with eyes that were something like her brother's but not quite as intense. 'Are you asking for a friend?' She gave a narrow-eyed grin.

Ouch. So much for being subtle.

'It's been tough at times.' The kids were back outside, doing cartwheels on the other side of the yard, and both women turned to watch them as Max spoke. 'Especially when he was a baby and I didn't have a bloody clue what I was doing. Mum was sick. If it wasn't for Mitch I'm not sure what I would have done. He stepped up, pretty much became a surrogate father.' She reached across and tapped Tess's wedding band. 'I didn't think *you* were doing this on your own.'

The ring was a constant reminder of what she stood to lose. What she may have already lost. 'I didn't either.'

'What happened?'

'Grace.'

Max's eyebrows arched. 'Really?'

She nodded, even though that wasn't strictly true. Grace's appearance in their lives had only widened the already existing gulf between Josh and her. Trying not to think about the situation was easy in his absence, but sooner or later it would have to be confronted. 'He doesn't want kids.' She sighed. 'And he certainly doesn't want somebody else's.'

'So he's back in Sydney?'

Now there was a question. He hadn't checked in for the last couple of days. She waved a hand, tried to sound nonchalant. 'He's overseas for work. In Brussels.' Or somewhere in Europe. Possibly on a plane heading back home.

'He might come around.'

'Maybe.' She squinted into the dying light. 'Anyway … is it hard, raising a kid on your own? Just asking for a friend.'

Max let out a belly laugh. 'Yes, it is. But it's also the best thing I've ever done. And if you can muster a little help from your family and friends you—and Grace—are going to be fine.'

'Mum, Mum.' Toby came tearing across the yard, Grace hot on his heels as a car cruised up the driveway and pulled to a stop. 'Sanjay is here.'

Max deposited her glass on the table. 'Won't be a minute. Toby's friend from school is coming for a sleepover. And his parents are joining us for dinner.' She headed over to greet her visitors.

Tess whistled out a lungful of air. It was a relief to have a few minutes to collect herself. So far she'd managed to avoid talking about Josh to anyone—apart from the one mention she'd made of him to Jules—and, in her usual style, she'd pretty much blocked him from her mind since coming to Weerilla. Time was ticking on. Five weeks had passed since she'd been notified about Grace and they still hadn't sorted themselves out. Sometime soon that conversation was going to have to happen.

She wriggled her shoulders and rubbed the knots from her neck. Over by the house, Grace was hovering behind Toby and two dark-haired boys, the taller one holding a large gift-wrapped box. The smaller one looked up at Grace, pointing to her face. Tess watched as she lifted her palm and pressed it against her cheek, said something Tess couldn't hear. If that kid was teasing Grace about her birthmark, he was going to find himself in big trouble. Grace shrugged and the boy smiled, and then the four of them ran up the steps and into the house in a riot of shouts and laughter. Just like normal kids.

Had Grace ever been a normal kid? From what Jules had said she'd always been quiet, too cosseted by Skye, too isolated from children of her own age. Now she had so much more to deal with than any child should have to manage. Yet watching her here, mixing with the others as if it was an everyday occurrence, it was almost possible to believe that she was just like any other ten-year-old.

Max returned, along with a striking woman wrapped in a turquoise pashmina and a bright-faced, bespectacled man in casual jeans and sweatshirt.

'Tess, this is Leela and Raj. Their son is Toby's bestie. When he's not here driving me nuts, he's at their place.'

Leela flashed a brilliant-white smile, her teeth almost blinding against her beautiful olive skin. 'We call him our third son. It's an honour to be invited to celebrate his birthday.'

'Nice to meet you both.'

Raj nodded politely then turned to Max. 'Where's that brother of yours?'

'Staying out of the way so I don't give him a job, I'm betting.' Max pointed towards the stable block. 'You'll probably find him in his office.'

Raj headed off and Leela clasped her hands together. 'Now, Max, what can I do to help?'

'Everything's done. Cake is in the fridge, skewers are marinating, salad is made, party pies and sausage rolls are in the oven ready to go.'

'Any other kids coming?' Tess had no idea about the plans for the night, but for a kid's birthday party it seemed unusually small.

Max heaved a sigh and shook her head. 'Nope. Toby is a bit of a loner at school. Although, you wouldn't know it right now.' Across the yard, the four kids were running around in circles chasing each other, squealing like banshees. 'I used to think it was because he doesn't have a father, like it was somehow my fault, but I've come to realise it's just his personality. He keeps to himself, apart from Sanjay and one or two others, so he only wanted something small. He and Grace have really hit it off, though.'

'I know, it's so weird.'

Leela gave Tess a puzzled look.

'Oh, I mean it's just that Grace is really shy, too,' Tess explained. 'Or at least I think she is. So it's odd that two such quiet kids would connect as well as they have.'

'Not really.' Leela's tone was soft and lyrical, rather than argumentative. 'They probably feel comfortable, understand each other.'

'Is Sanjay a quiet one, too?'

Her laugh was loud and not so gentle. 'Oh my goodness, no. He is much livelier, wouldn't you say, Max?'

'Totally. Life of the party. All the kids love him, so he can pick and choose who he hangs out with. Luckily, he likes hanging out with Tobes.'

'That's because Toby is divine.'

'Can't argue with that.' Max positively glowed. 'I'd better go check the oven. Saint Tobias will murder me if I burn his party pies.'

Toby did seem like a great kid, but Leela was the one who was so heavenly it was hard not to stare. The woman was drop-dead gorgeous, her smoky eyes rimmed with kohl accentuating the shape, shiny black hair flowing down her back. She would not look out of place on a catwalk. What was someone like her doing living in a backwater like Weerilla?

'Something you said before has me curious.'

Tess dragged herself out of her girl crush. 'What was that?'

'When you said you *think* Grace is a really quiet kid. Would you not know this?'

'Oh … well, I suppose I should.' She kept forgetting that people didn't know about the connection—or lack of it—between

Grace and her. 'She's only been with me for a few weeks. Her mother and I were friends, but we hadn't seen each other for a while before she died.'

'So sad.' Leela shook her head. 'Max has told me a little about Grace's circumstances. Such a horrible thing to happen to a young child. Still, she's lucky to have someone like you. Children are such a blessing. And our greatest teachers if we're willing to learn.'

A high-pitched wail reached them from across the other side of the yard.

'Oh dear, that's my Yash. Always in the wars. He was sent to teach me patience. Excuse me.' She gave a slightly exasperated smile and headed off in the direction of the noise, practically floating across the grass. Whatever had happened seemed not to be life-threatening, the initial scream now dulled to a light moan, an occasional sob thrown in for effect.

Sometime during their conversation, almost as if a switch had been flicked, night had fallen, and torches were being waved around in the same vicinity as the commotion. The troops were rallying. Should she go to help? Leela hadn't seemed too concerned. Probably better to leave her to it. She was one of those serene, wise women who always seemed to know the right thing to say, although the pronouncement that Grace was lucky to have such a wonderful guardian was certainly way off the mark. Her comment about children being teachers was curious, something Tess had never heard before.

What lessons could she learn from Grace?

If she was willing.

She really had to stop stuffing herself. Or do some exercise. Or both. Dinner was amazing—melt-in-your mouth steak, jacket potatoes cooked in hot coals and doused in butter, garden-fresh salad all washed down with perfectly chilled glasses of wine for the adults and plenty of green cordial for the kids. Max had refused any offers to help clean up, claiming there was little to do except clear the table full of dishes and plates, which she bribed the kids into doing with the promise of toasted marshmallows. Job done, they returned to the fire and sat, sticks in hand, waiting angelically. Grace sat by Toby's side, the flames casting an orange glow across her face, bringing a healthy radiance to her pale skin. She hadn't said much during dinner, but she seemed happy to listen in on the boys' conversation, completely content.

A mood that was apparently contagious. The pre-dinner sav blanc had been followed by another of shiraz and the sultry notes of the wine hit just the right chord. Mitch had brought out his guitar and was strumming away quietly after they'd all sung a rousing rendition of 'Happy Birthday'. Leela and Raj, it turned out, ran a local catering business specialising in home-cooked food with an Indian flavour. Raj was also the local computer repairman and together they had plenty of amusing stories about their experiences of small-town life. They didn't exactly fit the traditional demographic, but they'd been accepted into the community with only the occasional poorly disguised slur. Max didn't miss the opportunity to tell a few embarrassing stories about the birthday boy, who took it on the chin and retaliated with a few mum stories of his own. No one grilled Tess about her life, so it was easy to sit back and enjoy the company and the conversation. She didn't have to be anywhere, and there were no deadlines, meetings or messages to answer. For the first time since leaving Sydney, she was actually relaxed.

'Right, two more each then you lot have had enough sugar for the next decade.' Max presented the bag of marshmallows to each of the kids before offering them to the adults. *It would be rude not to take one.*

This was a whole new learning curve. Tess pushed her marshmallow onto a pointy stick, stuck it into the fire and waited. It came out charcoaled and bubbling and she shoved it into her mouth too soon, burning the tip of her tongue, then had to swig the last of her wine as an remedy. Once everyone had devoured their share of the sticky sizzling sweets, the Singhs bade them all goodnight and the kids re-tired inside for a movie, Max excusing herself to supervise the selection.

She should probably head home, too. But the fire was hyp-notic and it was Friday night, and it wasn't like there was anyone waiting for them back home. A gust of wind sent a shiver through her body despite the duffle coat and scarf she was wearing.

'Cold?'

'A little.'

'Hop up a minute.' Mitch rose from his seat beside her.

She moved to the side while he dragged both their seats— chunks of tree trunks fashioned into stools—a little closer to the fire. He threw a couple more logs on top, sending a shower of sparks dancing into the air.

'Thanks.' She sat again, the scent of smoke filling her nos-trils and the heat of the flames warming her cheeks. She tipped her head back. Stars filled the sky for as far as she could see, strewn like glitter across the dark blanket of night. If she reached out her arm surely she could touch one.

'Not bad, is it?' Mitch too was gazing upwards. 'Guess you don't get to see it like this in the city. Too many lights.'

He was so right. 'I don't think I've ever seen anything like it.'

'Never been camping?'

'Uh-uh. We were more of a resort type of family when we went on holidays. Mum didn't like sand. Or dirt. Or rain.' She laughed. 'Must be where I get my preference for hot showers, shopping opportunities and a cafe on every corner.' Funnily enough, she missed none of them.

She didn't have to look sideways to know Mitch was studying her. Probably thinking what a shallow piece of work she was. She kicked at a rock by her foot.

'It's good you came tonight.' *Where was he going with this?* She kept her eyes trained on a chunk of white-hot wood smouldering in the bottom of the fire. 'Toby enjoyed himself. He liked having Grace here.'

Okay. All good. 'I think she had fun, too.'

'She's a great kid.' He picked up a stick and poked at an ember that was threatening to fall from the pit. 'She's doing so well with the learning.'

'How can you tell?'

'The way she's managing the tasks I've given her, her confidence with the horse.' He tossed the stick into the fire and brushed his hands against the leg of his jeans. 'The discussions we've had after her sessions.' His eyes shone. 'Have you noticed any changes in her behaviour? I know it's only been a couple of days.'

'Nothing I can put my finger on, but she does seem more … settled? Maybe a little less sad.' She couldn't bite back the sigh. 'She still won't let me in, though.'

He glanced across at her, his voice low. 'Can I ask you a question?'

He was going to whether or not she said yes, so she turned towards him and waited.

'That first day when you came and I suggested the two of you have sessions together ... you practically ran out of here before I'd even finished talking.'

The blush scalding her neck had nothing to do with the fire, not that he'd be able to see it beneath her layers of clothes. She'd been an idiot that day, had behaved like a child. He'd have to have been deaf, dumb and blind not to notice something was wrong.

'What are you afraid of?'

She leaned forward, pushing all her weight into the balls of her feet, and stared into the embers. Vibrant orange, throwing off so much heat her face felt like it too was on fire. No matter how long she looked, the answer to Mitch's question wasn't there: it was locked deep inside her heart.

Mitch's face was a blur, but she knew he was watching her. Waiting. This was someone she could trust. Someone who genuinely wanted to help, if she could only find the courage.

She turned away. Tendrils of flame licked at the blackened stump fuelling the fire.

'It might help if you joined in on Grace's sessions.' His voice was a murmur, dulled by the crackling coals. 'Help you both.'

She closed her eyes, drew strength from the warmth pulsing through her limbs, from the idea of finally being free. 'Do you really think so?'

'I'm sure of it.'

She looked across at him, and for a long minute they held each other's gaze. She hadn't answered his initial question and he hadn't pushed for more. But they'd started the conversation, and for now, that was enough.

Grace was a complete nerd when it came to school work and Sundays were no exception. For a ten-year-old, the kid was super disciplined, following the timetable her mother had established without deviating. Occasionally, she accepted an offer of help and they'd work through a maths problem or a word definition together, but all in all she was pretty self-sufficient. Maddeningly so. It left an overabundance of time for Tess to wash and scrub and sweep, clutching the broom handle tighter each time she found herself anywhere near the old wardrobe. She'd lost track of the number of books she'd finished on her Kindle since she'd come out here, a luxury she usually only had time for on holidays, and the perfect distraction for a wayward mind. Diving into someone else's story was much more innocuous than revisiting her own.

Right now, she was skimming through the chapters of a historical romance. It was her current preferred genre, devoid of anything too disturbing, but cerebral enough to keep her mind engaged. Even the YA and fantasy books she generally favoured were too heavy on the dark stuff these days. It was so much easier to get swept up in a civil-war saga or take a turn around the room with Elizabeth Bennet.

Buddy, the magpie, landed at her feet, bobbing his head like a dashboard figurine. *Food, please.* He hopped along the verandah before lunging into the garden to nab a worm, holding up his prize for show-and-tell.

A noise from inside turned her head. Was she hearing things or was that the tinkling of piano keys? Grace hadn't played since that day before the funeral. *The Wizard of Oz* would forever now be tainted. Hopefully, this time she'd play something different. Tess pressed an ear against the weatherboards. One chord and then the next. *Ba da da da bom bom bom bom bom bi dom, ba dom bom bom bom bom*. It was vaguely familiar. She hummed along, stringing the notes together. That was it! 'Baby Elephant Walk'. Her fingers played along on an imaginary keyboard, racing ahead of the laboured tune. When the playing stopped, then started, then faltered again, she jumped to her feet, pushed open the door and peeked inside.

Grace sat, shoulders rounded, her mouth puckered like a prune as she frowned at the yellowing sheet music. Tess closed the door and stood motionless, considering her next move. This could go either way, but she had to give it a shot. Not daring to breathe, she walked across the room and stopped beside the piano, waiting there until finally, Grace glanced up.

She motioned to the vacant space on the bench seat. 'Okay if I sit?'

Grace shifted across, leaving just enough room.

Was this a good idea or would Grace think she was showing off? Only one way to find out. 'I used to play this one. It's fun but a bit tricky. Would you like some help?'

With Grace's head bowed, it was impossible to read her expression. Her hair fell over her shoulders, the long ringlets like silken corkscrews, begging to be touched. The room was deathly quiet. A few specks of dust shimmied into view, as if an invisible hand had given the curtain a shake. They bobbed through the air, floated past and disappeared from view.

'Yes, please.'

A small win; a tiny rush of joy. Tess wiped her palms over her thighs before she rested them on the keys. 'It's been a while, but let me see if I can remember.' Tentatively she picked out the first few treble notes, beginning to find her way after a couple of bars. 'Hmm, not bad.'

A glimmer of a smile in Grace's eyes. 'Can you do both hands?'

'Let's find out.' She peered at the notes, lifted her left hand to join her right and started again, tentatively at first and then a little quicker, fingers moving almost of their own accord as the jaunty rhythm came back. Muscle memory must really be a thing. She jerked her shoulders in time with the notes as she made her way through the first page and onto the second. Beside her, Grace also began jigging away, her leg bouncing up and down, and her fingertips tapping on her knees. 'Your great-grandma taught me how to play this, you know. On this very piano.' The words slipped out before she could censor herself. She watched Grace keenly to gauge her reaction.

'Did she really?'

Play and talk. Just play and talk. 'Uh-huh. She taught your mum and me after school.'

'Mumma said she always wished she'd kept learning. That's why she was teaching me.'

Tess played on, her fingers suddenly stiff and clumsy as she concentrated on her rendition. She'd avoided mentioning Skye ever since the funeral, couldn't stand to see that glazed, tortured expression haunting Grace's eyes. But right now, there was no sign of the torment accompanying any earlier references to her mother, so she pushed a little further. 'Well, she was right. I wished I'd kept learning, too.' She launched back into the song, pressing the keys harder, emphasising the beat more clearly. 'Can you guess why it's called "Baby Elephant Walk"?'

Grace shook her head and actually looked interested in knowing the answer.

'Picture a baby elephant hanging onto its mother's tail with its trunk. This is the rhythm they keep as they walk.' She slowed down, emphasising each note. '*Bom bom bom bom* ... see?'

Grace jumped off the seat. Reaching out her arms and lacing her fingers together, she lowered her head and marched around the room in time to the music, swinging her joined arms from side to side, stomping her feet to the beat.

'Yeah, just like that.' Tess quickened the pace, playing faster, somehow remembering the notes without looking at the keys. Grace sped up her actions, marching from one side of the room to the other and back again, collapsing onto the bed in a fit of giggles as the last bar of the song was played.

Without even thinking, Tess shot up from the piano and launched herself onto her back beside Grace, holding her sides as she laughed along. 'You are the best baby elephant I've ever seen.'

They lay there side by side, their chests rising and falling almost in unison until they'd both caught their breath. Grace rolled so she was facing Tess, their noses almost touching. 'Can you teach me how to play it like that?' Her cheeks were cherry-blossom pink, her eyes shining with an effervescent light.

'Of course I can.' Tess pushed herself upright, the bed creaking with the movement.

Grace sprang up and grabbed her hand.

They sat together at the piano. When Tess looked down at the black notes on the sheet, the heads and stems blurred, wriggling on the page like tiny tadpoles. The words she wanted to say caught in her throat, but inside, her heart was singing.

Twenty

Tess had chewed her cuticles so hard a couple had started bleeding. God knows what Grace thought of her juvenile habit. Thankfully, the little girl was too preoccupied with her own excitement about seeing the horses once again. Tess's feelings about their joint session at Affinity were exactly the opposite. If an animal darted across the road right now, it would definitely end up as roadkill because if she stopped, there was a good chance she'd make a U-turn and head straight back home. Most of the drive passed in a fog, her concentration completely focused on just getting there. When she pulled to a stop outside the stable block she couldn't even remember arriving, let alone opening the gate and coming up the driveway. This might have seemed like a good idea under the moonlight when she'd had a couple of drinks and the fire was making her head swim, but in the bright light of day it was already feeling like a huge mistake.

'Are you coming?'

She turned her head to the side, towards the sound. Grace was already out, her voice muffled through the closed door of the car.

Tess nodded. It was enough of an answer to satisfy Grace, who skipped away towards the stables. Now she just needed to swing her legs out, get herself vertical and mobile.

Mitch spoke to Grace and then waved to Tess, watching her long after he'd dropped his hand. *This was it. Time was up.* Her arm moved towards the door. She pulled at the handle, a stream of cool air greeting her as she swivelled around, placed both feet on the ground and stared down at her newly polished RM Williams boots. She was perfectly prepared. On the outside. As long as she could fake her way through the session and not let her guard down everything would be fine. After all, she'd had years' worth of practice.

Grace made a beeline for Whisky, who stuck her head through the railing and was enjoying an ear scratch. Those two had really bonded, which was probably what this stuff was all about: you make a connection with an animal, so you get an endorphin rush and *whammo*, you feel better. Grace bent forward and rubbed her nose against the horse's muzzle. Chemical reaction or not, it seemed to be working, at least for Grace.

Mitch was still there, waiting. 'Hi.' Her voice sounded normal. A good start. 'How are you doing?' He eyed her carefully as he handed her a small black notebook, the same one Grace had been recording her thoughts in after each session.

'Thanks.' She could always use it for shopping lists. Taking the path of least resistance was the order of the day.

'You guys ready?' Max called out to them from the stable entrance. 'We're going to start inside, then come out and do some work with the horses.'

Mitch moved to head in, Grace jumping in front and beating him to the door.

Smile. Say as little as possible. Play along.

'You joining us?' Mitch had stopped and turned around to face her.

Tess smiled. 'Of course.'

Grace was already seated, her journal open on her knees. Max and Mitch occupied the other two chairs, leaving hers ready and waiting. She pulled it slightly outside the circle and sat, then loosened the scarf wrapped in layers around her neck.

'Tess,' Max started, 'thanks so much for being here with us. We're really happy you've agreed to join in on the learning with Grace. I know it's only five days since your last session, but we'd like to start off with a few reminders about how things work.' Her voice droned on, running through the confidential nature of the sessions, inviting the two of them to be open to the experience and the possibility that strong emotions could be stirred. *Sessions*, she had said. Plural. There was some mention of team building and then a second voice cut in.

'Is there anything you'd like to share with us from your journal, Grace?'

Focus. Listen.

Without any hesitation, Grace opened her notebook and began to read.

'*I love Whisky. I love the way she smells and the way she licks my hand but doesn't bite. When we did the exercise where I walked around the arena and she followed me, it made me feel happy. Like she wanted to be with me. Like she loved me. Doing the obstacle course was fun. My favourite part was when we zig-zagged through the cones and then Whisky stopped right next to me at the end. I was really sad when I had to leave. I can't wait to go back again.*' She looked up at Mitch, beaming.

'That's great, Grace. Thanks for sharing with us.'

'So, Tess ...' Max again. 'What are you hoping to gain from coming along today?'

Her cheeks burned as she stared at an L-shaped crack in the concrete. Why was it so stuffy in here? Grace's head was turned in her direction. As long as she kept it simple all would be well. She forced herself to look up and Mitch gave her an encouraging smile.

'I'm hoping we—Grace and I—can become closer.' Her voice was steady, with no sign of the quivering jellyfish beneath the surface. 'And that she might feel more comfortable confiding in me.' Was that right? Or should she be using second person, talking directly to Grace? She turned sideways in her chair. Made sure she caught Grace's eye. 'Or at least that you could talk to me more. Trust me.'

Mitch nodded. 'Great. I'll be directing you through a series of exercises with the horses. Try not to rush through them, take your time and remember that you're in this together, so as much as possible try to work as partners, with each other and with the horses.' He paused. 'Any questions?'

Tess shook her head. The less talking the better.

He stood and led them out, then handed them a brush each. 'We'll start with the grooming exercise. Grace, repeat what we did last time and see if Whisky wants to work with you again. She may decide not to today.' Grace's face fell. 'But chances are she will.' She perked up again and headed into the arena.

Tess took the brush she was offered and opened the gate. 'So do I just pick a horse?'

'This isn't so much about picking a horse as you and the horse choosing to work with each other.' He rested his hand on her arm. 'And there's no hurry, Tess. Take your time.'

244

Grace was circling the horses slowly, one by one, eyes averted, as she'd done the last two times. This would be a piece of cake. Walk around, find a horse, brush it, go home. The smaller chestnut was her target, but it would be better to delay it, to make the choice look more impromptu. The huge black horse flicked an ear in her direction. Apparently, he'd been a stallion until recently. He might have lost his manhood, but everything about him exuded power. Strength. A shiver skipped across her scalp. She swallowed, chasing it away. She passed Grace, already teamed up with Whisky, who stood with head lowered so her mane could be brushed. The chestnut Tess had in mind was standing in the middle of the arena. No point prolonging the inevitable. She picked up her pace a little and approached the smaller gelding. The horse turned its head briefly, gave a sniff then edged away, playing hard to get. Tess took a step closer, but as she reached out a hand towards the horse's withers a hot breath fell across her neck. She froze. *What was happening?*

'It's okay, Tess,' a voice called gently, 'he's just letting you know he's there.' Mitch was speaking from somewhere behind her, but she couldn't turn around. 'Just relax.'

For a few long seconds, she let her eyes fall shut. She loosened her grip on the brush, let her hand fall from the chestnut's neck and tried to stay calm. She wasn't alone. Mitch was here. She opened her eyes again to see her chosen horse walking away, but the warm air continued to coat her cheek. One stuttering centimetre at a time she turned her neck, forcing her eyes to follow. The tall gelding's rubbery lips touched her face.

'He's giving you an invitation.'

An invitation?

The horse's face was so close to hers she could see the damp recesses of his nostrils vibrating. She willed herself to move, but every muscle in her body was rigid, as if his breath had turned her to stone. She wanted to run—would he chase her? Would he trample her? Pin her down? Put a knife to her throat and slit her from ear to ear. He'd said he would kill them both if they told. Her parents would never see her again. Jean would never see Skye again. They'd be gone and nobody would ever know what happened to them. His rancid, rum-drenched breath spilled over her again, mixed with the sickly musk of his aftershave. Her stomach lurched. Her hand flew to her mouth. Oh God, she was going to be sick. She curled into a ball, barely upright.

'Tess.' He was calling to her. *How did he know her name?* It was hot, too hot under all these blankets, but she couldn't throw them off.

'Tess, it's me, it's Mitch.'

Mitch?

She dropped her hand. Pulled herself up to meet his cool green eyes. It was daylight. They were outside. At Affinity.

He rested a hand on her arm. 'You're alright.'

She gulped down a mouthful of air.

'Are you okay to keep going?'

A few metres away Grace was watching her closely, even as she brushed Whisky's tail, a curious glint in her eye. She had no way of knowing what had just happened, that Tess's worst nightmare had materialised the minute the horse had sought her out. Had something similar happened to Grace in her sessions? Had the memory of finding her mother, cold and stiff in her bed, been dragged out for her to confront? Mitch had already backed away, leaving her to make the decision for herself.

The black horse was standing by her side, calm and waiting. She raised her hand and placed it against his neck. Warm muscle, a velvet-soft coat. Here and now. Real and grounding.

She ran her fingers along his spine. He blinked, long lashes feathering the sharp bones of his cheeks, and rolled his tongue around inside his mouth before reaching out and licking her, once, on the arm. She took a small step back so she could lift the brush she still held in her hand. *Brush, hand, brush, hand.* She alternated one and then the other over the horse's body, moving from one section to the next, drawing on his quiet strength, completely absorbed in what she was doing, her mind-numbing fear dissolving.

And something inside her, shifting.

'Can I help?'

Grace was standing beside her. How long had she been there? The flashback was so shocking, the movement of the brush over the horse's coat so mesmerising, she had lost all sense of time and place. She glanced up to see Mitch, a short distance away. His expression was neutral, but he was there. Not quite sure if she'd be able to speak, she gave Grace a nod and returned to her task, moving to the other side to cre-ate some room. As they worked quietly together Grace began to hum. 'Baby Elephant Walk'. Tess shook her head, smiling and joining in, humming along until the horse was gleaming from head to toe and the grin on Grace's face reached from ear to ear.

And then something occurred to her. 'I don't even know your name.' She addressed the animal as if he was a person and might actually answer.

'Samson,' Grace piped up. 'His name is Samson.'

'Perfect.' Somehow in the last twenty minutes, or however long it had been since the memory had forced its way so bru-tally into her consciousness, the tension inside her had eased. It was there, hovering in the shadows, but focusing on the horse's strong, solid presence and the repetitive motion of the grooming had brought her out of her head and back to the present. Back to herself.

'You two have stolen my thunder.' Mitch walked over and joined them. 'The next task I was going to give you was doing a grooming session together, but it looks like you already have that under control.'

'So what else can we do?' Grace was absolutely glowing.

Had she actually grown in the last half-hour?

'Well, if you both feel up to it …' He looked at Tess, waited for her nod. 'I've set up an obstacle course at the end of the arena. The idea is for the two of you to work together with one of the horses, guiding them through the poles and around the cones.'

'That's easy.' Grace moved off towards the course, a series of parallel poles set out in formation, two orange witch's hats at the farthest end.

'Not so fast.' Mitch took a step forward to block her path. 'There's a catch. Two, in fact. First catch is you can't use a lead rope or head stall, the horse will be at liberty.'

Grace squinted at Mitch, then back at the two horses who were both completely chilled, heads turned towards the human trio, as if they too were listening to what was required.

'And the second catch?' Although Tess was still a little shaky, she wasn't going to let Grace down. Not having a lead rope could be a challenge, but you could always grab them by the neck and push them around if worse came to worst.

He smirked, as if he'd read her mind. 'You can't touch the horses. And you can't communicate verbally with each other.'

Wasn't improving communication the whole point of Grace and her being here together? And now he was telling them *not* to talk.

'Can we use our hands and stuff?' The cogs in Grace's mind were ticking over. Tess could practically see them spinning.

'Hands, bodies, you can use the carrot sticks—those orange sticks with the strings on them—to direct them, too. But the idea is that you work with each other to get the horses to where you want them to be, which is on the other side of those cones.'

How hard could it be to get a horse to walk over and through a few poles?

'Can we start with Whisky?' Grace was obviously not daunted by the challenge.

'So, do we lead her up there to the starting point, like grab her by the neck or something?'

Mitch gave his trademark smartarse grin. 'Start from where you are, doing it the way I outlined.' He walked back to the other side of the arena and hoisted himself up to sit on the fence, his dusty boots resting against the bottom rail, arms folded.

Tess sighed. They were on their own. 'Looks like it's just you and me, kid.'

Grace pivoted on one foot to face Whisky. She meant business. Eyeballing the horse, she started off and took a few steps before looking back. Whisky snorted, standing her ground. Unperturbed, Grace walked to the side of the mare, raised her hands and began to wave them in the air. It was met with a slight turn of the head and shuffling of feet but nothing more.

This was supposed to be a team effort, yet Tess was stumped.

In previous sessions, when she'd observed rather than participated, the horse had begun to follow Grace after the grooming. Maybe she just wanted some TLC before being ordered around. 'How about—'

Grace pressed a finger to her lips.

Oh yeah, no talking. She reached down and picked up the two brushes, and walked over to the horse, wriggling her eyebrows at Grace. They worked together, grooming Whisky in the same way they'd done with Samson, taking their time. Being quiet and slow around the horses really did have a languid effect on both groomer and horse. After what must have been a good ten minutes, Grace angled her head towards the other end of the arena, pointed at Tess and then at the horse's rump. She was actually taking charge, working out how to get the nag to move!

Tess raised one arm, directing from behind. Somewhere, sometime she'd heard that horses had excellent peripheral vision, so hopefully Whisky would respond. She kept urging the horse forward and then, as if it had been her idea all along, the mare took one step and then another until she was following Grace to the other end of the arena. Stopping on the right-hand side of the poles, Grace lifted an arm to block Whisky from walking too far. The mare stopped in front of the parallel poles laid out on the ground and Tess positioned herself on the other side. Carrot stick in hand, Grace walked back a little and swung the string at the horse's backside without letting it connect. Unfazed, Whisky ambled through the poles. Tess ran to where they formed an L shape and blocked the exit, directing the horse around the corner. Grace bobbed up and down, bubbling with excitement, her hands scrunched into fists as if she was jumping a skipping rope.

Tess stifled a shriek. No point in breaking the rules now. There were a few more poles to work around, but they were almost there. Bit by bit they guided Whisky over the rest of the course, keeping each other in sight, signalling with hand gestures and body movements and finally getting her across the finish line between the orange cones.

'Yay!' Grace shouted. 'We did it, we did it.' She ran across and threw her arms around Tess's waist, holding tight.

Tess pulled her in, squeezing back just as hard, breathing in the absolute triumph of the moment. The rancid odour lurking in her memory receded as she rested her cheek on Grace's head. All she could smell was the peachy scent of freshly washed hair, the primal smell of horse and the unexpected, intoxicating scent of happiness.

By the time they turned to head back to the stables, a wave of exhaustion enveloped Tess, the excitement of working with Grace and her earlier unanticipated reaction to Samson drowning her in a backwash of emotional fatigue.

She collapsed into the chair beside Grace.

'You both did brilliantly out there.' Max was full of praise, with no mention of Tess's meltdown.

'I know! How good were we?' Grace was so puffed up with pride she was in danger of exploding.

Tess leaned sideways and bumped her shoulder against Grace's. 'You were amazing. Thank you for showing me what to do.'

'How did you find the experience, Tess?' Mitch drew her attention back to the circle. 'Is there anything you want to talk about?'

Dissecting her reaction was not something she could do right now.

'No.' She shook her head. 'No. I'm just happy that we got to work together.'

'Can we do it again next time?' Grace chirped.

'If you want to do another session together,' Mitch paused, watching for her reaction. She gave an ever-so-slight nod of her head. As difficult as it had been, there was also something liberating about the process, like a valve inside her chest had been opened and half a lifetime of pent-up emotion had been released. 'There are a few great trust and team-building exercises we could do, to expand on what you did today.'

Grace turned to her. 'Can we?'

There was no way Tess could deny the obvious bonding that had taken place between the two of them. Coming back and working together would be good for them both. And in the meantime, she could work on her own issues in private. She smiled. 'That would be great.'

Mitch nodded, but the narrowing of his eyes and the straight, thin line of his mouth made it clear he wasn't completely convinced.

Country quiet was so different to city quiet. In Sydney, even when she'd lived in the depths of suburbia, there was always some kind of noise—a pimped-up 1975 Torana doing a burnout at the traffic lights, a Qantas jumbo thundering through the clouds when surely it must be past curfew, a dog yapping at a guy in fluoro lycra squeezing in a late-night jog. Living in Surry Hills, Tess had heard all this and much, much more. But out here, it wasn't the noise that kept her awake. It was the silence. The ear-ringing, deafening quiet of living kilometres away from other people, away from roads and cars, away from any form of actual civilisation.

The kind of quiet that leaves the mind spinning.

Grace was sound asleep in her mother's bed, no frown lines creasing her brow, no restless tossing and turning. She looked so peaceful there was almost a hint of a smile on her slightly opened mouth. Tess leaned down and brushed a whisper of a kiss to the girl's forehead. She'd done so well today, been so proud of herself the way she led that horse through the obstacle course. She'd raced inside to fill in her journal as soon as they got back, then devoured her dinner and crashed out not long after.

The little black book was sitting right there beside the bed, begging to be flipped open. Tess pushed the pads of her joined index fingers against her lips. *So tempting.* A quick peek is all it would take to find out what was in Grace's head. But that would be an act of betrayal. No, she'd wait for Grace to read it to her at the next session or share it with her beforehand if that's what she chose.

'Are you going to write in yours?' Tess had been preparing dinner when Grace had thrown her the question. She'd given her a quick reply, an easy way to delay contemplating the answer. 'Maybe later.'

Now, it was later. Nine pm.

She ran the tip of her index finger over the embossed head of the horse on the cover. A series of curved lines formed the mane, a few shorter strokes outlining the face. Everything about the day had been so tactile—the brushing of that plush, warm coat, the unmistakeable thumping of Samson's heart beneath her splayed hand. So surprising and yet so comforting.

The rush of memories really wasn't so unexpected. Ever since the day the letter had arrived about Grace—about Skye—they'd started surfacing, like pieces of flotsam and jetsam washing in on the tide of her past. Being here in Skye's home, around her belongings, her daughter; finding the photocopy about Harrison and then those confronting images in the shed. All of it had dredged up her deepest fears, her darkest secret. Working with the horse had forced her to face them, once and for all.

A piercing pain stabbed at the space behind her temples. She couldn't talk about them after the session, not in front of Grace, but they needed to be dealt with or they'd only come back louder and stronger and more insistent than ever. She'd spent the last twenty years storing them away in the junkyard of her brain, but if she was going to be any sort of mother to Grace—if they were going to continue the progress they'd started to make—her own issues had to be sorted. Embers glowed in the pot-belly, but a thin film of ice had settled beneath her skin. She threaded her arms through the chunky wool sleeves of her cardigan as she took one more glance at Grace. Still sleeping peacefully. Lifting the chair so as not to disturb the quiet, Tess moved it over to the table and opened the journal, picked up a pen and began.

It was a Friday. Aunty Jean was away for the weekend visiting friends in Woy Woy, so I was sleeping over to keep Skye company. We were both fifteen, in Year Ten at school, and even though we were in different classes we still hung out on the weekends and walked home together every day.

When I thought about it later, the way she'd gripped my arm and pleaded with me to come for a sleepover, she'd almost begged. I laughed at her. Said it wasn't a big deal and of course I would, but I didn't think any more about why she was so frantic. It was only later I realised why.

We called by my house to pick up clothes and demolished a batch of choc-chip cookies Mum had baked for afternoon tea. When we arrived at Skye's he was on his way out. He'd been staying for a couple of weeks. He gave us this weird smile and said something like, 'I'll be out late tonight, don't wait up.' Skye didn't even look at him, but I heard her mumble under her breath, 'Fat chance.' I'd asked her about him a while before, when he'd first arrived, and she'd said he was her uncle, the black sheep of the family, whom her gran only tolerated even though he was her son. He was staying for a while after coming back from overseas.

We had frozen pizza, watched a few movies and went to bed around midnight. I was in the spare bed in her room, like always. Usually we'd talk for hours, but she said she was tired. I was kind of mad with her. She'd been acting strange all night, hardly saying a word. Made me wonder why she'd even invited me in the first place, but I didn't say anything. There was a tap dripping in the bathroom and I listened to the drip, drip, drip *as I went off to sleep.*

Sometime later a noise woke me up. At first everything was fuzzy. The room was dark, but there was a crack of light. When we'd gone to bed Skye had stared down the hallway and then closed the door, rattling the handle as if she was testing it was shut. I asked her what she was doing, but she didn't answer. Once my eyes adjusted, I rolled over and looked across to Skye's bed. I couldn't see her. All I could see was a dark shape, a figure, and then I heard those horrible noises he was making and straightaway I knew what was happening. I was too scared to even blink. My eyes began to sting. His hand was over her mouth and he was grunting like a pig. Did he think I wouldn't hear? Wouldn't wake up? Or did he just not care? I wanted to yell at him to stop, but the words were like bricks cemented in the column of my throat. Inside my head, I screamed at him to leave her alone. Only one word came out, in a strangled kind of moan. Stop.

He climbed off the bed and stood up. I knew without being able to see that he was looking right at me.

Hot tears welled in her eyes. The pen froze in her hand. This was as far as she'd ever let herself remember. If she didn't exorcise the rest of the memory now, would she ever be able to accept what she'd done and move on? From the far corner of the room, Grace rolled over and sighed. It was the push she needed to continue.

I squeezed my eyes shut, willing him to go away, hoping that this was some sort of horrible nightmare. I rolled myself into a ball, trying to make myself smaller, but then his mouth was on my cheek. The pillow ballooned around my face. His nicotine fingers were in my hair. A rough whisper scraped against my ear. So pretty. Such silky hair. I'd like a taste of you. *I whimpered, like a dog tied up on a chain, his hands pushing against my shoulders. He yanked my hair so hard my scalp burned.*

My eyes sprang open. He dragged the blankets away, crushing me beneath his weight. He pushed his filthy mouth against mine so I couldn't get any air, forcing his tongue so far into my mouth I gagged. He pushed my nightie up my body, lifting himself up somehow on an elbow while he pulled at my underpants. And then ... then he shoved his rough, filthy finger inside me, the friction burning as he moved against my body.

Nice and fresh, *he hissed.* Unspoilt.

The strange metallic sound of Skye's voice. Leave her alone.

He laughed and I learned what it means for your blood to run cold.

Leave her alone. I'll do whatever you want. *Skye's voice, barely more than a whimper.*

His body stilled. Sandpaper stubble scraped against my cheekbone as he turned his head. Well that's an offer too good to refuse. I'll save it for another night. When I've got you to myself.

He pushed himself upright. Pressed his foot against my stomach. You're off the hook, *he said,* but I know where you live, and if you tell anyone about our little secret I'll come through your window one night and you'll get the same thing she does before I slit your throats and bury you both where no one will ever find you.

Air rushed into my lungs. I wanted to be sick. I wanted to vomit. I wanted to run.

The sound of a zip. A belt buckling up. And then he was gone.

I shivered uncontrollably beneath the sheets, bile in my throat, a spasm in my gut as if he was still standing there with the heel of his boot against my middle. Everything hurt from trying so hard to disappear. I swallowed hard, covered my mouth with my hands and opened my eyes.

He was gone.

But Skye ...

My mind lurched to what he'd done to her. I pushed myself upright and peered across to her bed. She wasn't moving. I whispered her name. No reply. Skye. Please talk to me. Tell me if you're okay. *I sniffed, my face a mess of tears and snot.*

Go to sleep, *she said,* don't talk or he'll come back. *That same dead tone in her voice as before. She said it like she knew.* Go to sleep.

She rolled away from me and I lay there in the darkness, his voice in my ear.

I know where you live, I know where you live, I know where you live.

Tess dropped the pen to the table and stared down at the scrawl on the pages. Small patches of the paper were wrinkled, some of the words smudged. She swiped at her cheek. All this time she'd never cried, never thought about it long enough to let herself, but now the tears wouldn't stop. There was still more to write. The day after the night before.

I didn't stay for breakfast. Even though my stomach was empty, I felt too sick to eat. Skye wouldn't speak. She said she wanted to be alone, but she walked part of the way home with me. We stopped walking outside Mrs Lennon's house and the perfume of the roses made me feel worse. My eyelids were so sore. I'd made myself stay awake, in case the door opened again, the echo of his voice burrowing in my brain like a parasite.

Skye was white, transparent. More ghost than girl. Please, Tess, please promise you won't say anything.

What I wanted to say was stuck somewhere between my brain and my mouth. Not telling was wrong. I dropped to my knees and fell across the top of the fence, heaving into the dirt.

I lay my cheek against the cool concrete. I'd walked along this fence when I was younger, practising my balance, one foot in front of the other like a high-wire acrobat. I so badly wanted to be that little girl again. Couldn't we just go back in time and forget everything about last night?

Say a thing and I'll kill you both.

His stinking breath still lingered in my nostrils.

His rasping voice still vibrated through every cell of my body.

The feel of his hand between my legs, his fingers pushing inside me, still scalded.

I forced myself upright. Skye stared directly into my eyes, repeating her question without saying a word.

Okay. *I drew an X across my heart the way we used to when we were little. All those years ago.* I promise.

Every breath of air seemed to leave Skye's body. And we'll never, ever talk about it again, *she said.*

I watched a bull ant drag a struggling moth along the concrete fence. Not telling would be safer for us both. And if we didn't talk about it, it would be like it never happened, wouldn't it?

Skye waited at the corner while I walked the rest of the way home, but when I reached our driveway and turned around to wave goodbye she was already gone.

The convulsing in her stomach was sharp and insistent. She dropped the pen, bolted to the sink, knocking over the chair, the wooden legs clamouring against the floorboards. Over and over again she vomited, her chest on fire, her shoulders jarring, sweat beading her forehead, until she was completely and utterly spent. She kept her eyes closed for a minute before she turned on the tap, slurped in a mouthful of water and spat it back into the sink. She splashed her face and wiped her chin with the back of her hand before turning off the tap and inhaling a long, slow breath. Although her body was still shaking, the worst of it was over.

One careful step at a time she returned to the table and righted the chair, holding onto the frame for support. She'd made such a noise, yet somehow Grace was still sleeping, her long curls floating out across the pillow.

Behind her was the wardrobe.

Inside the wardrobe was the box.

And in the box, the envelope and the newspaper clippings.

He has a daughter.

The man who had violated her best friend—multiple times, Tess knew without having to be told—was alive and living in Melbourne, passing himself off as a pillar of the community, a bastion of family values. Somehow Skye had found out about him, about his life. What had she been planning to do with the information? She'd come all the way out here so he would never find her. Had turned her life inside out to protect her child.

Those images in the shed: Skye had painted her pain and literally locked it away.

All these years Tess had gagged and bound herself so tightly she'd stayed silent even when she'd known her friend was in danger. It had been so convenient to convince herself she was just keeping a promise. But that was a lie. An excuse. She'd been a coward. Too afraid to tell anyone what had happened that night in case he made good on his threat, sleeping with a night light like a three-year-old all these years because she was too afraid to open her eyes in the dark.

Never in all this time had she allowed herself to think about what Skye's words that night had meant: *I'll do whatever you want*. The sacrifice her friend had made to save Tess suffering in the same way.

Now Skye was gone. Possibly had taken her own life because of him and without ever getting justice for what he'd done to her—what he could have done to other girls, what he could still do to girls like his own daughter. Like Grace.

Blood ran hot through her veins. If he thought he was going to get away with passing himself off as someone who deserved a seat in government he was oh so wrong. The only place he was worthy of was a jail cell.

She took one last look at Grace as she walked around the end of the bed. So like her mother, even in sleep. Reaching up, she retrieved the key from its hiding place on the top of the wardrobe and with one flick of the wrist she opened the door, removed the box and headed back to the kitchen. Finally, she was going to make things right.

Twenty-one

She slid the photocopied article onto the table, ironing it out with the heel of her hand. One by one she pulled the other documents out of the envelope. More copies of news stories detailing Harrison's business dealings, wins in local politics and his aspirations of being elected to state parliament. The photos were a joke. So believable in his smart suits, holding his wife's hand in one photo, his daughter's in another. God, how it must have repulsed Skye to see these images, to read what a success he'd made of himself while she'd spent her life dodging his shadow.

How was it possible for such a predator to hide who he really was?

A violent trembling started up in her legs and she lowered herself into the chair as the answer came to her unbidden. Whatever it was inside her that was her actual self—her being, her soul—shrivelled up into an embryo. She waited. A second, a minute, an hour, however long it took for it to uncoil, poking its finger into the bony centre of her chest.

The only thing necessary for the triumph of evil is for good men to do nothing.

Those well-known words she'd first heard in her senior history class came back to her now with a much more personal resonance. She had done nothing. Harrison had gotten away with his evil because she had done nothing, because Skye did nothing. He'd bullied them into silence and they'd complied.

Pins pricked at her scalp as the two brief conversations she'd ever had with Skye about that night played themselves back. The very next day, paralysed by her own fear, how easy it had been to say yes to Skye's request. Even at Jean's funeral when Skye had begged her to take care of Grace, how convenient it had been to agree once more then walk back into her neat, organised life and not think about it again. To act like it had never happened.

But Skye could never forget. And here was the proof.

Tess reached inside the envelope and unfolded a multi-page document, the hitch of her breath echoing in the eerie quiet of the cottage. She flicked through the pages, then turned back to the front, her eyes zeroing in on the typed heading at the top. *NSW Police Force*, and underneath, *Statement of Witness. Skye Whittaker.* And right there in typed print the name of the man she was accusing of sexual assault.

Neil Harrison.

So, Skye *had* been to the police. The date recorded on the top right-hand side of the page was 28 April 2018, just two months before her death. Tess skimmed the rest of the page, registering the multiple assaults recorded, not just during those months, but during three other time periods when Harrison had stayed at the house.

The way-too-familiar taste of bile filled her throat.

So Skye actually had reported the bastard. Had he been arrested? There was only one way to find out. The statement had been given at Weerilla Police Station and it was signed by a Constable Turner.

Tess glanced at the clock through bleary eyes. Nothing could be done now, and as much as she didn't want to wrangle the beast of sleep, she needed to get some rest. She folded the papers back up and placed them in the envelope, taking it into the bedroom with her and leaving it on the bedside table. Her boots had been discarded hours ago, but right now she didn't have the energy to change. She climbed under the doona fully clothed and stared at the stars stuck to the ceiling, keeping her mind fixed on them, counting them over and over. Wishes that would never come true.

The last time she'd been in a police station was in her first year of uni when she'd been rounded up with the rest of the crew for being drunk and disorderly on the streets of Newtown. They'd been thrown into a cell to sleep it off. It had reeked of disinfectant, certainly less nauseating than it had smelled after her friend—what was her name again?—had puked all over the floor. None of it quite as frightening as her mother's meltdown when she'd come to collect her. Luckily, this station in Weerilla bore absolutely no resemblance to that inner-city lock-up. It was more like something from the set of an iconic Australian movie: a red brick house complete with a huge bare-branched tree in the front yard and daffodils about to burst into flower along the regency-green timber fence. If it wasn't for the electric-blue 'police' sign above the window, she would have walked right on past.

She stood on the street side of the rusty gate, the envelope in her hand feeling more like a ball and chain than a few sheets of paper. Once she stepped through this gate, walked through the door and up to the counter, she would be saying words she had vowed never to utter. But Skye had taken the leap, freeing her from her promise. It was time for the adult Tess to find the courage her scared, cowardly teenage self had so sorely lacked.

The hinges moaned as she swung open the gate. Five short steps to the porch; two more to the door. She held her breath just long enough to give her the extra push she needed to step inside. A bell chimed, announcing her entrance, and then there she was, standing at the counter.

'Hello there, what can I do for you?' A cheery middle-aged, uniformed officer appeared before her. She glanced at his name badge and her stomach did a quick flip. Constable Brad Turner.

'Um ... I ...' She'd rehearsed this over and over on the drive into town: *Start with the statement.* She lifted the tab on the envelope and slid out the copy, held it gingerly between her fingers. It quivered like an autumn leaf on the brink of falling. 'I'm here about an assault.'

The policeman frowned. 'You've been assaulted?'

'No.' She pressed her thumbs against the paper to steady her grip. 'I was a witness to an assault.' Why was she pussy-footing around? Why not say it straight, use the label she'd avoided even thinking for all these years. 'A rape.'

The officer straightened his shoulders, his smile fading. Tess handed him the papers. He studied them closely before looking up again, rubbing his free hand over his bearded chin. 'Where did you get this?'

'I'm a friend of Skye Whittaker's. Her daughter's guardian. I'm staying at her house, with Grace, and I came across this in some of her papers.' It sounded so lame, like she was handing over a shopping list she'd picked up off the floor.

'Right.' He drew out the word, over-emphasised the T. 'But Ms Whittaker is dead, so unfortunately any investigation based on this statement is now null and void.' He folded the papers and held them out towards Tess. 'And in any case, it's confidential, so I'm afraid I can't discuss it with you.'

This was it. Her time to speak up. To not do nothing. 'I was there.' She forced the words out, made sure she was speaking loudly, clearly, emphatically. 'I was there when it happened, well, at least one of the nights that it happened, and he threatened me, told me if I ever said a word to anyone he'd come back for me.' She had to get the words out before they disappeared. 'I promised Skye I wouldn't tell anyone. I should have said something, but I was too scared. We were only fifteen and he was, he was ...'

'I see.' Constable Turner withdrew his hand from where it hovered midair, holding the papers he'd tried to return. He placed them on the desk in front of him. 'In that case, you'd better come in and tell me exactly what happened.'

Telling the story out loud was even harder than she'd imagined. Constable Turner sat opposite, elbows resting on the table, shoulders hunched as he wrote down—and recorded—everything she said. He was sympathetic, almost fatherly, without any sign of cynicism or disbelief. Relaying the events of the night wasn't even the worst part. It was admitting her silence that left her winded. But he assured her the story was a common one: victims of assault—and he told her she was one, too, even though her own suffering could never be compared to Skye's—stayed quiet for many reasons, not least the fear of retribution. Was she worried about that now? he asked, and she thought about the answer long and hard before honestly saying she wasn't. For the first time in her life, it wasn't her own skin she wanted to save. What she wanted now was justice for Skye and protection for other young women—like Harrison's own daughter.

Like Grace.

By the time she pulled up outside Jules's place, her limbs were leaden, her head pounding. She checked her watch. Jules hadn't batted an eyelid when they'd shown up and Tess had asked her to mind Grace for an hour or two. She had just given that big, broad smile and placed an arm around Grace's shoulder. It was good to have people here who genuinely cared. Jules, Mitch, Max ... she'd never expected that when she'd landed in Weerilla those few short weeks ago.

Out back, Erin was in the studio, moulding a lump of clay on a potter's wheel. Grace looked on wide-eyed, her face filled with wonder, so entranced she didn't even notice Tess's arrival. Jules must be somewhere inside.

She ducked her head through the door of the main house. 'Anyone home?'

Footsteps sounded in the hallway and then Jules appeared, looking over the top of the glasses precariously perched on the end of her nose. It was a good thing she had them attached to that string around her neck. 'Come in, come in. I'll put the kettle on.'

'Large and strong.' Tess dropped her bag to the floor and collapsed into a chair.

Jules joined her at the table as the whir of the kettle started up on the bench. 'I don't know what they're doing out there at Affinity, but I could barely shut Gracie up today. She was showing me her drawings of the horses, telling me about her favourite one. Whisky?'

Tess nodded. The initial changes she'd seen in Grace had been almost imperceptible—a quicker bounce in her step, a brighter gleam in her eyes—but since their last session, the one they'd done together, the turnaround had been more obvious. 'I know, it's amazing. It's like she's a different kid.'

'Not different. More like herself.' Jules stood again and went about the business of making coffee, depositing Tess's order and sitting back down.

It was a good distinction. Tess picked up the cup, closed her eyes and let the hot liquid slide down her throat. 'Oh my God, what is that? It's divine.'

'Isn't it?' Jules held her cup between her palms, close to her face, the steam curling like a trail of smoke from a genie's lamp. Her laugh was almost a giggle. 'You won't believe what it's called.'

Tess took another sip. 'Try me.'

'Dark Horse.'

'No way.'

Jules drew an imaginary cross over her heart.

Tess let her gaze fall to the black surface of the coffee. It was all too much. The heart. The dark horse: the one who keeps their truth hidden, the one not expected to win. It was the phrase used in the newspaper article to describe Harrison's run for state government. Well, he certainly had something surprising headed his way, and she needed—no, *wanted*—to share the news. She inhaled as she looked up at Jules. 'I've just come from the police station. I was making a statement.'

'Statement?' Jules was studying her like an abstract art-work on a gallery wall. 'About what?'

'A sexual assault that happened twenty years ago.'

Jules sat up straighter, her brows furrowing.

'It happened to Skye and I was there. I was assaulted, too.'

Detail by sordid detail Tess relayed the whole story, telling it again exactly the same way she'd told the constable. 'It feels like I've been holding my breath all these years. I can only imagine what a relief it must have been for Skye to make her statement.'

Jules's mouth fell open. 'You never told your parents?'

She shook her head, the tightness in her chest momentarily returning. That was still a mystery she didn't fully understand.

'And Skye went to the police before she died?' Jules was piecing the puzzle together, trying to make sense of it all. 'This man, Harrison, he would have been told about her accusations?'

'Yep. But he was also notified that she'd died. He'd presume there was no one to give evidence against him.'

Jules's eyes sparked like flint as she nodded. 'But now there is. So even though it's all those years ago, they can still make it stick?'

'According to the police officer, the statement Skye gave won't be enough since she's no longer here, but my accusations should at least get him investigated.'

'That won't be too good for his political aspirations.'

'It certainly won't. The smug prick won't know what's hit him when the detectives knock on his door. Again. It'll be like groundhog day. He managed to keep it quiet the first time around, but that won't be happening again. I have an old uni mate in Melbourne who's a journo. I'm pretty sure she'll be happy to splash it across the front page of the *Melbourne Herald*.'

Mental note: give Petra a call.

Jules reached across the table and took her hand. 'This man sounds like he could be dangerous. If you don't feel comfortable out there while this is all going on, you and Grace are welcome to stay with me.'

'Thanks, Jules, but it's all good. He's in Melbourne. There's no way he could track me down all the way out here. Once it's all put into motion, I may have to go there and testify, but that's a while down the track.'

'Well, the offer's open if you change your mind.' The sound of laughter trickled into the kitchen from the studio outside. Jules turned towards the noise and then back again. 'It's a brave thing you're doing, for your friend and yourself.'

Tess rubbed at her collarbone, her fingers scratching against the woollen neckband of her jumper. She went to stand but then froze. 'You know, if Skye had found the courage to go to the police it doesn't make sense that she would have killed herself. Wouldn't she want to see it through? Make sure the mongrel got what he deserved?'

'I would have thought so.'

Skye's suicide was still unfathomable. 'Unless the pressure got too much.' The whispers in her ear came from nowhere. His reptilian voice, his insidious threats. She'd heard them only once in reality but over and over again in her mind. How many times had he uttered them to buy Skye's silence? How many times must she have replayed them over the years as she'd tried to get on with her life? Perhaps, in the end, it had all been too much. 'I just wish I'd been there for her. Helped her.' She hung her head, unable to meet Jules's eyes.

'You're helping her now, doing what you're doing. Looking after her daughter.'

The back door swung open and Grace burst inside.

Tess coughed and pasted on a smile. Jules was right, she was doing what she could.

Even if it was too little, too late.

Twenty-two

Rain battered at the window panes. The day was wild and wet. Perfect for staying indoors. While Grace pored over her school work, Tess kept herself busy cleaning. It had been over a week since her visit to the police station and she'd scrubbed the place from top to bottom. Her fingers itched to pick up the phone and call the constable for an update, but he'd assured her things would take time, promised to keep her in the loop. Except there had been news of a different kind via the newspapers. She stared at the black screen of her iPad resting on the kitchen sink. She already could recite the article word for word. Clutching the dishcloth, she willed away the sweet taste of victory the words elicited, the sensation like a craving she needed to satisfy.

A quick tap on the tablet and there it was again. '*State Senate Hopeful Neil Harrison Questioned by Police.*' Good old Petra had grabbed the story and bolted like a racehorse. '*Toorak businessman and Senate hopeful Neil Harrison is being questioned by police in relation to a number of sexual assaults. According to sources, the victims included a member of Harrison's own family who was coerced into keeping quiet. Harrison, a married father of two, has denied the allegations. Police are continuing to investigate the case.'*

Her heart stuttered for the zillionth time as she stared down at the report. So matter-of-fact. There were no names mentioned, but of course Harrison would have been told who had made the additional accusations. Would he even remember her? Remember that night? There'd only been that one time with the two of them in the room. Had he been bluffing when he said he knew where she lived? Or had he followed her home before that day without her knowing?

She glanced over at Grace, the tip of her tongue poking between her lips as she concentrated on her maths problem, oblivious to the whole horrible story. Making the statement had been the right thing to do. For all three of them.

The door rattled as a thump sounded from outside. Tess dropped the iPad to the bench. She hadn't heard a car, but the way the wind was howling that was no surprise.

Grace jumped to her feet. 'I'll get it.'

'No.' Making the statement had been a risk, but one worth taking if it meant keeping Grace safe in the long term. For the short term it put Tess on alert.

Grace shrugged and lowered herself back into her chair.

Another knock, louder this time, longer.

'Okay, I'm coming.' It was probably Jules, out and about and up for a chat. Her fingers wrapped around the doorknob. She sucked in a quick mouthful of air and pulled.

'Josh!' Was she hallucinating? He was standing right there on the porch, brown leather bomber jacket zipped up to his neck, jigging around like he needed the bathroom. 'What are you doing here?'

'Nice to see you, too.' His expression was deadpan, but there was a quirk to his lips. 'Are you going to let me in? It's fucking freezing out here.'

'Oh, of course. Sorry.' She moved aside and he shuffled in, blowing on his knuckles and rubbing his hands together. The cottage was warm and cosy, a complete contrast to the blustering weather outside.

He scanned the room as he leaned in to give her a kiss. 'Nice place.'

'We like it.' He stepped towards the fireplace and raised his palms towards the radiant heat. Dark denim jeans, boots the exact colour of his jacket, a navy scarf tossed casually around his neck. His hair, mussed a little by the wind, was styled differently to when she'd last seen him, longer on top but still perfectly combed. His cheeks were a ruddy pink against the olive tan of his face, the colour no doubt acquired on his European business trip. He looked good, like he'd just stepped out of a menswear catalogue. She waited for the tingling sensation the sight of him usually evoked, but there was nothing. Absence was supposed to make the heart grow fonder, wasn't it?

Grace rose from her chair and crept into the main living area.

Josh turned towards her. 'Hi, Grace. Good to see you.'

Grace's mouth twitched in response, though no words came out.

Josh turned back, mumbling, 'Nothing's changed, I see.'

God, he could be a spoilt brat sometimes. If only he knew. 'Coffee?'

He pulled a face.

'Oh yeah, you're a tea man.' His refusal to share in her love of the finer brew had always irked her. She moved past him into the kitchen, ignoring the way his eyes followed her, like he was trying to work something out.

Grace gathered her books and zipped up her pencil case. 'I'm going to my room to read.' She scooted past Josh like a mouse scurrying past a prowling cat and disappeared around the corner into her bedroom. Technically, it had become Tess's bedroom since Grace had elected to sleep in her mother's bed, but if she was more comfortable in there it was fine.

'So, how's it all going?' Josh took a seat while she organised the cups.

'Pretty good. And you?'

'More than good.' He nodded deliberately. 'I'll fill you in about that in a minute. Tell me what you've been doing.'

Where would she start? They'd had a few phone conversations since he'd come home but both had steered clear of anything vaguely difficult. She'd reported in briefly on Grace's progress without giving any details. He'd raved about his trip and promised to visit when he'd caught up on his workload.

She filled the two cups, overshooting on the second and splashing her thumb with the boiling water. 'Bugger.' She reached for the tap and let the cooler stream wash over the burn.

'You okay?'

She nodded. This was all so strange, having Josh turn up out of the blue. Turning off the tap, she returned to the task at hand. The pad of her thumb throbbed like hell, but she'd live.

It could have been a scene from a television dating show. Cups on the table in front of them. Josh sitting there with his ice-blue eyes. The square, solid line of his shoulders. That sexy dimple she'd always loved in his chin. Lots of small talk yet a distinct absence of chemistry.

'So, what have you been doing with yourself?'

'Not a lot. Getting to know each other, hanging out. Grace has been doing some art classes—and teaching me the piano.' She smiled. In reality, they were learning together. Their 'lessons' were her favourite part of the day. 'And we've been doing some equine-assisted learning, too.' She'd trained herself to use the correct terminology since Mitch's training wasn't classified as therapy and it totally got up his nose if she used the wrong label.

'What?'

She lifted her chin. 'It's a kind of counselling session, with horses.'

Josh's forehead wrinkled into a series of crevices and he gave a kind of snort. Self-reflection had never been his thing. Never been hers, either, until recently.

He laughed. 'You hate horses.'

'Yeah, well, things have changed.'

She stared down into her cup. Things certainly had changed.

'And how's that working out for you?' He was obviously feeling the distance between them, too.

'Really, really well.'

He lowered his head and took a mouthful of tea, running the tip of his tongue over his bottom lip. There was a little-boy-lost look about him. She probably should be slightly more forthcoming, try a bit harder. 'It's helped break down the barriers, brought us closer.'

'Maybe I should come along sometime.' He still wasn't meeting her gaze and his tone was unsure rather than wry.

Wind screeched around the corners of the house. A log broke in two and collapsed inside the grate. A long, heavy silence fell between them. Her heart was beating so hard she could feel it pounding through the wall of her chest. She should say something, take him up on his invitation, but she was suddenly, inexplicably protective of her relationship with Grace.

'And Europe? How was it?'

'Like I said on the phone, it was awesome.' He paused again. 'Missed you, though.'

'You didn't look too forlorn in your Facebook photos.' *Ouch.* She'd meant it as a joke, but that wasn't how it sounded.

'Well, I wasn't going to sit in my hotel pining.'

And now it started, the same old back-and-forth sniping that inevitably ended up with them kicking and screaming their way to the bedroom. Time to damp it down. 'Sorry.' She shook her head. 'I'm glad you had a good time. Did the business stuff go okay?'

The question seemed to temper the simmering anger in his eyes. 'Very well. In fact … that's what I came here to talk to you about.'

His hesitant manner started her alarm bells ringing. Usually he was so cool, so sure of himself, but the way he kept shifting in the chair and peering into his cup had her worried. If he had something to say, why didn't he just come out and say it? She folded her arms and waited.

'I know things weren't great between us when I left.'

That was an understatement.

He lifted a hand, palm upturned, then let it fall. 'I've been offered a job in Brussels. A two-year contract doing programs for an international software company, the place I've been doing the project for.'

Brussels? 'Don't you like working for yourself?'

'I do.' He shifted the chair around and rested his elbows on his knees, suddenly alive. 'But this is a fantastic opportunity.

It would put me in touch with businesses all around the world, the connections would be phenomenal. And the package they're offering is mind-blowing. Full rent, car, travel expenses. We could go anywhere we wanted in Europe for next to nothing.'

She peered at him. 'We?'

'Yes, we. I want you to come with me.'

'Hang on, let's rewind. The last time I saw you, you said you didn't know what you wanted.' Had he meant Grace or them? Either way, he'd been unsure.

He sat back and rested his hands on his thighs. 'Look, things happened fast. I felt … I don't know, like the life we were living wasn't the one I'd signed up for.'

And now? Had he considered it more while he'd been away? Changed his mind about being a father?

'It was so weird only talking to you in snatches. Even weirder coming home to an empty apartment. This would be a chance for us to start again. It would be like one big, long holiday. We're always at our best on holidays.'

He was right. They did holidays well: no responsibilities, no work distractions, plenty of sex. But that wasn't real life. Certainly not with a child. A child he hadn't mentioned once in this new life plan.

'What about Grace?' She was in the next room, could probably hear everything they were saying, but it didn't matter. What mattered most was his response.

He gave a half-hearted jerk of his shoulder. 'She could come. If that's what you want.'

'What do you mean if that's what *I* want?'

'You said yourself at the beginning you'd see how it all went before you made a decision one way or the other. So is it what you want? This whole foster-parent thing?'

Tess resisted the urge to pick up her mug and send it spinning across the table. Nothing seemed to have changed for him but for her everything had changed. 'Yes, it is.' She drew in a breath. 'But it's not what you want, is it?'

He shrugged again. 'I can live with it.'

Live with IT? Really? 'Josh, this isn't a rabbit or a budgerigar we're talking about. This is a child.' She lowered her voice. 'I'm all she has. She's already been through so much. Uprooting her and dragging her across to the other side of the world just won't work. She needs stability.' And love.

'What about me?' His face darkened. He stood and threw his hands in the air. 'Doesn't what I want matter?'

And finally, it all made sense. Everything had always been about him. What Josh wanted, what he convinced her she wanted. The flash apartment, the fancy cars, the expensive holidays. Just the two of them. Child-free. Unencumbered. He'd spun her the fairytale and she'd believed every word. Maybe it was what she'd wanted, back then. But things were different now. She had Grace. She had a responsibility to Skye, and more than that, she had a life she'd never imagined, a life she was absolutely loving. There was no one to blame. It was just the way it was.

'The truth is …' As soon as she said the words her marriage would be over, but even knowing that she couldn't stop. 'We just don't want the same things anymore. I don't want to go to Europe, I want stay here, with Grace.'

He had the wild-eyed look of an abandoned kitten. 'I can't live here, Tess. I need to take this job.'

'I know.' Two small, soft syllables signalling the end.

'So, that's it?'

She nodded. The truth was, it had been over weeks ago, the second she had torn open the envelope from FACS, but the cracks had appeared long before. They sat for a minute, not speaking, until finally he stood. 'You've changed, Tess. You're not the person I married.'

He was so right. And she was glad. He meant it as a criticism, but in fact it was probably the highest compliment he could have given her. He'd married someone who was only half functioning, who was shallow and self-centred. The mirror image of himself. Since Skye's death, and being here with Grace, Tess had discovered the part of herself she'd lost that night, the vulnerable self who cared deeply about others, who sometimes even put them first.

The decision was made, and while she knew they'd need to talk more about it, she had said all she could for now. She stood, looked directly into his eyes.

'Is there anything I can say to convince you to come with me?'

She gave a slow shake of her head. He sighed and she remained where she was as he walked to the door, a gust of wind whipping through the lounge room as he opened it and closed it behind him without another word.

Tears coursed silently down her cheeks like raindrops down a windowpane. She brushed them away, and when she dropped her hand, a smaller one held it gently.

'Hey there.' Tess smiled down at the sweet child by her side. There was a good chance she'd overheard the whole thing. 'You okay?'

Grace nodded. 'Are you?'

She sniffed, not really sure. 'Feel like watching a movie?'

'*Enchanted*?'

'Not again?'

'Pleeeease?' Grace hammed it up, clutching her hands together and looking up with eyes like saucers, one stop short of begging.

'You set up the laptop and I'll grab the hot chocolates.'

Grace bounded away, found the computer and set herself up in the bigger bed, making sure the disc they'd hired from the library was inserted and ready to go. It hadn't taken her long to work out how to operate the laptop. Their favourite movie-watching beverage was hot chocolate, tonight with extra marshmallows and sprinkles. Within minutes they were snuggled up under the blankets, wearing milk moustaches and matching grins. Spending a couple of hours cuddling up with her favourite girl wouldn't mend her broken marriage, but it might at least numb the pain.

As the fireworks burst into life over the Disney castle, the aftermath of Josh's visit began to fade, replaced by something indefinable, something solid and warm. Something that felt a lot like home.

And so they all lived happily ever after.

Julie Andrews's parting words as the credits rolled brought her back to reality with a thud. Life was no fairytale, but it had been nice to escape it for a while. And be a kid again along with Grace. The pause midway for toasted sandwiches and milk had been an excellent decision and set them both up for an early night. Tess closed the computer and was about to climb out of bed when Grace sat up. 'You can sleep here if you want.'

The hopeful tone stopped Tess in her tracks. 'As in, we both sleep here?' She pointed at the bed and then each of them in turn. 'Together?'

Grace underlined her nod with a small smile. She dipped her head and picked at some fluff on Toffee's head. Now that Grace was talking, it was nice to know the bear's name. The poor fellow really needed a wash. 'I know you've had a bad day.'

The reference to Josh's visit was impossible to miss and Grace had been witness to the distinct lack of a happy ending. The invitation to share her bed was a way of reaching out. Little by little the walls were coming down.

'Thank you.' Tess wrapped an arm around Grace and drew her close, their foreheads kissing, the fruity fragrance of kids' shampoo a vivid reminder of her own picture-book childhood. Those days had been magical, she really had been the spoilt Disney princess, the only girl, over-indulged by her father and fussed over incessantly by her mother. Was it a plus to live in a bubble like that? Or did it just make it tougher when you realised what a horrible place the world could be?

Reluctantly, she let Grace go. 'We'd better do the teeth thing first. Don't want them being all green and furry in the morning.' She pulled an ugly face and Grace squealed.

'Like caterpillars.'

'Big, fat, hairy ones!'

'Urgh, yuk.'

They raced each other to the bathroom, Grace blocking the door, both arms outstretched, laughing. 'You can't come in, you're gonna have caterpillar teeth.'

'Oh no, I'm not.' Tess reached out with wiggling fingers and tickled her under the arms, refusing to stop until Grace collapsed on the floor in hysterics.

'No, stop, stop. You win. You can come in.'

Tess eased off on the torture. 'You give in so easily.'

A pleasant ache echoed through her chest, along with a louder noise. Was that a knock at the door? She dropped her hands and became instantly quiet, tried to hear over the sound of Grace's rapid breathing as she recovered from her giggling fit and the faint crackle of the fire. The incessant shrieking of the wind drowned out every other noise. Maybe she'd imagined it? No. Grace was staring at the door with possum eyes. She'd heard it, too.

Another round of knocking began, louder this time. Grace's face was blank, but there was fear in her eyes. Tess had shielded her from her visit to the police station, but there was no way of knowing if she'd overheard any of her subsequent conversations with Jules. *Right, Tess, you're the adult, take control.* 'It's okay. I'll see who it is. You go brush your teeth.'

Not a movement.

'Go on.' She pointed in the direction of the bathroom and lightened her tone. 'Otherwise, those hairs might start growing.'

One more slight hesitation and Grace did as she was told.

Who would be knocking at seven-thirty on a night like this? Jules? Unlikely at this time. Apart from her, there wasn't anyone else around here who might make a house call. Not unless it was something urgent, something that couldn't wait. Her shoulders fell as realisation dawned. It was Josh. He'd probably booked somewhere in town to stay the night and was back to try to get her to change her mind. Or couldn't find accommodation and was looking for a bed. The dull headache that had lodged itself behind her eyes when he'd arrived so unexpectedly this afternoon began to throb. She was definitely too tired for another heart-to-heart. She marched to the door and turned the knob.

'Look, Josh ...'

A hand slammed against the door, forcing it open. Tess threw all her effort into pushing back. Her stomach lurched. Standing in front of her was the one man she'd hoped to never see again—unless it was in the courtroom during his sentencing. The same half-bald head as the photo, the short neck and round face, but instead of the fake media smile a flat, straight mouth and purple shadows beneath his blood-shot eyes.

'Expecting someone else?'

The scent of his aftershave blew in with the next gust, hitting her like a slap. Her legs had gone to jelly, but she had to stay upright. She tensed her calves, then her thighs, tightening her diaphragm so that when she spoke she would sound assertive, in control. All in a matter of seconds. 'You're not allowed to be here.'

'Says who?' He kept his hand on the door, equalising the pressure she was applying.

Says no one. She was in the middle of nowhere with not a soul she could call on for help. She was on her own. 'Says me.'

Beneath the film of stubble his jaw hardened. 'Who the fuck do you think you are?'

'Who is it?' Tess turned towards the small voice, her heart stumbling. She spun back around, followed the path of his eye towards the girl standing by the fireplace. A beating of wings started up in her gut, a swarm of locusts jostling for position. 'No one.' Her pitch was too high. She coughed and tried again. 'Go into your room and read for a minute. I'll be there soon.'

'My room? But you said ...'

She gritted her teeth. 'Just go. Now!'

Grace blinked, dropped her chin to her chest and did as she was told.

Tess took in a deep gulp of air and turned back to the man standing in her doorway.

'Cute kid.' He smirked. 'Yours?'

'Yes.'

The slight lift of his eyebrow told her he didn't buy the lie. Grace was the spitting image of her mother. His hand spread against the timber, the fat, stumpy fingers, the manicured nails. Being face to face with him made every millimetre of her flesh feel like it was crawling with maggots. She had to get rid of him. Fast. 'You have no right to be here. You need to leave.'

Crease by crease his frown softened, the lines around his eyes smoothing out so they were barely visible. It was like watching the beast morph into the prince. He angled his head, raised his free hand and flashed a conciliatory smile. 'I'm sure we can work this misunderstanding out. Can I come in so we can talk things through?'

Come in? Was he fucking joking? She had no idea how he'd found her, but if he thought she was going to invite him in for a cuppa and a chat he was seriously deluded. He clearly had something to say, though. Maybe he'd incriminate himself even further if she let him speak. Her arm was aching. She folded her arms and leaned her body against the door for extra support. 'No. You have one minute, so talk fast.'

His smile vanished, and then returned in an instant. 'Look, I'm not sure why Skye made these terrible accusations, but I suspect she had some mental illness and ...'

'Mental illness?'

'Her mother was bipolar, you know, prone to bouts of depression.' He barely disguised a snicker. 'Probably would have killed herself like her daughter did if the cancer didn't get her first.'

'Skye did not kill herself.'

'According to the coroner she did.' His smile made her want to be sick. 'Amazing what you can find out when you have the right contacts. My friends in the Victorian Police have come in very handy.'

The same friends who had no doubt accessed the files and advised him of her whereabouts. 'Even if she did, it doesn't change what she told the police.'

'She was a mentally ill single mother living like some *Deliverance* hillbilly. Do you think a court is going to take her word against that of a highly respected businessman about to be voted into government?'

Pins and needles numbed her hand, yet still she was not letting go of the door. He thought he'd won, but she still had cards of her own to play. 'It's not just her word, though, is it?' Her gut twisted. She'd wanted a showdown, but had planned on it being in a courtroom, in public. 'Skye was your victim and I was a witness.'

'Victim.' He spat out the word like a rancid piece of meat. 'Victim of an overactive imagination is about all.'

'So that's your tactic, is it?' His arrogance was making her bold. 'Denial? Blame the poor, mentally ill recluse who dreamed up the whole thing.'

'Got it in one.'

'And what about me? My testimony.' Keeping her voice even was a struggle. 'What you did to me.' Would he even remember or know what she was referring to?

'Easy.' He shrugged. 'Loyal—and equally deluded woman—trying to salvage what's left of her dead friend's reputation.' He licked his lips. 'And if it does go to court, when I get off—and I will—just remember I know where you live now.' He leaned forward, whispering. 'Where the kid lives.'

Her scalp prickled. Her blood sizzled. She dropped her arms, fists clenched and took a step forward. 'You lying piece of scum. You'll never get anywhere near her.'

'I'm here now, aren't I?' He drew himself up to his full height, thrusting out his chest like a parading peacock. 'Drop the charges.'

'Go fuck yourself.' She grabbed the edge of the door with both hands, throwing her body against it, but Harrison was too quick. One shove and he unbalanced her. Another and she staggered backwards, almost falling. 'Get out of here. Now!'

'Or what?' He laughed as he stepped inside. 'You'll call the police? That hasn't exactly worked for you so far.'

She was in her pyjamas. Pocket-less, phone-less. Her mobile was on the kitchen bench. He was slightly shorter than her but wider, stronger. The door was still ajar, but if she made a dash for it he'd overpower her in an instant. And then there was Grace.

He moved towards her, shoulders arched, elbows bent so that his hands hovered slightly above his hips. 'So what are you going to do now, Ms De Santis?'

'Tess?' Grace called her name from the doorway of the bedroom. Shit. This was exactly what she didn't want. She had to get him out of here somehow.

Harrison turned at the sound of the small, frightened voice. 'So much like her mother.' He reached out and picked up a few strands of her hair. 'So pretty.'

White noise crescendoed in Tess's eardrums. She lunged forward, throwing herself at him as if she was scaling a high jump. Her body crashed into his and sent him flying. A sharp pain shot through her shoulder as she hit the floor, her head bouncing against the timber, jerking her neck backwards. For a few, long, dizzying seconds she lay perfectly still. Was the room spinning around her or was it her spinning, like a bottle in a game of truth or dare? A hot tide of nausea swelled inside her stomach, but she forced her eyes open. Harrison reeled away from her, toppling over as he reached out to catch himself, his hand finding the squat shape of the combustion stove. His wail ricocheted off the walls of the room as he righted himself, clutching his wrist.

Tess tried to push herself up from the floor, but black dots spiralled before her eyes. She leaned up on one elbow, choking back vomit. Harrison staggered, his fingers stiffened into a claw, the glazed expression in his eyes turning to rage. Rabid and seething, he hurled himself forward.

'You bitch,' he roared, flinging himself on top of her and pressing his elbow into her throat. That same suffocating, sickly smell she remembered so close again.

Fight, she had to fight back. Her eyelids were leaden, her lungs on fire, her head exploding, but she could not let him win.

And then, an audible crack. A groan. The solid weight of him pinning her down. Burying her beneath his bulk. Had time warped and transported her back to that night? Was she reliving the nightmare?

A quiet sob brought her around as the pressure on her larynx eased. Air trickled through to her lungs and she coughed. Her eyes flew open.

Grace.

Harrison's face slipped to her shoulder, blood pouring from an open wound on his skull. He was lying on top of her, inert and limp. Looking down at them both was Grace, her arms hanging loosely by her side, the cast-iron fire poker dangling from her right hand. Her pale lips parted, she was staring at the sharply pointed end of her weapon.

With whatever skerrick of fight she had left, Tess pushed her hands against Harrison's chest and heaved. Pain ripped through her shoulder blade and her head swam. His body thumped to the floor. She inched away and hauled herself up onto her one good elbow, only to recoil at the sight of him lying there on his back, blood covering the entire left side of his face. His eyes were closed. Never in her life had she wished anyone dead, until now. She focused on his chest, saw the almost imperceptible rise and fall. He was alive.

'Grace.'

Not a movement. Glassy-eyed, open-mouthed, she was fixated on Harrison, the poker still gripped in her palm.

'Grace.' Tess had to get through to her, had to make her move. 'Listen to me. Get my phone … kitchen bench.'

A quiver of Grace's chin, a flicker of her eyelids. A connection.

'Go. Now. Dial triple zero.'

And then a nod. A movement. *Thank God.*

'Good girl.' She fell back onto the floor as the footsteps became faint, the room growing darker, smaller. She was flagging, disappearing, but she couldn't let go. If she tuned in on the sounds around her it might help. Wind whistling through the timber walls. Coals crackling. A small, distant voice saying something about needing help, and a bad man and please come now. Further and further away. But also strangely close.

'The police are coming.' A warm, soft hand on hers.

She had to stay awake.

For Grace.

Twenty-three

It was a postcard morning when they trundled out of Jules's car and made the slow journey to the front porch. Not quite spring, but the feel of it was in the air, the sky a translucent shade of blue, bees busy in the garden. Fresh green shoots, bulbs Skye must have planted, were pushing up through the earth, and the leathery branches of a cherry-blossom tree at the side of the house were already covered in buds.

Grace clung to Tess's side, guiding her up the steps. While her legs were perfectly fine, she didn't have the heart to deny the help. Her back and shoulder still ached three days later. The dislocation hadn't been too hard for the paramedics to repair, but the fracture in her collarbone would take a little longer, with the help of a sling. Gradually the concussion had eased, the lingering headache worse when she got tired, but essentially she was in one piece.

'Home sweet home.' Jules popped up onto the top step carrying the overnight bags she'd packed when she insisted Tess and Grace recuperate at her place. She pushed the key into the lock, waving her arm in an exaggerated flourish to usher them inside. 'Here we are.'

'Darling.' Tess's mother rushed forward, throwing her arms out as she burst into a flood of tears.

'Mum?' Tess winced, pulling her encased arm closer to prevent it being crushed. 'What are you doing here?' Her father was standing awkwardly, hands in his jacket pockets, looking on.

'Did you really think we wouldn't come once Jules called us?' Her mother released her from the embrace but was still standing too close for comfort, horror pooling in her eyes.

Tess glared at her friend. 'Jules told you what happened?' Hadn't she said she would tell her parents herself, once she was home and things were back to normal? Hadn't she specifically said they were not to be called?

Jules straightened her shoulders and stared her down. 'I have a daughter not much younger than you and if she had been attacked ...'

Tess scowled, tipping her head towards Grace.

'If she had been hurt,' Jules continued, 'I would want to know about it.'

So much for loyalty, but she didn't have it in her to be angry. There were more important things to spend her energy on. Her parents would have found out sooner or later, and maybe it was easier that she didn't have to break the news herself. Although, she knew she'd have a few other things to explain. She gave a defeated smile. At least Jules hadn't called Josh as well.

'I'll put the kettle on.' Jules had the audacity to look smug. 'Want to give me a hand, Gracie?'

Grace turned, seeking approval. She'd been like Tess's Siamese twin for the last few days, a complete turnaround from when they'd first arrived at the house.

'It's okay.' She gave an encouraging nod and Grace went on her way.

A thick silence filled the room. Tess swallowed, not game enough to look either her mother or her father in the eye.

'How are you feeling, Spud?' Her dad had aged a good ten years since she'd last seen him, the worry lines across his forehead deeper, the rings beneath his eyes more pronounced.

'I'm okay, Dad.' It wasn't entirely true, of course, but she could see the pair of them were already worried sick and she didn't want to make it worse. 'Might sit down for a bit, though.'

'Yes, you should.' He rushed towards the chair and plumped a cushion, looking totally relieved to have a purpose. Her mother hovered, arms crossed over her pale-blue twin set.

Tess slumped into one of the two old lounge chairs in the middle of the room, opposite the fire. For a split second, the memory of burnt skin seared her nostrils, making her stomach churn. She closed her eyes and shook her head to will it away. When she opened them again her mother was sitting on the edge of the opposite chair, her father perched on the armrest. Beth clasped her hands. She would be absolutely busting at the seams with questions, but to her credit she didn't say a word.

They both deserved to know what had happened and it would be better to get it over with. Tess glanced towards the kitchen. Grace didn't need to hear any of this, so she kept her voice low. 'The only reason I asked Jules not to call was because I didn't want you to worry. And I wanted to tell you myself, when I was ready.'

'Oh, Tessa, we're your parents—'

'Beth.' Her father frowned, resting a hand on his wife's shoulder.

'I know. I'm sorry.' Tess adjusted the sling, then placed her arm on the side of the chair for support. God, what a fright she must look. Her hair hadn't been washed for days, the bruising on her cheek, where she'd hit the floor, was turning a nice shade of aubergine, something like the door. But she was alive and safe. They both were and that was all that mattered. 'I don't really know where to start. What do you know?'

'Jules called and said there'd been an intruder.' Her father jumped in to answer. 'That you'd been attacked but had managed to get away and had been injured a little in the process. We read a few other bits and pieces in the paper.'

'Right.' Familiar noises leaked in from the kitchen. The boiling kettle. Cups clinking onto saucers. Jules chattering to Grace, keeping her busy. The normal, cheerful sounds of everyday life. Words hopped into her head and out again, like frogs in a pond, quick and slimy and hard to pin down. There was so much to say, so much she'd never told them. All the reasons she hadn't spoken up circled through her head. She took a breath. There was only one place to start. That night years before, with everything he'd done and said. The sacrifice her friend had made, the promise she'd begged her to keep; how her own fear, and then paralysing guilt, had kept her quiet. Why Skye had moved away. The box in the cupboard, the equine sessions, her decision to come forward and support Skye's accusations. And then, finally, what had happened right here in this very room only a few nights before, although the exact details were a little fuzzy. It came out in one long bumbling story, all of it slipping out now that there was no reason to keep the details secret.

'Why didn't you tell us?' Her mother's barely audible question mirrored the look of utter desolation on her face.

'I was so scared.' Her throat was raw, but if she let herself cry she might not be able to stop. 'He told me he'd come to the house in the middle of the night. And then Skye begged me not to tell anyone. I know it was wrong, but I pushed it all into the back of my mind, pretended it had never happened.' And turned into an angry, difficult teenager. An emotionally stunted adult.

'The bloody mongrel.' Her father walked to the window, stood with his back to them, gazing outside. 'He'd better get what's coming to him.'

'That poor girl.' Her mother's face was wet with tears. 'No wonder Jean never mentioned she had a son, if that's the sort of person he was. The poor woman would be horrified. How long had it been going on for?'

'I don't know, Mum. Skye never said. The only time she ever mentioned it again was at her Jean's funeral. He was there and she was beside herself. He was her only surviving relative and she had to make sure he'd never get his hands on Grace.' A tremor skipped down her spine. That was not something she could even contemplate.

Her dad turned back around. 'Well, from what the police said, you did a mighty fine job of protecting her, love.'

'You spoke to the police?'

He nodded. 'Jules gave us the number. The local fellow told us what he knew. Said you and Grace were like the dynamic duo.' He tried to muster a smile, but only managed a slight upward turn of his lips.

'I wish she hadn't had to go through that.' Her voice shook. She sighed, waiting to regain control. 'As much as I wish he was dead, it's probably a good thing he survived. Grace has had enough trauma without living with that for the rest of her life.'

Beth reached out and put her hand on Tess's knee, giving her a trembling smile. 'I'm just so glad you're both safe.'

'Me too, Mum.' Harrison was behind bars. For now. The attack meant new charges could be laid and it gave credence to both her statement, and Skye's. It had been the stuff of nightmares, but the end result was what mattered. 'When the story came out in the press, a couple of women who had worked for Harrison over the years came forward. He'd used the same MO, threatened to hurt them if they said anything. Told them they'd lose their jobs, that no one would take their word against his. Apparently, there's enough piled up against him now to send him to jail for a long time.'

'They should throw the bloody key away,' her father growled. She'd never seen him so angry. 'Prison's too good for bastards like him.'

'Poor Skye.' Her mother's eyes were glassy. She gave a weak shake of her head. 'She had such a tragic life. I suppose it all got too much for her in the end.'

'I'm not so sure it did.' Despite everything, the horrible paintings, the memories that must have tortured her for years, Skye's decision to speak out about Harrison, to actually press charges, didn't fit with her choosing to end her life. 'I really believe the overdose was accidental. Once she'd made the statement, she was probably terrified he'd find her, relied too much on the anxiety medication, the sleeping pills. She had so much to live for and I don't believe she would never have de-liberately left Grace.'

A giggle came right on cue from the kitchen.

Beth nodded, brighter now. 'Are you two getting along bet-ter these days?'

'We are. Or at least we were, until this happened.'

'Kids are resilient, sweetheart. I'm not saying things don't affect them, but with plenty of love and the right guidance they can get back on their feet.'

'I hope so.'

The tea was taking a suspiciously long time. 'Does Josh know what happened?' A text had arrived from him while she'd been staying with Jules, letting her know he was flying back to Europe for a quick trip to finalise his contract. She'd replied with a brief *Good Luck* and nothing more.

A deep breath from Beth and then, 'It wasn't up to us to tell him. You can do it when you see fit.'

Wow. Her mum really was trying. And was there a hint she knew things were over with Josh?

'It's a big thing you're doing, Tess. I know I didn't handle things well to start with.' Her mother swallowed, faltering. 'But your father and I are very proud of you. And we support you one hundred percent.'

'We do, love.'

The touch of her father's lips to her forehead tipped Tess over the edge. She hung her head and let the tears fall. All these years she'd been so tough on her parents, blamed them, her mother in particular, for being too controlling, too interfering, too this, too that, when all along her own issues had been the problem. Somewhere in the fathomless depths of her mind she'd known the truth, but making them the scapegoats had been easier. She'd told herself she would have confided in them if only they'd been less judgemental, more compassionate. The truth was no matter who they were, she would have stayed quiet. It wasn't their fault. It wasn't Skye's fault. It wasn't her fault.

It was Harrison's.

And now, finally, he was going to pay.

Hours later, Tess stood on the porch and waved her parents goodbye, promising she'd call if she needed anything. Seeing them had been, despite her initial misgivings, quite wonderful, but she was tired and her mother's fussing was too much. There were no beds for them here, so they were staying at a B&B in town despite Jules offering them a room at her place. Probably just as well—her mother would no doubt spend the night interrogating Jules, trying to find out more about what had happened, and really, what she knew was enough. In the end, it had been good to get everything out in the open, but endlessly rehashing it all would do none of them any favours.

'You're not too mad at me?' Jules lingered in the doorway, looking slightly wan.

Mad? It took a minute for Tess to work it out. Ah, the phone call to her parents. She could give her friend a hard time, make her squirm, but that wouldn't be fair after everything Jules had done for them. And her intentions had been good. Sometimes promises needed to be broken. If only she'd learned that lesson earlier. 'No, you did the right thing.'

Colour flooded Jules's cheeks. Her hair was pulled back from her face with a pale-yellow scarf, her silver curls falling softly onto her shoulders. She looked like a guardian angel. Actually, she was. They hadn't known each other long and yet Tess trusted her implicitly. It had been a long time since she'd had such a close friend.

Jules beckoned her over to the door. 'Look at this.'

She poked her head inside and there on the bed was Grace, cross-legged with Tiger sitting in her lap, fast asleep. Oblivious to her closed eyes, Grace was reading aloud to her. *Anne Of Green Gables*, a brand-new copy of her own, a gift from her nonna.

Warmth spread through Tess's limbs. Grace was already looking more like herself, the quivering fear that had taken up residence in her eyes these last few days beginning to fade. Her mother was right. Kids did bounce back. 'You two look pretty cosy.'

Grace lifted her head, nodded briefly and then returned to her narration.

'We'll just be out here if you need anything, okay?'

Another nod, head bowed.

Stepping back outside, Tess closed her eyes and turned her face to the sun, letting its heat ripple across her cheeks. There was something she needed to do—wanted to do—and now was as good a time as any. She straightened up and turned to Jules. 'You got a minute? There's something I want to show you.'

'Sure.'

She'd revealed pretty much everything over the last few days, but there was something she'd kept to herself and Jules was the person she wanted to share it with first. A soft breeze blew as she led the way around to the back of the house. Luminous yellow light kissed the line of gums on the horizon, casting the sky above in a perfect orange glow. It was so beautiful. Exactly the sort of scene Skye would love.

When she reached the shed she dipped her free hand into her pocket and pulled out the key. She'd nabbed it from the hook earlier, hoping she'd get the chance to bring Jules out. With one arm encased in a sling and her loose hand a shaking mess, undoing the padlock was impossible. 'Can you do the honours?'

Jules took the key and did as she was asked. Even though the prospect of seeing the images again made Tess sick to the stomach, and as much as she was no expert, the power in the pieces was obvious. She moved towards the second door and waited while Jules unlocked it silently. One flick and the naked bulb lit the cramped space. The blanket tossed over the canvases was slightly askew after her last visit, and her rushed departure. She reached out and whisked it away, letting it fall in a heap to the floor.

Jules's hands flew to her face. She drew in a sharp breath. 'Oh my God.' Her voice was rough, her eyes watering. She reached out and moved the frames forward one at a time. Her expression changed from horror to incredulity as she took in every brushstroke. Knowing why they'd been painted, what they represented, made them hard to look at, but the pain and emotion Skye had somehow managed to capture also made them totally compelling.

Eventually, when she'd reached the last one, Jules cleared her throat. 'These are amazing. I've never seen anything like them.'

Tess nodded. 'I know.'

'What are you going to do with them?'

She inhaled a long, deep breath. 'No idea. I certainly won't be hanging any of them over the mantelpiece. But I don't think I can just dump them, either.'

'Definitely not.' Jules let the paintings fall back against the wall, her lips pursed as she arranged the blanket back over the pile. She glanced up. 'These should be exhibited.'

'Oh, Jules I don't know.' Would Skye want her pain thrown out there, for the world to see? She'd always been such a quiet, private person, would she really want to expose herself?

'I know what you're thinking, but hear me out.'

'Okay.'

'Our girl was talented, one of the most talented artists I've come across in a long time, but she didn't believe in herself. I have a list as long as my arm of people who wanted her work, but Grace was her priority. I always knew that she was only scratching the surface with her paintings. You've seen some of them, they're stunning—the light, the way she captures a feeling though how you can't quite put your finger on it?'

Jules was right. There was an ethereal, other-worldly quality to Skye's work that drew you in.

'But these,' Jules tapped a finger against the covered frames, 'these are on a whole new level. This is raw, unfiltered emotion. They need to be seen.'

'Seriously?'

'Some people would pay big bucks for work like this.'

'To hang on the wall?' Why would anyone want to look at such harrowing images, have them hanging in a public space?

Jules's brows furrowed. 'We know the story behind them, but others won't. To the average buyer they'd be a curiosity, a conundrum. Why did the artist paint them? What do they mean?'

'Surely any idiot can see they're not happy snaps?'

'Not everyone wants happy snaps. They want emotion, depth. And these have it in bucketloads.'

'I don't know, Jules.' She had enough images prancing around in her head without any concrete visual reminders—displaying them so overtly was another thing again. Suddenly, the air in the tiny room was cloying, viscous, hard to draw into her lungs.

Jules followed her outside, closing the door and bolting it shut.

Stepping into the stark daylight made her giddy. Or perhaps it was seeing the paintings again. She steadied herself against the side of the shed.

'You okay?'

She nodded.

'It's up to you, of course. But these are too good to keep locked away. I'd be more than happy to organise an exhibition. You wouldn't have to do a thing. And I have some clients in Sydney I know would be interested in buying them. You could put the money into a trust fund for Gracie. At least there'd be something good coming out of all this.'

All of a sudden, Tess was bone-achingly tired. 'I'll think about it.'

Jules took her arm and they walked inside. A pre-cooked casserole was on the stovetop, and its rich aroma filled the house. Grace had fallen asleep, the book open on the bed by her side. It was almost the same position Tess had found her in during those first few days in Sydney, when they'd been such strangers, when Grace had been little more than an obligation. Things had changed so much. Her marriage had pretty much fallen apart, she hadn't worked for weeks and her living space was certainly not prime real estate. She'd faced her worst fears, to some extent conquered them, and she felt lighter, more buoyant than she had since childhood. A couple of months ago she couldn't have fathomed any of it being possible. Now, she couldn't imagine her life without this fragile, funny little girl, curled up on the bed beside her cat. Whatever life had in store for them both, the two of them were going to be okay.

Twenty-four

It was good to be back amongst the horses. Whisky whinnied as soon as she saw Grace, ambled over to the fence and stuck her head through the rails, looking for a carrot and a scratch. Tess raised her hand to block the sunlight from her eyes. Samson, standing idly at the far end of the arena, lifted his head and watched them closely. Once more, the sight of him quite literally stole her breath. But now, unlike when they first met, she wasn't afraid of his size and power.

'Hi there, strangers.' Max came striding towards them, a grin from ear to ear, throwing her arms around Tess and pulling her into a tight hug. A good thing her shoulder was now well on its way to being healed. 'It's so good to see you. How are you doing?'

'Good, we're good.' Grapevines flourishing the way they do, there was no need to go into details. Max would know it all. Weerilla had even made it into the papers and the nightly news when word got out about Harrison's visit—and subsequent arrest.

Max eased away, but her hands bracketed Tess's biceps. 'I'm so glad you're both okay. If you need anything, anything at all, make sure you let us know.'

Both she and Mitch had phoned in the days following the attack, but Tess had needed space and time to process things. Both of them did. Her parents had stayed for a week, leaving only once her bruises faded and the sling was relegated to the medical cabinet. Now the worst was over and she and Grace needed to get back to normal. Finish walking the path they'd started and get on with their lives. 'Where's Mitch?'

'He got called out to do some emergency shoeing.'

'Oh.'

'He should be back soon.' Max gave a coy smile. 'But we can get started if you like.'

'Sure.'

Grace skipped ahead of them to the stable, settling herself in a chair, relishing the familiar routine. Tess sat beside her, resisting the urge to reach out and take her hand. Since the events of 'that night' as she now referred to it, the two of them had shared Skye's bed, hung out together pretty much all day, every day, their mutual need to stay close unspoken yet palpable. Not that such co-dependence was healthy, for either of them. She shook away the random thoughts and listened to Max's preamble and instructions.

'Today's tasks are all about trust. Trusting each other, trusting the horses, trusting yourselves. We're going to start with an exercise where you lead each other around using only voice cues.'

'What does that mean?' Grace scrunched up her face.

Max blushed. 'Sorry, still getting the hang of the lingo. It means you'll be leading each other around by giving instructions, while the other person is blindfolded.'

'Leading with a rope, like we do with the horses?'

'Nuh-uh. Just your voice.'

Grace frowned, clearly not understanding. Tess on the other hand understood only too well. She'd done this stuff in her senior year at high school and had hated it, actually opted out when the blindfold had been tightened, feigning a gastro attack and fleeing to the bathroom. But she could see the point of it now. Maybe it was worth another shot? Everything they'd done here so far had worked, so why not?

'Who wants to be led first?'

Grace jumped to her feet. 'Me.'

'Righty-o.' Max placed a blindfold over Grace's eyes, tying it in a firm bow at the back of her head. 'Can you see anything?'

'No.'

'Good. Tess, you have ten minutes to lead Grace around using only your voice, no touching. I'll be here and if it looks like you need help I'll jump in.'

Right. She could do this.

She walked a few steps in front of Grace, directing her through the stable block, giving clear directions, but she ended up with her 'follower' about to walk smack bang into a wall.

'Whoa, Gracie, stop there a minute.' Max gave a rolling gesture with her hands.

Clearer instructions were obviously needed. 'Okay. Turn to your right, take one step, then stop.'

Grace did as instructed.

'Now, walk forward two paces, then turn to the left and take three more steps.'

One instruction, one step at a time, they manoeuvred their way around the yard, finishing at the fence where the horses were standing, watching with bemused expressions.

'That's it. Blindfold off,' Max called.

Grace whipped the mask from her face and giggled. 'That was fun. Your turn, Tess.'

As Max tightened the blindfold Tess's heart skittered. She lifted a hand to her chest to calm it down. There was something suffocating about the forced darkness, that old reflex she couldn't quite shake. She drew in a breath and listened closely, letting Grace lead her on a higgledy-piggledy path all over the stables and yard. It was pretty easy once she gave in and listened. Once she surrendered her need to be in control and trusted. It was astounding how much more acute her hearing became, attuned to the sounds around her, the horses chewing at the grass, a blowfly buzzing at her ear, the cracking of a stick under her heel. And then there were the smells: freshly harvested hay, the pungent scent of manure, the tread of footsteps and the faint aroma of something spicier wafting past, something that made her lips curve of their own accord.

They ended up back where they'd started, Grace cleverly directing her into just the right spot before getting her to sit down. When she removed her blindfold the source of the enticing smell was seated right in front of her.

Mitch gave them both a thumbs-up. 'Good work, ladies. I only caught the end of that task, but it looks like you led beautifully, Grace.'

'Thank you.' Grace's cheeks flushed pink as she sat perfectly upright.

'And you did a great job listening and following the instructions, Tess.' From anyone else it would sound annoyingly condescending, but Mitch had a way of giving praise that was completely genuine. It had been over two weeks since their last meeting and it occurred to her now that she'd actually missed seeing him. 'So, for our last session with the horses it's your choice of what you would like to do. There are obstacles out there, and lead ropes. You can do some liberty work or use halters, it's up to you. Max and I will be on hand if you need any help, but this is really about you two working things out together.'

Teamwork. That made total sense.

'Can we ride?' Grace asked.

'Not today. But you can definitely come back again and we can go on a trail ride. On a weekend, when Tobes isn't at school.' Mitch paused. He was asking Tess for permission. 'We could all go out together.'

'Yay. Can we, Tess?'

'Yep.' She directed her answer back to Mitch. 'Sounds good.'

When she entered the yard she approached Samson slowly, moving to the one side, and waiting for him to come forward. Unlike the last time, she was totally comfortable being in the same space as the horses. Even though the incident with Harrison had shaken her up, the closure his arrest had given her had brought with it an welcome clarity, a new confidence, as if she'd been living her whole adult life in a fog and it had now miraculously lifted.

By the time the session was finished, she and Grace had mastered getting the horses over the poles, around a heap of obstacles and had jogged the full circumference of the arena with the two horses trotting calmly along behind them. Tess's pulse was racing for an entirely different reason to an hour before, when she'd first been blindfolded. A sense of pure joy left her practically gliding across the grass. Working with the horses had been a humbling, blissful experience, for which she would always be grateful. She rested her forehead against Samson's massive neck, inhaled his strong, earthy scent and patted him gently.

'Thank you, my friend.'

'Can I go to pick Toby up from school?' Grace raced to-wards Tess across the lawn, almost falling over herself with excitement.

'Fine by me.' Max was waiting in the driveway, keys in hand.

'Okay. I'll hang around here until you get back.' They had nowhere in particular to be, and right now she was so relaxed she could easily stretch out under a tree and doze.

Grace ran off, then stopped, turned and blew a kiss.

'Who is that child?'

'Quite the turnaround.' Mitch stood beside her, waving in the direction of the disappearing car.

'Sure is.'

'So you've been stood up?' There was a wry gleam in his eye.

She laughed. 'Looks that way.'

'Fancy a beer while you wait? Light, naturally.'

She shrugged. Not a bad alternative to a nap. 'Why not?'

He vanished into the barn and she made herself com-fortable on the bench seat under the huge old jacaranda. Bright fringes of leaves dotted the branches. Spring was in full bloom and Sydney soon would be a riot of purple. The whole city alive with colour, even from the air. It was strange to think she wouldn't be flying anywhere anytime soon. Josh would soon be leaving for his new life in Europe. She'd called him and given a condensed version of what had hap-pened but declined his offer to visit. A small knot tugged in her stomach, the same way it did every time she thought of him, but it loosened almost instantly. She should miss him, miss her old life, yet bizarrely she didn't. There was an apartment of designer furniture waiting to be sorted; for the time being, at least, she had no inclination to be anywhere except here.

Mitch returned, handing over an ice-cold beer. 'Cheers.'

She clinked her bottle against his. 'Cheers.' They sat quietly as the afternoon light began to soften. Being here, side by side on the bench, their arms touching, felt completely natural; however, there was an uncharacteristic edginess about him today. He tapped the toe of one boot against the back of the other where his ankles crossed. The session with Samson and Grace had left Tess mellow; watching them had apparently not had the same effect on Mitch. If he had something to say she could give him the time he needed, there was no rush.

Finally he leaned back and squinted up into the tree. 'You seem to be doing okay, you and Grace, after ...' He scratched a spot on the back of his neck just below his hairline.

People found it awkward to talk about what had happened and Mitch was no exception. Funnily enough, she didn't have the same degree of discomfort about it all. If anything, the recent event with Harrison had been cathartic, and had helped her come to terms with what had happened years before. Her life with Grace was settling into a routine and they were getting to know each other on a whole new level. 'Yeah, we are. Shoulder's all healed, bruises are gone. Grace was pretty stunned for a few days, but she's recovered really well. We both have.'

He dropped his head. 'It must have been frightening.'

A swallow darted out from under the eaves of the barn, whirring its wings like a wind-up toy. Maybe it was the brain's way of curing you after a traumatic event, but when she looked back on it now it was all kind of a blur. 'You know, it all happened so fast, it was like some crazy action movie.'

Mitch laughed.

She joined in, tucked her ever-growing hair back behind her ears. 'It was, honestly. I'm not saying I wasn't scared.' A flash of Harrison forcing open the door, his beady-eyed gaze burning into her like a laser made her shudder. 'But once the adrenaline kicked in, it sort of … just happened.'

Mitch studied the bottle in his hand as if it was some strange ancient artefact an archaeologist might have found on a dig. 'Jules told me about what started it all off, when you and Skye were young.' He turned, his eyes warm with concern. 'I'm sorry you had to go through all that.'

'It was much worse for Skye. I wish I'd had the guts to tell someone at the time.' She gulped down a mouthful of beer.

'You were just kids. He was the one with the power.'

It was true, Harrison was the predator. But if she'd spoken up at the time, made herself talk to Skye about it, tried to get her to tell someone … things might have been so different. For both of them. Would she ever be able to let go of the residual guilt?

'Our father was abusive.' Mitch spoke softly, a slight quiver in his voice. 'Not to Max and me, but to Mum. I've never forgiven myself for not sticking up for her as I got older. He had this control over us all, we were too frightened to stand up to him. He never touched us kids physically, but he was hard on us. Too hard.' He let out a long, weary sigh. 'He died when I was fourteen. And the sad thing is I wasn't even sorry.' His eyes glistened. 'If anything I was relieved. It was better to have no father than to have him.'

'Is that why you're so close to Toby?'

His shoulders lifted. 'Yeah. Children deserve more than a roof over their head and three meals a day on the table.'

Was she doing the right thing? Trying to raise Grace on her own, when she actually had no idea how to be a parent? Was, in fact, still learning how to be an adult? Toby had both Max and Mitch looking out for him, had a real mother and an uncle who did a better job than most fathers. She rubbed at her index finger, feeling the absence of her wedding ring. 'I don't know what I'll be like at this.'

Mitch frowned. 'At what?'

'Motherhood.'

A ripple of understanding passed across his face. 'Oh, right.' And then a gentle smile. 'You're already good at it. All Grace needs is someone to love her. And you so obviously do.'

He was right, on both points.

'So will you be packing up and heading back to Sydney now?'

It was a question she'd pondered over and over in the days immediately following Harrison's attack. Her family were in Sydney, her business, the apartment she'd shared with Josh that needed sorting out, but every time she'd asked herself that question, the answer was the same. 'No. I'm going to be sticking around. For the time being anyway. Grace is happy here and I don't want to uproot her just yet. I've offered my assistant a share in my consultancy and she jumped at it. I'm going to work remotely, building courses and doing some reports and analysis.' If the dodgy internet service didn't send her batty.

As they talked, the heavy clouds of doubt lingering in her mind parted, leaving nothing but the bright light of certainty.

'Jeez,' he grinned, 'you're pretty smart for a city chick.'

She gave him a light punch on the arm. 'And you're pretty smart for a horse whisperer.'

'Equine-assisted-learning practitioner, thank you very much.'

'Oh yes, I forgot.' Of course she hadn't forgotten. How could she? She rested a hand on Mitch's arm. 'And a very good one. If I hadn't done the sessions—if you hadn't pushed me to join in with Grace …' It was hard to find the words. 'I wrote in the journal you gave me, that first day. Everything came pouring out onto the pages. It gave me the courage I needed to go to the police, to press charges. And if I hadn't done that Harrison would still be out there.' She huffed. 'Shit, he could even have been elected to state government. What a joke.' She shook her head. 'So, thank you. So much.'

'My pleasure.' He was so close. Those green eyes. The strong, angular tilt of his jaw. That spicy, sexy aftershave. She leaned in, a tiny fraction, letting her eyes fall shut. His lips against hers were warm and soft. Then the slick, smooth slide of his tongue inside her mouth. That old familiar electricity sparking between her legs.

She jumped back. 'Oh God, I'm so sorry.'

Mitch sat up. 'Don't be.' He grinned. 'You can thank me any time.'

'I don't know what just happened.' Her cheeks were on fire.

'It's called kissing.'

'Smart alec.' She could easily slap him. And kiss him again at the same time. 'I'm trying to apologise for being inappropriate.' She stood, needing more distance.

'You don't have to apologise, Tess. In case you didn't notice, it was a two-way thing.'

'Yes, I know, but you're my …' She was about to say 'therapist', even though she knew he wasn't.

'Our sessions are finished. Unless you want them to continue.'

'No. I'm done. I mean, they're finished.' This was crazy. What was she even trying to say? She took a deep breath, crossed her arms, uncrossed them again. 'I'm not saying that kiss wasn't great, Mitch.' She was still blushing, her body still humming. 'I'm just not really in the right place to get involved with anyone. I have to focus on Grace. Getting the two of us sorted. We're getting there, but there's a way to go and I ...'

'Tess, I get it.' The slight downturn of his mouth belied his words.

She reached out and took his hand. Rough and sturdy hands. 'But I could really use a friend, if that's okay?'

He grasped her fingers, nodding. 'Totally okay.'

They sat on the bench, sipping their beers, hand in hand as if it was the most normal thing in the world. He was a good man, kind and gentle, yet with an inner strength that radiated out through every pore. He wasn't like any man she'd ever been attracted to before, but then again she wasn't the person she used to be, either. Right now, although she wasn't quite sure exactly who she was, she was definitely on the way to finding out. And when she did, when she and Grace had well and truly bonded, she might be in the market for someone.

And who knew? Maybe Mitch could be that someone. One day.

'Tess, can I go to school?'

Grace's question dragged her out of the daydream she should not have been having as she drove home. She turned to her passenger, who was looking right back, her face earnest.

'Can I go to school? Like Toby.'

'Wow ... I ...'

'They do all this totally cool stuff, he was telling me about it. Running races, and painting, they have a choir and a vegetable plot. And sheep and pigs.'

This was completely out of the blue, but Grace seemed to be deadly serious. 'Do you think you'd like it?'

'Yes, I really, really do.' She sat back against the seat, her voice dropping almost to a whisper. 'And I could have friends.'

A sharp ache echoed inside Tess's chest. Grace was lonely. It was there in the wistful gaze as she stared out the window, in the way she relished every minute spent with Toby and the other kids she'd met in art class. She was safe. If there'd ever been a legitimate reason to keep her under lock and key, it was gone. Skye had chosen to homeschool for a very good reason, but this was Tess's call now. For the time being, Weerilla was where they needed to be. 'I'll call the school tomorrow and make an appointment to see the principal.'

'Really?'

'Really.' The idea of whole days at the cottage without Grace made her stomach turn. But she already had another idea forming about what she might do with herself. School would be good for Grace. It was what she wanted.

It was time for them both to move on.

It was a perfect day in the middle of November and the buzz in the gallery was electric. So many people. All crowded into the small building, champagne glasses clinking, chins wagging. Skye's paintings hung on every wall, the larger canvases forming the bulk of the exhibition, which Jules had titled 'Catharsis'. True to her word, she'd managed to entice some wealthy Sydney collectors out for the opening and a number of the paintings had been sold already. It was easy to see how people would be drawn to them, in awe of the raw emotion they portrayed, but Tess, standing in the middle of the room, surrounded by the images, could only see her friend's pain. The sooner they were sold the better.

'Nice dress.' Mitch's voice was low, and rumbled against her ear.

'Thanks.' She smiled. It had been forever since she'd glammed up. Her mother had brought some of her dresses up and this one, a simple black knee-length with a touch of lace on the bodice, was one of her favourites. Her bare arms were lightly tanned from days spent sorting out the garden, and her hair, almost to her shoulders now, had been given a tidy-up by the local hairdresser.

'Heels, too.' Mitch's eyes travelled down her legs to the black patent leather slingbacks.

'Nice to be out of the jeans and jumpers. Not looking too bad yourself.'

'Max made me spruce up.' He fiddled with the collar of his dress shirt. It was a light-blue-and-white check, a nice contrast to his eyes. 'Even had a shave.'

'So I see.' Her fingers itched to reach out and stroke the smooth edge of his chin. She resisted. They were friends. Mates.

'In case you hadn't guessed, art galleries aren't really my thing.' His eyes roamed the walls. 'These paintings are pretty ...'

'Disturbing?'

'Yeah, that. No offence, but I don't get why anyone would want them hanging in their lounge room.'

'None taken, I agree. Talking pieces, apparently. Better on their walls than mine.'

'All ready for your big speech?'

The butterflies in her stomach launched themselves into overdrive. 'Ready to get it over and done with.'

Metal dinging on glass cut through the noisy chatter. Jules was getting the official part of the day underway. 'Looks like that's my cue.'

He reached out and squeezed her shoulder. 'You'll be fine.'

Blocking out the murmur of the crowd, she made her way to the podium.

'And, here she is.' Jules looked lovely as usual, her hair long and loose, wearing a touch of makeup and a deep-crimson kaftan topped with a gold scarf. As Jules welcomed the guests, Tess steadied herself by looking around the room. Lots of un-familiar faces, well-dressed types from the North Shore and Eastern Suburbs, mingled with the more casual locals. Max, stunning in a long khaki jumpsuit, her hair arranged into an impressive up-do, gave her a wink as she did the rounds with the finger food. Leela and Raj had done the catering and the smell of coconut, curry, chilli and garlic would have made her hungry if her stomach hadn't been such a twisted mess. Peals of laughter floated in from outside, Grace's amongst them. She'd been at school for over a month now and had fitted in surprisingly well. The huge front lawn of the gallery made a perfect playground and it was good the kids were out there playing, good that Grace wouldn't be hearing her speech.

'And so I'd like to welcome Tessa De Santis to say a few words about the collection.' Jules's introduction was met with a round of hearty applause.

Whatever else her friend had said was a mystery. Now it was her turn to take the stage. She gripped her notes as she took the two steps up to the lectern. A sea of expectant faces greeted her as a hush fell over the room. Most, if not all, would know the backstory, would know the part she'd played in Harrison's arrest. But today was all about Skye. A celebration of her life.

'Thank you for being here.' The silver bracelet she'd gifted Skye all those years ago, repaired and polished, jangled on her wrist. 'Skye Whittaker and I were childhood playmates and even though our lives took different paths we remained best friends all our lives.'

She paused. It was a truth she'd taken too long to realise.

'Skye was a natural artist. You'd always find her in the art room at lunchtime, creating amazing sculptures and paintings. But then life took her in a different direction.'

Her eyes fell closed, a slow tear tracing the curve of her cheek. Murmurs in the crowd and there at the back of the room, a good head taller than most, was Mitch. He poked out his tongue, gave her a thumbs-up. Silly man.

She checked her notes before starting again. 'But here in Weerilla, with the encouragement of Jules Starkey, she found her art—and herself—again. The pieces you see today in the smaller rooms are witness to the happiness Skye found living here with her daughter, Grace.' She scanned the works hanging on the walls, her eyes shifting from one image to the next. 'And the self-portraits you see here are a reflection of the enormous pain Skye suffered at the hands of her abuser.'

Like a symphony audience in the seconds after the conductor taps his baton, the room held its breath.

'When I first found these canvases locked away in Skye's shed, I was horrified because I knew what they meant. At that point, I couldn't have contemplated showing them to anyone. But what I have come to understand, as the title of this exhibition reflects, is that by doing these artworks Skye was able to set herself free. By capturing the darkness, she was able to walk from the shadows and into the light.'

She gave herself a moment, sipped water from her glass.

'Sadly, Skye is no longer with us, but I am sure she would have been proud to have her paintings displayed here today. Half of the proceeds from sales will go into a trust fund for her daughter and the other half will go to 1800Respect, an organisation that supports victims of sexual assault.'

She scanned the room. Only a few of these people had known Skye, or thought they did, the woman who kept to herself, the gifted artist who may or may not have committed suicide and left a legacy of amazing artworks. But they didn't know the real Skye. The sweet, funny, serious girl who somehow found the courage to conquer her demons, who would live on through her paintings and through her daughter.

'Skye Whittaker was a beautiful woman. Not just in the physical sense, but in her heart, and in the depths of her soul, and I am proud to call her my best friend.'

She stepped down into a round of applause, making a beeline for the door. She needed space, she needed fresh air. Most of all, she needed Grace.

I miss you Mumma.

We went to the creek today and scattered your ashes. Tess said that's what you wanted, that you'd written it in your will.

It was a warm spring day, your favourite kind, and on the way we saw the echidna. You remember him? He was shy, turned his back to us and started burrowing into the leaves at the bottom of a gum tree. We weren't going to hurt him, but I guess he didn't know that.

Tess carried the urn.

A whole family of black cockatoos were in the old banksia tree when we passed. They took off in a rush, their wings stretched out like giant fans as they flew into the sky.

It was quiet when we got there. Just the noise of the water tumbling over the rocks, like the day we found the baby bird.

We sat on the sand for a long time with the urn—and you—between us. Tess looked at me after a while and I nodded. She carried it to the edge of the bank and we crouched down. It was heavy, so she kept a hold on it, too. When she took off the lid she looked at me again and tried to smile. She was trying to be brave, but I could tell she was sad. Together we tipped it up and your ashes fell into the creek.

And then the urn was empty, and you were gone.

We stood there for a long time and watched the sun dancing on the water. I closed my eyes and saw your face, and I remembered what Tess had said about the ashes just being your body. That the most important part, your soul, was in the place you loved the most and with the people you loved the best.

The creek.

Tess.

Me.

If you or someone you know is impacted by sexual assault, domestic or family violence, call 1800RESPECT on 1800 737 732 or visit 1800RESPECT.org.au

People affected by sexual assault, domestic or family violence can access support 24 hours a day, seven days a week. The services are available to people experiencing violence and abuse, as well as their support networks including family, friends and frontline workers.

Acknowledgements

There was a time when I didn't think this book would ever be seen by anyone but me. If it wasn't for the encouragement and support of my writing friends, my family and my readers it would still be sitting in a word file on my laptop, so please indulge me while I thank everyone I need to thank.

This is my fifth published novel and my first foray into the world of independent publishing. In so many ways it is a product of everything I have done in my writing career up until now, and I would like to thank Vanessa Radnidge and the team at Hachette for giving me the opportunity to have four rural fiction novels published with them over the last six years. I am so grateful for everything that experience has taught me.

It's hard to know where to start in thanking all those who have helped me birth *this* particular book baby. As always my first reader, Carrie Green, thank you for your unwavering support and honest feedback. When you said you couldn't put it down I knew I had to get it out there to a wider readership. Chrissie Mios, thank you for your thoughtful comments from both a reader and writer perspective.

Without my writing buddies I wouldn't be writing. That's a fact. To Monique McDonell, Joanna Nell, Penelope Janu, Angella Whitton, Terri Green, Laura Boon, Michelle Barraclough and Rae Cairns, thank you for being there every fortnight in the flesh and every day online to provide feedback, toss around ideas, nut out marketing strategies, share pages and generally make this whole writing business so much more manageable. And fun!

Special thanks to: Laura for your heartfelt encouragement—I'm so glad I made you cry on that first reading. Michelle, your insightful comments on my manuscript helped so much with revisions. Rae, thank you for always being on the other end of that phone line to help untangle plot lines and sort out characters. Your feedback has been crucial to creating the final version of this novel, and to keeping me sane. Sharon Ketelaar, thank you for your pick-ups during the almost-last revision stage. It's so good to have fresh eyes at a point where nothing much is registering anymore. Krystina Pecorari-McBride, thank you for all the writing chats over the years, for always being on hand to read my words and give honest feedback. I'm looking forward to holding your book in my hands one day soon. Lisa Hall-Wilson, even though we have never met in person, your wisdom and feedback helped me take my writing up a notch (or hopefully two) and I am indebted to you for taking the time to read and comment on my manuscript.

Over the years, I have made some amazing friendships in the writing community, and I am so grateful for the interest many of those friends have taken in me publishing this novel and for being there on the sidelines cheering me on. Your kind words have been so encouraging. Rachael Johns, Jennie Jones, Annie Seaton, Mel Hammond, Tess Woods, and so many more: thank you.

Meredith Jaffe, my *Storyfest* partner in crime, and Kel Butler, my dynamo *Writes4Women* partner, thank you both for always being there to listen to my woes and inspire me.

Natasha Lester and Kelly Rimmer, thank you for reading the manuscript at a very late stage, for your support and amazing endorsements. Your kind words for the cover brought me to tears. Thank you so much!

Jenn J. Mcleod, our writing careers have had many similarities and it's so lovely to be travelling down this road together. Thanks for our Friday afternoon 'info swaps'. I look forward to continuing the journey with you, both on the road and between the pages.

Kim Kelly, you have been my inspiration in publishing this book. Thank you for your wisdom, your insights, your guidance and for always being happy to answer any crazy question I throw at you.

To my agent Jeanne Ryckmans, thank you for supporting me in this venture and having my back in all things publishing.

Quite a bit of research was undertaken in the writing of this book and a number of experts were called on. Thank you to Lyn Jenkin and Pam Seccombe at *Horsanity*. The 'Seeing With Fresh Eyes' workshop I took with your herd gave me a direct experience with equine-assisted therapy. I'll be back. Thank you also to Sarah Ferguson for your advice and clarifications on aspects of equine-assisted therapy. Thanks to my fourth daughter, Liz Reid-Philip, for answering my medical questions and for making enquiries on my behalf, not to mention being part of my cheer squad. And my gratitude goes to my friend Robyn Flewin for helping with some of the legal/police questions.

Pulling this whole thing together in practical terms was a huge learning curve. Thank you to Joel Naoum from Critical

Mass for coordinating everything and for answering all my questions with grace and patience. I am indebted to my cover designer for her beautiful work. You know who you are—thank you. I hope we get the chance to work together again. And thank you to Alexandra Nahlous for your superb and insightful editing, and for putting up with all my 'buts' and assorted errors. Working with you was a dream.

To my family and friends, including my mum Gwen, brothers Peter and Gary, and sister Lynne, thank you for your ongoing interest in my writing and for cheering me on from the side-line. It's wonderful to have your support both in person and online.

To my husband, John, thank you for not only sticking by me for over thirty years but for joining me on this Wildwords Publishing ride. Here's to many more, on both fronts. And to my three beautiful daughters, Freya, Georgia and Amelia, thank you for always believing in me and never thinking I'm too old to follow my dreams. To Jack, my gorgeous little man, thanks for making me smile and for giving me an even better reason to meet my deadlines.

Last but by no means least: thank you to my readers. I can't tell you how many times I've been having a bad day, thought about chucking the whole writing thing in and then I've received an email or message from a reader telling me how much they enjoyed one of my books. Without readers, authors would not exist and without my loyal readers *Cross My Heart* would not be out in the world. I hope you enjoy my story and I hope to write many more for you in the future.

Also by Pamela Cook

From Pamela

Thank you for reading *Cross My Heart*. I hope you enjoyed it.

I love connecting with readers and would love to hear your thoughts on the novel. You can contact me via my website or any of the social media links on the About the Author page.

You can also find Bookclub Questions for *Cross My Heart* on my website.

If you loved the story I would appreciate you taking the time to post a review on Goodreads or wherever you purchased the book.

To find out what I'm writing next, what I'm reading and other snippets from my writing life you can sign up for my newsletter here.

Blackwattle Lake

When Eve Nicholls returns to her childhood home it's not long before she's confronted by people – and memories – from her past. She re-discovers her love of horses and of the bush, along with her old adventurous self, but memories and unforeseen events force her to face her demons – and more.

'Eve took a deep breath and stepped down from the kombi. Everything inside her was shaking. Maybe being back here wasn't going to be as easy as she'd thought.'

A story about forgiveness and courage, and finding a place to belong.

"Well written, with appealing characterisation and an engaging storyline, Blackwattle Lake is an appealing contemporary novel set in rural Australia which I truly enjoyed."

Shelleyrae at Book'd Out (via Goodreads)

Read now

Essie's Way

Miranda McIntyre thinks she has it all sorted. She's a successful lawyer, she's planning her wedding and ticking off all the right boxes. When searching for something old to go with her wedding dress she remembers an antique necklace from her childhood, but her mother denies any knowledge of it. Miranda is sure it exists. Trying to find the necklace, she discovers evidence that perhaps the grandmother she thought was dead is still alive.

Ignoring the creeping uncertainty about her impending marriage, and the worry that she is not living the life she really wants, Miranda takes off on a road trip in search of answers to the family mystery but also in search of herself.

'In the distance the sky and sea merged into an opaque sheet of black, the only light shed by a sliver of moon. A crack of lightning split the darkness, illuminating the cauldron that was the ocean for just a few moments. She tilted her chin up and stretched forward, straining to see. Something was out there.'

A captivating story of family, love and following your heart.

"A stunningly beautiful novel that perfectly captures rural Australian life."

Mrs B's Book Reviews (via Goodreads)

Read now

Close To Home

For Charlie Anderson the only thing harder than letting go is moving on.

Orphaned at thirteen, Charlie has been on her own for over half her life. Not that she minds – she has her work as a vet and most days that's enough. Most days. But when she's sent to a small town on the New South Wales coast to investigate a possible outbreak of the deadly Hendra virus, Charlie finds herself torn between the haunting memories of her past, her dedication to the job and her attraction to a handsome local.

Travelling to Naringup means coming face to face with what is left of her dysfunctional family – her cousin Emma, who begged Charlie not to leave all those years ago, and her aunt Hazel, who let her go without a backwards glance. But it also means relying on the kindness of strangers and, when she meets local park ranger Joel Drummond, opening her heart to the possibility of something more …

As tensions in the country town rise, can Charlie reconcile with the past and find herself a new future in the town she left so long ago?

The only thing harder than letting go is moving on …

"It's a story that you just enjoy reading, that flowed well and that kept this reader completely engrossed from start to finish with many confrontations within the story that are both nail bitingly well written and equally heart-poundingly shocking."
Talking Books (via Goodreads)

Read now

The Crossroads

Rosie O'Shea dreams of seeing the world. But right now the outback hotel she owns is falling down around her ears, her bank account is empty and family duty means she's staying put.

Drought is impacting hard on **Stephanie Bailey** and her family. They've already been forced to sell off most of their cattle. The rains aren't coming and Stephanie's husband is becoming more and more distant.

City girl **Faith Montgomery** is left reeling after a shocking discovery. Determined to uncover the truth and make sense of her life, she arrives at The Crossroads Hotel but soon realises deception isn't an easy game to play.

One family. Three women. Will the lies they tell and the secrets they hide lead to more heartache or will fate bring them together before its too late?

Moving your life in a new direction sometimes means taking the hard road.

"It has everything you want – battles against external factors, a race against time, love, loss and ultimately a happy ending. It would make for a great summer or holiday read."
Sam Still Reading (via Goodreads)

Read now.

Pamela Cook and Room to Read

Pamela Cook is a committed writer ambassador for Room to Read, a dynamic global organization transforming the lives of millions of children in low-income communities by focusing on literacy and gender equality in education.

Founded in 2000 on the belief that World Change Starts with Educated Children®, Room to Read's innovative model focuses on deep, systemic transformation within schools during the two time periods that are most critical in a child's schooling: early primary school for literacy acquisition and secondary school for girls' education.

Room to Read works in collaboration with local communities, partner organizations and governments to develop literacy skills and a habit of reading among primary school children, and to ensure girls can complete secondary school with the skills necessary to negotiate key life decisions. Since its inception, Room to Read's worldwide team has benefited over 16 million children in Bangladesh, Cambodia, Grenada,

Honduras, India, Indonesia, Jordan, Laos, Myanmar, Nepal, Rwanda, South Africa, Sri Lanka, Tanzania, Vietnam, and Zambia.

As Pamela says, 'Having visited Room to Read schools in rural India, I have seen at first hand how life-changing their programs really are. Where you happen to be born should not determine whether or not you receive an education. I truly believe that World Change Starts with Educated Children and that's why I support Room to Read.'

For more information, www.roomtoread.org.

World Change Starts
with Educated Children.

Room to Read®

About Pamela

Pamela Cook writes Rural and Contemporary Australian Fiction featuring complex women and tangled family relationships. Her first novels were Rural Fiction with Romantic Elements: *Blackwattle Lake* (2012), *Essie's Way* (2013), *Close To Home* (2015) and *The Crossroads* (2016) published by Hachette Australia. *Cross My Heart* (2019) is Pamela's first Women's Fiction title, continuing her passion for writing strong female characters and stories set in beautiful rural settings.

Pamela is the co-host of the *Writes4Women* and *Writes4Festivals* podcasts, and Program Director for the inaugural *Storyfest* Literary Festival happening in Milton, NSW, in June 2019. She is proud to be a Writer Ambassador for *Room To Read*, a not-for-profit organisation promoting literacy and gender equality in developing countries. When she's not writing, podcasting or festival planning she wastes as much time as possible riding her handsome quarter horses, Morocco and Rio.

Pamela teaches writing courses and workshops through her business, *Justwrite*. www.justwrite.net.au

She loves to connect with readers both in person and online. You will often find her lurking in one of these places:

www.pamelacook.com.au
www.facebook.com/PamelaCookAuthor
www.writes4women.com
Twitter @PamelaCookAU
Instagram @pamelacookwrites and @w4wpodcast

CPSIA information can be obtained
at www.ICGtesting.com
Printed in the USA
LVHW031814051119
636425LV00003B/321/P